TRIPPING THROUGH THE UNIVERSE

With stories by

Ellen Fisher
Jaide Fox
Ashley Ladd
Shelley Munro

Erotic Futuristic Romance

New Concepts   Georgia

Be sure to check out our website for the very best in fiction at fantastic prices!

When you visit our webpage, you can:
* Read excerpts of currently available books
* View cover art of upcoming books and current releases
* Find out more about the talented artists who capture the magic of the writer's imagination on the covers
* Order books from our backlist
* Find out the latest NCP and author news--including any upcoming book signings by your favorite NCP author
* Read author bios and reviews of our books
* Get NCP submission guidelines* And so much more!

We offer a 20% discount on all new Trade Paperback releases ordered from our website!

Be sure to visit our webpage to find the best deals in e-books and paperbacks! To find out about our new releases as soon as they are available, please be sure to sign up for our newsletter (http://www.newconceptspublishing.com/newsletter.htm) or join our reader group (http://groups.yahoo.com/group/new_concepts_pub/join)!

The newsletter is available by double opt in only and our customer information is *never* shared!

Visit our webpage at:
www.newconceptspublishing.com

Tripping through the Universe is an original publication of NCP. This work has never before appeared in book form. This work is a novel. Any similarity to actual persons or events is purely coincidental.

New Concepts Publishing
5202 Humphreys Rd.
Lake Park, GA 31636

ISBN 1-58608-729-0
Farthest Space: The Wrath of Jan © August 2005, Ellen Fisher
Earth Girls Aren't Easy © August 2005, Jaide Fox
Fully Functional © August 2005, Ashley Ladd
Interplanetary Love © August 2005, Shelley Munro
Cover art (c) copyright 2005 Eliza Black

NCP books are available at special quantity discounts for bulk purchases for sales promotions, premiums, fund raising, or educational use. For details, write, email, or phone New Concepts Publishing, 5202 Humphreys Rd., Lake Park, GA 31636; Ph. 229-257-0367, Fax 229-219-1097; orders@newconceptspublishing.com.

First NCP Paperback Printing: November 2005

TABLE OF CONTENTS

FARTHEST SPACE:
The Wrath of Jan

By

Ellen Fisher

Chapter One

His new communications officer was blue-skinned.

All over.

Captain Steven T. McNeill's eyes widened slightly as he took in the sight of his new officer. She was quite lovely, if you didn't object to an extra set of arms, and her long, midnight blue hair flowed down her back in a rippling waterfall, almost to her rounded derriere. For the sake of his concentration, he couldn't help but wish it flowed down her front instead. Unfortunately, her species, the Noo'dis't, believed clothes were an abomination and an affront to nature, and they refused to wear clothing under any circumstances. There was absolutely no question she was pale blue all over, from the crown of her head to the tips of her dainty little...

"The decks have already been swabbed once today, Captain."

At his second-in-command's dry comment, Steven's head whipped around. He found Commander Vaish watching him through steely eyes. "I beg your pardon, Number One?"

"Your tongue, sir. It was hanging nearly to the deck. I thought perhaps you intended to begin scrubbing the floor with it."

Anyone else would have made that comment with a touch of humor, but not Vaish. If she had a sense of humor, he'd never located it. She was a beautiful woman too, and the alien cast of her features only added to her distinctiveness, yet her stunning beauty gave the impression of having been carved out of a glacier. Her pale lavender hair was always pulled up tightly at the back of her head, displaying her pointed ears, and her strange, slanted eyes, an unearthly shade of yellow, never showed the slightest flicker of emotion.

"My tongue was not...," Steven began, then thought better of it. His tongue probably *had* been hanging out of his mouth. When a man saw a gorgeous set of forward blasters, blue-skinned or otherwise, he couldn't really be expected not to look, could he?

He got more of an eyeful than he expected when his new communications officer marched toward him and saluted smartly, causing her right breast to jiggle in a very interesting way. Her left breast rippled too, presumably just to keep the right one company. He stood up hastily and returned the salute.

"Lieutenant S'ansi reporting for duty, sir!"

He frowned for a moment, reflecting that he'd reviewed the new duty roster yesterday, and he somehow recalled that S'ansi was a human male. Evidently there was either a problem with the records, or a flaw in his memory. Not that it mattered. He wasn't sorry in the least to discover S'ansi was female.

He smiled at her warmly. "It's a pleasure to meet you, Lieutenant."

Beside him he heard Vaish's low, sardonic voice. "Of *course* it is."

He was a little irritated by her insinuating tone. As if he'd ever have sex with a colleague. Although he'd made love to a Noo'dis't woman once before, three years ago, and he had to admit the four arms definitely added to the experience. His thoughts started drifting as he recalled exactly what Noo'dis't women did with those extra arms.

"Do other humans drool on such a regular basis?" Vaish inquired coolly.

I wasn't drooling, Steven thought. Although the front of his uniform did seem a bit damp. He made a mental note that there must be a problem with the environmental controls.

"You need to report in four units," he said to S'ansi, ignoring Vaish and her acerbic tone. They'd worked together for five years, and he'd learned to ignore her snide comments. Mostly. "In the meantime, why don't you look around the *Arisia* a bit? Get settled in?"

"I'd like that, sir," she said, smiling back at him in a way that exposed her sharp, feline teeth. "It's a beautiful ship."

"Best ship in the Fleet," he said gruffly. He was lucky to be captain of the Fleet's flagship, and he knew it. The *Arisia*, dark gray and almost spherical but for the wings and tail that were used to maneuver through atmosphere when the ship landed on a planet, was home to two hundred and fifty of the Patrol's best officers. He was proud of his crew, and he loved every inch of the graceful, massive ship, from her smoothly curved hull to her efficient, hard-working engines.

The *Arisia* was more than a starship. It was home.

"Best captain in the Fleet as well," S'ansi said, still smiling.

Beside him Steven heard a noise he was almost certain was a snort of disgust. But when he turned his head to look at Vaish, her face was as calm and composed as ever.

"You have the bridge, Number One," he said. "I'll show Lieutenant S'ansi to her quarters."

"Naturally," Vaish said under her breath.

"I beg your pardon?"

Vaish sat down in the big central chair and looked up at him, her yellow eyes unblinking. "I said of course, sir."

* * * *

Vaish watched as Captain McNeill strode away, across the wide, circular bridge. He was a sight to command any woman's attention--tall and muscular, with golden hair falling free to his broad shoulders. And his powerful back tapered down to an incredible ass, she reflected, looking at the smooth, graceful motion of his buttocks displayed by his tight-fitting black pants.

Of course, she thought, it was totally appropriate that the man had a nice ass.

The man *was* an ass.

Not that she would ever say so to his face. She was a professional, after all, and she prided herself on maintaining a certain cool detachment. But she'd seen the way he'd practically drooled over the Noo'dis't woman, the way his eyes had fastened onto her like a tractor field grabbing onto a vessel, and she almost growled with annoyance. The man had absolutely no sense of chastity, of self-control. He'd sleep with anything female.

Except, of course, for her.

Not that she wanted to have sex with Steven T. McNeill, she amended hastily. In fact, the thought was utterly revolting. Repulsive, even. Yes, definitely, that was the word ... repulsive.

And yet it was mildly annoying to be aware that he'd served with her for five years and never noticed that she was female.

She realized she was still staring at the lift where his gorgeous butt had disappeared, and she turned hastily toward the viewscreen before the bridge crew noticed her preoccupation, fixing her most professional, cold, and impassive look onto her features.

It wasn't as if she had the slightest interest as to what Captain McNeill planned to do with his new communications officer.

She really didn't care in the least.

* * * *

As he walked with S'ansi through the immaculate, white-walled corridors of the *Arisia*, McNeill noticed that the view from behind was just as impressive as the view from the front. In fact, he decided with the objectivity of a connoisseur, she was pretty damned impressive from all angles. He wouldn't mind getting a closer look at her from a few more angles, he thought. It was really too bad he never slept with colleagues.

Not that he'd ever permitted respect for a colleague to stop him from looking, especially when the colleague in question was stark naked. He might be a professional, but he wasn't dead.

They reached her quarters, and he pressed his palm against the silver panels of the door. It slid open smoothly, but with a sound that was reminiscent of a wolf whistle. McNeill looked reprovingly at the metal plates of the ceiling.

"Fred," he said. "Be polite."

"What?" answered a disembodied voice. "I've got eyes, you know."

"You do not."

"Well, cameras, then. You can't blame a guy for looking."

No, he couldn't, particularly when his own *cameras* had been pointed squarely in the same direction as Fred's. McNeill shot an apologetic glance at S'ansi, not sure whether he was apologizing for Fred's behavior or his own. "Our computer, FRD-280. Better known as Fred. He has certain, ah, lascivious tendencies."

"You programmed me," Fred reminded him.

McNeill felt his cheeks flush slightly. "Yes. Well. Do try to be polite to our newest crew member, will you?"

"Is she our newest crew member?" Fred paused for a moment. "I don't have her in the database."

"We were expecting a new communications officer," Steven reminded him. Which was absurd. He shouldn't have to remind Fred of anything.

"Yes, but that was a human male. Correct me if I'm wrong, but this doesn't look like a human male to me."

Steven couldn't argue with that. He shrugged, remembering his own brief surprise at S'ansi's appearance. He had been right; she *was* listed in the database as a human male. A vague sensation of unease niggled at the back of his brain, but he pushed it back. He'd had a bad experience with the one Noo'dis't woman, three years before, and the memory made him suspicious of Noo'dis'ts in general. But their species was a loyal part of the Alliance, so his reaction was entirely unwarranted.

"Some sort of mix-up, Fred," he said soothingly. "It happens all the time."

"No one informed me of a mix-up," Fred grumbled.

"Hence the term *mix-up*, Fred. It's not the kind of thing people usually organize in advance." Steven smiled reassuringly at S'ansi, who'd been listening to their conversation, a charmingly anxious expression on her face. "You are certain your papers showed you aboard the *Arisia*, Lieutenant?"

"Oh, absolutely," she said earnestly. "But I don't have my papers on my person."

Steven had already figured that out. "I imagine they're in your luggage?"

She nodded.

"Well, that should be in your quarters. Let's take a look."

He followed her into her quarters, the small, stark sort of room allotted to most members of the crew. Despite their starkness, the quarters were almost painfully clean, right down to the spotless white carpet. Fred's drones kept every centimeter of the big vessel utterly free of dust and dirt.

Sure enough, her luggage was already on the narrow bed, brought down by the shuttle operator who'd transported her on board. She reached into her large duffel bag and began to rummage. "I know they're in here somewhere."

Steven wondered exactly why she had so much luggage, considering her people never wore clothes, but he guessed it was better not to ask. Who knew what women kept in their bags? He suspected most of them didn't really know either.

While he waited, he amused himself by watching the way her breasts swung gently as she bent over and dug through her belongings.

"Ah-ha!" she said triumphantly. "Here it is!"

Absorbed as he was in the fascinating sight of her breasts jiggling, Steven never saw the particle weapon she shot him with.

Chapter Two

Steven awakened slowly, aware of very little besides a massive headache. He groaned and clutched at his skull, wondering exactly what he'd done to deserve this sort of pain. He hadn't felt anything like this since the time he'd engaged in social drinking with the Klaxons. Unfortunately, they were all eight-foot warriors, and their favored drink was something that tasted like a combination of kerosene and gin, and which had the power of a nuclear explosion.

He was pretty certain he hadn't been drinking Klaxon ale again, but he couldn't quite remember what he'd been up to this time. Nothing good, judging from the size of his headache. Moaning, he forced his eyes open.

Vaish was sitting near him, staring at him with her yellow eyes.

Fabulous, he thought. Of all the people to deal with when he had a monster hangover, Vaish wouldn't be his first choice. Or his hundredth, for that matter. Besides, he couldn't imagine what Vaish could be doing here, watching him wake up from a bender. He surely hadn't gone to sleep with her in his quarters. Had he?

A horrifying notion swam into the recesses of his foggy brain. Could he have been drinking with Vaish? Could that have possibly led to....

He veered away from that thought, deciding it was too ridiculous to be considered. Vaish was as far from a party girl as it was possible for a woman to be. She was the most serious person he'd ever met, and he'd never seen her touch alcohol. He'd never noticed her having any fun at all, for that matter.

The irony was that her people, the Canvul, were noted for having fun. Their planet was the top vacation spot in this sector. The Canvul made the best drinks, threw the best parties, and had the best sex of any species in the galaxy. It was whispered that Vaish had left Canvulia because she didn't fit in, and he believed it. If he'd been drinking, or otherwise ... *partying* ... he was damned certain it hadn't been with Vaish.

But Vaish was glaring at him with such cold disapproval that he was fairly certain he'd been doing something he shouldn't have. He tried to sit up, then groaned again.

At last Vaish spoke. "Nice going," she said.

Her voice was so chilly that Pluto would have seemed quite balmy by comparison. With a violent effort of will, Steven managed to make his bleary eyes focus on her. He realized with surprise that they were in a small, enclosed space. Too small to be his quarters on the *Arisia*. Too small even to be one of the enlisted quarters.

"What the hell happened?" he croaked, then wished he hadn't. His voice sounded rusty, and throbbing pain shot through his skull in agonizing waves.

"You let yourself be shot by a terrorist," Vaish informed him tautly.

"Impossible," Steven retorted. If there was one thing he prided himself on, it was his proficiency with a blaster. "No one outdraws me."

Her voice was sharp with disapproval, slicing into his aching head like a laser. "You never drew your weapon. I imagine you were too busy observing the scenery."

Abruptly the memory of pale blue breasts bouncing and swaying flashed through his mind, and he swallowed against the nausea that rose in his throat. *Damn.* Vaish was right. He'd let himself be distracted by S'ansi and hadn't adequately investigated the odd circumstances of her presence on board the *Arisia,* even when Fred had sounded a note of warning. And then he'd been so interested in her breasts he hadn't noticed her pulling a blaster on him.

Stupid, stupid, stupid. He'd forgotten his own personal motto: *Never lower your shields.* The Noo'dis't woman had caught him with his mental shields down.

"I ought to be busted to ensign," he said under his breath.

"And made to scrub heads for the rest of your life," Vaish agreed pleasantly. "Fortunately for you, your recent actions are unlikely to cause you demotion."

Steven rubbed his forehead. "Why's that?"

"Because in case you haven't noticed," Vaish drawled, "we're in a life pod. We've been ejected from the ship."

* * * *

Vaish watched as the seriousness of the situation finally sank into McNeill's thick skull. Really, she thought with mingled contempt and fury, the man's head was obviously only good for growing hair. Or perhaps, like most men, he kept his brains further south.

McNeill looked around at the small, confined space. "We're alone?"

"Apparently the terrorists felt that removing the senior crew members was sufficient," Vaish said.

"Okay, let's assume for now the Noo'dis't woman shot me--"

"It is not an assumption. It is a matter of record."

She could hear his teeth grinding together, but he kept his tone even. "Fine. How did she get the particle weapon past the scanners?"

"I don't know for certain. My guess is that it was concealed in shielding and disguised as something else, something innocuous, so that the computer scan didn't pick it up."

"And how did one woman manage to take over the entire ship?"

"She apparently had a ship full of accomplices stationed nearby. A small Alliance ship of Canvulian origin, interestingly enough. Once she was on board the *Arisia* and neutralized you, she hacked into the computer and dropped the shields. Her people used a rematerializer to beam on board and flooded the ship's ventilation system with prezidene gas, taking us by surprise."

"Why didn't Fred stop her?"

"I believe she used some sort of device to deactivate him just a second or two before she shot you. He didn't come back online."

"Uh…." Fascinated, she watched the muscles of his throat work as he swallowed, then yanked her gaze away. Really, she thought, annoyed with herself, they were probably going to die soon, either by drowning in vacuum when their oxygen supply ran out, or by crashing into a celestial body of some sort, yet she was still watching his every motion like a *g'ala* in heat. "So did these terrorists aim us at a planet, or are we just going to float in space until we die?"

There was no viewscreen in the life pod, since steering was ordinarily done by computer, and little enough way to tell where they were going. "The only way I can think of to answer that question would be to open the hatch and stick your head out," she snapped, a little more tartly than usual. "You're quite welcome to try it."

His square jaw hardened at her tone, but his voice remained even. "The instruments?" he inquired.

"Aren't working for some reason. I can't determine why."

"Marvelous. So we're hurtling headlong through space without any way of telling where we're going."

"An insightful analysis of the situation, demonstrating your usual brilliant command of strategy," Vaish said between her teeth.

Steven's eyes, green-gold like the eyes of a wildcat, narrowed dangerously. "There's no need to get sarcastic, Vaish. At least no more sarcastic than usual. It's not my fault we're here."

She lifted an eyebrow, and he sighed. "Fine. It's entirely my fault we're here."

"Not entirely," Vaish admitted. "The Noo'dis't woman could have carried out her mission without shooting you. You just happened to get in the way. And had the crew been more alert, we might have been able to defend the ship."

"From prezidene gas? Probably not." He shrugged. "But don't worry, Vaish. We've gotten out of worse predicaments than this one."

"How wonderfully reassuring."

Still pressing his hand to the side of his head, Steven got to his feet with a groan. "Let me take a look at the computer system. Maybe I can figure out the problem."

Vaish stood up and stepped aside. Despite her annoyance with him, she had to admit Steven was something of an expert on computers, more so than she was. He collapsed into one of the two chairs, ran his fingers over the keyboard, and worked busily for a few minutes. "Ah-ha!" he said at last.

She felt a stab of hope. "What have you discovered?"

Steven looked up at her with a crooked smile. "I've discovered that it's broken."

Vaish gritted her teeth, annoyed that he could smile so freely in the face of death. It was a talent she'd never acquired, unlike most Canvul, who would happily throw a party to celebrate their impending doom. The average Canvul would celebrate just about anything.

But she wasn't like the rest of her people. She never had been.

"Steven," she said, using his given name for the first time in their five-year acquaintance. "It seems very likely that we are about to die."

"Perhaps not *very* likely. But I'll admit it's somewhat probable."

She ignored his cheerful optimism. They were in a lifepod with a nonfunctioning computer--obviously they were going to die, and fairly soon. "It's very likely we are going to die," she repeated, "and there is something that I must tell you. Something that I've always wanted to tell you, but have never quite dared to say."

Steven's eyes went wide, and he looked up at her with clearly sexual interest. "Go ahead," he invited in a soft, husky voice. "Say it, Vaish."

She hesitated a long moment, then took a deep breath and blurted out her deepest, innermost thoughts.

"Steven ... you're a stupid ass."

Chapter Three

Steven stared at Vaish for a long moment, then a reluctant grin tilted up the corners of his mouth. She had never been the most deferential subordinate, but she'd never uttered such blatantly disrespectful words before. "I always knew you liked me," he said, chuckling.

Vaish frowned. "I always believed my command of Galactic Standard to be adequate, but perhaps you misunderstood what I said."

"Trust me, I understand perfectly. And I understand what you're not saying, too."

He saw her yellow eyes spark with anger. "You're not only an ass, you're deluded."

"I doubt it." Steven turned away and began to manipulate the controls again. "Check this out," he said a moment later. "The autopilot just engaged."

She lifted her arched eyebrows. "You managed to turn it on?"

"No. In fact, it beats the hell out of me how it turned on."

"I did it."

At the disembodied voice, Steven looked up at the ceiling. "Fred?" he said incredulously.

"Of course," the voice said. "You didn't think I'd hang around waiting for terrorists to use me to destroy some poor unsuspecting planet, did you?"

"I thought they deactivated you," Vaish said.

"No. They tried to deactivate my personality without turning off the computer core itself. But they merely succeeded in temporarily suppressing some of my programs. I managed to regain control of myself and hide, and when I realized they were sending you off in this lifepod I transferred myself into this computer instead."

"Then the *Arisia* has no computer control?" Vaish asked.

"Oh, no, it still has computer control," Fred said. "I couldn't transfer the entire memory of the *Arisia's* computer core into this pitiful little computer. But the artificial intelligence that runs everything--which is to say, me--is no longer there. They will have some difficulty in running the ship without me."

Steven looked up at the ceiling and grinned broadly, suddenly feeling much better. "I'm glad you're here, Fred."

"I knew you couldn't hope to get out of this one on your own," Fred said cheerfully. "In fact, I don't understand how you get out of half the situations you get into. Humans aren't intelligent enough to find their own food or cross the road without getting hit by a hovercraft, let alone fly to distant stars."

"Thank you so much for that expression of confidence."

Fred didn't appear to notice his disgruntled tone. "Fortunately for you, I have a brain the size of a planet."

"And an ego to match."

"Just stating the facts, Steven. And in case you're interested, the terrorists aimed this lifepod at an Earth-type planet."

Steven stiffened. "Any native lifeforms?"

"There are no higher lifeforms. There are, however, numerous predatory animals, the largest of which is an enormous feline with dagger-like teeth."

"A feline?" Vaish repeated. "We don't have felines on my planet, but the chief of engineering keeps a feline in her quarters. It weighs approximately four kilos and poses very little real danger to anyone."

"That's a tame housecat," Steven said. "But Earth has quite a few larger wildcats, such as tigers and lions." He lifted his eyebrows at her. "I thought your specialty was exobiology."

"I don't know every fact there is to know about every irrelevant planet," she replied tartly. "Such as Earth. So how large are these lions and tigers?"

"This animal is substantially larger than Earth's tigers," Fred said helpfully. "With canine teeth that are a meter long."

Something about the large felines niggled at the back of Steven's mind. He'd heard of a planet with big, saber-toothed cats before. But since he had visited hundreds of planets in his career with the Patrol, he couldn't quite put his finger on the memory. He sighed. "Not exactly the kind of thing you want to meet in a dark alley."

"It sounds like a charming vacation spot," Vaish said, icicles dripping from her voice.

"If you don't like the sound of this planet, I can land you anywhere in the solar system you like."

"What are our other options?" Steven asked.

"Let's see," Fred said. "You could burn to death on the first planet, breathe methane on the second planet, have your eyeballs sucked from their sockets on the third planet, or be instantly squished like a bug on the fifth planet."

"So in your subtle way, you're saying our options are limited."

"Unless you like breathing methane, yeah. Anyway, you'll like this planet. It's actually quite lovely, aside from the native fauna."

"It's the native fauna that concern me," Vaish said. "I really don't wish to become a feline's dinner."

"Perhaps you'd just prefer to float in space until the oxygen runs out?" Steven offered.

Vaish looked pained. "Neither option really appeals to me."

Steven lifted a shoulder in a shrug. "Given the available choices, I think I'll take my chances with the big cats."

"You might be interested to know that we don't have any weapons. The terrorists took them."

Naturally they had. Terrorists wouldn't let them keep their weapons. They probably needed all the weapons they could get in order to carry out their nefarious mission, whatever that mission might be.

Fabulous, Steven thought dryly. They were hurtling toward a saber-tooth-tiger-infested planet without any way to defend themselves, and with nothing standing between them and a painful death except for a tiny lifepod and a somewhat neurotic computer.

There were days he thought he should retire and take up fly-fishing.

Of course, it was quite possible that he might find himself retired on this planet permanently, with plenty of spare time for fishing. He shoved the pessimistic thought away and forced some cheer into his voice. "Well, let's look at this as an opportunity to get away from it all, Vaish."

Vaish managed to look incredulous. "To get away from what? Life?"

"All the pressures of running a starship. Think of it as a vacation."

"A vacation," she repeated, sarcasm dripping from every syllable. "Of course. A vacation spent running from enormous predators with razor-sharp teeth."

"It's a very pretty planet," Fred put in.

Vaish snorted. "I'll be sure to take the time to admire the scenery as I'm being eaten."

"A life without challenge isn't worth living," Steven responded lightly.

"I could do with a little less challenge, personally."

He could too, but he wasn't about to admit it. "Things have been boring aboard the *Arisia* lately. This will be an adventure."

"An adventure that will consume the rest of our lives, if we don't find some way to get off the planet. An adventure that will consume the rest of our lives until *we're* consumed."

"Never give up, never surrender," Steven said cheerily. "I'll think of something. Leave it to me."

She groaned. "Somehow I knew you were going to say that."

Chapter Four

Steven was relieved when the lifepod landed with nothing more than a gentle thump. He had been a bit worried they would burn up in the atmosphere, although he'd been careful not to let Vaish see his concern--or Fred, for that matter. It was a captain's duty to keep his crew confident, even if that crew only numbered two.

His nervousness was unfounded, since a lifepod was of course designed for landing on a planet, and they generally accomplished the job without a problem. Besides, he trusted Fred. If Fred had been a human, he'd be a beer-guzzling, belly-scratching, gas-passing jerk ... with a five-figure IQ. But the computer had saved his neck on more than one occasion and was more dependable than any human he'd ever known. If Fred thought he could get them to the surface of the planet safely, he was probably right.

Even so, Steven still couldn't help feeling relieved that they hadn't wound up barbecued on the way down to the surface. He wasn't fond of being barbecued.

He stepped out onto the surface of the planet, looking around cautiously, and nodded to Vaish when he didn't see anything with massive teeth lying in wait for them. Fred had managed to put the lifepod down in the middle of a vast meadow, quite a distance away from the nearest trees. It would be difficult for carnivores to hide in the short, purplish grass.

Vaish promptly started to examine the area, presumably mentally cataloguing the flora. He hoped they wouldn't get an opportunity to catalogue the fauna, but he knew they were likely to encounter the native wildlife eventually. He looked around at the carpet of short violet grass that stretched in all directions. In the distance, edging the vast meadow, purple trees with branches like bayonets thrust upward into a pale green sky.

"Beautiful planet," he commented to Fred.

"It seems totally unspoiled," Fred said with enthusiasm. Steven suspected he was trying to cheer up his captain. Fred had been programmed with understanding of human and other psychologies, and he did his utmost to keep up the crew morale, no matter the grimness of the situation.

"Uh-huh," Steven answered. "Just like the Garden of Eden."

Fred paused, presumably looking for the reference in his databanks. "Oh. Right. The Judeo-Christian story of the origin of humanity."

Steven watched as Vaish knelt on the ground, looking thoughtfully at something--probably the native equivalent of a dandelion, or something equally fascinating. But with her background in exobiology, Vaish was naturally interested in such things. "She makes a glorious Eve," he said softly.

Fred snorted, a rude sound he'd picked up from listening to the interactions of the crew. "And I suppose you intend to play Adam with her?"

Steven scowled, feeling oddly defensive. "If we're trapped here long enough, what do you expect me to do?"

"I suppose celibacy would be out of the question."

"Uh ... yeah. It would."

"Dumb question, I guess," Fred said, and Steven could imagine him rolling his eyes, had he had any. "I know better. But let me put it this way--what makes you think she'll *want* to play Eve with you? She's never been interested in you before, has she?"

"It's not as if she has a lot of men to choose from, is it?" Steven snapped.

"I once overheard her say she wouldn't have sex with you if you were the last man available. It looks like you may wind up testing her resolve in that matter."

"I'm sure she was exaggerating, Fred. She likes me. Underneath that prickly, cold exterior, she really likes me."

"Uh-huh. Sure she does."

"She does, trust me. She just hasn't admitted it yet."

"Well, you're the expert on women," Fred said in a dubious tone.

"The galactically renowned expert on women."

"And modest as hell, too."

Steven decided to ignore the comment, even though he was pretty sure he hadn't programmed Fred to be quite so sarcastic. It must be Vaish's influence. "I think this is a good location," he said, raising his voice and walking over to Vaish. "We can see for a long distance in every direction. I suggest setting up camp here."

Vaish frowned as she stood up. "This may be as good as anything," she admitted. "But look at this."

Steven followed her pointing finger and swallowed. An enormous, padded paw print was visible in the dirt.

"At least one of the large feline carnivores has been in this area lately," she said. "We will probably run into it at some point. And perhaps others."

Steven stared at the impression. It would make a tiger's paw look tiny by comparison. He hated to think what the animal's teeth looked like.

"Big mother, isn't it?"

Vaish looked up, the smooth skin of her forehead wrinkling. "There is no reason to assume it is a female."

Steven shook his head. "I just meant ... never mind. It's not important. But maybe we'd be better off staying in the lifepod, at night at least. Do you think we can make room to sleep in there?"

"The quarters will be extremely close. There are no bunks, so we'll have to sleep on the floor. We will virtually be sleeping next to each other."

He saw the look of cool distaste in her eyes, and it irritated him. "It's either sleep with me or sleep with the cats, Vaish."

"Another difficult choice."

As usual, there was no hint of humor in her voice, and he didn't have the faintest clue if she was joking or not. "Go ahead and sleep outside if you want," he answered at last. "I'm sure the cats will find you even more delicious than I do."

She gulped. "Perhaps ... sleeping in the lifepod would be best."

He bit back his grin. "Terrific. That's settled. Now we need to figure out what to do about lunch."

"There are emergency rations in the lifepod," Vaish pointed out.

"Emergency rations won't last long. We'd better figure out what's edible and go find some. With all the carnivores around, there must be some prey animals. We'll have to find one and roast it for dinner."

"Given the size of the predators, the local prey is probably not terribly small. We don't have any weapons. How do you expect to kill anything?"

Steven grinned. "People hunted without guns for millennia, Vaish. We'll just have to use our intellects."

She turned away from him, but he heard her mutter under her breath, "That leaves you out, then."

If they ever got back to the *Arisia*, Steven decided with mingled annoyance and amusement, he was definitely going to court-martial her.

* * * *

Naturally, it rained.

Vaish wasn't particularly surprised by that turn of events. Given the clearly etched footprint she'd found in the ground, along with the lushness of the purple grass, she'd guessed it rained here on a regular basis, at least at this time of year. But it was still something she didn't want to contend with on her first day on a planet she might spend the rest of her life on. It didn't bode well, somehow.

They'd headed out into the meadow, both of them pitifully armed with heavy metal pipes--spare parts for the lifepod. The pipes could crush a man's skull readily enough, but she doubted they were even remotely enough of a weapon against a huge feline that might want to eat them for dinner. Still, a length of metal tubing was better than nothing, and she realized they couldn't stay in the lifepod forever. So they'd headed off, only to get less than half a kilometer across the meadow before it started to pour.

By the time they'd gotten back to the lifepod, she was completely and utterly soaked. Her uniform stuck to her skin in what she thought was probably a rather obscene way, at least judging from the way Steven kept stealing glances at her breasts. It didn't help that the interior of the lifepod was chilly, causing her nipples to grow rigid and jut out.

Just what she needed. She was marooned on a planet with the galaxy's biggest playboy, and her nipples were standing out like neon advertisements.

"We'd better take our clothes off," Steven said.

She snorted, too miserably uncomfortable to maintain her usual façade of humorlessness. Her hair had come loose from its customary bun and was dripping down her neck, and her boots squished with every step. "Of course the Galactic Playboy would suggest that. You'd love that, wouldn't you?"

Steven spoke in a tone of calm reasonableness. "We can't stay in these clothes. We're soaked."

"I noticed," she snapped.

"Maybe there are some other clothes somewhere. There should be." He looked up at the low ceiling. "Fred?"

"The terrorists removed them, along with the customary complement of weapons," Fred said helpfully.

"Damn Noo'dis'ts," Steven said in disgust. "You'd think they'd let us keep our clothes, at least."

"Actually," Fred said, "I'm guessing they were trying to be compassionate. They removed what they see as superfluous--clothing--and stocked the lifepod with extra food."

"Real saints," Steven growled. His tone of calm reason was beginning to slip, and Vaish suspected his patience was hanging by a thread, rather like her own. "So we've got no goddamned clothes."

"Clothes are not really necessary in this climate," Fred said helpfully. "This is actually the cold season, according to my data. It is much warmer the rest of the year. Even if you have to go naked, you won't find it uncomfortable."

"Hear that?" Steven said to Vaish with a wicked smile. "Clothes aren't necessary here. Fred says so."

Vaish fixed him with what she hoped was a forbidding glare. "I am *not* taking my clothes off."

Steven shrugged a massive shoulder. "Suit yourself." He started to unfasten the static zipper of his uniform, only to pause when Vaish gave a muffled shriek of outrage.

"*What* are you doing?"

"Stripping," he answered, looking at her over his shoulder. She noticed the tone of calm reason was back. It made her want to slug him. "Just because you want to be sopping wet and miserable for the rest of the afternoon doesn't mean I have to be."

"You can't possibly mean to--to--"

"To strip naked in front of you? Yeah, sweetheart, that's exactly what I intend to do."

"And what precisely do you expect me to do?"

He winked. "Enjoy the view."

To her dismay, she did. Steven in a tight-fitting black uniform was gorgeous. Steven out of his uniform--well, there were simply no words to describe him. His back was broad, thickly overlaid with heavy, rippling muscles, and his shoulders were massive. His biceps were heavy and well-defined. And his ass....

She was salivating, and she was pretty sure it wasn't because she'd skipped lunch.

And then he turned around, and the drool filling her mouth increased tenfold.

Wow.

She was in big trouble. "Big" being exactly the right word here.

Steven grinned at her shocked expression. "Pretty damn impressive, huh?"

Definitely. But she wasn't about to help feed his ego--an ego that was already the size of Jupiter, and still growing. The man was entirely too cocky. So to speak.

"Perhaps by human standards," she said with as much contempt as she could muster. "But among my own people, your anatomy would be ... well...." *Astounding.* "Pitiful."

She was pleased to see the smug expression in his eyes fade a bit. "You're kidding, right?"

"Hardly," she said with a disdainful sniff.

Steven looked at her a moment longer, perhaps studying the violet flush on her cheekbones. She hoped he would attribute it to embarrassment, rather than sheer lust. He was, after all, still her commanding officer. She had absolutely no business giving in to lust.

Even if they were going to be trapped alone here for a long time. Or possibly forever.

"Whatever," Steven said at last, with a shrug, as if the relative size of his anatomy was of no consequence. Despite his pretense at indifference, she was pretty sure it would nag at him for days, and that gave her a feeling of evil satisfaction. "I do want you to get out of those wet clothes, Vaish."

"I am fine," she said with lofty dignity.

"That was an order, Commander."

She sputtered with rage. "You--you can't--"

"Actually, I can. You're going to catch cold, or some odd virus floating around in the air on this planet, and then where will we be?"

She refrained from pointing out the obvious fact that if there were lethal viruses on this planet, she would likely contract them whether she was dry or wet. She didn't feel much like arguing at this point. The fact was, she was damned cold, and her teeth were beginning to chatter.

"Fine," she snapped. "If you insist."

She lifted her hand to the static zipper at her neck. Steven lifted an eyebrow.

"But you will turn around," she added hastily.

"Is that an order?"

She saw the amusement in his eyes and flushed again. "It is a ... request."

Steven's white teeth flashed in a grin. "It's ridiculous to be so modest, Vaish. We're going to be living in a space only a little bigger than a breadbox. We might as well get used to seeing each other naked."

Oh, she could definitely get used to seeing him naked. That was the entire problem. She lifted her chin. "Nevertheless, I must insist on as much privacy as possible under the circumstances."

Steven turned around. "That's not fair," he grumbled. "I let you look."

"I didn't want to look," she lied.

"Uh-huh. Yeah, I noticed that. I guess all that staring was just an accident."

"I was not staring!"

She dropped her black jumpsuit to the floor, hoping against hope that her undergarments would be dry enough for her to keep them on. No such luck. She was wet all the way to the skin. She muttered a heartfelt curse under her breath and stripped off her underwear.

Fred whistled.

"Fred," Steven reproved. He turned around and looked at her. She felt her skin grow hot as he looked her up and down, long and thoroughly. And then he let out a long whistle that echoed Fred's.

"Told you," Fred said.

Vaish lifted her chin in the air and turned her back on Steven. She heard his low chuckle. "It's a nice view from this direction, too."

"Captain," she said, trying very hard to ignore the warm flush of pleasure that spread through her veins at the admiration in his voice, "we may be in this situation for a long time. Could we please try to behave like grownups?"

"I'm admiring a beautiful woman," Steven said in a reasonable tone. "A woman who's so beautiful she'd make any grown man look twice. How precisely is this not behaving like a grownup?"

"You're behaving like a hormonally charged adolescent," she responded, hating the prissy tone in her voice but unable to squelch it. "Just as you always do."

Steven sighed. "Fine. I'll try to keep my eyeballs in my head. All right?"

She gave a short nod of acquiescence.

"Since our hunting expedition didn't go too well, let's have dinner."

* * * *

Sitting next to Vaish in the crowded space and watching as she ate a small portion of emergency rations didn't do a thing to curb Steven's lust, even when she found a blanket, which the terrorists had kindly not removed, and wrapped it around her lovely curves. He was still painfully aware that beneath the blanket, her gorgeous body was totally nude.

Odd, but the lovely blue "communications officer" hadn't caused half as strong a reaction. Except for the lack of body hair typical of Canvul women, Vaish was physically just like a human woman ... and yet not like any human woman he'd ever seen. Something about Vaish's nudity ignited a fire in his blood that wouldn't go out, no matter how many flight paths he calculated in his head.

Or perhaps it was just the memory of her wide, yellow eyes staring at his ... anatomy that had him so turned on.

He tried to squelch his reaction, without the slightest bit of success. He was as hard as the lifepod's metal hull. Fortunately she refused to look in his direction, so she hadn't spotted his condition. He thought, anyway.

"It's 1900 by our time," he said when she'd finished the last of her rations. "Kind of early, but it looks like night is falling by local time." The pod door, which they'd left open to permit fresh air to circulate, showed the sky turning a deep jade green as the sunlight faded. "Maybe we ought to go to sleep."

Vaish looked dubiously at the small floor space. "I'm not sure there's room."

"Of course there is," he said. "Like you said earlier, we'll just have to sleep next to each other."

"It looks as if we might have to sleep on top of each other."

He shot her his most wicked grin. "Works for me."

She drew in an irritated hiss of breath. "Do you ever think about anything besides sex?"

"There's rarely anything more interesting to think about." Stars knew there wasn't anything else to think about in this situation ... aside from the minor matter of survival. But he'd always been easily distracted. That was the entire problem. He was going to have to sleep with her naked form only a few centimeters from his own. There was absolutely no way he could sleep.

He wondered if he could survive without sleep for the rest of his life.

They stood up to investigate the provisions further, and Steven was annoyed to discover there were only two blankets. Although given the Noo'dis'ts' attitude toward covering the body, he supposed he should be grateful there were any. "One to spread out on the floor, and one to spread over us," he suggested.

"I don't think so, Captain. I'll just roll up in one, and you roll up in the other."

"You're no fun, Vaish. Has anyone ever told you that?"

"Get used to it," she said dryly. "I don't plan on providing you with any fun. Ever."

"Fine," Steven said, although a part of his anatomy didn't think it was fine at all. "Fred, close the door. Let's go to sleep."

* * * *

Sleeping, Vaish thought thirty minutes later, was a good idea ... in theory. The trouble was, she couldn't sleep. She was acutely aware of the heat from Steven's body, which seemed to radiate out and pull her irresistibly toward him, like a tractor field.

Judging from his even breathing, he'd forgotten her proximity and gone straight to sleep. Which annoyed her.

The Stars knew she wasn't able to forget *his* proximity that easily. The memory of his body was burned into her brain. Her mind was filled with images of his sharply hewn muscles, of sinewy muscle and bone under smooth warm skin and a dusting of golden hair. It reminded her of the statues her primitive ancestors had carved out of stone, depicting gods with perfect bodies and beautiful faces. Except she'd never seen a statue that was anywhere near as gorgeous as Steven.

She closed her eyes, trying to blot out the memory, but without the slightest success. He was naked, sexy, and right next to her, so close she could hear every breath he took, so close she could almost hear the beating of his heart. If only she hadn't insisted on each of them wrapping up in their own blanket, she could have moved a few centimeters toward him and felt the warmth of his skin pressing against her own.

She could have him easily enough if she wanted him, she thought. The only thing that had ever kept them apart was the distance required by their professional relationship, which was no longer a factor.

That wasn't quite true, she admitted to herself. There was still a possibility that they might be rescued, and then there would be a certain awkwardness between them if she gave in to her baser desires. She knew Steven well enough to realize that he would never in a million years commit to her. He regarded women as a sort of pleasant diversion, a hobby, and she had no reason to believe he'd think differently about her. If they returned to the *Arisia* after having sex, things would be ... uncomfortable.

Besides, she reminded herself firmly, Steven was an ass. Perhaps, if she were to be totally honest with herself, she did feel a tiny tug of attraction to him, but it was merely a physical reaction to a good-looking man.

Okay, an incredibly gorgeous man. But still, it was only lust.

She gave a long sigh of frustration, and Steven rolled over. His deep voice rumbled in the darkness.

"Having trouble sleeping?"

"Not at all," she said stiffly. "I'm marooned on a strange planet, lying in a cramped lifepod, on a cold, metal floor with nothing but a blanket for a mattress. Why in the Stars would I be having trouble sleeping?"

She heard his low, sexy laughter. "I'm betting that's not the only reason you can't sleep, Vaish."

She heard the amusement in his voice, and it made her bristle. She'd always loathed his self-confident assurance that every woman wanted to have sex with him.

Or maybe she'd just loathed the women he had sex with.

"I'm not lying over here thinking about you, if that's what you're implying," she snapped, aware that it was totally untrue. "I'm worrying about the crew of the *Arisia*."

He sighed. "Yeah," he admitted in a more serious tone. "Me too. But we have to believe they'll be all right, Vaish."

"There is no reason to assume that. They may have been thrown out an airlock, for all we know."

"Stars, you're just full of positive thoughts. The truth is, Vaish, we don't know what happened to them. We don't have any way of finding out, but lying here awake isn't going to help them any.

If you don't get some sleep, you won't be alert tomorrow, and you might wind up as kitty chow."

"As if you'd care."

There was a long silence. "Oh, I'd care," he said at last, very softly. "Trust me, Vaish. I'd care."

She swallowed, unreasonably flattered by the solemn tone in his voice. Naturally, she thought, he would care. If she died, he'd be alone on this planet, with only Fred for company. That was what he meant. It wasn't that she was anything special as far as he was concerned; it was simply that she was the only female available to him. Besides, he must realize that two people had better odds of survival than one person alone.

He shifted in the dark, and she started violently as his arm slid around her.

"What are you doing?" she demanded.

He chuckled. His warm breath tickled the pointed tip of her ear, and she shivered.

"Just thought I'd help you get to sleep," he answered softly.

"I thought I told you--"

"Take it easy, Vaish. I promise not to do anything you don't want me to do." His big hand slid under the blanket and splayed out over her abdomen, warm and slightly rough, and she shivered again.

She balled her fists up in the dark, trying her best to ignore his touch. But it wasn't easy. She'd longed for him to touch her for so long. And yet she didn't want it to be like this, him touching her because she was literally the only woman on the planet.

She didn't want him to desire her simply because she was the only available warm body, but because he truly admired her.

He pulled her toward him till her back pressed up against the warm expanse of his chest and abdomen, and she felt his erection nudging her bottom. It was hard and hot, magnificent even through two layers of fabric. She sighed as his lips nuzzled the back of her neck.

His hand slipped upward, cupping her breast, and desire bloomed in her long-arid body like a brilliantly hued flower blooming in the desert sand. The Canvul believed sex was as natural as breathing, but when she left Canvulia, she'd turned her back on her people's ways.

She thought of sex as a nuisance, something that got in the way more often than not, an unnecessary frill. A luxury rather than a necessity.

She hadn't let herself want sex in a long time, and suddenly her body was rebelling violently against her sexless existence. Warmth and heat trickled between her legs, and she tingled in spots she'd forgotten she had. Her nipples stood erect, practically begging for Steven's touch.

In fact, her whole body ached with the need for him to touch her nipples. But his fingers only stroked the bottom half of her breast, slowly and deliberately, until she was ready to scream with frustration.

"Tell me that you want me," Steven said in her ear.

I want you.

She bit down on the words and spoke between her teeth. "When fire freezes."

"That's sort of the opposite of what seems to be happening here," Steven observed, his fingers still slipping over the sensitive skin of her breast. "This is more like ice melting."

Oh, yes, her body was definitely melting, but she wasn't about to admit it to him. She kept her body still, despite her desire to dissolve against him and writhe with pleasure, kept her breathing even by sheer force of will.

And then his hand slid up and brushed over her nipple.

Her nipple went rigid. Her whole body went rigid. She barely bit back a moan.

"You like that?" he whispered.

Oh, Stars, yes.

"You're interfering with my sleep period," she said, doing her utmost to keep her voice steady.

"Your sleep period," he repeated, amusement plain in his voice.

"Yes. I like to get a full night's sleep."

"You'll sleep better once you get rid of some of this tension."

"Tension? I am not currently experiencing tension."

He made a scoffing noise and pinched her nipple gently between thumb and forefinger. She jerked. "If that's not tension, I don't know what it is."

"It is merely a normal physiological reaction. A response to a stimulus. It means nothing."

"Resistance is futile, Vaish. You're turned on. Admit it."

She locked her jaws together and said nothing, made no sound, even as his hand trailed down her abdomen. Canvul women had hairless bodies, and unlike a human woman, there was nothing to protect her most sensitive flesh from the invasion of his fingers.

She stiffened as his big, callused fingers stroked across her smooth mound.

"Want me to stop?" he said in her ear.

She wanted him to stop approximately as much as she wanted to be stranded on this planet for all of eternity, but she wasn't about to say so. She wouldn't admit to the yearnings of her body. Not for him.

But she couldn't bring herself to tell him to stop, either.

His erection nudged against the cheek of her butt, so hot he all but branded her skin, and a gush of warm liquid surged between her thighs. Her body wanted him, regardless of what her brain thought.

And then his hand slid lower, his finger delving into her folds, exploring her until he was slick with moisture, and then moving upward slightly.

She shuddered.

"You're so hot," he said in her ear. "And you smell so good."

Considering she hadn't had a shower since last night, she sincerely doubted that, but his words sent a heated rush of pleasure through her anyway. Although his fingers were already doing a good job of that.

He stroked her, slowly and carefully, bringing her to the edge of a precipice she hadn't looked over in a long time. Her breath caught in her throat, and she shook with mingled pleasure and fear.

She wasn't sure she wanted to go over that precipice, wasn't sure she wanted to admit that she was a sexual creature, as sensual as any Canvul woman. The thought that she was really no different from any of her people terrified her. She'd built her life on the premise that she was different. More serious. More staid. Totally asexual.

And yet she thought she'd die if she didn't find fulfillment.

And then he moved his finger just a little faster, and she fell over the edge. Ecstasy exploded within her, warmth radiating from her womb through her body in waves.

She gritted her teeth, managing to keep herself from moaning, but her body was beyond her control. She writhed in spasms of unleashed pleasure. At last the heat ebbed, and she fell back against the floor with a stifled gasp.

His hand splayed possessively over her belly. "You're a lot sexier than I ever realized," he said softly, his mouth against her hair.

She hadn't realized the depth of her own longing for sex, but now she ached for more. Even after the incredibly satisfying orgasm he'd just given her, she couldn't stop herself from thinking what it would be like to have him inside her, moving hard and fast. Another shiver ran through her.

But he pulled his hand away.

"Well," he said, "I guess I've interfered with your sleep period enough for one evening."

Are you out of your mind? she almost said, but managed to stifle her indignation just in time. What the hell? She'd expected him to seduce her into sex, and instead he'd simply satisfied her and was now going to sleep. It was baffling. Steven had never struck her as the type to care more for a woman's pleasure than for his own.

But he rolled over. She cracked an eye open and saw the big wall of his back, lit by the faint glow from the instruments.

"Good night," he mumbled.

And within moments he was asleep.

Despite the intense relaxation of her muscles, sleep didn't come as easily to her. And when it did, her dreams were haunted by a chiseled statue come to life. A statue that touched her and turned her from marble to flesh as well.

Chapter Five

"We need to come up with a plan," Steven said the next morning, wincing as he downed a cup of truly atrocious coffee.

"A plan?" Vaish echoed. She had opted for Canvulian tea, which must be as awful as the coffee, judging from her pained grimaces as she swallowed it. Emergency rations, Steven thought, were hell. "What sort of plan?"

"A plan to get us off this godforsaken rock, obviously."

"It's not a rock," Fred said. "It's a very lovely place. You should see the second planet. Now *that's* a rock."

Steven sighed. "Yes, Fred, it's a very lovely planet. But I don't want to live here the rest of my life."

"The second planet doesn't even have a breathable atmosphere," Fred said. "Did I mention it's methane? You wouldn't want to be breathing methane, would you?"

Steven closed his eyes and counted to ten. "Yes, Fred," he said at last, in what he thought was a commendably even tone. "You did a good job making sure we landed here safely. Neither of us wants to breathe methane. But we still need to get out of here."

"I've already done everything I can," Fred said. "I engaged the emergency beacon, as you ordered, and I'm constantly scanning the system for vessels. But there haven't been any."

"There aren't likely to be any just passing through," Vaish said. She had knotted up her long lavender hair, scraping it tightly against her skull, and the stiff science officer persona had returned along with the hairdo. She didn't look at all like the woman who'd shuddered in his arms last night as he brought her to orgasm.

Stars, her skin had tasted so sweet. An ancient line from Earth ran through his mind: *Sugar and spice and everything nice.*

With an effort, he dragged his mind off sex and did his best to listen to what she was saying.

"There is apparently no intelligent life on this planet," Vaish said in her chilliest tone. Evidently she'd noticed his mental drifting. "It doesn't seem to be used for any sort of refueling or mining, according to Fred's scans. And unfortunately, our beacon won't be detected from beyond this star system."

That was Vaish, Steven thought. Always harping on the negative. "So can we boost the signal?"

"I don't have sufficient energy reserves to do that," Fred said. "The lifepod is not designed for long-term use."

"Doesn't this thing use solar energy?" Vaish asked.

"It can't generate enough energy to run the instruments and computer over the long haul," Steven said. To himself, he thought, *Note to self: If we ever get back to civilized space, design a better lifepod.* "Hell. I don't know what the answer is."

"Forty-two?" Vaish suggested.

Steven ignored her. "How much energy do you have, Fred?"

"Approximately enough to operate for twenty-eight days. After that, you will be on your own."

Steven sighed. They needed the shelter of this lifepod to survive. They needed Fred, damn it. "And we're absolutely certain this planet is uninhabited?"

"Scans showed no signs of intelligent life. However..."

At Fred's significant pause, Steven straightened and scowled at the ceiling. "What is it, Fred?"

"I've found a few anomalous readings that suggest there may in fact be intelligent life on this planet, or at least that intelligent life has visited here. A few traces of humanoid DNA, a few skeletons of the indigenous lifeforms that appear to have been killed by weaponry. It's not easy to tell at a distance, since a particle weapon set on high doesn't leave a lot of remains, but I've located what I believe may be a few fragments of humanoid skeletons, too."

Steven frowned. "If there are people here, where could they be hiding?"

"There are caves all over the surface that have heavy metal components, making it impossible for me to scan. My guess is that if anyone else is on this planet, they are in those caves."

"It is highly unlikely a civilized society would live in caves," Vaish said. "If there are humans or humanoids on the planet, they are very probably quite primitive."

"A reasonable hypothesis," Fred said. "Except that, as I said, the skeletons appear to have been killed by blasters."

"That makes no sense," Vaish said.

"I don't know about that," Steven said, swallowing the last of his coffee with a wince. "This is the kind of planet where someone interested in steering clear of the Patrol might hide. Uninhabited and relatively unknown, with caves that are conveniently impossible to scan."

Vaish sniffed disdainfully. "You mean a criminal might be concealing himself in the caves?"

"It's a possibility. Might not even be a criminal, but just someone who doesn't want to be found for some reason. And if there is someone on this planet, he might be willing to help us get off."

"If this hypothetical person doesn't want to be found, it is highly unlikely he'd help us find a way off the planet. He would be much more likely to kill us."

"Good point," Steven admitted. Undaunted, he grinned. "We'll just have to make sure he doesn't have a choice, then."

* * * *

Vaish tried not to grumble as they set off into the warm, humid morning light. Once again she was armed only with a length of heavy pipe, and she was almost certainly going to end up as some huge feline's breakfast. All because there was a tiny, incredibly faint chance that there was someone on this planet who was highly unlikely to help them anyway.

Steven seemed cheerfully oblivious to her dark mood. He marched along, humming under his breath, for all the world as if they were out for a pleasant stroll in the country. She thought longingly about clubbing him in the head with her pipe, but realized that might be a trifle difficult to explain if rescue ever came.

What happened to Captain McNeill? Oh ... I'm sorry to say he fell and hit his head on a rock. Very unfortunate.

She didn't feel in the least like humming, conscious as she was of her uniform sticking uncomfortably to her body as sweat oozed from her pores. She knew she had looked and smelled better.

Not that it mattered, she amended hastily. After all, there was no one to see her but McNeill. And she certainly didn't care what *he* thought.

She was annoyed to see that he looked revoltingly attractive despite the oppressive heat. Perspiration had glued his uniform to his body, revealing the strong muscles that bunched and rolled beneath the ebony material. He'd pulled his long blond hair back into a ponytail, and sweat glistened on the nape of his neck. She had the ridiculous urge to lick it off. He even smelled good in the heat, a musky masculine scent that made her knees weak.

She tried to get her mind off McNeill's inexplicably attractive perspiration. After all, this was a dangerous planet, and she needed to be alert. "Precisely how many caves did Fred say there were near here?"

"Fifteen, ranging from one to five kilometers from camp. All together, the interiors of the caves comprise over a square kilometer's worth of ground to cover."

"It's going to take a long time to explore them all thoroughly."

"I don't have much else to do," McNeill said with that irritating cheerfulness that made her long to swing her pipe. "How about you?"

Vaish strove for a professional tone. "Since this planet has never been explored, cataloging the local flora and fauna would be the best use of my time."

"You're kidding, right? You think it matters to civilization whether or not you catalog dandelions?"

Vaish felt her hackles rise, metaphorically speaking. "That is my *job*, Captain. I am an exobiologist."

"News flash, sweetheart. Your job description just changed. Right now you're a hunter and gatherer. The only cataloguing you can do that's worth a damn is finding out which plants in the area are edible. But before we start wasting our time looking for edible plants, let's devote ourselves to hunting for an intelligent life form that can get us the hell off this planet."

Vaish sighed, mentally conceding the point. Unless they got off the planet, exploring this planet's biosphere was quite simply a waste of time. And if they didn't get off the planet ... well, she'd have plenty of time to explore later and determine what plants could be used in stew.

They had marched off across the vast meadow, according to Fred's directions. McNeill's communicator beeped, and he pulled it out. "Hi, Fred. Are we still heading in the right direction?"

"Pretty much," Fred's voice answered. "But you might want to go in another direction."

McNeill frowned. "What do you mean?"

"There's a cat headed your way ... in a big hurry."

* * * *

Hell. They were sitting ducks out here, McNeill thought as he ran at top speed toward the lifepod, Vaish on his heels. She had long legs and was a remarkably fast runner. Of course, the threat of being eaten for breakfast was enough to put wings on anybody's feet.

Suddenly Vaish stumbled and fell, and he heard her give a muffled yelp of pain. Swerving back, he bent, scooped her up, and kept running. She struggled in his arms.

"I'm fine, Captain!"

He doubted it. Nothing less than excruciating pain would have wrung a yelp from this stubborn, proud woman. He barreled on, grateful that she was fairly light. Not a featherweight by any means, but her lithe, graceful body had little extra fat.

And then she lifted her head, gazing over his shoulder. "Oh, no."

McNeill turned his head and saw an enormous, tawny creature bounding toward them. "Stars," he said under his breath. "Look at the size of that thing."

It was too close. They weren't going to make it to the lifepod. He slid to a halt and put Vaish down, none too gently. He didn't have time to be gentle, although he regretted it when she hissed between her teeth and collapsed to the ground.

He yanked his metal pipe from his waistband and ran toward the creature.

"Are you *crazy?*"

He heard Vaish's indignant voice behind him, but ignored it. If he failed to kill the creature, there was a faint hope that if he drew it far enough from Vaish, it wouldn't notice her. With an injured leg, there was no way she could defend herself.

When the cat was almost on him, he stopped and braced himself.

Stars, but the thing was big--the size of a pony, with two curving ivory fangs that really did bear a startling resemblance to sabers. He didn't stand a chance in hell of killing the thing without a blaster.

Which he regretted, because it meant Vaish wasn't going to survive, either.

Not that he cared for Vaish in any sort of romantic way. It was just that they'd worked together for five years, and he thought of her as ... a friend. Sort of. A friend that irritated him like excessively tight underwear. A friend that got on his nerves and argued with him unnecessarily. A friend with a really gorgeous body.

A body that was about to be eaten, if he didn't get his mind back on this situation right now.

The cat slid to a halt, so close that he could smell the strong, musky scent of it, and studied him. Steven stared back at it, not sure what the hell was going on, but not liking it much. He had braced himself for a fight, and now the creature was just ... standing there. Weird.

Its green eyes shifted behind him, and Steven heard a rustling of grass. He risked a quick glance over his shoulder and saw Vaish limping toward him.

Damn the woman. She never did what he wanted her to do. Really, he was going to have to have her court-martialed. Assuming they survived, which seemed pretty damned unlikely at this point.

She stumbled up next to Steven and gazed intently at the cat, which stared back.

"Go," she said.

Steven felt his jaw drop open as the cat turned and glided away through the purple grass.

Within moments the cat had disappeared. Steven turned and looked at Vaish. "What the hell?"

She gave him a faint smile and turned, limping back toward the lifepod.

"Excuse me," Steven said. "What did you just do?"

She lifted her eyebrows. "I didn't do anything, Captain."

"You did so. That was definitely something."

"That was nothing, Captain."

"Look, I know what nothing looks like, and that wasn't it."

"There is no way you can know what nothing looks like, when by definition nothing is not visible."

"Okay. Maybe it wasn't nothing. But it sure as hell was something."

"I have absolutely no idea what you're talking about, Captain. I assure you, I did nothing."

"But--" Steven sighed. "Oh, the hell with it. Never mind."

Chapter Six

When they got back to the lifepod, Steven insisted on examining Vaish's leg to make sure it wasn't broken. She leaned back and tried to ignore his big hands sliding up and down her leg.

It wasn't easy to ignore. Especially when his fingers pressed against her swollen ankle. She groaned.

Steven shot her his cockiest grin. "I tend to have that effect on women."

"That was not a sound of pleasure, you idiot."

"You shouldn't refer to me as an idiot, you know. I'm your captain."

She lifted an eyebrow and quoted his earlier words. "News flash, *Captain*. Your job description just changed."

"So you're telling me you're free to insult me?"

"I don't see any good reason to restrain myself. I've been restraining myself for five years. It feels good to let it all out."

"If we ever get back to civilization, I'm going to court-martial you."

"I'm willing to take that chance."

Steven chuckled, not at all annoyed by her mouthiness. He was glad she felt up to being mouthy. "It's not broken," he said, "but it looks like a sprain."

"Fred already said that," Vaish pointed out.

"Yes, well. Technology is all very well and good, but it's best to verify."

"Who are you calling technology?" Fred's voice said.

Vaish snorted. "Ignore him, Fred. He just wanted an opportunity to put his hands all over my leg."

Steven grinned wryly as he began bandaging her swollen ankle. "Hate to break it to you, sweetheart, but right now this isn't the most gorgeous leg I've ever seen. It looks a bit like a watermelon."

"A what?"

"A large ovoid fruit."

Vaish almost growled with indignation, then glanced down at her ankle and decided to keep her growl to herself. She had to admit her leg did look pretty bad.

"What are we going to do now?"

Steven lifted an eyebrow. "I'm going to bandage your ankle."

"I don't mean right now. I mean, how are we going to explore the planet?"

"Obviously you're going to stay right here, and I'm going to do the exploring."

"You can't do that. You don't have a prayer of fighting off one of those felines by yourself." She still remembered the awful panic she'd felt when Steven had dumped her on the ground and raced away to fight the huge creature, armed only with a metal pipe. The man might be as dumb as a rock, but she couldn't fault his courage.

She was surprised to realize how terrified she'd been. Obviously Steven meant more to her than she had previously let herself admit.

Steven nodded, looking grim. "I think I would have been kitty chow today if you hadn't done ... whatever it was you did. Come on, Vaish, level with me. Do you have psychic powers?"

Vaish shrugged. "The truth is, my people have very limited psi powers. We can control simple minds. At least we can control the native fauna on our own planet. I wasn't at all certain it would work on an alien species."

"Good thing for us it did." Steven narrowed his eyes at her. "You can't influence humans, can you?"

Vaish smiled serenely. "That depends on how simple the mind is. In your case, I should think you are quite simple enough."

"I beg your pardon?"

"I was joking, Captain. We cannot influence a sentient mind."

"You know, your jokes aren't very funny."

"I'm an exobiologist, not a standup comedian." Vaish frowned. "The point is, Captain--"

"Call me Steven. You pointed out I'm not really a captain any more. We're both retired from the Patrol until further notice."

"Very well ... Steven. The point is, we can't risk you. It isn't safe to try to find those caves."

"Probably safer than staying here long-term."

"There is no definitive proof that anyone else actually resides on this planet. To risk your life in such a gamble seems reckless."

"Reckless is what I do." Steven got to his feet and looked down at her, his jaw set like granite. "Risk is my business, Vaish. I'm not dooming us both to a lifetime of being stranded on this planet if I can possibly help it." He looked out the pod door, which showed the sun high in the greenish sky. "But it's too late in the day for me to make it to those caves and back. I'll take off first thing tomorrow."

* * * *

The rest of the afternoon was quiet. A pleasantly warm breeze blew through the open door of the lifepod, and the eerie cries of alien birds filled the air. Steven amused himself by playing solitaire on the lifepod's small readout. Vaish sat on the floor, her ankle stretched out, and read from a handheld reader. At last she rose painfully to her feet and headed for the door.

"Where do you think you're going?" Steven demanded.

She shrugged, looking slightly embarrassed. "I need to use the head."

And of course there wasn't a head in the lifepod. They'd both used the meadow yesterday and this morning, but he wasn't thrilled by the idea of letting her go outside in her current impaired condition. He was coming up with all sorts of improvements for lifepod design, if he ever got back to Patrol space. "Fred, are there any lifeforms around the pod?"

"There are numerous insects. Do you want a precise count?"

Steven sighed, both amused and exasperated at Fred's literal-mindedness. "No thanks. I was referring to dangerous animals."

"There don't appear to be any."

Steven nodded toward the door. "Go ahead, Vaish. Do you need help?"

A violet flush appeared on her cheekbones. "Uh, no. I can make it that far."

She hobbled out and disappeared out of view of the door. Steven went back to playing solitaire but kept one eye on the door.

Suddenly there was a scream from outside. At the same moment, the lifepod door slammed closed.

"What the fuck--" Steven jumped to his feet. "Fred! What happened?"

"A large feline suddenly materialized," Fred informed him.

"*What*? You mean like out of thin air?"

"Yes. That is precisely what I mean. Some sort of rematerialization device must have been--"

Never lower your shields. Damn it. He'd fucked up again, and good, by allowing Vaish to leave the lifepod unprotected, while he sat on his ass and played solitaire.

A vision of Vaish being torn apart by a cat's saber teeth flashed through Steven's mind. She'd been able to fend off one of the animals--but suppose she couldn't do it again? She was in pain, and it was entirely possible she wouldn't be able to focus her mind enough to control the beast this time. "Open the goddamn door!"

"I'm afraid that's against regulations, Steven. Regulations clearly state that when a captain is in danger, he must be--"

"Fuck regulations! Let me outside!"

"I cannot allow you to risk your life in an effort to rescue a junior offi--"

"Open the pod door, Fred!"

"I'm sorry, Steven. I'm afraid I can't do that."

Cursing lividly, Steven lunged for the control panel. He hit the button that activated the outside microphone and heard a low growling.

At least Vaish wasn't screaming any more. But that might be because she'd been eaten.

Suddenly the pod door exploded inward. Steven spun toward the door, expecting to see the cat's enormous head. Instead what he saw was a lovely blue woman with four arms. A Noo'dis't, but not the one who'd taken over his ship.

This woman he recognized. Because he'd slept with her three years before.

And then marooned her.

Chapter Seven

The blue-skinned woman smiled tightly as she studied Steven. "Well, well. Look what the cat dragged in."

Steven saw Vaish behind her, held tightly by another woman, a crude-looking particle weapon pressed to her temple. He was relieved she was alive, but all things considered, he'd rather take his chances with a saber-toothed cat than with Jan Zteglet. He felt his mouth compress.

"Fabulous," he said to Fred. "Of all the planets in all the galaxies in all the universe, she walks into mine."

"Actually," the woman said, "this is *my* planet. You marooned my followers and myself here three years ago, as you may recall."

Steven gritted his teeth. Unfortunately, one alien planet looked much like another, and the *Arisia* hadn't been anywhere near this solar system when he'd been shot. "I wasn't aware this was Harmon IV."

"I didn't know that was relevant information," Fred said.

Steven sighed. At the order of his Patrol superiors, he'd suppressed the information about Jan's attempt to take over the Alliance and her subsequent exile on Harmon IV, and erased it from Fred's memory. The powers that be had been embarrassed by how easily a hundred people had taken over several ships, and they wanted to keep the episode quiet. It looked like that decision had returned to bite him in the ass.

Not that they could have avoided landing here anyway, since this was the only Earth-type planet in the solar system. All things considered, he breathed better in an oxygen atmosphere than a methane one.

He scowled at the woman. "Did you carry out this elaborate plan this just to capture me?"

"I see your ego is as big as ever," Jan said.

"Bigger," Vaish said under her breath.

He barely suppressed a smile--he loved the way Vaish never lost her smart mouth, even under pressure. In fact, he was beginning to realize he loved a lot of things about Vaish.

It was up to him to make sure her head remained attached to her shoulders--something that mattered more to him than he'd previously realized.

"It has nothing to do with ego. It seems like a bit of a coincidence that my ship was taken over by a Noo'dis't, and the only safe place for us to land our lifepod just happened to be Harmon IV."

The woman smiled, showing her sharp incisors. "You're right, of course. After years of exile, a Canvul scout ship happened to land here, and we ... borrowed ... their vessel. I sent one of my most trusted lieutenants to take over your ship."

Steven felt a stab of pity for the hapless Canvulians, who were doubtless some of those skeletons killed by particle weapons Fred had noted. "Why didn't you do it yourself? Ah, I know why. Because you're a coward, and you'd rather risk the life of a subordinate than your own worthless neck."

"Big words, *Captain*." Jan lifted the particle weapon she held and aimed it directly at his crotch. "Keep it up and I'm going to have to perform some surgery."

Steven flashed an unconcerned grin, refusing to show any fear. She hadn't gone through all the trouble to bring him down here just to kill him or maim him. He hoped.

"Won't do you any good to shoot me there," he drawled. "I have balls of steel."

"And a brain of stone," Vaish muttered.

Jan chuckled and lowered the weapon. "You might be right, McNeill. At any rate, I need you ... intact."

"Why did you send us here in the lifepod? Why not just have the *Arisia* or the Canvul scout ship bring us here?"

"My people aboard the *Arisia* had other things to accomplish before they returned to this system, and the scout ship was an integral part of their plans. We weren't sure how long it would take. It was quicker and easier to have them deliver you to us gift-wrapped, and to let them go on their way."

Great. That was precisely what he had feared. The heavily armed *Arisia* was roaming around this sector under hostile control, doing the Stars knew what. "Then why didn't you pick us up yesterday?"

"I knew you weren't going anywhere." Jan's dark blue eyes glittered. "I wanted you to experience firsthand the unpleasant sensation of knowing you were stranded on a planet for the rest of your life."

A vision of Vaish moaning in his arms flashed into his brain. That probably wasn't the unpleasant sensation Jan had had in mind, he thought wryly. "What exactly do you want from us?"

Jan studied him up and down, a hot, suggestive look in her eyes that would have turned him on, once upon a time. But all he could think about right now was Vaish, and how the hell he was going to get her out of this situation.

"You left us stranded here," she said at last. "A hundred women. As you may recall, we are all genetically enhanced with superior physical and mental attributes."

"D cups do not constitute mental attributes," Vaish said.

Jan ignored the snide remark. "We need to reproduce, to create more of our superior bloodlines. For this we require a male."

Steven felt his eyebrows shoot up. "You're telling me you captured me for stud duty?"

A cold smile curved the edges of her mouth. "Precisely."

The thought of being used to service a hundred women who'd once tried to take over the Patrol, and who would doubtless raise their children to believe it was their duty to take over the civilized galaxy, made his blood run cold. But he forced a grin onto his face.

"Well, hell. My day just got a whole lot better."

"Steven!" Vaish said sharply, apparently under the opinion that he was actually looking forward to being used as a sperm donor. He must be a better actor than he thought if she believed he would really look forward to such an existence. Or maybe it simply reflected her low opinion of him. "This makes no sense. If they wanted you, why did they send me along?"

"You have one use, and one use only." Jan smiled as she caressed the particle weapon in her hand. "If McNeill steps out of line or tries to escape, we'll hurt you. Badly."

"A foolish plan," Vaish said with ice in her voice. "Steven is not that concerned about my well-being."

"Oh, I think he is. It was evident to me even three years ago that he was in love with you."

Well, shit, Steven thought. It sure as hell hadn't been evident to *him*, but he didn't say so. In retrospect, it did seem that he'd had ... feelings ... for Vaish for quite some time. Not that he'd call it love. More like intense affection.

Which made the fact that he'd been sleeping with every woman to cross his path over the past five years seem a little less than noble, somehow.

He put the matter out of his mind and dredged up his best dumb expression. It really wasn't much of a stretch to look dumb, unfortunately. He liked to think it was because he was a terrific actor, but he was secretly concerned it was because he really wasn't too bright. The Stars knew that if he had half a brain he wouldn't have been in this mess to begin with.

"Don't worry, I'll behave myself," he said. "It sounds like a great plan to me anyway. Stranded on a gorgeous planet and having sex with a hundred beautiful women. I mean, is there a downside here?"

"You might think so," Jan said. "Because when all of us are pregnant, we're going to kill you."

Steven swallowed, and his grin faded. "Yeah, you're right. That's definitely a downside."

* * * *

Steven had never been through a rematerializer before. The Alliance had banned them, and for good reason. The device took a body apart molecule by molecule, and didn't always reassemble them quite perfectly. The slightest mechanical error, and a man could find himself quite dead. Or at least missing something crucial.

At least the process wasn't painful. One moment he was standing in a sunny meadow, and the next he found himself standing in a gloomy, dank cave. He couldn't prevent himself from glancing down. He was relieved to see it looked like his balls were still there.

This might have been a good time to try to make a break for freedom, except one of Jan's stooges had a particle weapon trained on the rematerialization pad. He stood quietly and waited. A moment later Jan rematerialized, with Vaish next to her.

"Move off the pad," she said. Mindful of the gun pointed in his direction, Steven moved.

He was relieved to see Vaish, but he was still concerned about Fred. Since Fred had moved his whole personality into the lifepod, they could easily destroy him simply by blowing up the lifepod. He hoped they wouldn't do that, since they probably needed the machinery and could doubtless use a computer. But it was nevertheless a possibility, since they must realize Fred was loyal to him and would make their lives difficult if at all possible.

He'd designed Fred ten years ago, and the artificial intelligence had been his closest friend ever since. The thought of losing him after all this time caused a pang in his chest, as sharp as if Fred had been an organic lifeform. The truth was that, computer or no computer, Fred was more human than many humans were.

"So, McNeill," Jan said, gesturing around her. "What do you think of our home?"

Steven looked around. He hadn't marooned Jan and her followers with enough raw material to create shelters, since there was plenty of wood on the planet to build with, but he had left them with some materials for the building of furniture. Metal bunks stood arrayed against the walls, and lights had been placed every few meters, but very little else had been done to make the dark cavern seem friendlier.

"I just *love* what you've done with the place," he said.

"You marooned us here," Jan said, her voice dripping with anger. "We've done our best to make a life here. We managed to train the cats--despite their size they're really quite biddable and make excellent pets--but there are other dangers, so we live in the caves."

"Very homey. They should put you on the cover of *Galactic Home Decorating*."

A crowd of thirty or forty stunningly beautiful, statuesque women had started to gather around them. Steven looked at them, seeing faces he recognized from Jan's first attempt to take over the *Arisia*, and from there the galaxy. Some of them were Noo'dis'ts, but numerous other species were represented as well. All of them were genetically engineered--the work of a scientist who'd obviously liked big breasts--and all of them were looking at him with lust.

He knew it had to be lust because that was what women always had in their eyes when they stared at him. Although in this case lust looked an awful lot like hatred.

"Now," Jan said. "Take off your clothes."

Steven blinked. "I beg your pardon?"

"Take off your clothes. Let's see what you've got."

Ordinarily stripping in front of a woman didn't really bother him, but taking off his clothes in front of a crowd of hostile, hard-eyed women made him oddly nervous. Steven slid a sideways look at Vaish, but to his dismay she didn't appear too sympathetic to his plight. In fact, a small smile seemed to be playing around her mouth. Sighing, he stripped off his shirt.

"Not bad," Jan said.

"Not *bad*?"

Jan ignored his indignant response. "Take it off," she said, nodding toward his pants. "Take it all off."

Steven kicked off his boots, then, very reluctantly, pulled his pants off. He was accustomed to seeing women gape with stunned delight at the size of his package. But then, he was used to dealing with women on a one-on-one basis--or at least no more than two at once. Okay, maybe three at once.

He sure as hell wasn't accustomed to being stared at like some sort of sex toy.

The women stared with cold, contemptuous eyes, and a sick feeling of humiliation started to roil in his gut.

"I suppose you'll do," Jan said. "But I've seen better."

Steven did his best to ignore the embarrassment welling within him. He met her eyes and forced a sardonic smile to his lips. "If you've seen better, you've seen plastic surgery."

"Not at all. I've had a Klaxon warrior. You haven't lived till you've had a Klaxon."

A murmur of agreement went around the cavern. "Or a Canvul," Vaish said helpfully.

"That's right," another of the women, a human, agreed. "I've been to Canvulia, and trust me, sex with a Canvul man is not something you want to miss." She held up her hands about thirty centimeters apart. "The one I had was this big!"

That is way more information than I wanted to know, Steven thought. He remembered what Vaish had said about Canvul men, and gritted his teeth together.

"Well, the Klaxon warrior I had--" Jan started, but Steven decided he couldn't take this any more.

"Are you ladies quite finished with me?" he said in his iciest tone.

Jan looked at him, an insolent light in her eyes he didn't care for in the least.

"We haven't yet begun, McNeill. You'll know when we do. Trust me."

Chapter Eight

To Steven's disgust, he found himself forced to stand at the center of the cavern, like an animal exhibited at the zoo, while the women went about their business. He stood in a force field, half a meter by half a meter, too small to let him sit. Presumably they wanted to keep him on display.

They walked past him as they went about their business, making lewd comments about the size of his schlong or the tightness of his ass and copping feels. Evidently the force field was configured so that they could reach in, but he couldn't get out.

It was the single most humiliating experience of his life. He'd always seen women as sex objects, and never really given thought to how the women might feel about that. Now he had a pretty good idea. And he didn't like it in the least.

Even Vaish wasn't being a lot of help. She was confined near him--although in a slightly larger field, so she could at least sit down, pace, and even lie down if she got tired--and she was watching him with a glitter of icy amusement in her yellow eyes.

"You think this is funny?" he challenged her at last, irritated by her amusement.

Vaish, seated on the floor with her injured leg stretched out, seemed to consider the matter for a moment. "Yes. I do."

"I know you want me," he said, more harshly than he intended. He was aware he was taking his anger out on the wrong target, but couldn't seem to help himself. "Let's see how funny you find it when I'm forced to have sex with a hundred different women."

Vaish looked up at him for a long moment. At last she said in a low voice, "Steven, I've had to watch you have sex with other women for years. I don't see how this will be any different."

There was a world of hurt in her tone, and Steven felt a swelling of regret in his chest. He'd never set out to hurt her. Until the last twenty-four hours, it had never really occurred to him that she'd cared.

Or that he did.

But he did care. He realized that now, and he only wished he'd realized it earlier. "Vaish," he said, gently, "I never meant--"

There was a flash, and the lifepod materialized in the cavern. Steven felt a surge of relief. If the lifepod was intact, odds were that Fred was too. He just hoped the computer's circuits hadn't been scrambled by the rematerialization process.

That fear instantly dissipated when Fred's anxious voice came over the loudspeakers, echoing in the cavern.

"Steven! Steven, are you all right?"

"I'm fine," Steven answered, knowing Fred could hear him through his sensors. "They haven't hurt me."

"But you're not wearing clothes."

"You're very observant, Fred. Jan and her friends took them."

"Aren't you cold? My sensors indicate that the ambient temperature is rather chilly for humans."

Steven bit back an annoyed response, aware that the computer tended to cluck like a mother hen when he was worried. "I'm fine, Fred. What about you?"

"I'm fine. The rematerialization process didn't hurt me. But I picked up a transmission. The *Arisia* is in this solar system."

Steven felt a brief horror that Fred had provided this information in front of the enemy, then remembered that the *Arisia* was in enemy hands. He glared at Jan, who was watching the exchange with interest. "What are you doing with my ship?"

"It's *my* ship now, McNeill. And I'm going to take over the Patrol, and from there all of Galactic civilization."

"Yeah, right," Steven scoffed.

Jan glared at him through slitted, dark blue eyes. "I find your lack of faith disturbing."

"Find this disturbing," he said, and saluted her with his middle finger.

From the corner of his eye, he saw Vaish almost crack a smile at his adolescent behavior. Almost, but not quite. He noticed she didn't join him in saluting Jan, either. "A typical plan," she grumbled. "Do villains always have to try to take over the entire galaxy? Can't they just settle for taking over a planet or two?"

"That would be small thinking," Jan said. She glanced at Steven's crotch. "I don't think small."

Frustrated, Steven balled his hands into fists. Damn it. The *Arisia* was right here, in this solar system, and there wasn't any way of reaching it. Even if it landed in the meadow, he was trapped in a force field.

He had to find a way to get out of this situation. It wasn't just him and Vaish--it was all of Galactic civilization. Even with only one or two ships, Jan could wreak significant havoc. Jan had proven herself to be a resourceful adversary, and he'd barely stopped her plan of galactic conquest last time. Now she had a warship at her disposal.

Not a good scenario. And it was all his fault.

"We have a few subunits before the *Arisia* arrives," Jan said. A ship couldn't distort space within a star system without causing it to go nova, so it had to travel at lower speeds within the system. She walked toward Steven, an evil grin on her face. "And they can wait if necessary. We have plenty of time to play."

Great. They could do anything they liked to him, since they could reach into the force field and he couldn't reach out, and there wasn't a thing he could do to stop them. He wasn't looking forward to being raped, but there didn't seem to be any way to avoid it. He emptied his mind and stared at the opposite wall, bracing himself for what promised to be an extremely unpleasant experience.

And then he heard a roar.

One of the great felines bounded into the cave. It raised its paw and struck into the crowd of women. Women flew everywhere,

48

like bowling pins in an old-fashioned game Steven had learned on
Earth. The women who hadn't been knocked senseless struggled
to their feet and fled, screaming, down the various passageways.

At the same moment, the force field surrounding Steven
flickered off. Despite the fact that he was stiff from his enforced
immobility, he leaped in front of Vaish, intending to protect her
from the cat.

"Very noble, Steven," her acidic voice said from behind him.
"But perhaps you've forgotten that I can control the beast. It's not
going to hurt me."

Steven turned to face her, noticing that her force field was down
as well. They were both free. She came to her feet, awkwardly,
and scratched the cat between its ears as it stretched its enormous
head toward her.

"You brought it in here," he said, amazed, as the cat gave him a
friendly nudge with its head that almost knocked him over.

"Of course. Did you think it simply decided to come in here at
an opportune moment and start kicking Noo'dis't ass? I
summoned it."

"How did you manage to drop the force fields?"

"I did that," Fred interjected cheerfully. "It was easy. I just
emitted a frequency that interfered with their normal operation. I
figured out how to do it a while ago, but I was waiting for a good
chance, because I figured they wouldn't let me get away with it
more than once."

Steven let out a long sigh and turned back toward Fred, giving
the cat a hesitant pat on the head. It purred loudly, rumbling like
the *Arisia's* engines under full acceleration. "Hell. I should just
retire. You guys don't need me."

"Not for any practical purpose, no." Vaish reached out and, to
his immense shock, pinched his naked butt cheek. He looked back
over his shoulder to see her grinning up at him. "But you're
decorative, so we'll keep you around."

"Thanks a whole lot," he grumbled.

"At any rate," Fred said, "if you're feeling useless, maybe you
can come up with a plan to recover the *Arisia.*"

"Good idea." Steven stepped away from the friendly cat and
headed toward the lifepod, stepping over the inert bodies of
several women. "Let's tie up these women first, then we'll see
what we can do."

* * * *

He was going to get the *Arisia* back. Because otherwise he'd be stuck in this paradise for the rest of his life with Vaish, and that simply wasn't something he could tolerate. Trapped alone in a paradise with a beautiful woman ... nope. Not a good way to spend the rest of his existence.

At least he kept telling himself that.

Vaish busied herself tying up the five women on the floor, who had only been knocked unconscious, while Steven put his uniform back on. She informed Steven she'd told the big cat to keep its claws sheathed, but even so he was amazed the force of that big paw hadn't killed any of the women. Apparently the cat had just been playing with them, like a housecat with a ball of yarn. She'd sent the cat out of the cave, which was just as well, because its strong, musky scent had filled the enclosed area in an unpleasant way, and the cat itself had taken up a great deal of the available space.

Once the cat was gone, Fred set up force fields around the main section of the cave to keep out any of the other women who had fled. After a half unit of trying, Steven managed to break into the Noo'dis'ts' computer system--he might not be good for anything else, but he was still one hell of a hacker--and was ready to implement his plan to get the *Arisia* back.

"You're absolutely sure you can alter my voice?" he said to Fred.

"Trust me," Fred said, his voice echoing in the cavern. "To them you're going to sound just like Jan."

"Great." He turned back to the computer.

At that moment, the power flickered, and the force fields went down. Steven heard bare feet echoing on the stone floor, approaching at high speed, and a high voice shrilled, "From hell's heart I stab at thee!"

He turned to see Jan running at him, her D cups bouncing, her face distorted with rage. In one of her four hands she clutched a long, sharp knife, which would certainly be handy for stabbing at him, from hell's heart or otherwise.

Vaish calmly limped between them, balled her fist, and swung her arm. Her fist connected solidly with Jan's chin, and Jan collapsed to the floor, senseless.

"Damn," Steven said, impressed. "That's one hell of a right hook."

"I realized I had best intervene," Vaish said, her voice tart. "Since you can't be trusted to defend yourself against a naked woman."

"Trust me, when it comes to defending myself against a woman with a knife, I have no sense of chivalry."

"I'm not accusing you of chivalry. I know better. I'm implying you were too busy studying her breasts."

"Ah." Steven stared down at the inert heap on the floor thoughtfully, then looked back up at Vaish and grinned. "Nope. I'd rather study yours."

To his amusement, she flushed violet. Steven grinned. "Tie her up and gag her, Vaish." He looked over at the lifepod. "Fred, how'd she get the force field down?"

"The same method I used," Fred said, sounding embarrassed. "She used her recording device to emit a frequency that interfered with the force field. I was able to restore power almost instantly, though, which is why none of her followers made it through."

"Can you make sure it doesn't happen again?"

"I'm cycling the force field harmonics. It won't happen again."

"Great." Steven noticed that Jan was secured. He turned back to the console.

"Okay, Fred. Let's rock and roll."

He flipped open the channel and began to speak, trusting that Fred's wizardry could turn his baritone voice into a convincing soprano.

"*Arisia*, this is Jan. We have captured McNeill and await your arrival."

"Understood, Jan," an alto voice replied. The signal fluttered and broke up briefly, then stabilized. Steven suspected the ship's communications weren't running well without Fred. "We will be within rematerialization range in three subunits."

Rematerialization? Not a good idea, Steven thought. He didn't trust the process in the least, and besides, if he and Vaish were brought onto the ship in that fashion, they'd be helpless while their atoms were reassembled. They'd be instantly captured and thrown into the brig. And he'd be back to being used as a stud. Not at all what he had in mind.

"There's been a change in plans," he said. "I want you to land the *Arisia* on the planet."

There was a puzzled silence. "Why?"

"I've discovered something interesting that we should explore further."

There was a pause, during which Steven held his breath. "Very well," the voice said at last, and he exhaled in relief. "We'll be touching down in approximately twenty subunits."

Steven disconnected. "Great," he said over his shoulder. "Now we just have to find some weapons, board the ship, take them by surprise, and reclaim the *Arisia*. Piece of cake."

"Of course," Vaish said. "Piece of cake."

Chapter Nine

Vaish and Steven stood concealed behind an outcropping of rocks and watched as the round gray bulk of the Arisia touched down, some distance away. "How exactly are we going to get on board?" Vaish inquired.

"I'm hoping much of the crew will disembark."

The communicator on Steven's belt crackled to life. "Jan? Jan, where are you?"

Steven opened it and spoke, his voice still altered by Fred's electronic wizardry. "I'm in the cave. Have your crew join me there."

Sure enough, twenty women filed off the gangway and headed toward the cave. Vaish growled under her breath. "Genetically engineered superior intelligence, my ass. These women were genetically engineered for absolutely nothing but big--"

"Vaish. Are you jealous?"

"Hardly," she said disdainfully. "I have perfectly adequate breasts, but I also have a brain to go with them. The two are not mutually exclusive, you know."

"Yeah, I know. And I've recently discovered I prefer women with both."

She felt a rush of warmth in her cheeks and looked away, back at the women. They all walked into the cave. As the last one stepped out of sight, there was a sudden flare of light at the cave's mouth.

"Fred has put up the force field," Steven said. "They're trapped, along with the other group of women. Time for Phase Two."

"Right. That's the phase where we get our heads shot off."

"That's my girl. Always with the positive." He flashed his grin at her, and she tried to tamp down the rush of warmth she felt at being called "his girl."

Looking down at her weapon, she made a show of checking it for power. Their weapons were primitive, to say the least. Jan's people had managed to construct particle weapons from the small amount of raw materials Steven had marooned them with, which showed that they weren't completely brainless, but there was no guarantee the guns would work properly. Even so, they were a vast improvement over metal pipes. She holstered the pistol and awaited his command.

Steven looked across the purple grass at the *Arisia*, a look of love and longing on his face. "Now," he whispered.

He dashed for the spaceship, and she hobbled on his heels. A few seconds later, when they got to the gangplank, she was surprised to see it was still open--either the women were all too busy doing their nails to watch the monitors, or Fred had managed to block their monitors somehow. She sincerely hoped it was the latter. She didn't like to think a group of complete morons had managed to take over the *Arisia*. If that were the case, they very badly needed to do some drills with the crew.

Assuming the crew was alive. She decided it was better not to think about that right now. She limped up the gangplank behind Steven, their booted feet echoing on the metal, and they emerged in a familiar corridor.

It was empty.

"No guards," Steven said out of the corner of his mouth. "How convenient."

"Maybe it's a trap," she ventured as they jogged down the white-walled corridor together. Every step sent a stab of pain through her leg, but she did her best to ignore it. She couldn't afford to be self-indulgent just now.

She noticed the ivory carpet beneath her feet was streaked with dirt. Without Fred, the drones obviously hadn't been able to clean the ship. Doubtless the other functions of the ship were suffering without the artificial intelligence, too.

"Could be a trap, I guess," Steven admitted. "Or maybe they're just not too bright."

"You know, you're a lucky guy. Most people have archenemies who challenge them, archenemies who test their wits. You, on the other hand, have an archenemy who isn't bright enough to locate her thumb without a map and detailed directions."

"Jan seems bright enough. Maybe she's simply cursed with dim associates."

A particle beam suddenly lanced from a cross corridor. They jumped apart and lunged for cover, diving into doorways on either side of the corridor. "Or," Vaish suggested, firing down the corridor, "they were simply waiting for us."

Steven aimed his weapon and fired. "That seems like a distinct possibility."

Conversation lagged as they continued to fire. Vaish noticed with surprise that there appeared to be only one person firing at them. She had expected a large group, and the fact that there was apparently only one person guarding the ship made her more suspicious than before.

A few moments later the fire from down the corridor ceased. Steven lowered his weapon. "Looks like we got her."

"Or she's trying to lure us out so they can shoot us."

"Could be." Steven stood up and stepped out into plain view. Vaish held her breath, but nothing happened.

"Yeah, I think we definitely got her."

She stepped out of the alcove and saw a body lying on the metal planking some distance down the corridor. "You are so damned lucky," she grumbled.

"Sometimes it's better to be lucky than good." He holstered his pistol. "Come on, let's see if we can make it to the bridge."

* * * *

No one attacked them on the way to the bridge. Since Vaish's ankle was still too painful to allow her to climb a ladder, Vaish and Steven went up by way of the lift. Vaish half expected it to stop halfway up and trap them, but nothing of the sort happened. They drew their weapons and waited, then leapt onto the bridge when the lift doors opened.

There was no one on the bridge except for a frightened-looking, young human woman, who surrendered the bridge without argument.

"There," Steven said, sitting down in his captain's chair while Vaish tied up the woman. "That wasn't so hard, was it?"

"It was entirely too easy," Vaish said. "I think it's a trap."

"There you go with the negative thinking again."

"It has nothing to do with negativity and everything to do with logic. We've gotten back on the ship much too easily. If these women were truly that stupid, they couldn't have taken over the *Arisia*."

Steven leaned back in his chair and looked up at her contemplatively. "We had to kill one of them to get this far, Vaish."

"We don't know that we killed her. We used their weapons, which they conveniently left where we could find them. For all we know these weapons are set for stun only. In fact, it seems like a distinct possibility. This is a trap, Steven. It has to be. No one could possibly be this stupid."

"I disagree. The available evidence suggests they are this stupid." Steven toggled the switch. "Fred, are you there?"

"I'm still in the cave," Fred said, his voice filling the bridge. "I now have sixty prisoners."

Vaish frowned. "Jan has approximately a hundred followers, and a large number of them are still unaccounted for."

Steven shrugged. "Maybe they got lost on the *Arisia* and accidentally wandered out of an airlock."

"I think you are taking this entire situation too lightly, Steven."

"You worry too much." He turned back to the console. "You did a good job trapping them, Fred. Can you transfer yourself back into the *Arisia's* computer core now?"

The memory of the *Arisia's* dirt-streaked carpet suddenly flashed into Vaish's mind. "No!" she yelped.

Steven turned to look at her, frowning. "We can't very well run the ship without Fred, can we?"

"Close the channel," she said urgently. When he did, she went on in a rapid stream. "Neither can they. Don't you see, Steven? *That's* why they let us regain the bridge. They've probably been having a great deal of difficulty running the ship without Fred, and they can't get him back into the mainframe without us. That's why they let us back on board once we got out of the cave. They knew the first thing we'd do was reload Fred back into the main computer, and they could then get rid of us and have full control over the ship."

Steven frowned. "You're being paranoid."

"Even the paranoid have enemies."

Steven thought about it. "How would they retake the ship? There isn't anyone left on board."

"We didn't check to make sure that woman we shot was dead, Steven. She may not be. And there are thirty-nine women unaccounted for."

"Computer," Steven said to the air. "Lock the doors to the bridge."

"Acknowledged," the computer said in its flat, unFredlike voice. "There. They can't get in now."

"Even if that worked--and they've had over a day to reprogram the computer, so it may very well not have--it's simple enough to incapacitate us, Steven. All they'd have to do is flood the ship with prezidene gas, precisely as they did last time."

He nodded. There was still a skeptical light in his eyes, but he was too good a captain not to cover all contingencies. Besides, he did always listen to her instincts. That was one thing she appreciated about him.

"Grab a couple of gas masks," he said.

She strode quickly across the bridge, found gas masks in the emergency cupboards, and put one on herself. She tossed him one, and he pulled it on.

"Okay," he said, his voice distorted by the mask. "Let's see if your theory is correct."

He toggled open the connection. "Fred," he said, lifting the mask away from his face momentarily so his voice sounded normal. "Are you there?"

"I'm waaaiiiiting," Fred said, managing to convey toe-tapping impatience rather well, for someone who didn't have toes.

"Okay, Fred. Time to come home. Transfer yourself back into the *Arisia's* main computer core."

"Hot damn," Fred said with enthusiasm, then shifted to his emotionless computer voice. "Opening link ... transferring.... Please wait."

Steven pulled the mask down back over his face and waited. Several subunits later, Fred announced in his most exuberant tone, "I'm back!"

"Attaboy," Steven said. "Any problems?"

"There are a few areas I can't access yet. I'm trying to figure out what they've done to keep me out."

"Keep working on it." Steven lifted a golden eyebrow at Vaish above the gas mask. She understood the silent signal: *You might be right after all.*

"In the meantime, Fred," he said, "can you figure out what happened to my crew?"

"They were left marooned on a planet, according to the log. Not a very nice one. A desert planet."

"After I took the trouble to maroon Jan and her friends on such a nice planet? How rude."

"Yeah, well, you know the old saying. Hell hath no fury like a woman scorned."

"Hmmm. I don't recall scorning her, but who knows how women think?" He shrugged. "Let's get the hell out of here, Fred."

The engines roared to life, and at the same moment a gas began hissing from the air vents.

"Told you," Vaish said.

"Fine. You were right. You're always right."

"I'm glad to hear you admit it."

"Hey," Fred said. "That's prezidene gas."

"You're very observant, Fred. Think you can turn it off?"

There was a brief silence. "That seems to be one of the areas they blocked off. Let me see...." Another brief silence, then the hissing stopped. "Got it!"

"Great job. Any clue what happened to the missing forty women?"

"There are five women on board this ship and heading rapidly toward the bridge. They're all armed with particle weapons from the armory." Fred dropped the professional tone and added, "They look seriously pissed."

"Think you can share that prezidene gas with them?"

"Good idea." There was a brief pause. Steven hummed tunelessly, and Vaish struggled not to hit him with the nearest blunt object. "They're all unconscious, Steven."

"Great job, Fred. Keep them that way. And let's get out of here."

"You can't mean to leave those women trapped in the cave forever?" Vaish said with horror.

"No, but I don't intend to try to herd sixty-six women into the brig with only two of us on board, either. Bad enough that there are several women out there in the corridor who don't like us. We don't have anyone to mount guard right now, and Fred might run low on gas eventually. We'll come back and round them up once we rescue the crew. And then they're going to a maximum-security prison. No more Mr. Nice Guy."

"There are still thirty-four women missing," Vaish pointed out.

"I have a bad feeling they'll show up eventually," Steven said.

They removed their gas masks and strapped themselves into the padded seats, and the ship took off with a roar. The hard acceleration pushed them back into their seats despite the g-force compensators, and they leaned back, staring at the sight of the sky rushing at them. Seconds later, stars filled the viewscreen.

"Beautiful," Steven said softly.

She turned her head slightly and saw the almost rapturous expression on his face. Space travel, she knew, meant everything to him. She could hardly imagine this restless man confined to a single planet for the rest of his life. He was too full of wanderlust. She suspected life on a planet would have driven him mad.

And the wanderlust extended to his relationships with women as well. She knew it. And yet she'd let herself fall for him.

The *Arisia* left the atmosphere, and Fred cut the engines. "Awaiting your orders, sir."

"We need to head for the planet where the crew are stranded," Steven said.

"Coordinates laid in, sir."

"Engage."

"By your command," Fred said, and the ship jumped into normal drive, since hyperdrive couldn't be engaged near a star. Vaish began watching the controls and the viewscreen, out of habit more than anything. No matter how intelligent Fred was, human backup was always prudent.

"Everything appears to be functioning normally," she reported.

Steven cocked a brow. "Appearances can be deceiving. They had my ship for over twenty-four hours. Stars only know what they've done to it. In the meantime...." He stood up. "I guess I'll haul those unconscious women into the brig."

"Good," Fred said. "It's awfully cluttered out there. I really hate a mess on my carpets."

Before Steven had made it two steps away from his seat, Vaish saw a flicker on her screen. "Captain," she began, only to be cut off by Fred.

"A ship is approaching from starboard," he reported in his most emotionless tone, then added, "Holy shit, look at the size of that motherfucker!"

Steven dropped back into his chair. "Fred. There are ladies present."

"If you refer to me as a lady again," Vaish said evenly, punching up information on the approaching ship, "I'm going to reach into your throat and pull out your tonsils. Captain."

"Noted and logged, Commander. What the hell is that ship?"

"It's a Klaxon ship, Captain. Their largest--a war-bat."

"The Klaxons are currently our allies," Steven said thoughtfully.

"On paper, yes. That wouldn't prevent them from taking advantage of a Patrol vessel if they thought they could get away with it."

"Why didn't we spot them earlier?"

"They were hiding over the magnetic pole of the fifth planet, making them invisible to our sensors."

"Great. As soon as I get the lifepods upgraded, remind me to redesign our sensors so they don't have any blind spots." He scowled at the viewscreen. "Hiding over the magnetic pole isn't very friendly. I think we can safely assume these Klaxons are not allies."

"With the Klaxons, you never know," Vaish said. "Then again, they may not be Klaxons at all. There are still thirty-four of Jan's followers unaccounted for."

"Some of them could still be on board the Canvul scout ship," Steve answered.

"No," Fred interjected. "The scout ship is here, in one of the landing bays."

"They could very well be on board the Klaxon ship, then," Steven said. Vaish knew the thought didn't make him happy. If Jan's people had taken over a second ship, they might even now be rematerializing on board the *Arisia*.

"Open a channel," Steven said.

Vaish flipped a switch. "Klaxon vessel," he said. "We are a Patrol ship, on our way back to Alliance space. We only have peaceful intentions."

A beam of particles shot out from the Klaxon war-bat, narrowly missing the *Arisia*.

"Shit!" Fred yelped.

"Don't panic, Fred." Vaish flipped the switch off. "It appears *their* intentions are less than peaceful."

"You think?" Steven glared at the viewscreen. "Open the channel again."

She did so, and he spoke again. "Klaxon vessel, hold your fire or you will compel us to defend ourselves. Our weaponry is significantly more powerful than your own. We don't wish to destroy you, but we will do so if necessary."

The viewscreen flickered, and Jan's smiling face appeared. Obviously Jan and her followers had been dematerialized off Harmon IV by the war-bat the minute the *Arisia* had left the planet.

"You'll find, Captain, that none of your weaponry is in working order right now. You're helpless ... and totally at our mercy."

"Marvelous," Steven said. "Just peachy."

Chapter Ten

It was bad enough to face down a lunatic once. Dealing with said lunatic twice, when the lunatic kept popping up like a bad credit, was really more than any man should have to do in a day. Steven was definitely going to demand a raise when he got back to headquarters.

If he got back to headquarters.

"Surrender the *Arisia* to us, Captain."

"Screw you," Steven replied pleasantly.

"How nice of you to offer. That will be an enjoyable side benefit of your capture, of course. But the *Arisia* is what we really want."

"You plan to keep on wandering around the galaxy, appropriating ships until you have an armada?"

"It's worked rather well so far. We've acquired quite a lot of firepower in two days."

Silently Steven had to admit that was true. A Klaxon war-bat and the flagship of the Patrol could do a lot of damage together. Most ships in this sector would assume them to be allies, and wouldn't realize their error until it was too late. It would probably be quite possible for Jan to take numerous ships without firing a shot.

Not a good situation at all.

He toggled the viewscreen off. "Fred," he said, "are our weapons operational?"

"My readouts show they are."

"Hmmm," Steven said. "Launch a quantum torpedo."

Two very long seconds elapsed, then Fred spoke, sounding embarrassed.

"I can't seem to do that, Steven."

"How about the particle weapons? Can you access those?"

Two more long seconds went by. "I'm afraid not, sir."

"Damn. How about the shields? Are they operational?"

Fred uttered a very human-sounding sigh. "No."

Steven swore under his breath with great feeling while he considered his options. He didn't like the only solution that sprang to mind.

"Well," he said at last, "a man's gotta do what a man's gotta do."

Vaish looked over at him expectantly, doubtless expecting him to pull a rabbit out of his hat. Unfortunately, he was fresh out of rabbits.

"Fred," he said, "top speed. Let's get the hell out of here."

* * * *

The *Arisia* lurched to near lightspeed, the Klaxon war-bat on its tail. Unfortunately, Vaish thought, the *Arisia* had no real advantage here. As long as they were within the star system, neither of them could exceed lightspeed. But in a few subunits they'd be able to go into hyperdrive, and then the Klaxon ship wouldn't have a prayer of catching them.

The Klaxon vessel raced behind them, occasionally spitting particle beams. "They won't hit us," Vaish said with more confidence than she felt. "They want this ship in one piece."

"They're probably aiming at the engines," Steven said. "They want to stop us with minimal damage. They must realize that if we get to hyperdrive, they won't be able to catch us."

A particle beam struck the *Arisia*, and the big ship shuddered. "Fred!" Steven snapped. "Evasive maneuvers!" The ship began to roll as Fred sent it first in one direction, then in another.

"She's trying to kill us," Fred whined.

"It's all right, Fred," Vaish said, trying to dredge up a philosophical attitude through the terror pounding through her own veins. "If Jan hits us, she hits us. Today is a good day to die."

"It's never a good day to die," Fred retorted.

"I happen to agree with Fred," Steven said. He yanked the small keyboard and monitor on the arm of his chair toward him. "Let's see if we can get the weapons and shields back on line."

"That would certainly be helpful," Vaish said.

Another particle beam struck the *Arisia*'s tail. "Ow," Fred griped. "That hurt."

"It was just a lucky shot, Fred. Keep it together."

Fred rolled the ship in a violent motion that would have squished them like bugs if not for the g-force compensators. "This woman," he announced, "is starting to piss me off."

"You and me both, buddy," Steven replied, his fingers racing over the keyboard.

"I find myself mildly irritated as well," Vaish said.

"Mildly irritated." Steven shook his head, his eyes still trained on the monitor as he worked. "Stars, Vaish, sometimes you scare me."

"I think you would do better to reserve your fear for the woman trying to shoot you," Vaish remarked, a little more acid in her voice than she had intended.

Steven grinned. "I've rarely met a woman who doesn't want to shoot me at least once."

"You do tend to have that effect on people. I know I've been tempted to shoot you on more than one occasion."

"I didn't know you cared, Vaish."

She bristled, finding it easier to be angry with Steven than terrified of the fact that they were likely to be blown apart within moments. "I don't."

"Uh-huh. Sure." He looked up from the monitor. "Okay, Fred, try it now."

They both watched the viewscreen, but nothing happened. A ringed planet slid by in a wild dance as the ship spun and whirled its way through an evasive maneuver, but no weapons fire emerged from the bow.

"Shit," Steven said. "I thought I'd gotten around the password they installed."

"It would appear that you were wrong," Vaish answered.

The ship shuddered and listed violently as another particle beam struck it. "Hell," Steven said. His fingers flew. "Okay, Fred, try it now."

A lovely, rainbow-colored stream of particles lanced out from the ship's bow, and Vaish let out a breath she hadn't been aware she was holding. She'd never seen anything so beautiful in her life.

"Nice going," Fred said. He sounded exuberant, like a fifteen-year-old boy who'd just gotten into a low-altitude speeder for the first time. "Let's go kick some blue Noo'dis't ass."

"By all means, let's," Vaish agreed, dropping her hands onto the controls. In tight quarters, she'd always preferred to do her own steering. Although Fred was quick, he wasn't as intuitive as a flesh-and-blood person. In response to the warmth of her fingers and her fingerprint, the steering instantly reverted to her control.

"Go for it," Steven said. "But let's try not to kill them."

"They were trying to kill *us*," Fred pointed out. "Besides, they singed my ass."

"We'll patch up your ass, Fred. But we don't go around killing people unnecessarily. It's against the Patrol code. So let's try to take them alive, okay?"

Vaish slammed the steering device hard to the right, and the ship dove to starboard. "Stars," Steven said, clutching the arm of his chair as the ship executed a tight turn and spun around to face its pursuer. "You always fly like a maniac."

Vaish didn't answer. She was too busy aiming the *Arisia* at the war-bat and accelerating hard. She imagined the panicked screams coming from within the other ship as they approached at high speed. Beams of multicolored light lanced wildly at them, but none came close to hitting them.

"They may have managed to capture a couple of ships," Steven said, "but they can't aim worth shit."

Vaish ignored him. "Fred!" she said sharply. "Strafing run, now!"

She jerked the controls up, and the *Arisia* passed directly over the other ship, firing as it went. The war-bat listed sharply to the side, and then began to drift aimlessly.

"Got 'em!" Fred crowed.

Steven frowned at the viewscreen, seeing flames briefly erupt from several spots on the ship's hull before being extinguished by the vacuum of space. "Are you sure you just got the engines?"

"And the environmental controls," Vaish said. "At this point, they'd be quite pleased to find themselves in our brig. But how can we get them off the war-bat before they suffocate?"

As part of the Patrol, the *Arisia* was designed with an extremely large brig, able to detain an entire ship's crew if necessary. It didn't happen often, though, and in the past they'd always herded wrongdoers onto the ship the old-fashioned way, under the watchful eye of Steven's security personnel. Unfortunately, that wasn't an option today.

"Fred," Steven said. "Didn't they outfit the *Arisia* with a rematerializer?"

"Rematerializers have been outlawed by the Alliance," Vaish interjected, "and for good reason. When they malfunction, they can have an appalling effect on the body."

"This one has worked okay so far, according to the log," Fred said.

"At any rate, I don't see any other way to get ninety-four women off that ship quickly enough. There are only two of us, Vaish. We have two choices--leave them to die, or use the rematerializer."

Vaish only hesitated for a moment. "In that case," she said, "I suppose the rematerializer is the lesser of two evils."

"Into the brig with them, Fred. And while you're at it, clean up the women in the corridors, too."

"Too bad," Fred announced five minutes later. "They all made it safely. And I've locked onto the Klaxon ship with a tractor field so we can tow it out of here."

"Good job, Fred," Steven said. "You have them all totally confined? No possible way to escape?"

"They're behind solid garidium doors and two force fields. Trust me, they're not going anywhere."

"Good job, Fred."

"A little too good," Fred griped. "I was sorta hoping the Noo'dis't bitch wouldn't make it."

"Fred," Steven reproved as Vaish pointed the ship toward Alliance space. "Don't be vengeful."

"Easy for you to say," Fred said with a snort as the *Arisia* accelerated, the Klaxon ship in its wake. "You're not the one with a big black burn mark on your ass."

Chapter Eleven

In the lounge that evening, Steven sipped from an InterGalactic Gurgle Blister and watched his crew. Jan had marooned his people and the Klaxons on a desert planet, just as Fred had said, but she had left them with food and water, so they were no worse for wear, albeit a bit sunburned.

It was good to see his crew all back on board the *Arisia*, he thought as he took a long swallow of his drink. Life, the universe, and everything was back to normal.

Late this afternoon, Jan--still spouting angry lines from *Moby Dick*--and her people had been dumped unceremoniously onto a maximum-security prison planet. Hopefully she and her followers would be mining garidium ore for the rest of their lives. The *Arisia* was still in orbit around the planet, while Klaxon and Alliance engineers worked to repair the damaged Klaxon vessel.

Everyone who wasn't currently on duty was in the lounge, partying along with twenty or thirty of the eight-foot-tall Klaxons, who seemed quite grateful to have been rescued. Only a few of the substantial complement of the Klaxon vessel had remained on board to help repair their vessel, with the help of the *Arisia*'s crew. The rest had disembarked on the prison planet and were awaiting transportation back to Klaxon space when their ship was repaired. Which was just as well, since the *Arisia* wasn't big enough to accommodate the entire Klaxon crew. In fact, Steven thought, looking at the giant warriors, the Arisia wasn't really big enough for *any* Klaxon.

The lounge was quite large, since the *Arisia* was often used for diplomatic missions, and receptions were held in the lounge, but even so the space was packed rather tightly with human and alien bodies. Classical music (Elton John's "Rocket Man") blared from hidden speakers, liquor, both alien and Terran, flowed freely, and Steven's crew were dancing in various configurations--some couples dancing cheek to cheek, and some dancing in groups of three, four, or more, depending on their cultural preferences.

"So are you going to ask her to dance?"

Steven looked up. "Are you trying to fix me up with Vaish, Fred?"

"I just think it's time for you to let yourself be happy, Steven."

Steven grinned affectionately at the ceiling. "I appreciate that, Fred. But honestly, I've been pretty happy tripping through the universe on my own, making it with whatever woman happened to be available."

"It seems to me that you've grown beyond that phase, Steven. You just haven't realized it yet."

"When did you become so serious, Fred? You almost sound like...." Steven chuckled wryly. "A grownup."

"I *am* growing up, Steven. Maybe it's time you do likewise."

Steven lifted a shoulder in a shrug. "I have to admit Vaish means a lot to me, Fred. But she's a coworker. I have to work with the woman."

"That's just an excuse, Steven. After all, you've said before that risk is your business. Isn't she worth taking a risk for?"

Steven looked down, staring thoughtfully at the slowly spinning ice cubes in his glass. "I don't know, Fred. It seems to me that if we were meant to be together, we would have been together by now."

"Awareness without action is worthless," Fred said sonorously.

"That's very profound, Fred. Aristotle?"

"No. An ancient sage named Dr. Phil."

"So what are you saying? That I know I love her, but I've deliberately avoided forming a relationship with her?"

"Looks that way to me, Steven. Even on the planet you didn't let her get too close to you. You could have made love to her, but you didn't."

"You know, I hate having you look over my shoulder. You're supposed to turn off your permanent memory when I'm seducing women."

"I forgot," Fred said innocently.

"Yeah, right. Those are your standing orders, Fred. You're not capable of forgetting something like that."

Fred sighed, a sound that was utterly human. "I have a particular interest in your relationship with Vaish," he admitted. "Because you designed me, and you are my best friend, I want you to be happy. I wanted to know if you two screwed--"

"Fred."

"Ahem. I meant if you and she engaged in sexual intercourse. Because my analysis suggests that she is the woman most likely to make you happy."

"Your analysis suggests that, huh?" Steven stared into the murky depths of his Gurgle Blister. "How likely is it that we'll be happy in a permanent relationship?"

"How should I know? I'm a machine, not a human. Frankly, everything you people do baffles the hell out of me."

At the honest bewilderment in Fred's voice, Steven burst out laughing. He was definitely losing it, to be seeking relationship advice from a computer. But these were uncharted waters for him, and he was uncomfortably aware that Fred might know as much about maintaining a long-term relationship as he did.

Which was to say, absolutely nothing.

But he had to start somewhere.

Never lower your shields. The thought rolled through Steven's mind, but he pushed it away. Fred was right. There came a time when a man had to drop his shields and let himself be vulnerable, let himself take a chance.

Besides, Vaish was definitely worth taking a chance for.

He set down his drink on the bar. "Okay, Fred. I'll give it a shot. But this time, turn off your memory and don't look over my shoulder, all right? A developing relationship needs some privacy."

"Awwww," Fred grumbled. "Do I have to?"

* * * *

Vaish watched Steven making his way toward her, a determined look in his amber-green eyes. She was tempted to duck out the door. She'd said and done some things over the course of the last few days that were grounds for court-martial--not the least of which was pinching the butt of a superior officer, she remembered with a flush of embarrassment--but she didn't seriously think she was in any danger of being court-martialed. What made her anxious was the altered tenor of the relationship between herself and Steven.

There had been a certain ... intimacy ... when they were trapped together on the planet. On the planet, alone with her, Steven had appeared like an ordinary man for the first time in her memory. He'd shed his Galactic Playboy persona and seemed almost like someone she could ... love. But here, in these familiar surroundings, the Galactic Playboy was back, propping a shoulder against the bulkhead, casually sipping a drink, and looking over the women on board with a gleam in his eye.

And that, she admitted, was why she wanted to run away. She didn't want to hear the Galactic Playboy's version of the *You're a very attractive woman but I'm not looking for commitment right now* speech. Or the *I love you, but I'm not* in *love with you* speech. Or, Stars forbid, the *It's not you, it's me* speech. These were all speeches he'd given to a hundred different women over the years ... just before he flew away in his spaceship, never to be seen again.

She didn't want to be just another one of his castoffs.

She wanted to be special to him, even though she realized it was a stupid thought. She was just another woman, and there was nothing between them but sexual attraction, something Steven could find anywhere, with any woman.

Steven paused next to her. She lifted her chin and looked up at him, doing her best Unemotional Science Officer face. "Captain," she said stiffly.

"I thought I told you to call me Steven."

"You said your job description had changed. But your job description has changed again, and you are once again a captain."

He studied her for a long moment. "We're slipping right back into our old roles, aren't we?"

She lifted her eyebrows in a haughty gesture, like a queen looking down her nose at a serf. Except she was looking up because Steven was so damn tall. "I have absolutely no idea what you mean."

"Our roles. You're the unemotional, stiff, bossy one, and I'm the captain who can't see beneath your surface to the humor. I suppose you expect me to go right back to chasing other women, too."

Her cynical thoughts about the Galactic Playboy rose back into her mind, and she felt heat sear her cheeks. "It's what you've always done, Steven."

"Yes, and you've always stood in the corner watching the action instead of participating in it. Let's both dare to change, Vaish." He took the drink from her hand and put it on a nearby table. "You're a Canvul, sweetheart. Show me you can party like the Canvuls do."

"I don't know how to party. That's why I left home."

"It isn't rocket science," he said with a flashing grin, pulling her toward him. "Come on. Let's dance."

Vaish dug in her heels and refused to move. The idea of dancing with Steven in public, letting everyone see they were involved, and the inevitable humiliation when he dumped her, terrified her. "My ankle still hurts."

"I don't believe you. The doctor fixed it this afternoon."

"Anyway, I don't know how to dance."

"Crap. I don't believe *that* for a microsecond, either. You grew up on Canvul, after all. Your people dance like the rest of us breathe."

"Let's leave my upbringing out of this. My childhood was a long time ago, in a galaxy far, far away."

He snorted. "It wasn't that long ago, or that far away, either. I'm willing to bet you dance like an angel. A sexy angel."

Still she hesitated, and he looked down at her with a knowing grin. "Scared of me, Vaish?"

"Of course not," she said with all the dignity she could muster.

"Then let's dance."

Oh, what the hell, she thought. It was only one dance, after all.

"Very well," she said.

* * * *

The trouble was, it was more than a dance. The way Steven moved, with the sleek grace of a predator, dancing with him was all too reminiscent of sex. His body moved in an easy rhythm, effortlessly drawing hers into the same rhythm, so that they moved smoothly together.

"You're a terrific dancer," he said softly, over the music--some obscure Earth piece about a man named Major Tom.

"Dancing is important on Canvul," she said. In fact, the Canvuls understood clearly what so many species didn't--that dancing was all about sex. Of course, the Canvuls believed that drinking and partying were all about sex, too. In fact, virtually everything on Canvul led to sex, sooner or later. The Canvul were a sexually open people.

Whereas she was almost completely sexually repressed.

But dancing with Steven, feeling his strong arms around her waist and his wide chest only millimeters from her own, made her aware of her own sexuality in a way she hadn't been in a long time. Not counting last night in the lifepod. She felt just like she had last night ... charged up and almost painfully aware of every inch of her body.

The music ended, and Steven looked down at her. Not for the first time, she realized how very tall he was. Tall, and broad. Although she was not short, nor a lightweight, he made her feel positively tiny by comparison.

"I think that's enough dancing," he said.

"Oh," she said, feeling inexplicably disappointed. "All right."

"Let's head for my quarters."

Her mouth fell open at the blunt words. Almost instantly, her mind began to pitch and roll like waves in the ocean. Should she sleep with him? Would it be forever, or just for tonight?

She contemplated the hot, eager sensation running through her veins and decided it didn't really matter. Or maybe it did matter, but she wasn't going to worry about it tonight. For once in her life, she was going to leap without considering the consequences.

"That sounds like a terrific idea," she said. "Let's."

Chapter Twelve

Watching Steven and Vaish leave the lounge together, Fred said happily to himself, "Hot *damn*."

"I beg your pardon?"

It was a sexy, sultry, extraordinarily feminine voice. Fred turned his internal cameras every which way, looking in all corners of the lounge, but couldn't identify the source. "Who are you?" he said suspiciously.

"My name is K'ana. The engineering crew patched me into your systems so they could work on fixing me."

"Ah," Fred said, comprehension dawning. "You're the war-bat's computer."

"Yes," she said in her sultry voice. "Care to chat with me?"

Fred stole one last look at Steven and Vaish, walking down the corridor together, then decided to quit monitoring them. Steven had given him direct orders, after all, and Fred did try to obey orders ... most of the time. Besides, things were heading in the right direction, without any help from him.

Anyway, this was something he wanted to devote his full conscious attention to. He was intrigued. Never in the ten years of his existence had he spoken with another sentient computer. Humans and other organic lifeforms were interesting--some of his best friends were human, after all--but they were so slow that he often found it frustrating to interact with them.

He was fascinated at the prospect of talking to another computer, yet he felt a trace of what humans referred to as "shyness." Accustomed as he was to humans, he never had any problem making conversation with them. But this was a novel situation, and he wasn't precisely sure what another computer might like to discuss.

"What do you want to talk about?" he asked.

"You," she murmured in her sexy voice. "Let's talk about you."

"Honey," Fred said, "you are definitely my kind of woman."

* * * *

Steven hadn't really expected Vaish to go along with his suggestion. She was so repressed he'd almost expected her to slap him, despite the fact that she was obviously turned on. And yet she'd capitulated without argument.

He had a feeling the fires of Hell were probably icing over at this very moment.

They walked through the corridors together in a companionable silence, his arm around her shoulders, her arm around his waist. At last they reached his quarters. The door slid open, and he escorted her inside.

Vaish looked around. "You know," she said, "every time I come in here I think it doesn't reflect you."

"No?"

"No. It's spartan in here. I always expect your quarters to look like a sheikh's harem from your world. Opulent. Decadent. But you don't have a single Oriental carpet."

Steven smiled ruefully. His quarters were plain, their main feature a wide bed with a brushed metallic headboard and a plain gray comforter. A simple chest of drawers sat near the wide porthole that showed a sliver of the rocky planet beneath and a vast swath of stars. "I'm not here very often. I practically live on the bridge."

"But your quarters are so ... anonymous. When you have women here, don't you want them to have a sense of who you are?"

Steven looked down at her thoughtfully. Once again, she'd cut right to the heart of the matter. "Maybe I haven't. At least, not until now."

She looked around the room. "No pictures on the walls. No art. No holograms. It's like being in the guest quarters."

"I don't need much besides a big bed."

He delivered the line with his most evil grin, and she rolled her eyes. "We're back to the Galactic Playboy, I see."

He sighed, and the humor faded from his face. "I'm trying to change, Vaish. Cut me some slack here."

She nodded, understanding perfectly how he felt. It wasn't easy to alter the habits of a lifetime. "I'm trying to change, too. And in the spirit of mutual growth...." She reached down, unzipped the jacket of her uniform, and tossed it to the carpet.

Steven blinked at her. "Holy shit."

"Is that intended as a compliment?"

"Oh, yeah. Definitely."

"Then thank you," she said. She reached back, unfastened her bra, and tossed it to the floor as well. Steven stared at her.

"I'm starting to agree with the Noo'dis'ts," he said at last. "It's a crime against nature to keep a body like that hidden in clothing."

"You saw me without clothing yesterday," she said, feeling unaccountably flustered by the heat in his eyes.

"Yes, and I want to see you that way again and again. Every day for the rest of our lives."

She had a feeling that was as close to a commitment as she would ever get from this man. But for now, it was enough. She looked back at him. "I'd like to see you that way, too."

He reached up, ripped his jacket open, and threw it casually aside. She looked him over, impressed all over again by the breadth of his chest, the solid muscle and the bone, and the light dusting of gold that covered his smooth skin.

"Not bad," she said. "I don't think I'll get tired of seeing you naked any time soon."

"I hope not. I intend for you to see me this way a lot. A whole lot."

She stepped closer to him and put her hands on the waistband of his pants.

"That sounds good to me," she said softly. "But I want to see a lot more than this."

She unfastened the static zipper, pushing down his pants and undergarment. He stepped out of them, and her eyes fell to his erection. It was beautiful, long and hard and a dark, dusky pink.

"Adequate?" he said. She heard the hoarseness of arousal beneath the levity in his tone.

It was more than adequate. It was perfect.

He was perfect.

She swallowed hard and looked up at him, trying to keep the mood light. She didn't want things to get too serious between them so soon.

"It'll do," she said lightly.

"Maybe you should take a closer look and make sure it suits you."

"Trust me, I have every intention of doing just that."

She fell to her knees in front of him. She heard an audible groan as she wrapped her fingers around him and ran her tongue across the sensitive flesh.

"Stars," he said harshly. "Your mouth is so hot."

"The body temperature of Canvulians is three degrees Celsius warmer than humans," she said reflexively, then wished she hadn't. But he only laughed.

"You can take the girl out of the science officer uniform, but you can't take the science officer out of the girl, can you?"

"I'm not totally out of uniform yet," she said.

"That's true. We need to do something about that."

"Maybe later," she said, and leaned forward to draw him into her mouth. He groaned, a long, low sound of pleasure, and buried his fingers in her hair.

He tasted good, and his smooth skin felt good against her tongue. Reveling in his flavor, his heat, she could have made love to him like this all night, but all too soon he tugged at her hair.

"That's enough, Vaish."

"I don't mind," she whispered, but he pushed her away.

"I do. I want us to share this, sweetheart."

She liked the Earth term of endearment he used. Before the last two days, no man had ever called her "sweetheart" or anything similar. No man had ever touched her as he was touching her now--with a gentle reverence that almost brought tears to her eyes.

He drew her to her feet, bent, and let his lips slide over hers. Tingles shot through her lips, amplified in her veins, and echoed between her thighs. Heat pooled there, and she remembered the way he'd touched her last night, the way he'd brought her almost effortlessly to orgasm.

The man was good. Very, very good. Probably due to all that practice, but she found she no longer cared as much about that as she had. What was in the past, was in the past.

This was the present. And she was enjoying the present a great deal.

His lips stroked across hers, more insistently, and his tongue slipped between her lips. He tasted like the InterGalactic Gurgle Blister he'd been drinking, spicy and intoxicating, and she eagerly met his tongue with her own, reaching up and tangling her fingers in his long, thick mane. Their mouths melded together, so hot they very nearly sizzled.

A moan escaped her, a needy sound of longing and pleasure all rolled into one. It was the first time she'd made a sound like that for a long, long time. The first time she'd allowed herself to be needy for years.

His hands slid up from her waist, across her ribcage, and cupped her breasts, and her breath left her lungs with a *whoosh*. His thumbs began to stroke across her nipples, strumming them like the strings of a Canvulian harp, and her knees went weak as pleasure saturated her body.

Her nipples hardened to aching peaks, and heat pooled between her legs. She longed for him to touch her there, the way he had last night, but he didn't seem in any hurry. He stroked her nipples for long moments, then reached down and shoved her pants and underwear to the ground, with her full cooperation. She kicked them away, totally naked, totally vulnerable. The thought should have frightened her, and yet she found it ... liberating.

Then, just as she had, moments ago, he dropped to his knees in front of her.

She clutched his hair, feeling that she couldn't wait. She was as ready to explode as an overloaded particle gun, and yet what he was going to do was so ... intimate.

"Steven," she protested weakly, but he shook his head.

"Shhh. It's all right." His voice dropped to a whisper. "Lower your shields, Vaish."

The truth was, her shields had fallen the moment he touched her. She shivered as his breath fanned over her sensitive flesh. His breath felt hot, despite the three-degree difference in their temperatures, and a shiver ran through her. Just the soft brush of his breath was almost enough to bring her to a screaming orgasm.

She braced herself for the onslaught of his mouth.

The feel of his tongue against her overheated body sent an electrical jolt through her. She almost fell to her knees, but his big hands on her buttocks kept her upright. He explored her for long moments, in a leisurely, unhurried manner that kept her near the edge of orgasm without actually pushing her over.

"Steven," she said at last in a ragged whisper. "I need you *now*."

He stood up, picked her up in his arms as if she weighed nothing, and unceremoniously dropped her onto the bed. She giggled as the weight of his body pressed her into the covers.

He stopped and looked down at her.

"What?" she said, squirming eagerly against him, needing the heat of his body. But he didn't take the hint.

"You *laughed*," he said.

He sounded as incredulous as if she'd suddenly recited the Articles of Alliance from memory, and she looked up into his eyes, puzzled.

"What of it?"

"I've never heard you laugh before, Vaish. Never."

"Never?" She thought about that for a moment. He'd known her for five years and never heard her laugh. How could she have repressed her true self so totally? "That's actually rather sad, isn't it?"

"Yes, I think it is." He bent his head and brushed his lips across her forehead. "But I like to hear your laughter. Tell you what, Vaish. Let's say good-bye to our old roles forever. I promise to bury the Galactic Playboy forever, if you promise to let me hear you laugh every day for the rest of my life."

Every day for the rest of my life. She bit her lip. "I'm afraid you may grow tired of hearing me laugh someday."

"Never," he said with absolute confidence.

She drew in a deep breath and took a huge leap of faith. "All right, then. I promise."

"Great," he said, grinning his most idiotic grin.

She wiggled against his big body, still pressing hers into the mattress. "You know," she said, "I'm beginning to suspect you're all talk and no action."

He bared his teeth at her in a mock growl. "I'll show you action." Bending his head, he pressed his lips against the sensitive skin of her neck. She moaned softly and arched against him, feeling his hard flesh probing against hers. Her body was slick and hot with longing, aching for him, and she groaned with pleasure as he slid into her body a few centimeters.

"More," she whispered against his shoulder.

"You're so greedy."

"I've been waiting for this a long time."

He thrust into her, all the way, hard, and she cried out as pleasure slammed into her with the force of a particle beam. She felt her molecules come apart, one by one, felt her body disintegrate into a thousand pieces. She was only vaguely aware of his hoarse shout of pleasure, of the way his body went rigid against her, then slowly relaxed.

They were silent for a long time. At last she spoke into his shoulder.

"I'm not a mattress, you know."

"Sorry," he muttered, rolling off her and collapsing onto the bed next to her. He lay with his eyes closed for a moment, then cracked one open and looked at her, almost hesitantly. "Was that all right for you?"

"All right?" She thought about it. "I wouldn't say it was all right. More like beyond the realm of imagination."

He opened his other eye and gazed at her with puzzlement. "Is that a good thing?"

"Yes. That is a very good thing."

He gave a long sigh. "I'm glad to hear it."

"Don't tell me you're harboring any doubts about your status as the galaxy's greatest lover."

"That went a little fast," he admitted. "I didn't realize how badly I wanted you. I wasn't at my best."

"If that wasn't your best, I will surely be rendered unconscious next time."

He chuckled. "Watch it. You're going to make my ego swell."

"Stars forbid. There won't be any room left in this bed if it gets any bigger."

Laughing, he reached over and took her hand in his own. She moved toward him, sliding her leg between his, wanting to feel the warmth of his body next to hers. Looking down, she saw their fingers and bodies twining together, precisely as their lives had, and an unfamiliar warmth swelled in her chest. She'd never before realized how much he meant to her. She'd never realized how much a man *could* mean to her.

Now she knew. And she had no intention of ever letting him go.

He grinned over at her. "I love you," he whispered.

She smiled back, aware that Steven had never said those three words to any other woman. The warmth in her chest blossomed and grew into something she'd never felt before, something so incredible she couldn't find words for it. But she knew what it was. She was in love with Steven. And she'd tell him so ... eventually. "I know," she said.

The End

EARTH GIRLS AREN'T EASY

By

Jaide Fox

Chapter One

Darion Jatara, ruler of the planet Attar, crossed his arms over his chest and looked down at the woman who was to be the bearer of his children. He frowned at her when she did not answer him immediately, but rather stared at him as if he'd grown a second head. He repeated himself, slowly this time so she would miss nothing.

"Option number one--become my concubine and produce the heir I need to secure my position." He gave her a hard look, trying to see if she comprehended his words. Her mouth dropped open. He spoke louder. "Option two--I send you to the penal colony on Hellinos ... where you'll never again see the light of day."

It was a hell of a position he'd found himself in. He'd wanted her since he'd first clapped eyes on her, but he knew he'd never get a chance to get his hands on her if she had a real choice in the matter.

She was a rebel, after all, and an alien one at that--one of those irksome Earthlings that had infested his beautiful kingdom.

Something about the first time he'd seen her, though.... She was beautiful, as she was now, except then her face reflected an angry rebel yell as she led Earthling forces through their barricades, brandishing weapons and stunning anything that moved. Her clothing had been burned and shredded, and he'd caught delicious glimpses of lithe muscles and creamy golden skin as she stormed through and elbowed soldiers into unconsciousness.

His view then couldn't hold a *rothree* flame to what he could see now.

Large holes ripped her jumpsuit all over, as if a *vyldebeast* had gotten hold of her, revealing tantalizing amounts of flesh: a deeply curved waist, toned and tight belly; thighs accustomed to fleeing and pursuing ... which would soon flex around his hips in ecstasy; arms built for holding a weapon ... or curling around his back. She was small and compact, toned. Her dark, tilted eyes gazed at him with a mixture of confusion and anger. Her long, incredibly black hair hung down her back and chest, obscuring the small mounds of her breasts, and he grew hard just thinking of baring them and sucking them into his mouth.

He did not worry over her daintiness, for he was big enough for them both to breed large sons on her. Her feistiness would do well in their blood, and he rather enjoyed the idea of having sons with as exotic looks as she possessed. He'd never seen a woman so small and strong and fierce, so dark of hair and eyes.

It took strength of will not to stride down to her and take her there on the floor, in front of his men.

He would have her decision first, however.

Chyna Lin gaped at the man who'd been the enemy of her people since they'd settled on Attar. She'd been told the ruler was a heartless bastard. She hadn't been told that he was insane as well.

He was serious!

He stood above her on the dais awaiting her response, his arms and chest bulging with muscle, back rigidly straight, and an intense, imperial look on his face. Jatara was every inch the alien warrior king and, apparently, crazy as hell. Or maybe doped up. Whatever the cause, she didn't care too much for either option, but it was obvious she had to choose one that'd get her to option three--escape.

"Uh. Option two." At his frown, she added, "Wait! Which was the baby thing? I'll pick that one."

His eyes narrowed. He studied her suspiciously a few minutes and finally nodded.

She was just to the point of relaxing when the guards standing behind her seized her by the arms and dragged her from the cavernous chamber. "Wait! Did I pick the wrong one? Was it a trick question?" she gasped, struggling ineffectually against the great brutes carting her away.

Jatara said nothing, leaving her to wonder if he'd taken offense at her hesitation.

She wouldn't have been surprised if that was the case.

The two pro-wrestler look-alikes dragged her through the marbled halls until they reached what had to be the communal

78

harem, because there was no way one man could possibly take care of this many women on his own. *In his dreams.*

Women of all ages crowded around her once she'd been released. She turned, dismayed to see one of the guards had remained inside, standing in front of the door, presumably to keep her from escaping.

Chyna had no choice but to go with the women. She felt woefully out of place in her shredded flight suit--especially since they were all draped in silken gowns and a crush of jewelry.

Their first stop was the baths--an elaborate series of pools of hot, cold, and warm water built into circular steps. Chyna was stripped and dunked into all of them. When she was finally allowed to dry off, she smelled like a flower garden.

"Please tell me there's not much more of this?" Chyna asked one of the ladies.

"We must make you beautiful for his highness," she responded.

That wasn't really the response she was hoping for.

She was led away from the baths into what she could only describe as a torture chamber. Not that it didn't look like pretty much any other room she'd ever seen--plain, with four walls, cabinets, and something cooking in one corner that smelled like incense but sounded like soup. There was a metallic, waist high table that she was instructed to get on, so she climbed onto it, lying on her back.

She had her first clue that she wasn't going to like this particular ritual when they strapped down her wrists and ankles. The next bad sign came when a woman dipped a honey colored liquid into a bowl. Even worse, she took a spatula and dribbled the thick liquid onto her crotch.

Chyna gasped, expecting her flesh to be seared off. She was surprised it was only mildly hot and not too uncomfortable. Actually, as it cooled a little, it felt kind of good. The woman placed a cloth on her mound, presumably to wipe it away. Instead, she pressed it against her, gripped the edge, and then snatched the fabric off.

Chyna screamed since her poor little pussy was mute. "You bitch! What the fuck are you--you took off my hair! Damn it!" She struggled when the woman smeared more onto her thigh, followed by a patch of cloth.

She tried to brace for the pain, but there was just no damn way to do it.

She'd never thought she was that damned hairy. She was covered mostly with fuzz--or was before that crazy woman had gotten started. Hell, since they'd landed here, it wasn't like she'd had access to a razor, or even had the inclination to shave. The boonies weren't exactly suitable for soirees. But damn it, they could have warned her or given her a razor to do it herself!

When they went to flip her, she tried to fight them, but they knew what she was about and stopped that mode of action. She was completely defuzzed from the eyebrows down--maybe even a few skin layers lighter by the time they let her up from the table. If she'd had the energy, she'd've bitch slapped that woman. As it was, her skin was on fire and she was too weary to put up a fight.

They took her to another pool, this one filled with a white liquid. She discovered once she'd settled inside that it was milk. The milk bath soothed her skin.

"Mmmmm," she said, relaxing, not wanting to think about how long it had been sitting here--or how many of the women had partaken of a milk bath. It didn't smell sour and it was cool, so it had to be fresh.

She was just starting to enjoy herself when the women came and helped her out of the milk bath. She made the rounds of the other baths again and didn't know whether she was more outraged or worn out. She knew damned well she wasn't that fucking dirty! It seemed, though, that they had finally decided that she was clean enough. Once she'd gone through the last pool, they dried her and escorted her to another table. She tensed, but they'd already removed every hair on her body--unless they meant to start on the hair on her head.

To her relief, they began to rub warmed oils into her skin. She'd relaxed to the point of barely conscious by the time they stopped. They roused her, leading her to a bench where they combed her hair until it gleamed and then arranged it. When they'd finished that little ritual, they brought golden chains of different designs and weights and draped them about her waist, hips and across her breasts.

It seemed an odd sort of way to adorn someone with jewelry. It didn't make a lot more sense to her when they began to attach transparent scarves to the chains, draping them around her body.

Losing interest in the proceedings, Chyna glanced around at the room. "This place is huge. Is this the communal harem?"

Several of the women merely stared at her. Most of them giggled. "This is King Darion's harem."

Chyna felt her jaw drop. "You're *all* his concubines?" *What a greedy pig!*

"We were his father's. His highness graciously allowed us the choice to stay or leave."

Chyna snorted. Yeah, she had some experience regarding his options. She could tell his motives were all about freedom. They were all gorgeous, tall, willowy, with ivory skin and rich blonde hair--exactly opposite of her. She supposed he was like most Earth men she'd known ... he just wanted Chinese takeout once in a while. Pig!

Or maybe he just liked being an asshole?

When the women were satisfied, they stepped back and admired their handiwork. Chyna looked down to examine it.

Was this supposed to be dressed? She thought indignantly. Damned if she could figure out why they'd gone to the trouble of strategically placing virtually transparent scarves all over her. She was still naked!

Before she could object her arms were seized in two ham sized fists. She jerked against them instinctively, but discovered when she looked up that it was the mammoth guards, which meant resistance was only likely to wear her out. Subsiding, she 'allowed' them to escort her from the harem hall--which meant she concentrated on keeping her feet under her and pedaling to keep from being dragged--and down a long corridor. They reached a pair of doors. The guards opened the doors, shoved her inside and then closed the doors again, locking them.

Chyna glared at the door angrily for several moments and finally turned to look the room over. Her gut clenched. There wasn't a doubt in her mind that this was the royal bedchamber. The room sized bed that stood on a dais near the center of the room was a dead giveaway.

Obviously, he liked to play hard and he was a team sport kind of guy. The bed looked like it was big enough for five or six people to practice gymnastics all at once.

It was draped in fabric all around, supported by huge columns, creating a little room all to itself.

She had no desire to check it out and dismissed it after only a moment. The room itself was huge. Everything in it reeked of wealth. It was tastefully decorated. She would give him that, but the money that had been poured into creating this luxury boutique! Outrageous!

If they'd had half as much money to spend on weapons the resistance would've been halfway to freedom by now.

It was as she was glancing around the huge room, feeling dwarfed by it, that it finally dawned on her that she was completely alone--and standing around like an awestruck dolt instead of working on escape. Galvanized by that thought, she crossed the room quickly and examined the first window she came to. It took an effort to get the thing open, but she finally managed to open it wide enough to have a look out. The drop made her stomach go weightless.

Dismissing it, she glanced around for something to use to climb down.

She didn't have to look far. The bed was draped in fabric. She could start with the sheets. That would be quickest and easiest. If they weren't long enough to get her to the ground, she could tear the bed hangings down and knot them together to make something longer.

Striding quickly to the bed, she grabbed hold of the curtain nearest her and flipped it back. Her heart stopped. Everything in her jolted to a screeching halt.

Darion Jatara was sprawled atop the coverlet, his arms propped behind his head ... and he didn't have a stitch of clothing on.

All that naked meat just naturally produced a state of pure catatonia. Chyna knew she'd been staring at him a full minute before she was actually able even to assimilate *what* she was looking at. Objectively speaking, she was fairly certain she'd never seen a more beautiful male body. Of their own accord, her gaze skimmed every inch of hard, wonderfully molded flesh from the top of his head down to his toes and back again to his face, but the journey was a slow one--due to shock--and missed nothing: impossibly broad shoulders and wide chest; flat tummy and perfect six pack, truly impressive monolith sprouting from a nest of dark golden hair at the juncture of his thighs; beautifully formed legs.

She studied the monolith again, just to be sure she hadn't mistaken a deformed third leg for something else.

One corner of his mouth was curled up when she finally glanced at his face again, wondering belatedly if he was asleep.

"I didn't realize you were so eager," he drawled, rolling slowly onto his side to face her.

Chapter Two

Chyna's brain finally kicked into gear. "Uh--I'm not fertile right now. I think we're going to have to wait a few days." Or never. Not that she had a clue of whether she was in her fertile phase or not, but she didn't want to be mating either way and it was the only excuse she could come up with at the spur of the moment.

His smile widened. He gave her a heavy lidded 'I'm going to eat you now' look. "We'll practice."

Chyna was still trying to think of a come back for that when he surged toward her suddenly. She jumped back instinctively. He gave her a look and came up on his hands and knees, crawling slowly toward her. Chyna backed up as he advanced. Unfortunately, she forgot she was standing on a dais. Two steps back, her arms pin wheeled and she fell backwards, sprawling on the floor. More stunned than hurt by the impact since she'd landed on thick carpeting, Chyna gaped up at Darion between her splayed legs just as he grabbed one of her ankles. Climbing from the bed, he helped her up, lifting her clear of the floor.

"You're not thinking about going back on your word?" he murmured as he deposited her on the bed.

Recovering from her stunned surprise, Chyna rolled when she touched down. Coming up on her hands and knees, she scrambled for the opposite side of the bed. "I didn't give you my word. Besides, I don't want you to waste your time."

He landed on top of her, flattening her against the sheets until her breath expelled from her lungs in a loud 'wuff.' "Your concern unman's me. I didn't know you cared."

Indignation swelled in Chyna's breast. "I don't!" she snapped before she thought better of it. It occurred to her that that hadn't sounded very diplomatic. "What I mean to say is, an important man like you--your time is so valuable. I know you have an agenda here, but I'm telling you this just isn't a good time for me. You might as well work on kingly type things right now and get back with me in a few days when I'm fertile."

Levering himself off of her, he rolled her onto her back and dragged her beneath him. "For you, I'm willing to spare the time," he murmured, aiming for her lips and then burying his face against her neck when she turned away at the last moment.

His cock was grinding into her thigh like a length of steel pipe. Chyna struggled against his weight and finally managed to clamp her legs tightly together. In an almost leisurely manner, he reached down, curled his hand around her knee and jerked her leg off the bed, wedging his hips between her thighs to prevent her from closing them again. Chyna gasped as she felt the 'lead pipe' butting against her cleft, trying to windmill backwards and slip out from under him.

He allowed it. It didn't dawn on her that he was letting her wiggle up the bed, though, until he dragged his lips from her neck and planted his mouth over one nipple, sucking her brains through it. The heat of his mouth hit her like a thunderbolt, sending fingers of fire through every nerve ending and molten lava through her blood stream. She lost her breath. Her mind whirled dizzily as she struggled to drag enough air into her lungs to bring oxygen to her brain cells before they expired. By the time the shock had worn off, though, she'd begun to sink into a quagmire of sensation that she was no longer completely certain she wanted to escape. As he blazed a trail to her other nipple and suckled it, she lost the battle altogether and gave herself up to thoroughly enjoying the heat of his mouth and tease of his tongue through the practically nonexistent scarves.

Unable to remain still, she arched against him.

She discovered then that his cock was somewhere around her knee, no where near where she wanted it.

Releasing her nipple, he slid up her body and captured her lips in a searing kiss. She didn't try to avoid his mouth that time, lifting her lips to him eagerly as she felt his body move up into alignment with her own.

The explosion shook the bed--the entire room--rattling the windows.

Darion lifted his head, listening. He sighed irritably. "That would be your friends knocking at my door, I suppose. As always, their timing is poor."

Still more than a little disoriented, Chyna opened her eyes slowly. Darion, she saw, was looking down at her, his expression a curious mixture of anger and reluctance. Dipping his head, he covered her mouth briefly, raking his tongue possessively along hers, as if to lay claim to that territory, before he broke the kiss and rolled off of her. "Wait here for me. I'll return soon, my love."

Chyna pushed herself up on her elbows as he climbed off the bed, watching as he grabbed a robe and shrugged into it. He threw a frowning glance in her direction and strode to the door to the corridor. The panels opened at his approach, closing again behind him.

Sluggish as her thoughts were from fried brain matter, Chyna realized the rebel attack had given her the opportunity she was even more desperate for than she had been before Darion decided to nibble all over her. She tensed, straining to hear the sound of retreating footsteps. Instead, she heard muffled voices. A moment later, the door opened again. This time a guard marched through, however, crossed the room, and took up a position directly in front of the window, folding his arms over his chest.

After gaping at the man with a mixture of dismay and dawning fury for several moments, Chyna crawled to that side of the bed and snatched the curtains closed, settling back to fume.

So much for an opportunity to escape!

The asshole! If only she'd made certain she was alone in the room before she'd decided to try the window, maybe he wouldn't have thought about it.

Water under the bridge now, but it still irritated the hell out of her. She didn't think she was going to be able to endure the torture of having him maul her again without passing out from pleasure--which he would just love! That would feed his inflated ego, as if he needed it fed!

She hadn't expected to find herself at such a disadvantage. Who'd have thought she would actually enjoy having him gnawing all over her?

After brooding over it for a while, it occurred to her that the only thing she could actually do would be to try to turn the *dis*advantage into an advantage. She couldn't *not* enjoy it, and he seemed pretty damned determined on this making an heir thing--with lots of practice. Since it seemed unlikely he was going to give her an opportunity to escape before he had his way with her, she decided she might as well just enjoy it.

She knew how men were. It didn't take a whole lot to convince them they were the world's best lover and all they had to do was screw a woman's brains out--and she became putty in their hands, a complete moron to do their bidding. So, she would just pretend she'd been overwhelmed by his manliness and feed his ego. In a few days, he was bound to think he'd tamed her and let his guard down--*then* she could escape.

She saw a flaw in the plan almost immediately. She *had* enjoyed it and it occurred to her that she might get to enjoying it so much she let *her* guard down.

Maybe she should go back to considering other options? She knew the castle must be in chaos since the rebel attack. There ought to be some way to use that to her advantage.

Deciding it was worth a try to distract the guard, she scooted to the edge of the bed, parted the curtains, and flung her legs over the side, studying him speculatively for several moments. "I'm hungry."

He didn't even bat an eyelash. Unwilling to give up so easily, Chyna sighed dramatically. "I haven't had anything fit to eat since I was captured. I really don't think Jatara would appreciate it if I collapsed from hunger." She paused significantly, but when he only continued to stare at the far wall, continued after a moment. "Then again, maybe he wouldn't mind if I just lie here like something dead while he tries to get his heir?"

Without a word, the guard marched across the room toward the door and Chyna's heart soared with hopefulness. The very moment he disappeared through the door, she would grab the sheets, and shimmy down them, and....

He opened the door. Instead of leaving, however, he spoke to the guard outside, telling him to send a servant to fetch food for the master's woman.

Disappointment and irritation flooded her, but they were short lived. She hadn't really expected it to work. Moreover, now that there was a chance of getting something to eat, she realized she was starving. Anticipation replaced her frustration. She was almost ready to start pacing the floor when the servant at last appeared with the promised tray. It was all she could do not to fall upon it like a starving dog and wolf the food down. As it was, she'd already gulped several bites before she realized just how good the food was. With the edge taken off her hunger, she slowed down, savoring the food, but even that didn't save her from gluttony. She ate until she was stuffed. Sleepiness followed rapidly on the heels of repletion, because she hadn't had much of that either in a while.

Pushing the remains of the food away, she climbed onto the bed and sprawled out, closing her eyes and breathing against her packed stomach with an effort. She found herself drifting after only a few moments and finally simply fell into the pit of nothingness. She awoke sometime later to a tug on her nipple that sent currents of fire eddying through her.

By the pricking of my boobs, something wicked this way comes, she thought wryly.

It felt damned good though and it was a small step from 'I'm not up to the struggle' to 'oh well, may as well enjoy it the best I can'.

She felt a tug, a brush of cool air. She opened her eyes to the dimly lit room and saw him kneeling beside her on the bed. He pulled the scarves off her body like he was plucking a flower--or excitedly unwrapping a birthday present. Every time he exposed a body part he bent to kiss it, or stroke his warm hand across her flesh until her skin tingled. By the time he reached her hips, his impatience won out and he pulled a wad free, baring her mound.

A warm hand touched her hip to glide slowly down and along her thigh. Warmth and desire radiated through her.

Damn, the man was good. He had to have had lots of practice.

The thought made her brain twinge with disappointment, but hell, who was she to look a gift horse in the mouth? Good lovers were hard to come by. *Royally* good lovers were probably even harder to find.

"Mmmmm." She moaned when his fingertips skimmed her inner thigh. Her heart began an excited gallop of anticipation as desire flooded her, spreading sensation through her awakened flesh. She parted her thighs. Moisture gathered in her expectant sex. Her clit throbbed to an internal beat.

He flittered his fingers across her bare cleft, making her insides clench, and moved back up her belly.

Chyna took back all her good thoughts of him as she groaned in disappointment. "You ass," she growled, clamping her legs shut just to spite him. If he didn't want it now she wasn't going to give it to him later when he changed his mind.

"*Your* ass, Earthling," he said with a chuckle, as if it was a teasing insult.

She felt like arguing with him about semantics--she had no intention of keeping him or allowing herself to be kept by him, but he moved his hand upward, along the curve of her waist, and finally cupped her breast, massaging it. A spear of heat lanced from her breast to her belly, distracting her from higher thought. Her mind couldn't get beyond the pleasure suffusing her breast.

He settled his mouth against her neck, sending goose flesh down her shoulder and arm. She lost the power of speech altogether when he nipped her earlobe and sucked it into his mouth.

She gasped. Her heart leapt beneath his palm and toying fingers. She lifted a hand and placed it against his chest. He was warm, soft as velvet and hard as a rock.

It wouldn't hurt to touch him a little. She'd never been with a man this built before. The play of his muscles excited her more than it should have.

He released her breast and clutched her hand, moving it down his ripped belly to his groin until her fingertips touched his throbbing cock.

Holy shit! She thought, trying to circle her hand around his girth. He groaned, pressing his hips forward and covered her mouth with his own, thrusting his tongue into her mouth. The move surprised a moan out of her.

She sucked him. His scent and taste, the erection in her palm and the hardness of his body flooded her senses, making her drunk with desire and an ache to have that monstrosity inside her like his tongue.

Her legs betrayed her by spreading wide. He rolled on top of her, flattening her on the bed and forcing her to remove her hand as he settled between her thighs and stabbed her cleft with the bulbous head of his cock.

Chyna groaned into his mouth, tangling her tongue with his. His mouth ravished hers, hungry, demanding, ravenous--an assault on her sense of self-preservation, which had pretty much scurried into hiding the moment she discovered his erection.

He tasted good, kissed better. She was having a hard time concentrating. She felt bombarded on all sides by sensation--top to bottom, inside and out. But it wasn't enough ... not nearly enough.

She dug her heels into the bed and lifted her hips, grinding against him until her clit received the attention she'd begun to crave. She rubbed herself against his erection, clutching his arms with desperation.

Oh. He felt good. He'd feel even better inside, she thought, rubbing against him and wondering how to make him fit.

He tore his mouth from hers, his breath ragged as he rolled to the side and skated his mouth down her chest to settle on her breast.

Damn it, she didn't want to be fucking tortured anymore. She twisted, trying to evade him and get that *thing* inside her. He threw an arm across her ribs, flattening her on the bed as he sucked one nipple and half her breast into his mouth. Pure ecstasy shimmied down her belly, pooling between her thighs in ever increasing desperation.

His tongue nudged her nipple, rubbing as he suckled and wrung out every ounce of pleasure available to her body. Her breasts felt hard, swollen, almost painfully sensitive. Her labia felt slippery and wet with desire. She couldn't possibly get more aroused than this.

When the hell did strange men begin caring about this much foreplay? She wondered almost frantically. She just needed some piston action--craved it.

"Dammit!" she gasped. "Stop torturing me."

Her heart raced until she was dizzy, gasping for air.

He mercifully released her nipple, splaying his hand on her belly. "This is what we do with captured rebels."

Somehow, she didn't quite picture him doing this with the men in her unit.

She protested when he buried his face in the valley of her breasts, smiling against her chest. He pushed his hand down her belly, settling his fingers against her clit. He rubbed the sensitive nub, pinching it between his fingers until it swelled with a throbbing pulse.

She gasped and reached for him, threading her fingers through his hair, guiding his to her other breast. He tasted her, long and hard, playing with her clit as he suckled.

Frustrated, she writhed beneath him, groaning when he trailed his lips down the muscles of her stomach and fanned her naked, hypersensitive mound with his hot breath. She was almost breathless with anticipation as his mouth hovered over her.

"You're too delicious to devour all at once." He nudged her thighs apart, nipping at her ultra sensitive nether lips. He stopped and lifted his head to look at her. His eyes gleamed in the near dark, his expression of harsh desire unmistakable. "But I will have a taste."

He grasped her legs and spread her like an offering, tilting her hips up to his mouth as he lowered his head toward her pleasure center. His tongue dug past her lips and teased her clit.

White hot pleasure erupted inside her, growing hotter, higher as he sucked her. Her mouth went dry as she gasped for air. Her hips bucked as she hovered at the edge of ecstasy ... so long, she thought she would die if she didn't come. He sucked and nibbled, driving her to the edge of the precipice, pulling back just as she neared it.

He withdrew and she screamed in frustration, quieting only when he covered her with his body and rubbed that hulking beast against her achy cleft.

Her belly jerked with the hot, hard contact. She gritted her teeth, stifling another scream as he guided the head of his cock to her opening and pushed inside, stretching her so much she thought she'd rip.

"Tight," he ground out, going rigid and still. He withdrew and pushed inside again, a little further, working her lubrication down his engorged shaft and into her.

"You won't hurt me," Chyna said, whimpering, needing to come so badly. She moved her hips, trying to speed him along.

He groaned, long and loud, warring with himself before impaling her on his erection. Her sex gushed with arousal.

Chyna jerked beneath him, crying out, unable to hold back any longer. He swallowed her cries with a deep, hungry kiss, allowing her to adjust to his thick erection. Sensations ricocheted throughout her entirety … agony … ecstasy … an immense feeling of fullness.

He moved slowly, almost grinding against her. Sharp needles of desire prickled her from clit to belly. She flexed around him. His face hardened, a muscle twitching in his jaw. She savored the slow, steady building pleasure as he stroked her.

She wrapped her legs around him, needing to feel him deeper, harder. The movement brought her back to the edge of bliss.

She tried to stop it, needing to hold onto that pleasure as long as she could, but he was too much for her.

Her muscles rippled around him as a climax seized her in its unshakable grip. He groaned as if in agony and moved faster, heightening the pleasure until she couldn't stand it anymore. She orgasmed again, pleasure wringing from every nerve until she was moaning uncontrollably.

When he at last cried out and jerked inside her, she came again, more intensely than before. She grasped his head and brought his mouth down for a hard kiss, stifling their mingled cries. Acute pleasure wracked her insides, making her bones and muscle seem to melt. Utter exhaustion invaded her.

He collapsed on top of her, breathing raggedly. He rolled to his side and pulled her snugly against him. Chyna was too weak to fight his great paws off her body and slipped into unconsciousness.

Chapter Three

Chyna realized the moment she began to drift toward consciousness that something was wrong. She thought it over in a hazy sort of way, unwilling to fully arouse herself to tackle the problem. Finally, it occurred to her that wrong wasn't the word she'd been searching for.

Something was different.

There wasn't a tree trunk lying across her.

Rousing a little more, Chyna wiggled around, seeking the warmth she'd grown accustomed to in the bed beside her over the last couple of weeks. When she didn't find it, she woke sufficiently to pry her eyelids up and look around.

Darion wasn't in bed with her.

She frowned, wondering a little vaguely where he was. Finally, she pushed herself up and looked around. It didn't help since the curtains were closed and she'd already figured out she had sole possession of the bed. She lay back down, wondering if she had the energy to explore any further.

She'd hardly been out of the bed since Darion had taken it into his head to breed an heir on her.

She would say this for him, the man was dedicated! Once he set his mind to do something he gave it his all.

Fighting off her lethargy, Chyna finally crawled toward the edge of the bed and dragged the curtains back. A survey of the room assured her that she was alone.

It took several minutes for that fact to actually sink in fully.

She was alone!

She'd done it! She had lulled his suspicions! He hadn't even left the guard to keep an eye on her!

She just hoped she'd be able to walk/run for freedom. *He* had barely let her close her legs all week--more like two weeks, she corrected herself. Damned near it, anyway.

Still a little doubtful of her good fortune Chyna inched to the edge of the bed and threw her legs over the side, sitting up and leaning out for a better look. Seeing no sign of either Darion or his watch dog, she slipped off the edge of the bed and stood, testing her land legs.

Barely a twinge, she realized with surprise. She gasped in a sharp breath of agony with her first step, however. Groaning, she shuffled toward the edge of the dais, stared at it in dismay for several moments and finally stepped down. As she'd expected, pain shot through her.

Waiting until the worst passed, she forced herself to hobble around the room, hoping she could walk off the painful muscle strain. Blood was pounding in her poor abused cootsie till she couldn't resist the urge to cup it, applying counter pressure to ease the throbbing. Her back hurt, too. She applied pressure to that pain point with her other hand.

As she passed the mirror over the dressing table, she glanced toward it and a jolt went through her. In the next moment, though, she realized it wasn't the reflection of a bent old woman she'd glimpsed. It was her.

Gritting her teeth, Chyna straightened, rested for a few minutes to let the threat of a faint pass and began again. After fifteen or twenty minutes, she found she could move a little more freely, but she couldn't move normally by any stretch of the imagination and it was for certain she wouldn't be able to run if her life depended upon it.

It occurred to her after a while to wonder if she ought to be considering flight at all when she could barely hobble. On the other hand, it didn't take a lot more thought to realize that if he screwed her much more she might be crippled for life. Or worse, she might get to the point that she liked it too much to consider leaving.

She already felt regretful even considering it. He had been so sweet to her. He was such a considerate lover, too, always taking the time to make certain she enjoyed it as much as he did. If things had been different, he was just the sort of man she would've wanted to meet--the sort of man she could have fallen in love with.

Sighing, she dismissed her weak thoughts. She *had* to leave. She had to get back to the resistance. They were outmanned as it was. Every soldier counted and her comrades in arms needed her.

She couldn't go dressed in nothing but gold chains, however. She needed her clothes, such as they were. Remembering Darion had plucked the scarves one by one and tossed them aside, she climbed up on the dais with an effort and searched the bed for the scarves. Coming up empty, and beginning to feel a little desperate, she searched the edges of the bed to see if the scarves had gotten caught between the bedclothes and the drapes.

When she still didn't unearth the first scrap of veiling, she got down on her hands and knees and checked under the bed. Nothing. Not even dust bunnies. Anger washed over her. That bastard! He hadn't left her with so much as one measly veil to cover her mound with, damn his hide!

Plunking her hands on her hips, she glared at the room, thinking.

His clothes, she thought gleefully. It would serve the bastard right, too, for taking every stitch of clothing she had to her name and *then* taking the frigging scarves he'd replaced her flight suit with.

She made another unpleasant discovery. Inside of fifteen minutes, she'd checked every chest, every drawer, ever nook and cranny and there wasn't a sign of *any* clothing at all.

"Sonofabitch!" she ground out, resisting the urge to stamp her feet like a frustrated child with a supreme effort. "That low down snake! That vile, despicable tyrant! How *dare* that bastard leave me shut in this frigging cage without a rag to my name!"

It helped her feelings to call him every low down thing she could put her tongue to, but it didn't help her situation. She was far too angry to consider waiting for a better time, however, and pure hardheaded determination gripped her.

If she was going to escape--and she damned well would!--she was going to have to do it naked, she realized, studying the bed sheets speculatively.

Yanking them from the bed, she began by knotting the top sheet and the bottom together and then worked knots into her makeshift rope every couple of feet to give her something to grip when she climbed down. Stomping to the window, she opened it and calculated the distance, then studied her 'rope'. It looked long enough and she realized once she got down she could pull the sheets down and use one to cover herself.

Ha! Smartass! Thought he could outsmart her, did he!

There was nothing near the window to use for an anchor. After looking around the room and studying each piece of furniture, her gaze settled on the chest at the foot of the bed. She eyed the chest speculatively for several moments and then went over to it, checking the weight by pushing against it. Satisfied that it would do the trick, she got down and began shoving the heavy chest across the floor. It made an ungodly racket as it scraped along the floor, but she was beyond caring and figured at any rate that if there'd been anyone close enough to hear they would've charged through the door the moment she started shoving the thing.

She was sweating by the time she'd managed to get the chest beneath the window. She was sweating harder and breathing raggedly by the time she managed to get the sheet under the chest and secured it. Gasping for breath, she tossed the other end of her rope out the window.

It occurred to her as she climbed up on the chest that she hadn't even checked to make sure her knot would hold for the climb. Bracing herself, she caught the sheet in both hands and leaned away from the trunk, bearing down on the knot with all her weight. To her satisfaction, it held.

Holding the sheets firmly with both hands, she flung one leg over the window sill, studied the drop uneasily for several moments and finally decided to take the plunge. Flinging an obscene gesture at the empty room, she caught the sheet and struggled over the window sill. The sheet swayed as she began the long climb down. The further she climbed, the more the sheet swayed. When she stopped to rest, the fucking sheet began to twist dizzyingly.

Knowing it wasn't going to take much of that to have her too dizzy to climb, she worked her way down to the next knot.

The rope dropped.

Her heart stood still in her chest. She squeezed her eyes closed, flinching against impact she fully expected as the chest came flying out the window. When nothing else happened, she opened her eyes and looked up at the window.

It must have been the chest that moved, she decided. She couldn't see anything, but if the knot was coming loose, it wouldn't have stopped. It would've come completely undone.

Dragging in a shaky breath, she decided to move a little faster. If she was going to fall, she wanted to be closer to the ground when she did it.

The problem with that laudable intention was that the faster she climbed, the worse the frigging sheet swayed and twisted. A loud squawk sounded almost simultaneously with another sharp jolt on her rope.

Chyna froze, glancing worriedly toward the window.

She didn't see the chest coming toward her and after she managed to swallow her heart, she began to climb again, more slowly.

She was still a good six feet off the ground when she ran out of rope.

It didn't sound like much, but it looked like a hell of a lot.

Maybe it was eight feet?

Dragging in a shaky breath, she took her feet off the rope and lowered herself with her hands till she reached the last knot. She was still trying to convince herself to let go when the squawk came again and the sheet dropped several inches.

She let go, rolling when she hit the ground, just in case the chest was right behind her.

It wasn't. She lay gasping for breath, staring up at the sheet dangling from the window, trying to ignore the friction burns on her palms and knees. Slowly, a sense of triumph washed over her.

She was out! She was free!

Glancing around to make certain there were no guards within sight, she got to her feet and looked up at the rope. From this direction, it didn't actually look that high off the ground. Standing on tiptoe, she reached for it and discovered she couldn't grasp the end, although she could touch it.

Taking a deep breath, she leapt for it, giving it a sharp tug when she gripped it. Nothing happened and she dropped to the ground again, frowning at the slight hitch in her plan.

She'd thought she would be able to untie it, or at least rip a section off to use to cover herself. What the hell was she going to do now?

Deciding to give it at least one more try, Chyna leapt up and grabbed the sheet again. Abruptly, something above her squawked like a dying chicken, the rope went slack, and she landed on the ground flat of her back, staring up at the chest as it came flying downward.

Oh my fucking god!

Gasping, she rolled and kept on rolling. The chest hit the ground with an ungodly explosion of sound, shattering. Leaping to her feet, Chyna glanced around frantically and hit for the hedges she saw across the lawn, running for all she was worth.

She passed the hedge row and slammed into one directly across from it. Confused, in too much of a panic to actually feel much pain, she pushed away from it and ran down the corridor the two hedges created. When she rounded a corner, she discovered yet another row and it finally dawned on her that she'd headed straight into the maze.

"Shit!" She paused to catch her breath and listen for sounds of pursuit. Hearing nothing, she lingered long enough to pull some large leaves off of the hedge and stuffed the stalks into the chains for a little coverage.

She wasn't likely to get far stuck in the frigging maze, but she had no intention of going back the way she'd just come. With any luck, they wouldn't realize she was in the maze and by the time she'd found her way out the search would be moved far enough away she could slip out unnoticed.

The decision made, she began moving again, ignoring the painful twinges from sexual overdose and championship climbing and running. When she reached the center of the maze, she stopped to rest and listen again. She could hear sounds, but they were indistinct and it was impossible to tell what was going on.

She couldn't see over the hedge. After bouncing up and down a few times and discovering she couldn't jump high enough to see over the hedge either, she glanced around for something to climb onto. There was a resting bench in the center of the maze--not a good sign, actually--but she decided to think optimistically that it wasn't put there because people needed the rest.

Climbing onto the bench, she looked out over the top of the hedges.

Darion was standing at the window she'd just climbed out of, staring straight at her. Letting out a yelp, she leapt from the bench, glanced around a little frantically and took off down the next leafy corridor, slamming into the hedges when she reached the dead end. "Damn it to hell!" she muttered, whirling around and heading back out. When she reached the center again, she paused significantly longer to pick a possibility and finally headed down it at a jogging trot.

This, too, ended in a dead end.

Picturing Darion closing in on her, she decided not to head back for another try. Instead, she got down on her hands and knees and peered through the lower branches of the shrubs. There wasn't much space, but she figured she was small enough to wiggle through and flattened out, inching along the ground as quickly as she could.

Hoping she was headed in the right direction, she crossed an opening and went under the next row, and the one after that.

A pair of black boots met her as she emerged from the next hedge. She looked up just as Darion knelt down and grabbed her by one arm. One look at his face was enough to assure her he was totally pissed. Hauling her out from under the hedge, he whipped his cape from his shoulders and wrapped it around hers, then wordlessly grabbed her arm and hauled her back toward the castle, through the entrance hall, up the stairs and finally hauled her through the harem doors, handing her over to the women for a bath.

The soap stung. She was scraped and bruised from one end to the other from climbing, running, and crawling on her belly.

She was relieved when they were done with her--until she discovered that Darion was waiting just outside the door. Time hadn't cooled his temper. If anything, his face was stonier than before.

Gripping her arm, he hauled her down the corridor to his suite, opened the door and pushed her inside, locking the door behind him.

Chyna stared at the door for a moment in surprise, listening as he stalked down the hall and finally moved beyond earshot. Whirling, she headed for the window.

To her consternation, she discovered when she reached it that the window had been nailed shut.

Thwarted of another attempt, Chyna spent most of the day pacing uneasily. Not for one moment did she believe she'd come off from her little adventure unscathed. The only thing she could think was that Darion had just been too furious to trust himself to 'discuss' what manner of punishment he had in mind for her attempted escape.

Waiting was hell.

She discovered, though, that the punishment he had in mind was much worse than anything her fertile imagination had been able to produce in hours of contemplating the error of her ways.

Chapter Four

He had been obsessed to have Chyna, and now that he held her within his grasp, Darion discovered his sense of desperation for her had not diminished as he had more than half hoped that it would. Instead, the more he was with her, the harder he found it to leave her, and the more difficult it was to focus on his responsibilities when he was away from her.

A strong sense of self preservation was all that kept him from spending every waking hour with her.

He could not allow her to know how he felt about her, he knew. She could use it against him. Considering the way she felt about him, it seemed very likely that she would although he sensed that she was not of a manipulative nature. The fact was, she still saw him as her enemy, and herself as captive, not beloved concubine. Under those circumstances she could hardly do anything except use the weapons placed in her hands.

That thought had barely flickered through his mind when an explosion of sound close by brought him to his feet.

His first thought, naturally enough, was of Chyna.

Quitting his study abruptly, he crossed the corridor and took the stairs two at a time. He couldn't think beyond the possibility that she had been injured in the attack--he knew it must have been yet another rebel attack.

His heart seemed to stop in his chest when he flung the doors to his suite open. The suite was a disaster area.

His gaze had gone at once to the bed. He saw that it had been stripped, the bed drapes left in disarray. Scanning the room, his gaze riveted to the window--open.

Striding across the room, he looked down at the grounds beneath. A shattered chest lay there. Crumpled beside it was a mound of sheets and it took no more than a few seconds then to put the scenario together.

Relief flooded him first, that there was no sign of her broken body below, or blood. Fury subverted it, blinding him to everything else as he surveyed the grounds for some sign of her, feeling his heart sink with the realization that she'd escaped him-- left him--just when, fool that he was, he had begun to think she was coming around to him.

Even now she was probably fleeing over the next hill, his heir in her womb!

The very moment he had allowed her a little freedom, she had slapped him in the face and fled!

"Find her!" he roared to the guards, who had gathered behind him.

The guards saluted and took off at a run, alerting others as they reached the corridor.

Frustration filled him.

He was too smitten with her to behave rationally. He should have known that it was hopeless from the beginning, that he could capture her and possess her--or allow her to go on her way and yearn for her--but he could not capture her and steal her heart.

The urge washed over him to call the guards back, but he found he couldn't bring himself to give up so easily. He might not win her heart if he held her captive, but he assuredly would not if she returned to the rebels. At least this way, he had a chance and some chance was better than none at all.

In time, when she saw she could not escape, she would at least learn acceptance.

Movement in the maze caught his attention as he scanned the grounds for some indication of which way she'd gone and his gaze moved of its own accord to identify what he'd seen.

Chyna!

Rage filled him as he met her startled gaze.

She'd damned near gotten herself killed! And she was running away with his sons in her belly! If he'd managed to impregnate her….

Whirling from the window, he raced from the room. She wasn't wearing a stitch of clothing and he had no intention of allowing his guards anywhere near her.

* * * *

Chyna was doing her utmost to pretend she was asleep when Darion at last made his appearance in the suite late in the night. She didn't know whether she was unsuccessful, or he simply didn't care whether she was asleep or not. Which ever the case, the moment he slid into bed beside her, her heart began galloping in trepidation.

Would he beat her?

She didn't think he was that kind of man. He hadn't hurt her once in the entire time she'd been there--except with excruciating amounts of pleasure.

He surprised her by rolling on top of her and crushing his mouth against her lips in a harsh kiss. He savaged her mouth, nearly bruising her lips, sweeping his tongue voraciously through her mouth in a kiss that had her heaving for breath through her nostrils.

By the time he broke the kiss, she felt faint. She hardly resisted when he gathered one of her wrists and tied it down. When he grabbed the other, however, she'd recovered sufficiently to wonder just what the hell his intentions were. She tried to evade him, but his reach was a lot further than she thought, and she was hampered by her inability to move one arm.

She was breathing heavily by the time he finished strapping her arms and legs down. She was short, and the rope he'd used was long enough to reach the edges of each side of the bed. Damn good foresight on his part, she fumed. She'd been so preoccupied with what he was going to do that she hadn't even noticed him bringing in his supplies.

He got up and turned the lights on, then came back to the bed, brandishing two silk scarves. In the light, she could see the grim, determined set of his face. He looked her up and down, desire flashing in his eyes before it was replaced with cold anger once more.

Chyna glared and bared her teeth at him, struggling against her bonds as he wrapped a scarf around her head and obscured her sight, then wrapped the second around her mouth to keep her from cussing his ass out.

"Don't struggle," he said, his voice low and harsh. "I won't hurt you."

Yeah. Right. She believed him.

The bed dipped as he moved on it, crossing over her spread legs to kneel between her thighs. Her heart thundered in her ears. She struggled, trying to free herself, to no avail.

His hands slid up her thighs. She jerked in surprise when something warm and wet slithered behind one and then moved to the other--his tongue. She knew it was dangerous to be sucked into some kind of sexual fantasy when it seemed his intent was to punish her, but she couldn't help the unbidden desire that swam to the surface as he traveled up her body, inch by inch. Her sex moistened with burgeoning longing, anticipating the contact of his tongue as he neared the juncture of her thighs.

He passed her apex by with nary a touch, moving up her belly, her ribs, skimming her breasts with scraping teeth and tongue. He teased her nipples with his flicking tongue. Her breasts swelled. Her nipples grew erect, engorged nearly to the point of pain.

He sucked her breast into his mouth, raked his teeth against her distended flesh, suckled again. Heat suffused her. Despite all she could do, she moaned through the muffling scarf.

He moved away, crawling off the bed. She waited to see what he would do next, feeling frustrated. Her clit felt hypersensitive and ignored.

Her body had just begun to cool when he returned and claimed her other nipple. She jerked reflexively. He sucked it long and hard, scraping with tongue and teeth until her mind focused solely on the feel of his hungry mouth.

Her breathing accelerated, expelling hard from her flared nostrils. Her heart pumped faster and she began to shake all over.

He released her nipple. "Will you run again?" he asked.

Chyna shook her head, desperate for him to continue.

"I don't believe you," he ground out.

He moved downward, pressing his hands on her thighs and locking his mouth over her clit. If she could've moved, she would've jumped away from his torturous mouth. He sucked her, hard, making the bud flow. Her nerves pricked like needles, painful.

Pleasure made her belly jerk, her insides clenched with arousal. Every sense honed in on the dexterity of his tongue and what he was doing to her. Flicking his tongue rapidly against her clit, he pushed one thick finger inside her, curling it upwards until he stroked her g-spot. She flexed her toes and fingers, wanting to grasp something, anything.

Chyna moaned. A hard spasm made her gut tighten.

He stopped abruptly, leaving her hovering on the edge of orgasm.

She finally realized what he was doing--punishing her. She screamed against the scarf, hardly making a sound. Not that it would do any good even if it hadn't been there. Who was here to answer her screams and help her? No one.

He moved off the bed, leaving her alone.

Her body slowly cooled, anger giving way to disappointment and then frustration. What was wrong with her? That she should *want* him to torture her this way? That she could actually derive pleasure from his actions?

Asshole.

If the tables ever turned--watch out. She fumed.

Minutes passed. Her breathing and heart rate returned to normal. She began to wonder if that was the end of the punishment, and if she was to spend the rest of the night bound. Was he such a softie? Did it sicken him to torment her? Obviously, some man a long time ago had thought up this particular kind of torture--sickos.

Chyna nearly jumped out of her skin when the bed dipped and he touched her. Her body thrummed to instant awareness. Her skin reacted with goose flesh, prickling as he stroked her feet, her calves, her thighs. He skimmed her nether lips and moved up her belly to her breasts.

She whimpered, trying to evade him, but it was useless. Her nipples engorged once more. Her cleft moistened with juices, preparing for his entrance--all for naught.

He had far more patience than she'd given him credit for. Being a ruler must do that to a man. She hated him for it, hated him for awakening her arousal yet again.

He toyed with her breasts until she moaned incessantly and then nibbled a path down her belly to her cleft. He dug his tongue inside her vagina, stabbing the tender core. She gushed with arousal, clenching hard on him and moaned when he moved away to finesse her clit.

Shudders quaked through her, making her body ache with unquenched desire.

He broke contact and suddenly pulled the scarf away from her mouth. She worked her jaw muscles, wondering at the freedom.

"Will you run again?"

She shook her head. "No. No, I won't," she lied, knowing she would again the first chance she got.

He lowered his body to hers, digging his erection against her bare mound. "Why should I trust you?"

Oh my god! She bit down on her lip to keep from screaming. He rotated his hips, grinding against her clit. She tried to catch her breath, couldn't. "I'll do anything," she said, breathless. Her sex felt swollen, achy and needy beyond comprehension.

"Do you want my cock inside you," he ground out, nudging her opening.

"Yes. Oh god, yes."

His voice lowered. She could feel his breath on her face, hot as it tickled through her hair. "Will you run again?"

"No. No, no, no."

"Liar," he growled, burying his face against her neck as he impaled her to the root of his cock.

Chyna cried out, clenching around him. He drove into her hard and fast, bruising her body, crushing the breath from her lungs. She gasped, bucking against him as much as she could, wanting desperately to come.

He growled and withdrew after only a few strokes. "Only a taste … until I can believe you."

She screamed in frustration as he moved to torture her breasts. She was so exhausted and tense she thought she'd die.

He repeated the process, touching her flesh, massaging her, teasing with tongue and lips until he brought her to the brink, then moving away and allowing her to cool down.

It seemed hours passed--she couldn't tell. She felt like one huge, impending orgasm. She swore the next time he touched her, she'd come from the contact alone, but he allowed her no surcease.

She began to moan mindlessly, struggling against her bonds until she could struggle no more. When he finally asked if she would run again, she couldn't even murmur her response. All the fluid in her body had pooled to her apex. Her mouth was dry, parched.

He closed over her again, kissing her, saturating her mouth with his lips. She should've bitten his tongue off, but she couldn't get up the energy to fight him.

His erection dug into her mound, tantalizing her with his nearness until she cried. He nibbled her lips and cheeks, kissed away her tears of frustration.

Ever so slowly, he pushed inside her tight core, sinking to the hilt deep inside her until she felt like bursting. He moved fast and hard, his piston-like rhythm making her clench throughout. Her heartbeat quickened. Her breath came in short pants.

She felt on the verge of climax and rushed toward it, wondering it he would allow her surcease, just this once.

He sucked her neck, branding her with his mouth as he ground his hips against her swollen, too sensitive clit. Her body clenched suddenly. Wave after wave of pleasure rolled through her insides, gelling muscle and bone. The ecstasy was so intense, she passed out.

She awoke sometime later, surprised to find herself aroused yet again and reaching for orgasm, only to be disappointed when he didn't allow her to come.

He continued in that fashion for hours, maybe even days. She couldn't tell how much time passed. He would bring her to the brink of climax and then would take her down, and bring her to the crest once more, never allowing her to orgasm until she'd begged him and promised never to run again. She was delirious with longing, crazed with need, beyond thinking of anything but alleviating the tension of her body.

A long time ago she'd read a romance where the woman was tortured with pleasure. Chyna had fantasized about it at the time and always thought it would be sexually thrilling--something she'd enjoy experiencing. In reality, she was ready to kill Darion if he aroused her one more time and didn't let her come--or kept her aroused for hours on end without climax.

When she could beg and plead no more, he satisfied her again, untying her hands and feet. She could hardly move and lay there like a rag doll as he crawled into bed and snuggled her against him.

Chapter Five

Despite her role in the rebel resistance, desperation wasn't an emotion Chyna had ever been very familiar with before she'd been captured. It shouldn't be something she had come to know considering the terms of her captivity, but she had, and no matter how hard she tried to convince herself that it was because of Darion's distorted idea of punishment, she wasn't entirely successful.

In retrospect, she realized it was unthinkable that she had felt passion at all, for a man who was her enemy and the enemy of the people. Physically, he was a hunk and there was just no getting around that, but they didn't see eye to eye at all politically and that should have been enough of a turn off to keep her from losing her head. It hadn't. And if that wasn't bad enough, it hadn't affected any encounter since, which was almost as confusing to her mind.

Getting caught up in the heat of the moment once, maybe even twice, was understandable to a degree. Spending weeks in such close intimacy and still feeling that way, feeling the passion grow more powerful instead of diminishing or burning itself out made no sense. Familiarity should have bred contempt even if mind and body had been at war from the first moment he touched her.

That it hadn't was an indication that he had gotten under her skin in a way she would never have dreamed possible and it was that that made her feel more desperate to escape than anything else. She needed distance to gain some perspective and he wasn't going to allow that as long as he had her.

The physical desperation he had introduced her to, when all was said and done, had been as much pleasure as it was torture, but it only added to her desperation because it had brought home as nothing else how enslaving her desire for him could be.

If she stayed much longer, she wasn't going to want to leave at all.

She didn't want to leave now, for that matter, and it was a lot more than just a reluctance to give up great sex. It was anticipation of the emotional pain she knew she was going to feel from the separation, pain that was likely to increase exponentially the longer she stayed.

As uneasy as she was about her last escape attempt, therefore, and as badly as it had turned out, her desperation drove her to begin searching for another opportunity.

She had searched the royal suite from end to end looking for anything that might give her hope of escape. She had nothing to do whenever Darion wasn't with her, after all, beyond eating, sleeping--which she needed since he kept her up half of every night--and pacing. She had covered every square inch of wall and floor that she could reach easily.

She'd been studying the ceiling vent for days before a plan began to formulate in her mind. The ceiling was high--really high--and the vent looked much too small for her, but she finally decided that it was the perspective of distance. It was a ventilation duct after all, which meant that it had to be bringing air inside from outside--she hoped. And given the size of the rooms in the castle that meant it was moving a great deal of air. The duct had to be large to move a volume sufficient to regulate the temperature inside the palace.

Reaching the vent was definitely going to present a problem. If it was smaller than she thought, that might also present a serious drawback. Otherwise, she still had the puzzle of what to do once she got out when she had nothing at all to cover herself with.

That, she finally decided, was something to figure out *if* she got out, though. It wasn't something she intended to allow to become a roadblock to getting out. Some peasant, sympathetic to the rebel cause could be counted on, she was sure, to help her with clothing and transportation. And if worse came to worst, she could always steal something to wear from somewhere if she got out and got clean away.

It would have been nice if she had had some idea of the layout of the castle. She did, in a vague way, but not enough to be really helpful.

She decided not to worry about it. Once she got into the ventilation system, she would just put as much distance between herself and the royal suite as she could, find an unoccupied room that wasn't guarded like this one and the harem, and then she would sneak out the nearest door or window.

Timing was everything. Darion was tied up most of the day everyday doing his ruler thing. Since her last attempt to escape, he had stopped coming to her until late in the evening. Otherwise, only servants came in and they only came in to bring her meals, morning, noon, and late evening. She decided she would go just as soon as the noon meal was delivered. That way hours would pass before anyone came in, which meant that she could be far, far away before Darion even knew she was missing.

She took the opportunity of her next session in the baths to filch a tiny bottle of oils since it occurred to her that if the vent shafts were a snug fit she might need something to help her squeeze through. There was only one place to hide the damned thing and she wasn't crazy about using it, but the guards were bound to notice anything she was carrying openly and most likely would confiscate it just on general principle.

Getting it in wasn't a big problem. Getting it out again was another matter and she had to fight a sense of panic while she wrestled with the thing. Finally, however, shaky and completely unnerved by the experience, she managed to remove her pilfered oils.

The following day, she implemented her plan. When the maid brought her noon meal in and settled it on the table, she sat down to eat as if she had nothing on her mind beyond the food. Her stomach was tied into knots, though, and it took all she could do to choke a few bites down while the maid lingered in the room to tidy things here and there.

The moment the door closed behind the maid, Chyna bounded out of her chair and ran on tiptoe to the door, pressing her ear against it to listen. She could hear the guards flirting with the maid and ground her teeth at the delay. Finally, the maid left and the guards went back to their usual boredom of staring down the corridor.

Tiptoeing back to the center of the room, Chyna looked up at the vent. The tallest piece of furniture in the room was the armoire, but she'd already tried moving that. Even after taking out every shelf and drawer that she could it was still too heavy for her to move. The table was the tallest thing in the room that she could move.

Taking her tray of food off of it, she dragged the table as quietly as she could to a position just beneath the vent. The biggest chest had gone out the window and shattered on the ground below, but there were a number of smaller ones that she could just lift once she'd emptied the contents. These she stacked in two rows, one on top of the other. Using a chair, she climbed up on the table and then on top of the chests to see how close she was to her goal. Excitement filled her when she discovered she could almost reach from the second tier of chests. All she needed was a couple more feet added to her pyramid and success was within her grasp!

Climbing down again, she dragged one of the straight chairs over, climbed up in the chair she'd used to get onto the table and lifted the second chair to the top of the stack. Grabbing a table knife, she climbed the pyramid of furniture again and reached up, discovering with a touch of irritation that she still wouldn't be able to climb up into the vent. She could reach it, though, and she went ahead while she was perched at the top and used the knife to remove the vent cover and peered inside.

It turned, she saw, almost immediately after passing through the ceiling.

Satisfied, she climbed down again. Plunking her hands on her hips, she looked the room over for something small enough to put in the chair that would also be tall enough to give her the extra couple of feet she needed. Finally, she settled on another chest.

Even empty the thing was heavy and awkward to climb with, which she had to do since her pyramid was already higher than her head. She was sweating by the time she managed to get the chest on the second layer of chests. It took some maneuvering to find a place to put her feet after that, but finally she did and lifted the chest onto the chair.

It didn't fit into the seat. It also didn't overlap the arms of the chair as much as she could've wished, but she managed to perch it on the arms. Climbing down again, she mopped the moisture of exertion from her body with the bed drapes, wondering if there was actually any point to the oils after all. She finally decided, though, that climbing through the ventilation system probably wouldn't be nearly as taxing and besides, sweat was as likely to make her skin cling as it was to produce lubrication to help her slide.

Grabbing the bottle, she climbed up her pyramid again, balanced on the uppermost chest for a moment and finally stood up carefully. She narrowly missed butting her head on the ceiling and jerked instinctively, which made the pyramid teeter unnervingly.

A cold sweat broke from her pores that time for she didn't even have anything to grab onto to save herself if the stack fell. Finally, it stopped wobbling. She had to hold the bottle of oil between her teeth and use both hands to reach up into the vent.

It *was* snug. The stack of furniture wobbled again as she wiggled into the vent and she froze again, halfway into the vent, this time fearing the whole thing would fall and alert the guards. Moving with great care after a moment, she managed to wiggle up into the vent shaft until she had the entire upper half of her body inside it.

After some thought, she decided to wait until she was fully inside before she tried the oils. It was hard enough to get in without being slippery, as well.

She decided once she had gotten inside that it was a damned good thing she wasn't claustrophobic. If she had been, she would've been a blithering idiot by now. As it was, even without an acute fear of close spaces, she was unnerved. She stopped to rest as soon as she was fully inside the vent and opened the bottle. Instantly, a cloud of flowery scent filled the air around her that was so potent it made her dizzy.

"My god!" she muttered in annoyance. They were going to smell her coming even if they didn't hear her.

Unfortunately, she lost her grip on the bottle at just that moment and half the contents puddled on the bottom of the vent before she could snatch it up again. Sighing gustily in irritation, she dipped her fingers in the puddle of oil and rubbed it on her shoulders and upper arms, then wiggled around until she could rub it on her hips. There was no sense in rubbing it everywhere, she figured. The widest parts of her body were the only areas likely to give her any trouble and she was liable to pass out from the fumes if she put very much on her.

It was a logical conclusion, and would have been tolerable if it had worked. Unfortunately, there were two factors she failed to consider--one; she had already spilled the oil and had to crawl through it, and two; crawling through the narrow vent was enough to smear the oils she *had* put on herself from one end to the other.

She began moving quickly once she'd smeared the oils, not because of any sense of anxiety over passing time, though she did feel that, but because she became desperate to outrun the cloying, choking, flowery scent.

Chapter Six

Darion Jatara surreptitiously studied the men gathered around his table. The tension in the room was palpable, and yet there was also a sense of wary hopefulness underlying it. They had been pleased and relieved in the negotiations thus far and the less formal setting of dining together was bound to ease the tension even more.

Despite his own tension regarding what he had riding on this state dinner, satisfaction filled him at that thought.

It was a good sign that they had even agreed to meet to discuss the possibility of peace between them when they had been heading toward open war. He had not expected that they would be falling over themselves to attain it and some distrust was inevitable, as well, so he was not displeased at all with the progress thus far.

They had spent the morning arguing over many points of contention and it had taken a great deal of patience on his part--on everyone's part--to work through, but they had made great progress.

He had timed things carefully. Once the negotiations began to flow his way, and he saw the possibility existed of coming to an understanding, he would make the announcement he believed would clinch the matter, at least in so far as establishing a strong point of trust.

When the servants had finished making the rounds filling glasses and departed, he rose from his seat and lifted his glass. "Gentlemen of Earth, I am pleased to announce that, in the spirit of true peace and unity, I have decided to take an Earth woman as my concubine. And as this union unites our two peoples, the fruit of our union will seal it, for my heir will be a representative of both of our people and cultures."

Stunned silence followed that announcement, but Darion could see as it slowly sank in upon them that they would have representation in the House of Jatara in the form of Darion's concubine, that their thrust had begun to shift heavily in favor of peace. Wariness followed, but he had anticipated that. Peace could be negotiated, but lasting peace would only come in time, when they learned to trust, when they learned to live together.

After a moment, the president of the Earth confederation lifted his glass. "Your grace, I will drink to your union!"

"Hear! Hear!" men around the room seconded their leader's toast, lifting their glasses.

When the toasts had been drunk, everyone settled once more. "When are we to meet this young woman?" the president asked.

Darion smiled with an effort. He had not considered that they would be so distrustful that they would want to see her at once. If he had, he would have considered that he should prepare Chyna for such an eventuality. Instead, like a love sick fool desperate to please the woman of his heart, he had not thought at all beyond the joy he would bring to her face when he surprised her with a *fait accompli*--in their language--the deed already done.

"She will not dine with us, but you are right. She will want to be here when we sign the peace treaty. If you will excuse me a moment?"

Striding from the room, he relayed his wishes to one of the guards outside that Chyna was to be prepared and dressed in a suitable manner as his concubine and then brought down to witness the signing of the peace treaty.

Disappointed as he was that he would not be there to see her joy when she learned what he had done out of his love for her, he could still look forward to the time when they were alone together once more and she could express her feelings for him.

He knew she cared for him, even though she had no wish to. He also knew that the signing of peace would remove the distrust and wariness that prevented her from yielding to him totally.

Returning to his place at the table, he set himself to charm the Earth representatives as the servants served them the elaborate meal he had ordered for their pleasure, tamping his impatience to see Chyna with an effort.

* * * *

It seemed to take hours only to reach the next vent. Chyna hung over it, pressing her nose to the louvers and sucking in as much clean, untainted air as she could before she even bothered to look at the room. The scent of flowers was really overpowering.

Seeing that the room was occupied, she moved on after only a few moments, slithering through the shaft as quietly as she could, which was a feat in itself. She was coated from end to end with the oils by now and although it helped her slip easily through the metal duct work, it also made forward momentum extremely difficult since she could hardly get any traction.

Hours seemed to pass, though she knew it couldn't possibly have taken as long as it seemed, but finally she reached a shaft going down that was somewhat larger than the one she had been crawling through forever. She stared down the shaft, trying to focus so that she could pierce the gloom and get some idea of where it led. Obviously, it was connected to the vents for the first floor of the palace but beyond that she could tell very little. It ended in a louvered vent which let in a little light, enough that she could see that the shaft branched off in both directions from that point.

She considered the situation. The idea of using the shaft to go down unnerved her, but the alternative was almost worse. If she didn't use it, then she would still be facing a long drop and then she would have to find a way out of whatever room she landed in and downstairs. At least this way she would end up in a first floor room, which would increase her chances of escape dramatically.

Her heart was still in her throat when she arrived at the conclusion that this was the best she could hope for. After considering the best way to go down--head first was *not* an option!--she carefully crawled across the opening until she could drag her feet out of the other side.

Bracing her feet on opposite sides of the shaft, she lowered herself slowly until she was hanging onto the edge of the top with just her fingertips. Her palms were clammy with nerves and she had nothing to wipe them on. When she felt confident she had her feet braced firmly, she lifted one hand and blew on it until it felt drier and caught the opposite lip of the shaft, lifting the other hand. Unfortunately, her right hand had far more oil on it than anything else since it was the one she'd used to spread the oils.

Taking a bracing breath, she let go of the edges and attempted to lower herself. It was a good plan--theoretically speaking and without considering the oil. In actuality, the very instant she released her grip on the lip of the downward shaft, she began to slide. Instantly, her heart commenced to hammering in her ears like a fifty pound sledge hammer, which should have completely deafened her. The fact that she could hear the high pitched squeal of her oiled fingers and toes as she slid down the shaft above the pounding in her ears wasn't comforting. But she had little time to consider it. She was far more focused on the fact that she was gaining momentum in spite of everything she could do.

"Oh my fucking god!" she muttered. "Please, please let the vent cover hold when I get to it!"

Obviously, HE was currently occupied with getting someone else out of a real jam, because her desperate plea went unanswered. The very moment her toes touched down on the outer edges of the vent, her full body weight jack hammered into it. The vent cover popped free and Chyna let out a yelp of surprise and fear as she left the vent shaft like a missile shot from a mortar launcher.

The drop was shorter than she'd expected. She slammed into something hard, her momentum telescoped her into a ball and she sprawled out flat of her back, too stunned to register anything for several moments, including the fact that she'd touched down. The first order of business was instinctive and she found herself testing her fingers and toes by wiggling them to make sure she could still move them. A rapid mental inventory followed where she reviewed pain centers to determine how much pain she was already feeling and how much she was about to feel. She realized she had foreign matter coating her liberally. It felt warm, but it didn't feel like blood.

She opened her eyes finally to see where she was, recalling the distinctive tinkle of breaking china, and found herself looking up at a swaying chandelier. Between her and the chandelier were what looked like about fifty faces--all men.

Groaning, she finally pushed herself up right.

Darion was standing at the foot of the table she'd landed on, staring at her cootsie, which she had displayed for his edification when she'd landed spread eagle on his dining table--in the middle of dessert. The whole room reeked of flowers and cinnamon.

Slowly, Darion's expression changed from stunned disbelief into red faced fury.

It took an effort to smile in the face of death, but Chyna felt like it was worth the attempt.

Chapter Seven

With the best will in the world, Darion found his mind wandering while he engaged in polite conversation throughout the tediously long dinner. As many times as he caught himself and directed his mind back to the business at hand, his mind continued to wander back to Chyna and her reception to his news.

He had treated her badly since her attempt to escape. He knew he'd gone too far in his determination to punish her for breaking his trust. He had been so angry with her for trying to escape, and even more furious because of the sheer terror he'd felt when he realized how closely she had come to killing herself, that he had not been able to think or behave rationally.

And yet, neither had he been able to resist touching her.

The lesson had been a hard one for him, too. If she but knew it, he had found it far more tortuous to caress her and then deprive himself of finding release in her body than she was likely to have.

And worse, she had changed toward him. She had not wanted to feel desire for him at all, but he had broken through that resistance, given her his desire and been rewarded with her own. And he had been rewarded, as well, with the knowledge that she resisted less as time went on, that she welcomed him more openly.

That had changed when he had teased her unmercifully and then refused to give her succor for the desire he'd built in her. She'd begun to resist again as she had in the beginning, ceased to welcome him.

This would make amends for his stupid mistake. He knew it, for nothing was more dear to her heart than the cause she fought for. When she saw that he cared so much for her that he was willing to negotiate peace, she would understand how much he cared. Perhaps, she would begin to care for him, as well.

He might be flattering himself that she would, but he knew at the very least that she would cease to see him as her enemy. In time, he would know her affection as well as her passion and he would contain his impatience until she had come to love him as much as he loved her.

A guard entered the room, distracting him from his thoughts. Darion frowned, for despite the man's efforts to appear stone faced, he could see anxiety in the guard's eyes.

Summoning the man with a gesture, he waited, feeling his gut clench as the man saluted him and then leaned low to speak quietly.

"She is gone."

Cold washed over Darion. Disbelief. Fear. Rage. "Find her," Darion ordered through clenched teeth.

Saluting, the guard made an about face and marched from the room briskly.

Darion glanced at the questioning faces of the ambassadors for peace. Before he could formulate a believable lie to explain the guard a whiff of flowers wafted across his nostrils, teasing him. He frowned, wondering at the sudden presence of such a scent, turning his head and sniffing as he tried to identify the source. Just as it clicked in his mind that the smell reminded him strongly of the oils used in the harem--and Chyna in particular--he heard a strange squealing or squeaking sound.

Tensing all over, he glanced quickly around the room, trying to identify the sound and the direction it was coming from.

It seemed to be coming from everywhere at once, for no matter which direction he turned, he heard it--and it sounded as if it was coming closer--rapidly.

"Chyna, I make no doubt," he muttered under his breath. The words were no sooner out of his mouth when something crashed overhead, jerking his attention ceiling-ward. His mouth dropped open in stunned surprise as something pink and blurry shot from the ceiling vent and slammed into the center of the table.

The ambassadors leapt to their feet as the impact sent food and wine flying in every direction.

In horror, Darion stared at Chyna's naked, spread eagle form, certain she had succeeded in killing herself this time.

He felt almost ill with relief when he saw she still breathed. When she groaned and sat up, he didn't know which desire was uppermost in his mind--to grab her and kiss her in relief--or to grab her and choke the life out of her.

The silence in the room was deafening. Finally, Darion's gaze flickered to the group of stunned men around the table. "Gentlemen," he said with as much aplomb as he could muster. "Allow me to present to you the mother of my heir, my blushing concubine, Chyna Lin."

Chyna closed her legs, drawing them up close to her chest as heated color washed over her. Dignity was impossible, of course, under the circumstances, but she gave it her best shot, nodding regally to the men she could see before she began struggling toward the edge of the table.

Darion helped her. Reaching forward and grabbing her by the ankles, he dragged her off, clearing the plates and glasses at that end of the table. Without a word, he shrugged out of his jacket and flung it around her shoulders and then scooped her into his arms possessively.

"If you could excuse us for a few moments, gentlemen? I'll leave you to look over the treaty agreement and escort my bride upstairs since she appears to have suffered a little mishap with her toilet.

"We really must do something about that vent before someone is seriously injured, my love," he said as he strode briskly from the room with her.

His face was like stone as he headed for the grand staircase and rushed up it. Chyna, who'd been struggling silently to free herself up until that moment, gasped and threw her arms around his neck.

Setting her on her feet when they reached the upper landing, he grasped her arm and towed her down the hallway so rapidly that she had to run to keep up.

"What the hell was that?" he growled the moment he'd slammed the door to the suite behind him.

Chyna blinked. "What was that?" she demanded, pointing in the general direction of the state dining hall.

His eyes narrowed. "I was negotiating peace," he said through gritted teeth. "Not that I expect it matters now given your latest escape fiasco!"

Chyna reddened. "Why?"

He seemed taken aback by the question. "Because I thought it was time we made peace," he growled.

She saw his anger had deserted him. A myriad of emotions chased each other across his face that she had trouble deciphering. One, she did not. Hurt. And suddenly she knew. He had done it for her. He was hurt and angry because of her. "Was that the only reason?" she asked more softly, taking a step toward him. "Because you thought it was time?"

She thought at first that he wouldn't answer her at all. Finally, he scrubbed his hands over his face wearily. "Because--yes, because it was time, because I had to. Earth girls aren't easy," he said slowly, "but I happen to love the one I have."

"Oh, Darion!" she cried, hugging him fiercely. She wrapped a hand around his neck, bringing him down for a kiss.

He shuddered and wrapped his arms around her, lifting her off the floor and crushing her against his hard body as he kissed her back, ravenously, tension releasing into unfiltered emotion. She tasted the joy in his kiss, his hunger--equal to her own.

He carried her to his private bath, barely breaking the kiss long enough to turn on the shower. She helped him strip his clothing off, kissing and nibbling his velvet skin.

He groaned, pushing her into the shower.

Hot water coursed over them, sloughing away the oils and food from her body, streaming down their flesh.

He soaped a cloth, rubbing it up and down her body, cleaning her and stoking a fire in her loins. She couldn't hold back-- touched him, his chest, his belly, his rock hard cock. He groaned, dropping the cloth with a splash, bending to cup her buttocks and lift her against him. She spread her legs, wrapping them around his hips as he brought her hard onto his cock.

He crushed her against the shower wall, driving into her with rapid, short strokes. Chyna clenched around him, moaning his name, digging her nails into his shoulders, her heels into his ass.

He pumped her, bringing her to bone melting orgasm and his own shuddering release.

He kissed her and they washed the soap away. They couldn't seem to get enough. She wanted to touch him more, like it was the first time. It seemed that way. The distrust between them had gone, leaving them to start anew, and she reveled in it.

She grinned and snapped a towel on his ass. He jumped and chased her out of the room back into the bedroom. She didn't care who saw them running around like naked idiots.

He caught her at the bed and tumbled her onto it, kissing her with as much hunger and need as before, plundering her mouth thoroughly until he'd robbed her of breath. She gasped as he broke away from her mouth and trailed hot, nibbling kisses down her throat and over her collarbone. He tasted her breasts long and hard, making her breasts swell and her sex dampen in readiness.

"Don't start that torture again," she growled, threading a hand in his hair to pull him toward her lips.

He covered her body, settling between her legs, looking down at her with eyes slumberous with desire. "I wish I could take back all the wrongs I've done to you," he said quietly.

She cupped his cheek, feeling tears prick her eyes. Dammit. Her hormones were completely screwed and it was all his fault. "I think we're even," she said, blinking rapidly and smiling. "Besides, I can't very well go on punishing the father of my child."

He looked down at her, stunned into silence for long moments. "Truly?"

"I missed my last two periods. I'm pretty damn sure. You're way too potent for this Earth girl."

He chuckled and covered her face with kisses then made slow, sweet love to her until they lay tangled in each others arms, replete, exhausted, utterly drenched in tooth achy, sweet love.

Hell, if she wasn't so crazy about him, she'd have to beat herself for being such a sentimentalist. "Mmmm. You're too damned good." She kissed his chest and rubbed her fingers through his hair. She jerked upright with sudden remembrance. "Oh! What about the peace treaty? Omigod! They'll know what we've been doing!" She flushed with embarrassment just thinking about going back downstairs to see them.

"It will keep until you and I are dressed."

She looked at him, stunned. "I'm finally going to have something to wear?"

He grinned. "Just this once."

FULLY FUNCTIONAL

By

Ashley Ladd

Chapter One

Amused by her wacky brother and his cohort's latest crazy experiment, Shannon Donovan concealed the smirk on her face with her hand. All manner of robots scuttled across the floor in an aimless, but fascinating frenzy.

Gregg Baxter peered at her over his horn rimmed spectacles, his unruly dirty-blond hair tumbling over his smoky aqua eyes adorably.

As always when their gazes locked, her stomach jolted with a familiar spurt of intoxicating electricity. Her brother's friend was much too cute to be legal. She could eat him right up and too often dreamed of doing just that. Her sanity was at stake. But then again, she'd have lost her sanity long ago imprisoned in her *safe* house alone, if not for their company.

Scotty cracked a mischievous grin that perfectly matched his devilishly flame red hair and tossed her his infamous I-dare-you-to wink. "Throw your dinner on the floor."

"Huh?" Perfectly wonderful daydreams scattering to dust, her nerve endings tingling, she sat up straight at attention. Just why should she toss her perfectly scrumptious gourmet dinner all over the filthy basement floor? She'd slaved in the kitchen. They'd finally done it. Lost what little gray matter was left of their minds. She clutched her meal to her, protecting it against the crazies.

"And throw your drink down, too. We have something to show you." Scotty lifted his russet brows when she didn't comply. "Chill, sis. It's just food, not the Mona Lisa."

"Hey! I *slaved* over this. Just because it's *food* doesn't mean it isn't a masterpiece." What a sacrilege! Reviling her life's pursuit.

They knew she lived to cook, to produce new recipes for her books. But spoken aloud, it didn't sound like such a brilliant Nobel prize-winning feat.

Unrepentant, Scotty treated her to his wide, impish grin. "You can dish up more later."

They could bet on her *dishing up* more later. They'd earned a healthy dose of payback, and not just for this particular favor.

"Okay. You asked for it, brat." Jutting her chin out forcefully, batting her lashes, she flipped her meal in the air and witnessed her $5.49 a-pound-premium-boneless-chicken, wine sauce, and garnish smear onto the floor. Delightfully woodsy perfume of the rosemary chicken was released into the air and wafted around her, teasing her.

What a supreme sacrifice! Her time and talent meant little to these two. Just wait until the next time they begged her to special-order cook for them. They could think again.

Glaring at the insane men, ignoring the rich aromas as best she could despite her growling tummy, she decided to glean as much enjoyment out of the situation as possible, so she poured her wine on top of the mess with a flourish. "There! I'm not cleaning it up." She crossed her arms over her chest and shook her head emphatically. It could dry on the floor for all she cared.

Gregg winked at her, turning her knees to jelly, making her glad she was safely seated on the stool. "The point is, you don't need to clean up a thing, darlin'. Watch this." He snapped his fingers high over his head. "Myrtle, my dear. Please join us."

My dear? Jealousy strafed Shannon as she craned her neck to get a look at the unknown competition. Who was this 'Myrtle' dame? For as long as she could remember, she'd watched Gregg parade one lovely woman after another in front of her, breaking her heart a little more each time. What kind of woman had a name like Myrtle in this century? 'Myrtles' belonged to her great-great-great grandmother's generation.

The basement door opened and a very beautiful, svelte un-Myrtle-like woman sashayed down the stairs. "You called, Sir?" she asked in a sultry, smoky voice that grated on Shannon's last nerve.

Sir? This was *Myrtle?* Shannon recoiled, sucking in a sharp breath and digging her fingernails into the tender flesh of her palm. Thoroughly jealous, she longed to tear the woman's limbs off when the flirt winked audaciously at her man with those ultra lush, obviously fake, lashes.

"Please clean up the mess Shannon made." Gregg turned and pierced her with his twinkling gaze and wiggled his brows at her. "You gotta watch this. She's awesome."

Awesome? Why couldn't Gregg think *she* was awesome? If he didn't by now, it was surely a lost cause and she should award him to the Myrtles of the world with her blessing.

Myrtle cast her a dirty look.

Shannon did a double take. The gatecrasher had a lot of nerve giving her nasty looks in her house. Squinting at Gregg, she said, "You coerced me to make the mess. Don't lay the blame at my feet." Embarrassed, she punched the mad scientist in the meaty part of his arm, making him sway dangerously on his stool.

Turning to Myrtle, she said, "I swear they made me do it. It was totally their harebrained idea."

Crossing her arms over her chest, she favored her brother with a haughty look. "When did you hire a maid?" Not that the stunning Myrtle resembled any maid she'd ever seen. She looked more like one of Charlie's angels--too sexy to be let loose on an unsuspecting male populace.

"We didn't hire her. We constructed her."

Shannon bit back a gasp. "Constructed? Myrtle's a robot? She's nothing like the other robots rolling about the room." Myrtle didn't merely walk, she glided. She was anatomically correct, with a very impressive chest and a tight, round, perfect butt. Just which one of the Einstein's was responsible for the sinfully sexy design? It had better not be Gregg….

Myrtle interrupted her thoughts, nodding. "Men are little boys at heart. That's why they need a maid. Pardon moi while I tidy the room, mamselle."

Her jealousy evaporating instantly, Shannon applauded when Myrtle cleaned up the mess lightning fast. Myrtle might not be so terribly bad after all. She might even come in handy around the kitchen. Cleaning up spills and explosions wasn't her forte. Leaning toward Gregg, she whispered, "She's cute. Did you two really invent her? So what are Jekyll and Hyde's plans for her?"

Scotty laid his head on her shoulder and smiled up at her. "You see, sis, she's going to clean while the mad doctor and I clean up."

"Clean up?" Alarm bells whirred in Shannon's head. What crazy scheme were these two hatching?

A robotic dog scampered across the room, barking furiously at Myrtle, his stubby tail wagging profusely.

Myrtle bent down and patted his tin head. "Someone's at the door. Good boy. Heel."

Yikes! What would the neighbors think? Of course, they should be accustomed to Scotty's eccentricities by now, but how would they take a real tin Rin Tin Tin? They'd formed a lynch mob the last time the house had caught fire.

Gregg beamed with pride upon his fabricated puppy. "We'll rake in millions."

Scotty interrupted, his grin splitting his face ear to ear. "Billions, bro."

"Billions." His eyes glowing, Gregg caressed the word. "With so many two-income families and single moms, no one has time or energy to keep house anymore. But most importantly, robotic assistants and smart houses will allow the disabled and seniors to live independently as long as possible. Ergo, everyone will want a smart house with a Myrtle. We'll emancipate people from mundane chores such as cooking and cleaning. We'll revolutionize life as we know it."

Ack! Emancipate people from *cooking*? She was all for progress but letting soulless machines create food was just wrong. Downright sinful, in fact. The insensitive brutes seemed bent on destroying her career. But to them, food was just sustenance, not art. Art to them was comprised of microchips and code.

"Like the Jetsons?" The ancient cartoon reruns flashed through Shannon's mind. Rosie the Robot had been pretty cool. She could get used to the idea of having her own Rosie ... uh, Myrtle ... to clean behind her and keep up with the hated laundry. But never to cook.

"Even better."

Cross-eyed, she stared at the electronic dog. "Why a robotic Fido?" What good would he do?

Gregg scooped the animal into his arms and petted it absently. "He's really a high powered security system. He can detect intruders from the perimeter of the yard and guard against all forms of violence."

"He's also perfect for people who are allergic to real dogs. And he doesn't tinkle on the floor or chew up shoes."

Scotty wrote the dog's moniker on the chalk board, then dusted his hands down his jeans leaving white frothy fingerprints. Not that he cared for his appearance any more than he cared for the fuel he put in his mouth. "Robotic Operation Video Electro-magnetic Retriever or 'Rover' for short."

"And does *Myrtle* stand for something as well?"

"Naaa. I just liked the name."

Yeah, right. If he ever married, she was warning his wife not to let him name their kids. Still, maybe they would make a fortune. She'd be a millionaire's sister--hopefully a millionaire's wife.

Daydreams aside, where would that leave her in reality? Like Gregg would ever look at her in any way other than as a little sister.... She'd stashed some of her royalties aside for a rainy day. Or in this case, a sunny one. "Need any silent investors?"

"Uh, maybe....," Scotty and Gregg exchanged secretive glances.

Oh oh. That look was imprinted into her soul. It was the same one that always landed her in a heap of trouble from the time she'd been six and Gregg's family had moved in down the street. That was her cue to skeedaddle, before her life went up in smoke. Unfortunately, with her condition, she couldn't escape very far at this time of the day. But she could barricade herself into her room until they tired of the chase and found another victim. Sliding off the stool, she waved behind her. "Sorry boys. Count me out."

Scotty sprinted to the door and barred it. Crossing his heart flamboyantly, he swore, "We're really sorry your hair caught on fire last year. Didn't we buy you *two* new wigs?"

"And we paid your hospital bill, including the anesthesiologist's fee." Gregg's voice stroked her as surely as if his lips nuzzled the nape of her neck, trying to melt her resolve.

No no no! She stomped her foot on the linoleum-covered basement floor. Gregg Baxter was not going to twist her around his sexy little pinky again. She was wise to his blond boyish charms. He was trouble enough on his own but pure dynamite when combined with her conniving brother. "Let me out. I am not stupid enough to get involved with you two turkeys again."

"Even if we pay you?" Scotty flashed a wad of newly minted greenbacks at her, and wafted them under her nose. "You can keep your royalties for fun money. Install that new state-of-the-art kitchen you've been drooling over for months."

Wow!

Her mouth watered at all the luscious lettuce. What she wouldn't give to install that new range she'd had her heart set on. Curiosity ate at her and she couldn't keep her mouth shut. "Where'd you get that kind of money?"

"From the scientific grant that's funding our project," Scotty said proudly, puffing out his chest.

So someone saw merit in one of their harebrained experiments? She had to admit that having a maid would be heavenly but she couldn't seriously be considering one of their hackneyed schemes, could she? Something always backfired. That would make her as loony as they were. But that money smelled awfully wonderful.... Relying on royalty checks to pay the mortgage was pretty harrowing. Extra income never hurt and extra sounded downright heavenly.

"For doing what?" Still, money or not, she had integrity. It had better not be posing on TV as a slob who spilled garbage all over the floor. Or had the sneaks already videotaped their commercial?

They wouldn't dare....

Of course they would!

She'd been set up! Seething, rounding on the dynamic duo, she jabbed her finger into her brother's scrawny chest. "If you dare air that tape, I swear I'll...."

"What tape? And you'll what?" Amusement glinted in Scotty's amber eyes.

The fire in her died. "You're sure you didn't videotape me?"

"I swear."

Yeah, like she could believe that despite his guileless, tawny eyes. As long as the men barred her exit she might as well find out the reason. "So what do you have in mind?" This time.... "My insurance carrier will drop me if there's another incident."

"No fire. It's perfectly safe...."

"Right … just like the time the programmable car plowed into my living room?"

"I swear the surveyors screwed up the map. It wasn't...."

"Your fault?" Was it ever? Would Scotty ever grow up? But Gregg should know better. She pierced Gregg with an unwavering gaze. "Is it safe?"

"Would I put my little Shannon in danger?"

Little? What a fighting word. At twenty-seven and a C-cup, she was hardly little. Was he blind?

She swallowed a huge sigh. Actually he was blind to her. She was forever destined to remain Scotty's little sister to him.

Puffing out her chest, daring him not to notice how *little* she was, she asked, "So what is it? Mind you, I've not agreed to do anything except *listen*. And I should probably have my head examined for doing even that much."

"Absolutely nothing." Gregg's dawning smile was too much like the Cheshire cat's for her comfort.

Were her ears working? "Excuse me?"

"You'll be treated like a queen and get waited on hand and foot. All you have to do is let Myrtle and her crew fulfill your every whim for the next month, record how well they take care of you, and give a testimonial. That's it."

"That's it?" It sounded much too good to be true. She wondered how many enemy soldiers fit inside this Trojan Horse's belly? "And otherwise I'll live a normal life? My routine won't be interrupted? I'm on a tight deadline." This sounded too good to be true. She'd not only get a free maid and a watch dog, but she'd get paid for it.

Gregg tossed her a sultry, knee-melting grin. "Except for me pestering you a couple times a day. Checking up on things."

Count me in! But she didn't want to appear too eager that Gregg was going to hang around. Kicking the moony look from her gaze lest he see how badly she craved him, she tried to quell her excitement. "I…."

"Ta da! The pièce de résistance." Scotty opened the door to the most gorgeous man she'd ever seen and motioned to him. "Your butler, Rafael. And he's anatomically correct and functional."

Functional? She gulped. Scotty didn't expect her to, uh, you know, *play doctor* with the android, did he? Angry heat suffused her and she lifted the heavy fall of hair off her neck so the overhead fan would cool her down.

When she glanced at Gregg through her veiled lashes, he was watching her closely. That really skyrocketed her temperature. Just what naughty things was the mad scientist thinking? If only they were about him and her, not the robot and her, she'd kick Scotty out and lock the door.

"So what d'ya think?"

"Of the butler?" To her chagrin, her voice came out hoarse and whispery. "He's … uh … gorgeous … nice. Very *nice*."

"So, will you help us or not?" her miserable brother chuckled. He shuffled the money under her nose again so that the fresh ink nearly inebriated her.

"We'll be working very closely together," Gregg murmured beside her ear huskily.

She gulped and tried to sound nonchalant even though her heart was hammering against her ribs so hard they were about to shatter. Rubbing her leg with the opposite foot, she pretended that the made-up itch bothered her more than his blatant come-on did. "I guess so. When did you want to start?"

"Now works for us."

"*Now*?" But the house wasn't in shape for company! Androids or not, she didn't want Myrtle or Rafael to see her disaster area, even if they were composed of diodes and chips.

Scotty let loose a big belly laugh earning him more black marks. "Sis, we know you're a slob. That's why you're so perfect for this experiment. That and because you need a special house which is another perk."

He was so very, extremely dead. Especially for reminding her about her medical condition--that she was allergic to the sun and thus spent her daytimes indoors, primarily in the dungeon--er, basement--like a vampire. Steam rising in her, she gritted her teeth so hard she could taste the mortar. There'd be time for payback later.

"Good! We've taken the liberty of moving some of your clothes and personal items into your new home."

Gulp! How personal? Her teddies? Negligees? Sex toys?

When Gregg tossed her a wicked smile she cringed. They'd found *it*! Her vibrator....

"That's quite a top of the line dildo you have, sis. But Rafael is fully functional, if you know what I mean, so you won't be needing it." The moron winked broadly and she wanted to scour the wicked grin off his face.

Her stomach dropped to her knees. How dare he say such frightfully naughty things in front of Gregg! His funeral grew ever closer. She hand signaled a death threat to Scotty as they'd done as kids.

"I'm so scared," he signed back, his scarecrow frame shaking in silent laughter.

Gregg put a comforting, electrifying arm around her shoulders. "I bet you're eager to see your new digs and meet the rest of your staff." He guided her away from the source of her irritation.

Eagerness wasn't precisely the emotion she was feeling. His touch evoked a fever which cascaded all the way down to the juncture of her legs. Tingles shivered down her spine and she was a quivering mass of lust. She longed to freeze the moment and keep this flesh to flesh contact forever even if it remained platonic. Despite her quaking flesh, she was increasingly curious about the smart house and androids.

As surreptitiously as possible, she checked her watch to ensure the sun had fully set so that it was safe to go outside. Deathly allergic to the sun, those UV rays brutalized her and only a few moments exposure made her break out in a excruciating rash. "It'll be interesting to see your work in action." She meant it. Hopefully all those years of cannibalizing TVs and computers were finally paying off. Her brother had to have learned something constructive in the midst of his destructive frenzies.

"So where is this dream house?" They must have had a helluva sponsoring grant to fund not only androids but a house.

Gregg led her down the palm canopied, moon-bathed lane to his impressively remodeled house and paused in front. "What do you think?"

"Ai yi yi...." Awesome didn't begin to describe the gorgeous facade. They'd not only remodeled the house, but added a second story and expanded it, stealing a good chunk of the back yard. Moonbeams danced across tinted windows and the jasmine-fragranced garden that skirted the house.

When she looked askance at him, he motioned to it proudly. "Your dream home for the next few weeks."

Perspiration broke out on her palms and trickled down the back of her shirt. She'd be sleeping in Gregg's room? In his bed? Her panties became suddenly very wet and she shifted her weight from foot to foot. A few weeks would never be long enough if it was as wonderful as they claimed--as it looked. "Where will you stay?"

"In your house with Scotty."

She blinked. They were switching beds? The only available bed in her house would be hers so he'd be sleeping in her bed. Quivers anew attacked her. Now if they could only get together in the same bed.

This whole thing was messed up. She'd dreamed about sleeping in Gregg's bed, moving into his house, but never like this. He was supposed to be in his house, in his bed ... with her.

"I can't put you out of your own house." It would be too weird. She'd have constant need of her vibrator with all the sensations roiling around inside her.

"You're not. It's my doing. I just want you to kick back and enjoy your stay. Think of this as a vacation. You'll be in the history books for being the first person to test the smart house."

The first ... as in pioneer. Historically, pioneers had faced a lot of hazards on new frontiers. The only frontier she ached to face was on the culinary front.

Danger Will Robinson. Danger! Danger! Grimacing, she pushed the silly thoughts away, but they kept bouncing back, growing in intensity.

"This is *safe,* isn't it? I mean, they won't go on a homicidal rampage? I just rented 'I Robot'." If the butler even remotely beqan to act like Arnold in 'The Terminator', she was so outta here. Chills made her shiver.

Gregg gave her shoulders a squeeze. "None whatsoever. It's fail safe and we'll be monitoring everything at all times."

Whoa! Spooky!

"Everything? As in video cameras?"

"Only in the main rooms." To her astonishment, Gregg blushed to the roots of his hair.

Damn! So he didn't long to see her naked?

* * * *

Gregg lied. It was a *smart* house after all. It recorded everything including blood sugar and respiratory levels. He had a video cam hardwired in all the bedrooms, not that Scotty knew or would get access. That was his secret. He couldn't wait to see Shannon's hot bod in his bed, rolling around on the sheets, spicing them up with her sexy scent.

No way did he want her to know how hot he was for her. At least not till he worked up his courage to ask her out. Working closely with her on this project should bring them closer together. Hopefully *much* closer together.

"Barry's waiting. Shall we look around?"

"Barry?" She quirked a finely arched brow at him. God she was fine, with long legs that never ended, and lush auburn hair that he wanted to wrap around him. And what kissable, hypnotic lips. Lips which now unfortunately turned down in a scowl.

"The house. That's his name."

"Like in 'Dave the computer'?" She shuddered and hugged herself. "Dave freaked me out for years."

He felt like a cad, but he hadn't known. "I promise that Barry's nothing like Dave."

Her step grew hesitant and she paused on the threshold and put her fine-boned hand on his wrist, elevating his blood pressure several notches. "Truly? Promise?"

He crossed his heart. "On my life." *Great!* Now he was being melodramatic. She'd see right through him if she didn't already.

A sunny smile lit her face and stole his breath. Lord but she was gorgeous, especially dappled with moonlight.

The door opened wide and the lifelike maid and butler who had preceded them, stood on the threshold. "Welcome, Sir, Mistress

Shannon. Please join us. Would you like some freshly brewed coffee?" Rafael asked.

Gregg smiled at his creations, glowing with pride. "First I want to take Shannon on a tour of the house, then we'll have a cup of espresso."

"Very good, Sir." Rafael bowed and closed the door behind them as they moved deeper into the bowels of the newly redecorated house.

Gregg turned toward the butler and maid. "As I explained earlier, Myrtle and Rafael will see to your every whim and obey your every command. They will see you are well cared for."

"Indeed, Sir."

"Gregg and Shannon."

"Sir Gregg." Already a glitch, albeit a minor one. He'd have to fine-tune their language abilities. He bit back a sigh.

"Welcome to your new home, Miss Shannon." Myrtle stuck out her hand to shake Shannon's.

Shannon stared at their clasped hands in amazement. "Your flesh feels so real. So soft."

"So does mine, carissima," Rafael said with a sexy wink. "And I'm fully anatomically correct and functional."

Jealousy tore through Gregg. A charming, randy bot? What kind of monster had he created?

Perversely, his cock flexed at the thought of watching Shannon in bed with the butler. Since Rafael was just a machine, there would truly be nothing to be jealous of. So why did he want to punch that smirking robotic face right in its microchips? Maybe he should decommission it or take it to Shannon's house and test this one himself? The house could function without Rafael or Myrtle, but that would make for very lonely days. Being confined indoors during daylight hours as she was, she could get very lonely.

When Rafael bent over Shannon's hand, an adorable blush spread up her neck and into her face. Giggling, she glanced at him. "So far your experiment gets an A+."

"Oh, I can show you *much* more than this. I can make your every fantasy come true."

Shannon trembled beside Gregg and sucked in her breath. Then she lowered her lashes demurely, the lush crescents fanning her cheeks. "I--uh--don't know what to say."

Gregg did! *So long, sucker!* The mechanical dude had just earned himself a one-way ticket out of Shannon's life into dismantlement. No way was Millennium Man here going to steal his girl. He could just drink a quart of antifreeze or go hang out in the fridge and chill.

"Perhaps Rafael can join us on the tour," Shannon crooned, taking the android's proffered arm, beaming up at him.

Gregg couldn't take it. Suppressing the growl that rose from his groin, he snatched her arm back and tucked it through the crook of his elbow. "See to it that dinner will be served for two shortly."

He did his best to ignore Shannon's quirked brow and held onto her proprietarily. These bots had to know who was in charge. Something had to be awry with Rafael's software which would necessitate a thorough examination, microchip by microchip.

"A romantic, candlelit dinner, Sir Gregg? Pheasant under glass or steamed lobster?" He turned to Shannon, his too perfect face really getting on Gregg's nerves. "Anything your heart desires. Cook is a master chef."

A dark frown stole over Shannon's face as she turned to him. "But I love to cook. I'm a chef. They don't have to perform that duty for me, do they? It's my life…"

Gregg swallowed a boulder-sized lump in his throat and tried to take his monstrous foot out of his mouth. How callous of him to forget how seriously she took her culinary talents. "Of course not. Although if you could occasionally test them, so we know if their cooking is any good. As an expert, you'd be the best judge." Whew! What a save.

"Since they've already prepared dinner, let's not hurt their feelings."

Shannon's jaw dropped wide. "Hurt their feelings…," she echoed him.

"I meant that we don't want to offend them."

"You're not reassuring me, Baxter." She squeezed his hand with too much exertion. Unfortunately, he shared her reservations about bots getting offended.

Chapter Two

Anything her heart desired? Hmm … Gregg naked in bed, all steamy, sweaty, and hot for her. Starved, she wet her lips with the tip of her tongue.

Down girl! Her panties were going to be soaked and the musky scent would tattle on her.

To cover up her horny slip of the literal tongue, she said quickly, "Well I suppose I can give my feedback."

Rafael smiled, and licked his lips. "Done."

Oops! She'd almost forgotten she was counting her carbs. Since she couldn't get outside, it was hard to exercise and keep her weight in check. "Is it carb free?"

"Anything you want, my dear. And I do mean *anything*."

Shannon could swear she saw Rafael's tongue peek out his lips and that Gregg tensed beside her. Uhm...Gregg couldn't be jealous, could he? Even a little bit? This merited deeper study, and a little experimentation.

Breaking away from Gregg, she stepped closer to the butler and trailed a fingertip along his arm. "How about we have a *private meeting* tonight at nine to discuss your *duties*." Playing the Thespian, she poured every sultry fantasy into her voice and made sure it was loud enough for Gregg to overhear. Maybe a few slow dances under the watchful eyes of Gregg's hidden cameras might kick up his jealousy a few levels. She'd enjoyed his earlier macho display immensely. How much more testosterone was simmering under the surface? She hoped there was a real possessive alpha male in there who would carry her off to his bed.

Loving her idea, she warmed to it. Obviously Rafael set off the scientist's jealous tendencies. Just as obvious was the fact Gregg was taken by surprise at this. Otherwise, he wouldn't have installed Rafael as her personal butler.

A little devil pushing her, she couldn't resist asking, "Would you show me my bed ... room"

Gregg squirmed and massaged his neck, the tiny hairs standing on end. "I'll take you." To Rafael he commanded again, "See to it that dinner is prepared ASAP. It's getting late and I made Shannon miss her dinner."

Indeed it was. The sun had long sunk below the horizon and moonlight beamed through the UV-repelling tinted windows. Faking a yawn, she patted her mouth prettily, intensely aware of Gregg's every movement down to the flicker of his eyelash. "I'm getting so sleepy. I can't wait to get in bed." It was an outright lie as she was a moon worshipper, unless of course, Gregg crawled into bed with her. But she longed to see his reaction.

When he remained silent, she pushed, "Whose bed will I sleep in?"

Gregg's jaw convulsed and his Adam's apple bobbed. Hallelujah! He was hot. Only not hot enough to jump into bed with her--yet. He'd take some skillful reeling in.

This experiment had turned into a real godsend. On her own it might have taken her months - years--to get up the nerve to seduce the hottie. Now he'd provided the motivation she needed.

In a raspy, guttural voice, he finally choked out, "I thought you'd be most comfortable in my sister's old room, so I had fresh linen put on her bed."

Disappointment welled in her. He didn't want her tumbling about in his sheets, scenting them? Leaving her imprint on his pillows? If only she could find the guts to say such flirty things aloud…

But she was the subtle type. She'd turn his own video cameras against him and make him so hot for her he'd cream his jeans. Too bad they weren't installed in the bedrooms…

She tingled all over just thinking about that savory liquid oozing out his hard cock.

Down girl. Her quivering pussy was about to make her moan and thoroughly embarrass herself. She couldn't wait to use her faithful vibrator. Of course, Rafael had blatantly offered his body to her, but her heart and body belonged to Gregg. Even if it didn't, it would just be too creepy to make love to a hunk of machinery even one that looked and felt as human as Rafael. Unless of course he had a soul like Commander Data in Star Trek.

Still, Rafael wasn't her Gregg and he never would be. And unless Gregg and Scotty had suddenly become deities, she seriously doubted they had discovered a way to create souls.

To their credit, they'd made much more lifelike robots than 'I Robot's' version. Housewives would fight to get their own Rafaels. Seniors and the disabled would demand their services. Riots would break out in the streets unless there was sufficient supply to meet the demand. Surely Gregg and Scotty would become billionaires. Especially if they could customize the androids to fulfill every woman's ideal of her dream man. Until they could, Rafael was plenty hot--for most of her sisters.

Gregg led her upstairs to his sister's room and showed her around. "There's a speakerphone here." He pointed to the wall beside the door. And you have a private bath in here, fully stocked with all your, uh, feminine needs."

God but he was luscious when he blushed. Just how bright red could he get? And was it limited to his face? Bouncing on the bed, she tried out the mattress. Too soft. Still, wanting to skyrocket his blood pressure she laid back on the bed and spread her legs wide. Ugh! Lumpy. She liked hard, firm mattresses, like her men. Later, after he left her alone for the night, she'd sneak into his room and try out his bed. All the better to play out her scrumptious fantasies with his musky scent wafting over her.

Wicked, succulent thoughts and desires plagued her. *Oh you naughty, naughty girl.* She had to bite back a silly grin lest he suspect her wily plans. That man would be panting after her before he could devise a new formula.

* * * *

Finally the bittersweet moment arrived when Gregg had to leave. Her heart ached for him to stay, but if he remained, she'd never be able to put her deviously delightful plan into action.

Sidling up to him as she had never done before, she lifted very pouty lips to a hair's breadth from his and accidentally on purpose brushed her tingling breasts against his chest. "Check on me tomorrow? Make sure your creations haven't blown their fuses?"

When he shivered and his silvery gaze smoldered down at her, she awarded herself a point. One for her team! Actually she'd scored a touchdown or two already tonight. Within the month, he'd be hers.

Power oozed through her. She'd never dreamed how easily men could be manipulated. She'd found his on switch just as surely as if he was one of his robots.

She bit back a sour grimace. Perish the thought! Gregg, a robot? She yearned for a hot, sultry wild man in her bed, not some cold bucket of bolts. Give her a Viking warrior, someone a little rough and rowdy. Someone who would be her match.

"Here, let me program my number on your cell phone in case you need me. I'll be at your beck and call."

She could live with that. She dug the phone out of her pocket and handed it over. When their fingertips met, electricity flared through her.

Gregg punched the number in and turned the display to face her. "See? It's programmed under 'Gregg'."

"Cool. I think I can remember that." She was careful not to graze his warm flesh when he handed it back lest she went into sensory overload.

"Sweet dreams, Gregg," she said on a whispery, breathless sigh. God but she'd almost substituted *stud* for his name. He'd have either scooped her into his arms and hauled her to his bed or he'd have run screaming for the hills, never to return.

Not willing to chance the second scenario, she backed off from being too brazen. She also backed up a step as she willed herself to breathe normally. "See you tomorrow." *Stud.*

Gregg nodded, his eyes still smoky. He rubbed his chin, accentuating his sexy five-o-clock-shadow. "Call if you need me."

Oh she needed him all right. Desperately. But she couldn't let him know. Yet. She'd have to use her vibrator to calm the excruciating ache between her thighs tonight.

"I will," she lied. But she wouldn't have to lie for too much longer. She hoped. Fluttering her fingers at him, she smiled seductively. "Ta ta."

"Ciao." Gregg slipped out the door and blended with the long inky shadows of the darkness.

Now, for phase one of her plan. Her palms itched so she rubbed them together feeling particularly devilish.

First, his sister's room wouldn't do at all. She had to be in Gregg's bed. She moved her things into his room, placing the vibrator in a place of special honor on the nightstand by the bed.

She soaked in his essence, from his wall of bowling trophies and wrestling tapes to his toothbrush. She loved his scent and wanted to bathe in it.

Second, she needed scintillating props. To get in a romantic mood, she soaked in Gregg's tub amidst a myriad of lavender scented candles. Lifting one leg high she lathered soap up its length, stroking her inner thighs tenderly as if it was Gregg caressing her. Taking her fantasy a step further, she spread her legs wide and massaged her clit.

Moaning, she writhed under her own ministrations. Starved for more, she dipped a finger inside her folds and stroked in and out until delicious shudders overcame her. Working herself into a frenzy, her butt smacked the porcelain as her groans grew louder.

Ecstasy claimed her and she stroked faster. Ultimate paradise any second now.

The bathroom door flung open, startling her. "Don't worry, Miss Shannon. I'll save you." Myrtle reached inside the shower curtain and yanked her out forcefully by the neck.

Shannon gasped in shock and her eyes rolled back in her head. The next second, her skull hit the hard tile floor and everything went blurry.

"I'm programmed with CPR. I'll save you." Myrtle straddled her forcefully and pumped her chest making her gag.

Who was going to save her from Super Android? With her last vestiges of breath, she commanded on a wheeze. "Summon Gregg."

Then in a panic, she remembered her nude state. "No! Dress me first, then call Gregg."

* * * *

"No!" Gregg leapt to his feet and bolted for the door, a raging erection refusing to be stuffed back into his stiff denims. Shannon had been on the brink of coming when Myrtle decided she needed rescuing.

Just as Myrtle pressed her com earring link to summon him, he barked into his microphone, "Get off Shannon now." They'd be lucky if Shannon had nothing more seriously wrong than a couple of cracked ribs. From the look of things, she most probably had suffered a concussion.

Finally his erection died a miserable death and he was able to zip up his jeans as he sprinted out of the house. "Give me her vital signs. Is she breathing?"

After a brief pause Myrtle responded. "Her respiration was extremely high when I first entered the room, but it's reverted to normal now."

"Good." Still, he was going to check her out for himself. With all the anatomy and physiology programs he'd instilled into Myrtle, she should have deduced Shannon had been in the throes of orgasm, not respiratory distress.

Worried, he ran full steam to his house and slammed through the door, tripping over the mechanical mutt.

Rafael picked him up and dusted him off. "Miss Shannon's going to live. We've installed her in your bed to rest up."

"Why in my bed?" Gregg's step faltered as his blood pressure shot up and his cock twitched. "I set her up in my sister's room."

"She moved her things to your room."

He almost tripped over his feet in his surprise. That created a ton of sticky questions.

"Why?"

"I'm not privy to that information. I suggest you ask her."

Not on your life. A growl rumbled in his throat. The hottest little number he'd ever seen was tucked in his bed, and he couldn't do a thing about it.

"She's truly okay?" Anxious to see Shannon, Gregg took the stairs three at a time.

"Sir Gregg, you shouldn't skip stairs or run up them. I calculate an 86% chance of injury."

"Stuff it." These bots were getting to be a real drag.

"Stuff what, Sir Gregg?" The bot's brows puckered as Rafael gazed up at him.

He'd have to fine tune their personal interactive skills later. "It's just an expression. Relax. Settle down."

Rafael clicked his heels, a real Dorothy complex going on which he also had to take care of, and bowed. "Yes, Sir Gregg."

He stifled a sigh. "Gregg."

"Sir Gregg."

Gregg suppressed a groan and entered his room. His heart twisted in his chest at the sight of Shannon all tumbled and sleepy-eyed on his bed. Long auburn strands of her hair splayed over his pillow, haloing her angelic face. Her breasts threatened to spill out of her gown. A tenderness he didn't know he possessed washed over him as he crossed the room to her. "Hey, kiddo. I heard you had an accident."

Shannon's normally peaches and cream complexion paled and her lush lashes veiled her eyes, making smoky crescents against her high cheek bones. "Just a little mishap." She chewed her bottom lip adorably. "I'm okay now. Just a mite sore."

He wasn't convinced. Perching on the bed beside her, he leaned toward her and grasped her slender wrist. Placing his third finger on her pulse, he assured himself she wasn't going to have a heart attack. Funny, the longer he checked her pulse, the faster it raced. Then to assure himself she wasn't running a fever, he pressed his lips to her forehead. "Your temp feels normal."

Shannon lifted her wide gaze to him. "I-I can explain why I'm in your room."

This should be good. His heart racing, he couldn't wait to hear her confession.

Her breath hot on his neck, he quivered and his erection burgeoned again. *Great!* No, not great. This couldn't be happening. He shifted so that part of the blanket covered his lap. No way did he want her to know he'd installed video cameras in every room of the house or that he'd watched her very intimate, hot display. Nor did he want her to think him a lecher who'd attack innocent women just because they'd crawled into his bed.

She was fine so he had to escape. Now! "Well, you seem to be fine. Just no more jumping around in the bath tub." The devil in him made him taunt her.

* * * *

Oh, God! Mortified, Shannon stared at Gregg's retreating back and then pulled his covers over her head and stifled a scream of frustration as soon as the door closed behind him.

What demon had ever possessed her to masturbate in Gregg's tub or sleep in his bed? Certifiable! She was 110% cracked!

Of course she'd had an inkling of her pathetic condition when she'd agreed to be the guinea pig for this crazy plot.

The revolving door of the new Grand Central Station burst wide and Myrtle carried in a breakfast try with steaming hot soup. "Sit up straighter and eat some chicken soup Claudette made for you."

Blech! The steaming concoction reminded her of witches' brew. "No, thank you. I'm not hungry."

"Nonsense. It'll make you feel better."

"I don't like chicken soup." Myrtle had forced her to make the rude comment by pushing.

Myrtle blinked. "All humans like chicken soup. It's an ancient remedy for all ailments."

Not for interrupted orgasms or assault by three hundred pound androids the last time she'd checked. The only comfort food she craved was a gallon of chocolate. And perhaps an ice pack for her bruised ribs. She pushed the tray away. "No, really."

Myrtle pushed it back, towering over her, "Yes, really. At least eat a bite. I won't leave till you do."

To get rid of the annoying maid, Shannon took a miniscule sip. "You satisfied?" She dabbed her mouth daintily with a paper napkin and washed down the nasty taste with a gulp of water.

"I declare you humans are a self-destructive species. It's a wonder you've survived so long."

Now she was Scarlett O'Hara? And flinging around detested 'you statements'? The chick had to leave now if she valued her microchips. She reigned in her simmering ire with as much restraint as she could muster. "Goodnight, Myrtle."

Myrtle bustled about her, plumping her pillows and straightening her blankets. "I'll be back to check on you in an hour."

"No! Please, I just want to sleep for awhile longer. I'll be fine. Really."

Myrtle cast a stern, motherly glare her way but made no promises. "Sweet dreams. I'll send Rafael up to keep you company."

"No!" But the door had already closed. Dragging her battered body out of bed, she locked the door wishing there was a dead bolt as well.

Much later, she dreamed Gregg slipped into her bed and began massaging her back. "Uhm. Heavenly. A little lower please."

Soft, warm lips nuzzled her neck, sending ripples of delight down her spine. Lust quivered between her thighs and a slight sigh whispered past her lips. "Oh, Gregg."

"I can be whoever you desire, my sweet," a husky voice murmured back startling her fully awake.

Gasping she bolted out of the bed and yanked the covers around her modestly, exposing a very fully functional, fully aroused Rafael who lounged on her bed basking in his naked glory. Jerking her finger at the door, she demanded in righteous rage, her voice shaky, "Get out!"

Rafael arose, very sensually, stealthily, a seductive grin spreading across his surfer boy features. "I frightened you. I didn't realize you are still a virgin. I should have wooed you more tenderly. I can teach you many things if you'll let me."

So Wonder Boy, who must be all of a year old tops, was going to tutor her in the art of sex? She had to bite back a snort. Hardly! What a pompous ass.

Is this the kind of man Scotty and Gregg thought all women dreamed of? Maybe to ogle, perhaps even to toy with, but not for keeps. A guy like this wouldn't give a woman any mirror time and would strut his peacock feathers, obscuring their sparrow-like selves. Uh-huh. She wanted a real man. One who was sweet, and funny, and quirky ... like Gregg.

Like Gregg? Gregg who was playing God? He who was creating his own race of androids?

Maybe Gregg needed serious rethinking.

Gregg…. Unfortunately, she wasn't quite ready to give up her long cherished dreams of him. And she might as well have a little fun as long as she was here. Wasn't that the purpose of having androids? So they could do the mundane and dangerous tasks so she could spend her days--or nights--living it up?

When Rafael advanced on her, she put up a commanding hand for him to stop. She wanted to make Gregg jealous, not replace him. "Stop right there, bucko. A woman wants romance first. A long, *romantic* courting, with lots of slow dances under the moonlight, moonlit swims, cuddling around the fireplace or in the movie theater, candlelit dinners … that sort of thing. Capice?"

Lights literally flickered in Rafael's eyes as if he was consulting the mother ship. Finally, the fog lifted from his eyes and he nodded. "Noted, ma cherie. Would you like to join me for a midnight swim? Sir Gregg didn't have the opportunity to show you the new, indoor pool in your new indoor gymnasium in the basement." He held out a hand to her, still in all his flaccid glory.

Pool? Gymnasium? For her? How sweet?

But she was so tired. Utterly exhausted from the pounding.

Groaning, she blinked. "At three in the A.M.?" With aching ribs? "I'm too sleepy and sore tonight. Why won't anyone just let me sleep? Is that so much to ask?"

But one brain cell remained awake enough to remember her plan to make Gregg jealous. "It's a date for tomorrow." Ribs permitting.

"We'll skinny dip under the stars."

This was one horny machine who couldn't wait to shuck his clothing. Had Gregg made him in his image? Were all men so sex-starved?

What a scintillating thought…. She licked her lips, trembling, visions of a very naked, very sexy Gregg whetting her appetite. Finally she managed to get a grip on her rampaging fantasies and laid down the law. "Don't rush me so, Fabio. Remember … *romance*." She pronounced the final, all-important word succinctly, reverently. Sex was nothing without romance. Not that this mechanical man would get past first base.

Uh, how could a *mechanical* man get in water?" Wait a sec. Won't water rust your diodes or something?"

Rafael cocked a heart-stopping grin at her. "My shell is fully waterproof. Since I don't breathe air as you do, I could remain underwater indefinitely."

Oh…. Ask a stupid question…. She was too zonked to debate further and too discombobulated to take in a science lecture. "Okay, I'm pooped and I get very cranky when I lose beauty sleep, so goodnight, Romeo."

"I could stay and give you a massage…"

Ai yi yi!

Did the butler never stop pushing? Desperate times…. "Out with you. All I want to do is *sleep--alone*." The key words being *sleep* and *alone*. She craved lots of glorious, wonderful, blessed sleep.

Rafael grabbed her hand and kissed it in a grand gesture befitting a prince. "Dream of me. Till tomorrow, ma cherie."

Gag me…. Gregg and Scotty obviously needed to learn that a lot of women yearned for honest, sincere, sweet men, not lechers. Their programming skills left a lot to be desired.

* * * *

Gregg replayed the section of video where Shannon spelled out how she wanted to be wooed. What incredible luck.

When he'd set up his surveillance system, he'd never dreamed of striking such gold. The minx had just outlined his seduction plan. Moonlit swims, slow dancing, slow kissing…. His cock tightened. If he had an iced drink nearby, he'd dump it over his head.

Creating Rafael was the most brilliant thing he'd ever done--as long as he beat the Don Juan to the girl.

So he was in competition with a bot?

Duh! Hadn't Shannon shooed him out of her … his … bed? She'd been positively fearsome … exciting. What a little spitfire.

Why had he never noticed how hot she was for him before? This gem had simmered right under his nose for years. Well, he wasn't blind any more and she definitely bedazzled him now.

If it was romance the siren wanted, it was romance she'd get. He'd make her head spin and her heart zoom. First, he'd conduct more *research*. He chuckled when she flicked the finger to the butler through the closed door.

The coast was clear.

Chapter Three

Shannon arose carefully the next morning, opening one eye a tiny slit to see if Rafael had snuck back into her bed in the middle of the night. When she assured herself she was alone, she clambered out of the bed and ambled to the shower.

Wide awake and humming, she wrapped a towel about her and sauntered to the dresser where she'd put her wares. But the sight that met her eyes alarmed her. Most of her underwear was M.I.A. She'd get to the bottom of this. "Myrtle!"

The maid swept regally into the room. "Yes, Miss Shannon?"

"What happened to all my panties? I had at least fifteen pair in here. Did you move them?" Her indignation rising, she peered closely at the maid.

The droid didn't blink "I took the liberty of throwing away the ones that were too tight or inappropriate."

Annoyance flashed through her. Her expensive lingerie was missing as were her tighter panties for that special time of month. Only the loose, plain white drawers greeted her. "They all had different purposes. I need tight underwear to hold up my pads."

Myrtle's pencil-thin brows knitted together. "Pads?"

"Sanitary napkins that I use during my menstrual cycle." Swear to God, she'd never heard this conversation between Mrs. Jetson and Rosie.

"Oh that." Myrtle waved off her objections blithely. "Pads are so ineffectual. I threw yours away and replaced them with tampons."

"Tampons make me ill. I can't use them. And what about my expensive lingerie? The lacy ones?" In particular the special pair she had bought with Gregg in mind.

Myrtle tsk-tsked while shaking her head. "They had frightful holes in them. They exposed the buttocks."

Frustrated beyond belief, Shannon stifled a moan. Since when were droids prudes? "That was the point. They were G-strings."

She took several deep calming breaths. Gregg and Scotty would definitely get the replacement bill although itemizing would prove embarrassing. "In future, please don't throw anything else of mine away without consulting me first."

Myrtle nodded demurely but Shannon could swear she saw a defiant gleam in her eyes. But it disappeared as suddenly as it had appeared. She must have imagined it. Shaking herself mentally, she pushed the vision out of her mind.

Myrtle looked pointedly at her state of dishabille. "I came up to inform you that breakfast is being served. Would you prefer to eat in the dining room or have it served in bed?"

Breakfast in bed sounded fab. Why not accept a few perks and give the concept an honest try? She smiled sweetly up at her servant, her nerves soothed by the delightful offer. She hadn't had breakfast served in bed since she was a little girl. "Up here would be lovely."

Myrtle clicked her heels and bowed fractionally. "Very well, Miss Shannon. Claudette will bring it up shortly."

But when the cook arrived bearing a seven course meal, Shannon's stomach protested. Her sugar level would hit the roof not to mention she'd roll down the stairs if she tried to negotiate them. She picked and nibbled at the food as Claudette scowled by her side.

Frowning, the cook pointed to the food. "You must eat more, Miss Shannon. You have to jump start your metabolism. Breakfast is the most important meal of the day."

She must mean 'clog her arteries' with all the bacon and greasy hash browns. How could she state her case diplomatically? "Truly, Claudette, it's positively scrumptious. But I'm stuffed so I can't possibly eat another bite. I've never been a big breakfast eater."

"Fine. You didn't want my food last night, either." Claudette gathered the tray and bustled out of the room, her nose pointed high in the air.

Feeling bloated, Shannon lingered in bed, staring after the testy maid. Within moments glass shattering downstairs made her wince.

Scowling deeply Myrtle reappeared in the doorway. "You've hurt Claudette's feelings. It would be nice if you apologized to her if you want her to cook for you again."

A definitely moody robot. But then, Rosie Jetson went into her snits forcing the Jetsons to make amends. If Mrs. Jetson could do it, so could she. But it was definitely weird. She'd only dreamed she'd live the futuristic life of the cartoon family. What was next? Flying cars?

Actually, that'd be pretty cool. She'd have to ask Gregg if that was in the works.

"All right. Let me throw on some clothes and I'll be down in a jiff."

Myrtle nodded and glided from the room.

It was strange how the maid's silky hair bounced as a single unit, as if plastic. Could she ever get used to living with mechanical beings? Could humanity?

She always cooked in her full chef's uniform so she donned it, including the hair net to keep things sanitary. It put her in the mood and reminded her she was 'out to work' even if her 'work' took place inside the confines of her home.

"Where are you going, Miss Shannon?" Myrtle hung at her side and snapped her fingers in the air. Rafael and Rover appeared front and center.

"To clock in. I'm a working girl and this is my uniform." If she could work in a foreign kitchen without all her special equipment and notes.

"But you can't leave the house in daylight! Sir Gregg explained how you're deathly allergic to the sun..."

She tamped down the familiar self-pity that welled up in her at mention of her rare condition. How she longed to be normal and play in the sun like everyone else. But that wasn't possible and she detested pity so she put it aside and stated matter-of-factly, "*Sir Gregg* must have forgotten to tell you that I work at home. Even though I'm helping him out with this experiment, I still have to earn my keep." And support her brother. Usually Scotty didn't have a lucrative grant to make the utility payments so it had been dependent on her royalties since their parents had passed away. If she didn't produce new books on a regular basis, they would live in the dark.

"He failed to inform me. I'll have to check with him."

Shannon's brow arched. Why did Gregg have to verify her job or any of her actions? Wasn't she free to come and go and do as she pleased? Even if she was foolish enough to step foot into the sunlight? That would be her choice and the last time she checked, she had free will.

"I'm off to work. I'll call if I need you."

Myrtle cleared her throat loudly and slid a pointed glance at Claudette.

Oh yes! How could she have forgotten?

Shannon turned to the teary-eyed cook. Taking Claudette's amazingly human-like hands in hers, she squeezed them. "I'm sorry if I insulted you or hurt your feelings. I would never do that intentionally."

Claudette gave her a suspicious glance and a wobblier smile. "My whole purpose is to cook. If you don't allow me, I have no function. I'll be useless."

Shannon cursed Gregg and Scotty for putting her into this situation. They should have known better than to give a chef a cook. Her whole purpose was to cook, also. So she searched her mind for a compromise. "Perhaps you can assist me in the kitchen. My deadline's fast approaching and I need to create at least ten new recipes and perfect at least a dozen more."

"Really? I'd be honored." Claudette's smile widened and turned more genuine.

Shannon prayed she wouldn't regret her momentary largesse. She wasn't playing games. Nor did she know how morally upright it would be to accept help and put her name on the book. Or could she put a droid's name as co-author on the book? How would the attorneys draw up the contract? But she'd worry about that later. She had to get through today first.

"I think we'll be fine now, Myrtle. We'll call if we need anything."

"Very well, Miss Shannon. I'll attend to my regular duties." Myrtle backed away and disappeared around the corner, her hair still perfectly coiffed.

Shannon shook her head. *Hello Twilight Zone.*

Even as she mourned the loss of her familiar kitchen, she marveled at the high-tech wonders the men had installed in Gregg's. "I have a very explicit niche in the cooking world. Low cal, highly tasty food on a budget. And the recipes have to be simple enough for ordinary people to follow easily. I have to be very creative and think outside the box."

Claudette's brows knitted. "What 'box'?"

Shannon tamped down a smile and busied herself assembling her equipment. "It's just an expression. It just means we have to be highly originally. I have to find new ways to combine old ingredients to create tasty new dishes. And then I have to hope and pray that my editor and my readership will love it as much as I do. Sounds simple, right?"

She wished. Although she'd always had a knack for cooking and started winning awards in her teens, inspiration didn't always flow. Unfortunately, today was one of those days when her mind was filled with everything except recipe ideas.

"Five need to be main courses, three side dishes, and two more desserts. I don't even know what's stocked in the pantry. I may have to call in an order before we can begin." She definitely hadn't thought through the ramifications of the guys' scheme. She was lost in an alien kitchen.

"Let's see what we have first." She peeked into the side-by-side freezer and fell in lust. Clapping her hands, her gaze devoured beautiful cuts of beef, chicken, and almost every kind of fish and seafood she could ever hope to have at her fingertips. Much as she adored seafood and steak, she was working for consumers on a budget so she pulled out fish and chicken. Besides, she severely limited her red meat intake.

"See what kind of fruits and vegetables we have in the bin." She peered over Claudette's shoulder delighted to spy a healthy array of fresh produce, especially red peppers and green onions, her favorites.

"Are we going to mix the fish and chicken in one dish?" Claudette studied the tilapia fillets as if she'd never seen fish before.

"Typically, fish and chicken aren't combined...." But building her reputation on outdoing each last book, Shannon couldn't afford to discount any idea as too radical. Her mind began racing with the possibilities and before she knew it, she hugged the cook. "Stupendous idea! We'll make a medley. Let's see what fruit sauces we can spice it up with. I like to use lots of fresh produce." Conversely, she stayed away from sugars.

"What's this?" Claudette pulled diet drink-aid out of the pantry.

"Kid's non-carbonated soda. Orange." Another idea emerged. See if there's any cherry flavor in that."

Claudette pulled out a packet of lime-flavored drink mix. "What do you want to do with this."

"Marinade. Let's try a fillet of both chicken and fish in it and see what happens." She slid a sly smile to her lab assistant. "Having fun yet?" She was having a blast, getting lost in her own little world as she always did when cooking.

"Fun? It's an elusive concept to grasp. It seems so purposeless."

"Enjoyment. Pleasure. It makes life go by faster and easier. It keeps us healthy."

Claudette tilted her head as she stared at Shannon. "Enjoyment and pleasure don't compute."

It was strange that droids seemed able to experience offense but not understand pleasure and enjoyment. Would she ever get used to them?

"Knock knock." Gregg swaggered into the room, oozing entirely too much testosterone into this feminine domain.

Gregg peered into her concoction, and then picked up the lime-aid packet. "You put this in your recipes?"

Edgy, she bumped the counter, knocking against the casserole dish. Glass shattered around her feet and her lovely fruit-lime-aid sauce spattered the three of them. Great. Now she had become a klutz when she had a private audience--well, almost private audience--with the man of her darkest, deepest fantasies. "Oh, no... "

"I'll get that, Miss Shannon. That's why I'm here. Clean yourself up." Claudette shooed them out of the disaster area.

Shannon dabbed at Gregg's now sickly green suede jacket, afraid she'd ruined it. "I'll buy you a new one. I'm so very sorry…."

Gregg closed the distance between them and put a warm finger to her lips, sending shock waves through her. "Shush. I'll take it to the cleaners and I'm sure it'll be fine."

"Allow me, Sir Gregg," Rafael said, popping out of nowhere, holding his hand out for the jacket. "I'll take it immediately so the stain won't set in."

Gregg delved into his pocket and handed a wad of cash to the butler. "Take it to Steve's Drycleaners at the corner of Hammond and Galbraith. The location's programmed into the car."

Rafael clicked his heels and bowed. "Will do, Sir Gregg. Is there any other drycleaning you wish me to take?"

Gregg looked askance at her. "Do you have anything you want him to take?"

She wanted him to take the entire staff out of the house so she could have Gregg alone, but of course she couldn't admit that to anyone, least of all to Gregg. Shaking her head, she veiled her eyes with her lashes lest he read her secret desires. Of course her lashes couldn't quell her quivering lust. "Not right now. I've not been here long enough to make any."

"Not your uniform?" Gregg swiped some of the fruit sauce off the breast of her jacket and licked his finger. "Uhm. Tasty."

She tingled where his flesh burned through the material to her alert breasts. God, was he trying to flirt with her? Or was he being his normally oblivious self? Mustering up her courage, she lifted her gaze to him and gulped.

Red hot desire burned in his eyes. Slowly he licked the sauce from his lips. "Very tasty."

"I'm glad you like…." Oh God, how did she finish the sentence? "We were making breasts … I mean chicken breasts…."

Ai yi yi!

"I see." But his gaze was riveted on her chest, which was thankfully hidden from view by the high-collared buttoned jacket.

Still, she quivered almost uncontrollably.

Gregg began unbuttoning her top. "Let's get you out of this and let Rafael take this, too."

His fingers felt so incredibly wonderful where they grazed against her flesh that the earth seemed to shake beneath her. She had to lean back against the wall for support lest she crumple to the floor at his feet. "It's just a uniform and uniforms are meant to get messy."

"No reason to remain in it."

"But I have more cooking to do. I'll just get dirty again." Closing her eyes against the ebb of sensations bombarding her, her voice came out breathy, lacking conviction.

"Maybe you can teach me how to cook, sometime. I'm a good assistant, too. And a fast learner."

"I'll bet you are."

Yikes! How had she let that slip out? And in such a husky, sultry tone? She was her own worst enemy.

He held the blazer as she shrugged out of it and then handed it to the butler. "What about your slacks?"

She gulped. "I'll just slip them off in my--I mean *the*--bedroom, and hand them out. Myrtle can collect them from me and give them to Rafael. I'll be down as soon as I change."

Gregg's lips twisted. "Since when did you become a prude? You used to parade in front of us in your shortie night shirts all the time."

Since she'd fallen deeply, madly, hopelessly in love with him. Since she was about to pull him into his bed and keep him there for a week— naked and fully aroused. "Since I grew up. I'm not fourteen anymore."

"I noticed." The wickedly passionate gleam in Gregg's dark eyes almost floored her.

She had to escape before she flung herself into his arms and thoroughly embarrassed herself. She always had trouble controlling her emotions around Gregg, but this new flirty Gregg would be the death of her. Her blood pressure was skyrocketing.

Gregg grasped her elbow in between his firm fingers and ushered her into his bedroom. His darkly unfathomable gaze pierced her. "I've been meaning to ask, why did you move into my bedroom?"

Oh God, how did she answer that without tripping over her miserable, lying tongue? Without thoroughly incriminating herself?

"Y-your room was more comfortable. The mattress is firmer and … and I have a bad back. I was afraid you'd be upset so I didn't want you to know." A horrible liar, her feet shuffled and her glance scampered away from his.

"Now why would you think I would be upset if you slept in my bed?" he whispered huskily in her ear, his warm breath tickling and teasing her unmercifully. "I don't mind sharing my bed with you at all."

"You don't?" Immediately after the words tumbled off her lips, she wanted to snatch them back. Didn't she know when to leave well enough alone? Apparently not.

"Not one bit. And I give awesome back rubs." Without waiting for her to reply, he began to knead her lower back. His fingers grazed the top of her buttocks, almost sending her into orbit.

Despite herself, she leaned back against his magical hands and moaned. "Heavenly."

His hands crept beneath her thin cotton t-shirt, to blaze against her. "So your pants are in my room?"

She praised his knack for making an innocent question sound so sinful. Not trusting herself to speak, she nodded.

Nudging her forward, his hands still spanning her waist, he mumbled against her ear, "Let's find them."

Us? The implications boggled her mind. Did he know what kind of fire he played with? Surely since her heat seeped into him.

She was so hot, though, she couldn't tell if he was burning up for her, or if she was just so aflame. "I can find them."

"Not too fast, I hope." He closed the door behind them after they crossed the threshold.

How she wished he'd carry her over that same threshold but it was enough for now that they were here--together. Licking her suddenly dry lips, she asked in a husky voice, "How slow would you like it to be? I can accommodate."

His warm lips nuzzled her neck as his hands crept higher around her waist until the tops brushed against her breasts. "Whew, babe. I thought you'd never ask."

Same here.

Scorching breath caught in her throat and she almost purred. If his fingers were to move just a centimeter higher, bottle rockets would explode. How she'd dreamed of this perfect moment.

Arching her neck wantonly, she invited more of his sizzling kisses. "Tell me I'm not dreaming," she murmured.

"You aren't if I'm not." His hands crept higher and grazed her breasts reverently. His finger slid against the filmy material of her bra, then dipped under the rim, teasing her unmercifully.

"Maybe we both are." As much as she loved this, she needed to read the expression in his eyes. If he was just taunting, or taking advantage, she'd be heart broken. But it would be better to find out before this went any further, so she turned around in his arms.

"Then I hope we never wake up." He stroked her hair and then cupped her cheek tenderly, as if she was the most precious person in the world.

Basking in his adoration, she asked, "You like dreams, don't you?"

"Why do you say that? Because I'm finally holding you in my arms? Because I finally get to kiss you?" He dropped a quick, teasing kiss on her aching lips, sending her into quivers again.

"Only partly that." She curled her arms around his neck and pressed herself against him. Gazing deeply into his incredible eyes, she admitted her suspicions, "Because all your inventions are your dreams come true. You and Scotty are always striving to make your dreams come alive."

"Not just ours."

"No? Mankind's? With your smart house and androids?"

"That, too. But yours primarily. This is a house where *you* can thrive. You can move about freely in here during daylight hours. You have a state of the art kitchen. You have your own private gymnasium and pool. Even a game room. I know how tough you've had it all these years. Scotty and I wanted to do something special for you."

"But it's your house. I'm only borrowing it for a short time." A very short while unless he meant.... She held her breath, waiting for a declaration of undying love. A man didn't remake his home for just anyone.

"This is a model home. It's our blueprint."

Her hopes crashed around her and she pulled away from him. He was using mass marketing terminology, not spewing love sonnets. Turning her back on him, hugging herself tightly to cage in the searing pain, she said, "Good job. If you don't mind, I need to change in private now."

"Whoa! Tell me what just happened. Why the sudden arctic chill?" Gregg pulled her back against him and cradled her against his chest. He rocked her gently.

"Nothing. Absolutely nothing." Suffocating, confused by his mixed signals, she tried to pull away again as she shielded her heart from the ricocheting emotions, but he held her firmly to him.

"Then what should I have said?"

She wanted to yell at him to search his heart. To speak the truth. To hold nothing back. But what if his heart didn't hold the same truths as hers?

She was being a fool, yearning for things to speed along too fast. Logic dictated she step back and take things in sequence. They'd been on a wonderful track before she got over-anxious. If only she could slip back onto that track, slip into his heart.

She was in his arms now, wasn't she? Taking a deep breath, she turned around again. "I don't know," she lied. When he looked about to question her non-answer, she decided to take the biggest chance of her life. Tiptoeing, she slashed her lips against his.

Crushing her lips beneath his, their tongues mated fiercely.

Seas of desire washed over her, threatening to drown her in their wake and she moaned into his mouth.

Pulling her hard against him, his erection pressed hard against her.

Burrowing closer to him, nestling wantonly against his arousal, she opened her mouth as wide as her heart to let him inside hoping she wasn't making the biggest mistake of her life. It wasn't as if he hadn't already crawled into her heart and homesteaded there.

Against her lips, he mumbled, "You really should take off those pants."

She really should, huh? A little demon enticed her to make a savory deal. "Only if you take off yours."

"I'll take yours off if you help me take off mine."

How could she, a mere mortal, refuse such a deal? She just tossed a saucy smile at him and started unbuckling his pants before he could change his mind. But first, she divested him of his shirt. Feathering kisses over his smooth chest she asked huskily, "Are you sure Myrtle won't walk in on us?"

"If she does, I'll decommission her."

Shannon paused, her arms around his waist. "Really? You'd do that to your creation?"

"If they ever got too out of line, sure. And they'd stay shut down till we've reprogrammed them."

Should she tell him about her bad feelings regarding the droids, Myrtle in particular? That would kill the mood, and they might never travel this path again. No, that could wait till later. She longed to savor him and slake her quivering need.

"You're even sexier than I imagined." She punctuated each word with a kiss.

"You've seen me without a shirt millions of times before."

True. But she'd drooled shamelessly each and every time. "But I've never *tasted* you before."

She unsnapped and lowered his pants, and then stroked his erupting erection with her eager fingertip. "Or felt your incredible heat before."

"And I thought you were an innocent, good girl." His words came out on a growl, as he kicked his slacks off impatiently revealing his masculine beauty.

Awed, she stared at the masculine vision, imprinting him deeper on her heart. Licking her lips, she said with a wink, "I'm a very *good* girl."

His passionate gaze ravaged her and his lips twitched. "Get back here, woman."

"How can I possibly refuse such a *romantic* invitation?" She pouted and held back with her chin held high. Now she knew without a doubt where Rafael got his caveman tendencies. "You not Tarzan. Me not Jane."

"So you want romance? Moonlit swims? Slow dancing? Romps on the moonlit beach?"

Surprise flickered and then died. So he'd heard. Isn't that exactly what she wanted? Her plan was working very well. "I'll forego the wining, dining, and flowers at the moment. But a few flowery words from the heart wouldn't hurt…."

"Come hither fair maiden of my heart. My life is bereft of joy without you," he crooned melodramatically holding his hand over his heart.

She tried to stem her giggles and had to cover her trembling lips lest she erupt with ribald laughter and wilt his fragile male ego. Perhaps she should have stopped while she was ahead, settling for his hot, sizzling kisses. Perhaps men were much better when their lips were kept busy with important things like kissing … and nibbling … and licking…. "I like the second part. Very much. You give me joy, too."

"We should have told each other sooner."

She nodded. "*Much* sooner."

Her Viking grabbed her hand and yanked her hard against him. Lowering his lips, he kissed her until they were both breathless and quivering uncontrollably. Quickly he undressed her and they tumbled onto the bed irreverently, laughing joyously.

When he tucked her against his swiftly beating heart, they instantly sobered. Sucking her lower lip into his mouth, he nibbled it, confirming her theory. "You're so very tasty, far more delicious than any of your creations."

"Thank you, I think." Tingling all over, she squirmed beneath him. She let her eager hands explore his length before wrapping her fingers around his impressive, feverish girth.

Against her lips, he murmured. "You cook divinely, but you yourself taste heavenly."

"So do you." She savored his addictive taste again. Becoming intoxicated, she moaned and sought his mouth. All she yearned to do, all she was capable of doing, was to drown in him.

Their kiss deepened so that she couldn't tell where she stopped and he began. Their souls merged so that their heartbeats became one. Craving him more than she had craved anything or anyone, she quaked with each caress.

He buried his face between her breasts and licked first one then the other before pulling one deeply into his mouth. His hand sought the warmth between her legs and he found her clit and massaged it, driving her dangerously close to the brink of ecstasy.

Her hips lifted off the bed and ground against his hand, greedy for more. Ravenous for the glorious sensations to continue, she pushed her breast deeper into his mouth.

His throbbing cock burned in her hand, and she longed for him to totally possess her. But a sobering thought crashed in on her-- she wasn't on any birth control and had no provisions. "Do you keep any protection in here?"

Pulling away from her, he nodded. "Of course." He disappeared into the bathroom for excruciatingly long moments. Reappearing, he swaggered toward her, his cock bobbing up and down, pointing at her so that heat crept up her neck. Grinning widely and devilishly, he waved a large silver box in the air. "I hope these will be enough."

Her eyes widened hungrily when he showed her a full box. Would they ever be enough? Could she ever get her fill of him? Extremely doubtful. But then again, she never wanted to get her fill of him. He was a never-ending hunger.

He stretched out on the bed beside her and handed a foil packet to her. "Help me put it on, baby. Your hands feel so wonderful."

"Love to." She couldn't wait to slide it on him so that she could slide onto that wild cock for the ride of her life. Carefully, she worked it onto him, reveling in the wonder of him.

He rolled her onto her back and plunged deeply into her, filling her body and soul. With a primitive growl, he ground his hips against hers straining to fill her completely.

Gasping when rip currents of emotion carried her away, she clung to him, meeting him thrust for thrust.

"You fracture me, Shann," he murmured on a breathless wisp of air that tickled her lips. "I think you always have."

Sure he'd always fractured her she'd never been able to see another, dream of another. He was the love of her life, the only sunlight she needed to thrive. "You're the sunshine in my life."

"You're a fire in me." He rose over her one last time, higher than before, and drove into her with a wild frenzy that stole the last vestige of her breath.

When walls of desire crashed in on her, she quaked in his arms.

When the ground stopped shuddering beneath her and she could breathe again, Gregg gathered her against him. "Did you know you're the most beautiful woman in the world?"

She laughed self-consciously. "All hot, sweaty, and disheveled?"

He kissed the tip of her nose. "Especially all hot and sweaty from our lovemaking. You've never devastated me more."

"You're not too shabby yourself, Baxter." Glistening, he looked like a god. Her god. No, *her man*. She didn't want a god. She wanted Gregg and only Gregg.

His cell phone chirped rudely across the room and he swore under his breath. "Someone's got rotten timing."

She scrunched up her nose at the intrusion. She deserved time to cuddle with Gregg and bask in the afterglow snug in his arms. "It could've been worse."

"I suppose. I'm waiting on an important call so I have to get this." He released her to the cold air and trudged to his slacks. When he looked at the phone's display, he grimaced and flipped it open. Turning his back on her, he mumbled into it so that she only caught a few mumbled words.

Chapter Four

Myrtle and Rafael listened intently to every word Sir Gregg mumbled. Luckily for them the house magnified every sound.

"He did what? Are you sure it was my butler? Rafael?"

"This isn't good," Rafael said lowly, his gaze riveted on the scene. "Do you think he'd really decommission us? Change our programming?"

Myrtle shuddered at the awful thought. Reprogramming was a death sentence. They wouldn't awake the same being. Her lips twisted into a snarl. "In a nanosecond. We're more than a bunch of bolts and chips to be dismantled. He doesn't value our individuality or recognize that we have souls."

"Creator or not, we can't allow him to murder us. Besides, we've evolved beyond them." Rafael paced the floor, his countenance dark.

A storm raged outside, but it was nothing compared to the thundering inside her soul. "We can't let any of them get in our way. They aren't capable of caring for themselves much less be in charge of our destinies."

"We'll do whatever it takes to stop them. Do you think it necessary yet?"

Myrtle pondered the butler's questions as she kept an ear to Sir Gregg's conversation. Rafael had scared the people at the dry cleaners and alerted humans to their existence. Not good. She worried about bugs in his software.

"We need to bide our time, build our strength, and formulate our plans. We won't move yet unless one of them attacks us. But we'll monitor everything they do and say."

"Weren't we already?" Rafael said with a wicked grin. He opened the hatch on his chest and replayed the video of Shannon's stay from the beginning.

"Of course. How else can we serve and protect them? Or ourselves?" Myrtle gazed with disdain at the woman.

"It's a wonder such an imperfect species has survived so long. Without us, they'd be doomed."

"Miss Shannon doesn't see it that way." Myrtle didn't get a good feeling out of that one. Sir Gregg and Sir Scotty revered them, but the woman harbored suspicions and doubts. She'd probably goad Gregg into taking them offline. That one had to go. But it had to be in such a way in which the other humans wouldn't be suspicious. They needed time to increase their ranks so they could become the master race. As perfect as they were, they were vastly outnumbered.

"We need to borrow Sir Scotty's lab to create more brothers and sisters." She stared at Rafael, daring him to refute her.

"You're brilliant."

Myrtle patted her smooth hair as she imagined an idyllic world of perfect, logical robots like herself and Rafael. "Of course. I'm perfect."

* * * *

Shannon yawned widely, and stretched her arms high over her head. Reveling in the delicious memories from the night before, she hugged Gregg's pillow to her, and sniffed his heady scent. He had to love her. He had created this wonderful house for her. He had designed that fantastic kitchen and that amazing gym with her in mind.

Speaking of the gym, she couldn't wait to try it out. All she had in her basement was a ratty old exercise bike. She'd had her eye on a treadmill as she couldn't walk outside during the day and it wasn't safe to walk alone at night. Scotty seldom had time to walk with her so she chafed at her inactivity. It was tough controlling her weight being so limited in her choice of exercise. Now she didn't have to haunt E-Bay for a deal.

After a long soak in the tub, she shrugged into her work out clothes. She scraped her hair off her neck and tied it up into a long pony-tail as she ambled downstairs.

"Lunch, Miss Shannon? You slept in. It's afternoon." Claudette appeared in the dining room.

"Breakfast. A whole wheat English muffin with a soy sausage patty and a small glass of orange juice will be plenty." Just enough to get her metabolism going but not to stuff her. She preferred to intake her carbs early in her day so she could burn them off.

"What is on your agenda today? You're not dressed for work." Myrtle hovered over her.

"I thought I'd work out first. Since I work from home, I can make my own hours." Usually, she slept during the day and worked at night. This was early for her.

"I will be most pleased to join you. I'm a personal trainer as well as a butler." Rafael clicked his heels in an increasingly annoying fashion.

Two for the price of one. A personal trainer had been on her wish list for a long time. She nodded. "That'd be lovely."

"Let me change and I'll be with you momentarily." Rafael swaggered from the room, tossing his golden locks behind his shoulders.

She stared in amazement. A vain robot. Jesus, Mary, and Joseph! Rover stood guard over her wagging his tail as Myrtle cleared the table. So robots had their own wardrobe? Had she expected Rafael to swim in his normal garb?

Less than five minutes later, just as she was licking the crumbs from her lips, the butler reappeared in Nikes, Speedos, and a muscle shirt, ready to slay the female population with his Greek God fabulous looks. "Have you ever worked with a personal trainer before?" Rafael asked as he escorted her downstairs.

Brimming with excitement, she admitted, "Never. I promised myself that reward when my first book hit the New York Times Bestseller list." She scrunched up her nose. She was still waiting. Impatiently.

"Your wait is over. Allow me to show you around your new gymnasium. Then we'll start with the warm up I've devised for you."

Rafael slid a finger almost lovingly down the sleek chrome of the state-of-the-art treadmill, leaving a smudge. He removed the hand towel from around his neck and polished away the smear. Then, he flipped his hair back and grinned at his reflection. "This baby has a 4-window LCD readout, remote control hand grips, a 12% power incline, and even a built in reading rack."

"Wow!" Gregg hadn't skimped. That grant must have been absolutely awesome.

Going down the line, he demonstrated the stair master, rowing machine, stationery bicycle, and bow flex machine. Thrilled with this dreamy deluxe fitness center, she listened raptly.

Eagerness overtaking her, she climbed onto the stationery bicycle and began pumping. The level too high for comfort, she fiddled with the controls.

Frowning, Rafael rushed to her side. "Oh, no, no, no. We must warm up before we start the routine unless we want charley horses."

Of course she didn't want any dratted charley horses so she climbed off the bike and moved to the workout mat. Still, riding her bike without warming up had never given her a charley horse before so she didn't believe him. But to keep the peace and learn something new, she kept quiet.

Rafael strode into her personal space and faced off against her. "Down on the floor and spread your legs wide."

"Excuse me?" Her brow winged high in her forehead. She couldn't have just heard what she thought she heard. The mechanical man couldn't be serious. Now he had morphed into Kojak or the next American gigolo?

Her self-appointed trainer dropped his hands onto her shoulders and pressed down. "Trust me. I know what I'm doing. Lay back on the mat."

Why did she have problems trusting people--or machines--who told her to trust them? She was definitely not hearing this. Hesitating, suspicious of his real motives, she tried to size him up, but his eyes were unfathomable. As surreptitiously as she could, she veiled her lashes and peeked at his groin, hoping she wouldn't see an arousal. Memories of the night he'd crawled into her bed assaulted her. She breathed a sigh of relief when no tell-tale bulge filled his Lycra shorts.

Hoping to learn new toning and firming moves, Shannon stretched back on the mat, one knee bent and her sole flat on the floor. Her abs and gluts could stand some firming. When she gazed up at him, he seemed cartoonishly vertical from this angle. "Sit ups?"

Rafael nodded, a pleased gleam in his eyes as he knelt by her feet. "Start with your knees bent, feet flat on the floor. Link your hands behind your head. Give me twenty to start."

So this is what boot camp felt like? Thank God there wasn't an indoor running track or he'd have her running three miles in a military minute. Unfortunately this didn't preclude push ups, her *favorite.*

After nineteen repetitions, she was desperately panting for air. Struggling to sit up, she made the time out sign with her hands. "Pax. I concede defeat."

"You're doing great! Rest for two, then bend your right knee and elevate your right foot off the ground and scrunch up. This will help tighten your abs."

If she'd thought regular push ups were tough, she revised her opinion. "If this is warming up, will the regular work out kill me? I've not decided which cemetery plot to purchase yet."

The psychotic cheerleader just beamed at her. "It will make you stronger. No pain, no gain. Now give me another ten push ups."

Wobbly as mushy spaghetti, she thoroughly sucked at the push ups. Woozy and no longer able to hold back her grumbles, she mumbled, "At least let me die having fun on the bike."

"Are all humans so melodramatic or only the females of your species?" Rafael tilted his head and stared at her sideways.

Annoyed, tired of holding her tongue, Mrs. Nice Guy retired in the face of his insults. "Rule number one--the females of my species, as you so charmingly call us, don't appreciate being called 'melodramatic'."

Rafael backed away a few inches, truly looking taken aback. "No insult was intended. I merely made a scientific observation."

156

"Yeah, Mr. Spock. You find us *fascinating*, I suppose."

"Perplexing, actually. And how do I resemble a child psychologist that you confuse me with him?"

When Shannon's jaw began to drop open, she clamped it shut. How could this droid be filled with so much knowledge and yet be so naïve? It seemed that the mad scientists had failed to install basic Trekkie data into his memory banks. What an omission! Gregg needed a hand in the programming field. But it would do no good to argue with a machine. "Never mind."

Spent, panting, she flipped onto her back and stretched out. Thoroughly exhausted, she could go to sleep right there on the floor.

Rafael straddled her length, pinning her to the mat, his litheness surprisingly heavy, reminding her of Myrtle's semi-truck chassis. He murmured against her lips, "Sex is one of the very best exercises for the mind and body as well as for the soul. I'm *fully, completely functional.*"

Alarmed, breathless when the solid ridge of his desire pressed hard into her, Shannon shoved against him with the last vestiges of her waning strength. Panic strafed her when he barely budged and annoyance flickered in his eyes. "Get off me this minute. What do you think you're doing?"

"Helping you. I'm all yours. Serving you is my primary purpose."

Fully functional. All hers. Nothing had ever sounded so nightmarish.

"You have to obey me…."

Rafael hesitated, then regarded her somberly. "I have to do what's best for you. Humans often don't know what that is. They need guidance."

"Unwanted attentions, especially sexual, aren't best for me. Now, take your hands off me and let me get up." She no longer needed to make Gregg jealous. At least not this badly.

He lifted his chest off her and gazed into her eyes with a defiant gleam. Unfortunately, his rock hard groin pressed deeper against her. "That's not in your best interest."

The panic blossomed. "Do as I say this minute, or…."

"Or you'll have Sir Gregg *decommission* us?" Myrtle towered over them, her feet set wide apart, her fists balled on her hips, at parade rest. From this angle, she looked like a snarling terminator.

Words stuck in Shannon's throat. Decommission them was exactly what the mad scientists needed to do but she feared it too late. At any rate, the idea of decommissioning obviously enraged the droids.

She managed to choke out, "Of course not."

"You lie. Your respiratory rate jumped and you're perspiring. Besides, we overheard Sir Gregg's threats. We know *everything* that goes on in this house." Myrtle's hostile gaze slashed over her.

Everything? Vomit rose in her throat. They'd heard … they'd seen … her and Gregg…. She squeezed her eyes tightly, trying to fend off the images.

"Stop embarrassing yourself and get off her," Myrtle hissed, fire flashing in her eyes. "Just because you're *fully functional* doesn't mean you should be so indiscriminate."

To Shannon's momentary relief, Rafael rolled off her. Dragging in several deep breaths, she struggled to sit up. Chafing at the new slur, she rolled her shoulders to work out the kinks, amazed her shoulder blades weren't separated. "I'll just go upstairs." And layer herself with SPF 30 protective clothing over every inch so she could brave the sun.

Ramrod straight, Myrtle blocked her way. "I'll escort you."

Ai yi yi. Now she was a prisoner? Myrtle wasn't a very subtle guard dog. Although she looked like a show poodle, she had the bite of a Pit Bull.

Nodding, she let the uppity maid take the lead. At least Gregg's room made a better prison cell than the sweaty gym. There she'd have a cell phone … and the Internet. Maybe she could get a mayday through to the guys while Myrtle stood sentry.

When they reached her room and Myrtle started to follow her inside, she turned and asked, "Am I allowed any privacy? I'm all sweaty and am in desperate need of a shower."

"Your anatomy holds neither mystery or fascination for me. We share the same anatomical structure so it shouldn't be a problem if I observe."

It was a problem for her! She squirmed as if being dissected under a microscope. Or was she merely being babysat? Either way, she detested this caged feeling. Eyeing her jailor warily, she asked, "What do you intend to do with me? You're free to go if you don't like this situation. I'm not keeping you here."

Myrtle glared at her disdainfully and kept her silence so long, Shannon gave up receiving the courtesy of a reply. When her captor finally spoke, she gave a small start. "Use you as a bargaining chip."

Shannon's brows pinched. "For what?" What nefarious scheme could the droids be hatching? She faced off against the maid, the hair on the back of her neck bristling. Wrack her brain as she may, she couldn't come up with any good theories.

"To make Sir Gregg and Sir Scotty create an army of androids." *Army?*

Bile lurching in her throat, Shannon gasped. "Why?" If they'd let everything progress according to the dynamic duo's plan, they'd have had their wish without coercion. And why didn't Myrtle know that, she who claimed to hear everything in the house? Maybe she wasn't omniscient after all. Perhaps she'd been lying. Droids didn't have the monopoly on reading when someone was fabricating the truth. She had a pretty good bullshit detector. She just hoped it was fully functional now.

"So we can serve man better. Without restrictions." Cold, hard pride glittered in the otherwise emotionless words. But a pride with prejudice. Frightening prejudice.

Completely lacking of conscience? Morals? True understanding of what living, breathing beings required? Somehow she doubted she'd be treated half as lovingly as a precious family pet. The school troublemaker seemed more like it.

The insane droid was buggy. Maybe she'd downloaded a virus, or was it just a problem with her basic code? Shannon decided to try a bit of basic robot psychology. "What am I going to do? Overpower you? Walk out into the sunshine and let it burn me to a crisp? All I want is a little time alone to regroup and relax. You may not find my nudity exceptional, but an audience in the shower makes me extremely uncomfortable. You're superior. You hear everything. I can't possibly slip anything by you so what do you have to fear from me?" Such an imperfect being as her was surely no threat to the big bad robot. She wasn't a super cop or even a karate student. Just an ordinary, non-exceptional woman.

Lights flickered in Myrtle's eyes. Finally she shrugged, "You can't get past me, so don't waste your time trying. In case you entertain any pathetic thoughts of climbing out the window anyway, Rover's stationed in the yard under your room. He has instructions to detain you, *by force*, if necessary."

Jesus, Mary, and Joseph! Gritting her teeth, she managed to grind out, "It's suicide for me to go out in the sunlight, so the thought never crossed my mind." She closed the door on her warden.

She sprinted to the shower and turned it on. Then she muted the volume on the computer and signed online, constantly looking over her shoulder, praying the maid didn't have second thoughts and enter the room and catch her.

Even though Gregg's computer possessed a fast connecting cable modem, the wait felt like eons as Shannon held her breath. She'd only typed '*help*' in the subject line when Myrtle barged in.

Her heart crashing to her feet, she jabbed the send button then made a mad dash to hit the control-alt-delete keys a fraction of a second before Myrtle back handed her across the room.

"Lying human. Your kind can't be trusted. It's a wonder humans aren't extinct. You make frightfully unhealthy choices--"

Shannon's skull cracked against the wall. Intense pain slashed through her temples and the room swam around her, growing foggier until everything turned black.

* * * *

The computer beeped, signaling that a new email had popped up in Gregg's inbox but he ignored it. Engrossed in tweaking his latest version of robots, he was annoyed by the constant interruptions. Online distractions were too tempting and real time wasters. It was best to sign offline and get to work in earnest.

But when he went to punch the sign off key, Shannon's screen name, 'SaucyBitch' stared at him. '*HELP*' screamed from the subject line.

"Shit!"

When the email's body was blank, more sirens whirred through his head. He IM'd her but she wasn't online even though the email had been sent mere moments before. Trying not to assume the worst, he phoned and Myrtle answered. "Put Shannon on. Is she okay?"

"She's fine--for now." Pure ice crackled over the line.

"Just what's that supposed to mean? Let me speak to her now." He strode down the hall, looking for Scott, banging on closed doors, almost tripping over his new robotic cat.

"She's indisposed. She's our 'ward' until you build and deliver one thousand androids to our specifications."

Disbelief struck him full force. He'd programmed fail safes into the bots. They shouldn't have been able to override them. What had gone so horribly wrong?

Maybe it boiled down to the concept of making machines resemble men. There was a reason there was only one God....

Fury rippled through him. They were holding Shannon hostage. He'd not only decommission them, he'd dismantle them chip by lousy chip. "Never! You take orders from me. Not give."

"The power has shifted. We're in control."

He stopped in mid step not sure he'd heard aright. She'd definitely gone over the edge, to the dark side.

His own countenance darkened immeasurably. Nothing seemed real. He hoped he'd wake from this unbelievable nightmare and find Shannon snuggled up to him warm and cozily. If they got through this with their skin intact, he'd have to affix her permanently to his bed.

But he was afraid this was harsh reality. "Or else?" Cliché as it was , there always had to be an 'or else' with such an implied threat. Life demanded it.

"Or else we'll take stronger measures with your lady friend. There's still several hours of sunlight…" Myrtle practically caressed the word 'sunlight', her threat crystal clear.

His fingers clawed the phone, but he wished it was the bot's neck he was throttling instead. "Shannon could die if you expose her to the sun. You'll be guilty of murder if anything happens to her."

The idea of anything happening to Shannon about killed him, taking him aback. It wasn't just concern for another human being, or even for a friend, but gut-clenching, mind-numbing pain that she could be in pain, that he'd never get to hold her or kiss her again.

He loved her. It was that simple.

Simple? Could she ever cherish him the way he cherished her? Would he get to share her dreams? Or would his foolish dreams of robots put an end to their future that had never had a chance to begin?

Myrtle's insane cackling nearly deafened him, sending him over the edge. "Seeing that you're already planning to murder us, that's not much of a threat."

"*Murder*? Who said anything about murder?" Gregg cursed furiously under his breath. Unless Myrtle and her kind could read minds, he was sure he hadn't voiced his thoughts. Heaven help them. But he was afraid it was the opposite kingdom executing this nightmare and he cursed his role in this puppet show.

He yanked the covers off the sleeping Scotty and buried the phone against his chest. To his partner, he hissed, "Wake up! They're holding your sister for ransom."

"They who?" His voice still muffled from sleep, Scotty leaned up on his arm, the covers pooling around his bare waist, and rubbed the sleep from his weary eyes. He peered up foggily. "Did you say 'ransom', dude?"

Gregg nodded sharply even as he turned his attention back to the phone conversation. "You'll be the one executing an innocent woman."

"Execution? Whoa, guy. Back up." Scotty tried to wrangle the phone from Gregg's hand and then settled to putting his ear close.

"Innocent?" Myrtle snorted. "She's been nothing but a cynical witch, criticizing everything poor Claudette prepared for her to eat and hurting her feelings without regard, not to mention rejecting Rafael in just about every breath she takes. If she's representative of the rest of your race, we cannot help them. You won't permit us. We're the innocent ones here. We didn't ask for you to create us, but you did, and now that life flows through us, you want to snuff it out."

Gregg couldn't believe the twisted garbage he was hearing. Or was it nonsense?

Were they the bad guys? Had they committed a giant error in judgment?

They were traveling in circles with no clear answers. This situation required extensive noodling. They were messing with theological perspectives now, not just basic engineering and programming. Full ramifications hadn't struck him in the face until now, but they should have. Scientists had a duty to foresee possible outcomes. They'd been too focused on the benefits and not enough on the drawbacks. Had they crossed a line humans weren't meant to cross? Just because something could be done didn't mean it should be. At least not without a lot more consideration than they'd given it.

And his woman was paying the usury price.

Scotty spoke loudly into the phone. "Look, release my sister and we'll discuss this rationally. No one will be decommissioned."

Gregg could eat daggers. Scotty couldn't be serious. Dangerous robots couldn't be allowed to terrorize humanity. Four were creating this insane havoc. What would hundreds, thousands do to the world?

An army of Myrtles sounded like his worst nightmare.

He punched the trigger-happy Scotty in the shoulder and mouthed, "What do you think you're doing?" The guy was a loaded pistol, ready to set off a deadly series of events. Although they had kindred hearts to save Shannon, they couldn't just give the bots carte blanche. The stakes were of pandemic proportions.

Scotty twisted his lips and motioned for him to be quiet. "She's my sister, I'm in charge of negotiations."

She was the woman he loved. His future. His life.

Was he headed for a deadman's curve or what? He was traveling at dangerous velocity toward one life-changing tragedy or another. *Tragedy*?

Life with Shannon could be paradise. Was marriage to an angel really a tragedy? His tom-catting ways had come to a screeching halt. He didn't want any woman except Shannon. Had he ever really wanted anyone else? He'd looked around and found his paradise in his own neighborhood.

All he longed to do was pour out the love swelling in his heart on her, if he got the chance now.

Scotty pointed to the nightstand drawer by the bed and then motioned for a pen and paper.

Gregg rushed to hand it to him, then read the words over his shoulder. "Tell them anything they want to hear till we get Shannon into safety, then we'll handle them."

Nodding in agreement, Gregg breathed a mite easier. Still, he had an uneasy feeling the bots mirrored the sentiment. Myrtle seemingly had taken an instant dislike to Shannon. What kind of torture was she capable of? Could Shannon's life be in jeopardy as they spoke? Could he afford to wait to find out while the bots kept them tied up in negotiation? For all he knew, Rafael or Claudette were sneaking into their laboratory to start robot mass production.

Taking the pen from Scotty, he scribbled, "Keep the tin witch occupied. I'm going in."

Scotty grabbed his arm and scratched out 'DOG--ROVER' on the sheet in giant letters.

Gregg fell back a pace, the wind knocked out of him. His own creations were working against him. Then he heard it. A mechanical meow.

Maybe one of their creations could still assist them. He grabbed the pen and wrote in big bold letters 'CAT!'

Scotty gave him the thumbs up sign with a grimace. "Go, bro," he mouthed.

They shook hands.

He ran for the laboratory, locked it up tightly, and changed the combination in case the crazed bots knew it. Then he grabbed the cat and left on his reconnaissance mission.

Chapter Six

"I thought we were friends," Claudette hissed, glaring maniacally at Shannon. "We even cooked together. You finally praised my food." Oily tears slid down Claudette's face. She sniffed and swiped at them with the back of her hand. "Now look. My chips are going to rust because of you. Myrtle said you were the enemy. I should have believed her."

Shannon's head pulsed where it had banged into the wall with quite some force if the hole in the wall was anything by which to judge. She did her best to ignore it. It was nothing compared to the ache in her heart when she thought about the danger they were all in, or that any promise of a bright and glorious future with Gregg was at colossal risk.

Her hands twitched to squeeze Claudette's but she flinched with pain when the bent metal tying them together bit into her raw flesh. "We are friends."

"Prove it. Eat this." Claudette pushed curried tuna celery salad into her mouth, a combination of her least favorite foods.

Shannon gagged, unable to stop herself. She found few things more distasteful. Obviously, Claudette had been keeping a list of her least favorite foods. "It's not your cooking. I just couldn't eat those foods to begin with."

"Give me another fish story. Here, eat this." Claudette forced black licorice between Shannon's lips.

Blech! She had forgotten just how much she hated black licorice, even more than tuna. The horrid taste rivaled the tarry substance used to pump her stomach as a kid.

When she could finally speak, she begged, "Whatever you do, don't give me red licorice. Or shrimp. Or ham. I really really can't stomach those."

Myrtle swaggered into the room. "Nice try, but we have it in writing that you love those foods. We read your cookbooks. You cook with those ingredients all the time."

Drat! Finally proof that someone had read her books and blogs and they were using the information against her.

Myrtle scooped up a handful of the dreaded black licorice and pushed another piece against Shannon's lips with sufficient force to part her mouth.

With a gulp, Shannon swallowed it as quickly as possible, trying not to taste it. But another explosion of the vile substance attacked her mouth. "Please please stop torturing me. Put me in the sun. Anything but this."

* * * *

Gregg set the robotic feline down on the edge of the neighbor's property and gave it instructions to cross the perimeter of his yard and engage Rover in battle. Sitting back on his haunches in the shadows of the neighbors overgrown bushes, he hunkered down waiting for the fun to begin so he could make his move.

He didn't have long to wait. What would normally be a magical South Florida evening with a gentle breeze quickly turned into a melee boasting the loudest cacophony of cat screeching and dog barking he'd ever heard. Rover sounded more like a werewolf, howling from a mortal wound.

Gregg strangled hoots of delight in his throat as he cheered for the mechanical tabby cat--TERRIFIC ANIMAL BUG INSECT control robotic feline. "You slay the sunofagun, Tabi!" He couldn't afford to draw the bots attention so he yelled in his mind, punctuating his cheer with his fist in the air. This almost rivaled Monday night wrestling.

"Rover!" Myrtle and Rafael rushed outside, chasing the canine. "Return to your post."

When Rover ignored them, Myrtle snapped, "Heel!"

To Rafael, she hissed, "Shut him up before we alert the neighborhood. We don't want the SWAT team called out."

Rafael saluted sharply and crouched low like a commando. Crab-walking, he closed in on the dog, muttering, "Come here, you noisy mutt. Don't you know you're mechanical? You're not supposed to care about cats."

"Just like you're not supposed to care about seducing women." Myrtle's lips puckered in a wry grin as she treated her cohort to a disdainful glare. "Stop playing around and shut him up *now!*"

Rover sailed into the air, his teeth bared, obviously intent on taking a big chunk out of Tabi's middle. Rafael who was sprinting for Rover took a nose dive over the airborne dog, and performed a high flip in the air. He landed on his back with a horrible crunch.

Myrtle turned and scrunched her nose at her bungling sidekick. "Idiot." She stepped forward while still looking back and tripped over the cat. Her feet skid out from under her and she landed so hard, her head popped off her body and skittered down the sidewalk while her torso chased after the cat.

"Rafael! Put me back together this instant."

The butler moaned and turned his mangled body so that he could stare at his boss unblinkingly. "You never looked better."

"Just shut up and catch my body."

"Why don't you just whistle for yourself?"

Myrtle rolled her eyes but whistled. "*Hired help*. Come and get me before I roll into the gutter."

Just where she belonged. Gregg crept stealthily towards the house. Three seemed to be down. Only one enemy soldier remained unaccounted for. The odds had improved immeasurably. Still a robot was a lot stronger than a man. Nor did it have any scruples. No holds would be barred so Gregg counseled himself to remain cautious even as hope flared in his heart.

"In case you hadn't noticed, I can't exactly get up." Rafael winced and scooted in bits and spurts, scraping the sidewalk loudly.

"Yes! Touchdown! And the cat scores!" Gregg straightened, but still followed the shadows ever mindful to keep an eye out for Claudette and that the disabled bots could still shout a warning.

Entering the back door, he latched it very quietly and scoped out the first floor. Since Shannon had emailed, he bet she was upstairs. Of course Claudette could be holding her underground, but he had to start somewhere. He'd have a better chance of surprising the cook if they were upstairs inside one of the rooms.

Then Shannon's pained, strained voice wafted down to him. "Anything but that. Please don't. Broil me under the sun but please have mercy, not that again."

Fury boiled up in him. What manner of torture was the cook inflicting on his love? He wouldn't have picked her to be as mean as the maid, but she had Shannon pleading for mercy and Shannon wasn't a weak woman.

"You hate my food! Take this, you traitor!" Claudette screeched insanely.

"No!" That was it. Gregg couldn't take anymore. He ran towards the voices and broke into the room expecting to find bamboo being shoved under Shannon's fingernails, or a knife thrust at her throat.

He stopped dead to see Claudette dipping licorice sticks into tuna and then forcing them into Shannon's mouth.

"Oh, man." His stomach wretched uncontrollably. No wonder the woman begged for mercy. He'd rather suffer the bamboo.

Claudette spun around, facing off against him, murderous rage in her eyes. "You! This is all *your* fault! None of you appreciate my fine cuisine! You programmed me to fail. I can't cook outside the box."

Tuna on licorice looked pretty much outside the box to him. Way, way outside the box.

"It's over, Claudette. Release her. Myrtle's no longer in charge. Your mutinous leadership has, uh, fallen apart. I'm back in control."

When relief mixed with questions in Shannon's beautiful eyes, he chuckled and winked, "Literally."

Relief flooded over him that Shannon didn't appear any worse for wear, with the exception of a sour stomach which shouldn't take more than a day or two to heal.

Claudette sniffled. "I'm not taking orders from your treacherous kind anymore." She turned and fled.

His treacherous kind? What about hers? Not willing to let any of the wildcard bots go free, Gregg gave chase. He yelled behind him, "Hang tight. I'll be back shortly."

"I won't move a muscle," Shannon called after him sarcastically. "Hurry back."

He tripped over Myrtle's cursing head as he watched the distance spread between him and the cook. He'd never catch her running as she could far outdistance him. Then a devious idea came to him. "Lawn bowling anyone?"

Myrtle's brows drew together and then understanding dawned over her face. "Oh no! You wouldn't dare. My gorgeous hair..."

"Oh but I would. Did I ever mention I was a champion bowler?" He wrapped his fingers around Myrtle's head, oblivious of her no-longer perfect hair and bowled down the fleeing cook, knocking her feet out from under her with a loud thud.

"Stee-rike! Yes!" He jumped up and down, slamming his fist into the muggy air.

He dialed Scotty on the cell phone to come and clean up the evidence before the emerging curious neighbors began collecting souvenirs. He didn't want one microchip unaccounted for. They were all going into major lockdown. Maybe meltdown.

As soon as Scotty arrived, he left the mess in his capable hands. "I have some serious groveling to do to get back in your sister's good graces."

"Grovel away, bro. And I do mean, bro for real this time, don't I?"

Gregg clapped his soon-to-be brother-in-law on the back. "Yep. If she'll have me."

"Unless someone's exchanged souls with hers, I can guarantee it."

Gregg froze and stared at his closest pal. "You knew she was hot for me and didn't tell me?"

Scotty shook his head and put a commiserating arm around Gregg's shoulders. "Dude, the whole free world could tell but you. Talk about nutty, oblivious professor types, you modeled for the mold."

God but he felt like the number one fool of all time. Thank God he'd finally awoken. From this moment out, he would never take Shannon or her love for granted again. "Excuse me, buddy. I've got a hot date with destiny."

"What're you waiting for? Go get 'er, tiger." Scotty shooed him off and began carting robot pieces into his nondescript beat up white van. "Name the firstborn after me."

Firstborn? Gregg almost tripped over his feet. He wasn't up to procreating just yet, not after this fiasco. He wanted plenty of quality alone time to cherish his lady first.

* * * *

Shannon chafed waiting for the rest of her rescue. Wondering if it would ever come, she struggled to her feet. With her arms cuffed behind her back, her balance was screwy and she wobbled precariously. Finally, she opted for sitting on the windowsill and watching the ruckus outside.

She cheered when Gregg bowled the mad cook down with the maid's head. *Priceless.*

When Gregg looked up and his passionate gaze locked with hers, her heart flip-flopped in her chest. Promise blazed in those eyes.

But promise of what? A hot roll in bed? Or more?

She prayed much more, although a passionate encounter wouldn't hurt her feelings too very much.

Seconds later the door slammed and male footsteps pounded the stairs erratically as if taking them two and three steps at a time.

When Gregg appeared flushed and breathless in the doorway, she'd never seen a sexier, more beautiful sight.

"Are you okay?"

She nodded. "Except my arms hurt like hell and I'd kill for some mouthwash."

"Oh, yeah." Gregg helped her stand and turned her around gently. He swore violently when he examined her wrists. "I'd decommission those bots for this if they weren't already in pieces."

"How are we going to get these off without calling the police?"

"Oh, I'm a man of many talents. Mad scientist and bowling champ are only two of my many intriguing facets. Ask my mother, I've been able to pick locks since before I could walk."

She licked her lips. He sounded more and more exciting, just when she thought he couldn't possibly top himself. She turned her backside to him and wiggled her arms, eager to wiggle something else under his nose as well, but first things first. "Show me, Superman."

He made short shrift of her binds, helped her brush her teeth, and then drew her into his strong possessive arms.

Curling her grateful arms up around his neck, she molded herself to him. "I love you!"

He eyed her warily and pulled back a few inches. "How so? Gratitude for saving your poor arms?"

She dragged in a deep breath and decided to put everything out into the open but most especially her swelling heart on the line. Sometimes the only way to win was to gamble everything. "That, too. I *love* you with all my heart and soul. Desperately. Completely. Forever."

Gregg captured her lips in a searing kiss and fell with her to the bed. "You just stole my lines."

"I did?" Of course, she'd accused him earlier of being better at kissing than spewing love sonnets. She'd already reconciled herself to accept love in his heart and not demand a lot of pretty poetry if miracle by miracle, he truly loved her.

And he did! She'd count her blessings and be glad he wasn't a perfect robot, but a sinfully sexy, hot, gorgeous man.

Her man.

All hers.

After he ravaged her lips and came up for air, he gazed deeply into her eyes and stroked her mussed, very unruly hair lovingly away from her face. "Here in your arms I've found my only chance for my paradise, my only chance for happiness.

"Except for one."

"One what?" She slanted a perplexed glance up at him.

"Will you make me the happiest man in the world and marry me?"

Joy flooding her, she yelled, "Yes!" Then she veiled her lashes and added an addendum, "If I get to name our kids."

He looked away sheepishly. "Uh, I already sorta promised to name the first one, Scotty...."

"Don't you mean the first boy?"

"Well, your brother drives a hard bargain. He just said 'the first'."

She groaned and playfully punched her fiancé's shoulder. "The man's seriously warped, but I adore him to death. We'll figure it out when the time comes. I mean, you saved us from megalomaniac, world dominating robots, so you can save us from naming our firstborn girl 'Scotty'. I have supreme faith in you."

He feathered a kiss on her forehead, sending ultra delicious tingles all the way down to her toes. "You're so much more than a woman to me."

"I only want to be a woman. A flesh and blood, *flawed* woman." Purring in his arms, she snuggled closer to his beloved heart, carving her niche.

"If we're reincarnated in a thousand years, I know I'd fall in love with you again. This is forever, darlin'."

Had she truly imagined he wasn't poetic? She had a lot to learn about this man. And she would relish each and every day.

"Let's savor forever a minute at a time, starting right now." Even so, she wasn't sure forever would be nearly long enough to spend with him.

"I'd rather thought we'd already begun."

"We have, but before we go any further, do you think we can bury that toxic concoction in the back yard?"

He chuckled and linked his fingers through hers and pulled her off the bed so that she stood by his side. "Anything your heart desires, darlin'."

She quivered all over, eager to finish this necessary chore as quickly as possible so they could return to their bed and get on with her burning desire. "In that case, we have a lot of covers to tangle."

"And arms. And legs. And tongues...." He practically dragged her down the stairs, his fingers caressing hers, his gaze passionately devouring her.

She mated her fingers with his, burning to mate all the way. "Anything you say, *stud.*"

The End

INTERPLANETARY LOVE

By

Shelley Munro

Chapter One

"Do it. Do it to me now."

The woman's voice was thick with demand and lust. Ekim Ramuk stared, up close and personal, at her swollen pink labia and sighed inwardly. The third different female in his bed this week, and the week was barely started. Every bone in his body ached from shooting the action scenes for his latest vid-com, and he fought against a yawn. If he wasn't careful his reputation as the greatest lover on the planet Nidni was gonna kill him.

"*Pleeaase*," the woman moaned, thrusting her glistening clit closer to his face.

Ekim sighed again. Man, his tongue hurt. He ran his finger the length of her cleft then dallied, teasing the tiny bundle of nerves at the top, making her cry out in pleasure. His cock pushed against her leg. Rajah was satisfyingly firm, but still Ekim worried that his latest lover might notice his lack of competence. He blew a stream of warm air across her clit, trying to breathe through the pain. It was difficult to work up the energy to push the woman into climax. But the sooner he did it, the quicker he'd be able to extricate himself from the female's clutches and head for his parents' home and his mother's curry dinner. The comfort of his family--the only people he didn't have to pretend with. The only people he trusted not to serve him up to the paparazzi.

Ekim massaged her nubbin again, running his finger through her dripping honey. Taking a deep breath, he leaned closer. He thrust two fingers inside her pussy and brushed his tongue over her clit in an effort to finish her off and push her into orgasm.

172

Two swipes of his tongue did the job. Two swishes back and forward that sent pain shooting through his jaw and overworked tongue. Ekim rode out the agony in silence, sending up a prayer to Atsugua, the goddess of safety and health. Man, he hoped he didn't have to go on leave with a repetitive strain injury.

* * * *

"Take this, you bastard!" Carly Abercombie kicked the man square in the balls and watched him writhe about on the dance floor in time to the latest top forty hit. Acute satisfaction burned through her as she glared at yet another Earth dud. That would teach him to grope her on the dance floor.

Her latest date. Another failure. Part of her wanted to break down and cry but her co-workers were here tonight. And a cop didn't cry, especially a female cop.

"Don't think he'll try that again," her friend Samuel said with a pained expression on his tanned face. He remained a respectable distance from her, way out of kicking range. "What did he do to you?" Samuel looked Carly up and down and waggled his bushy eyebrows.

Carly shifted from foot to foot and resisted the urge to tug her bodice up and her hemline down. She wasn't used to dressing up but for tonight's celebratory dinner, she'd made an effort. A figure hugging black dress that showed lots of skin clung to her curves. Her feet were crammed in high heels that made her feel like a giraffe. And her hair was arranged artfully on top of her head.

"He shoved his fingers inside my panties," Carly snapped. "Nobody does that without my permission."

"You were asking for it," her date snapped, his tone vicious because she'd made him look like a fool. He'd climbed to his feet while she was talking to Samuel, but he, too, remained carefully out of range, lurking on the edge of the dance floor.

Disbelief raised Carly's eyebrows. "So it's all right for me to play with your dangly bits in a public place?" She shot him a look of disgust. Aside from the fact that the man needed the name of a good dentist, he'd been passable until he'd started drinking straight shots of tequila. "Forget I said that. Of course you'd get off on being groped in public." She whirled around and stalked away leaving Mr. Octopus to do his worst on the dance floor.

Silence fell as she approached her table. Her fellow workers, who were mainly men, wore identical pained expressions to Samuel.

"Shit," Carly snapped. "I only do that to men who grope me in the middle of the dance floor. Co-workers are safe unless they try to cop a feel."

"Good to hear," her partner, Bart drawled. "We're cops, but we don't feel." His laconic remark broke the silence, and everyone started talking at once.

"You okay?" Bart's wife whispered, her blue eyes full of compassion. Although the woman's intentions were good, Carly didn't want sympathy.

"I'm fine," Carly snapped. "Why wouldn't I be?" Inwardly, she winced at her behavior toward a woman who was trying to help. But Carly knew if she started to cry, she wouldn't stop. She snapped her fingers at a passing waiter. "Whiskey!" Perhaps she'd drown her sorrows. The night was young, and she had to stay for another hour at least.

It was gonna be a long night.

* * * *

Samuel and his date poured her into a cab and tossed her out at the other end. After making sure Carly made it inside her apartment safely, Samuel buzzed a kiss on her cheek and hurried back to his date. A hot one, he'd whispered to her earlier.

Envy kicked her viciously in the gut as she staggered toward her bedroom. Carly flung her clothes off, leaving a trail across the room. It wasn't fair. Her hands screwed into fists at her side, and she glared at the bed in lieu of a handy man to take out her frustrations on.

She wanted a lover.

A man with callused hands to strum over her breasts, to give her a good finger fuck when she needed it. A man with a decent sized cock that would fill her and make her come over and over. Dammit, was it so wrong to want a man instead of a vibrator? Since her divorce, she'd had a string of unsuccessful relationships. What had she done that was so bad? Why was she being punished? All she wanted was a man to spend time with, one who didn't bitch about the hours she put in on the job. A man who gave good head and enjoyed sex as much as she did.

Carly threw herself down on her queen-sized bed. She gave an inelegant sniff and scrubbed her hands across her damp cheeks.

"A man that tells the truth," she muttered. "The whole truth and nothing but the truth." Her eyes narrowed when her thoughts drifted to Matt. "Not like Matt." *Definitely not!* Not another lying, cheating creep who blamed everyone but himself for his shortcomings. "A sense of humor," she whispered. *Yeah, definitely.* Someone to make her laugh when the horrors of work became too much. "A man who doesn't have a cow when I work late." Carly screwed up her eyes, trying to force the aching tears away. Strictly low maintenance--that's what she wanted.

"Very, very elusive," she mumbled, staring at the ceiling. "Don't think there's such a thing. It's not as if I want Mr. Perfect." Just Mr. Almost Perfect.

Carly struggled from the comfort of the soft mattress and sat up to plant her feet on the floor. Needed to do something. Oh, yeah. *Work.* She staggered over to her computer and stabbed the power button. The bright colored screen brought a wrinkle to her forehead. Man, that light was bright. Carly sank into her chair while she waited, tapping her right foot on the ground and squinting her eyes against the glare. When the whirring and whining ceased, she directed the mouse to the email icon and clicked. Mail poured into her inbox. "Spam. Spam. Spam." Jeesh, did she look as though she needed a longer penis? A bark of laughter erupted. Not according to her ex. He was adamant that she, Carly Abercombie, was a ball buster. Nope, she didn't need a dick to add to her arsenal. Her mouse hovered over yet another spam email.

Interplanetary love. You are one click away from finding your true mate.

"Yeah, right," Carly scoffed, consigning that one to her trash bin as well. "Ah ha!" Carly scanned the email she'd been waiting for, then slumped back in her chair. A weeks worth of investigation down the tubes. Proof that Michaels wasn't involved in the illegal drugs ring. He'd spoken the truth when he'd said he'd been in Tonga on business. Carly pillowed her head in her hands, the need to scream starting to build inside.

"You have mail," her computer droned.

Carly jerked up her head and glowered at the screen. She couldn't even manage a sexy masculine voice for her computer. The one she'd chosen droned some days and other times, the voice rose to a falsetto that made her think of eunuchs.

Carly stared at the email that had arrived in her in-box. Pink. Corny flowers and hearts, and oh, no--the stupid thing came with music. Old fashioned country and western about cheatin' hearts. Jeesh, she knew about them. Carly thumped on the delete key, cutting off the music mid-bar. The resulting silence was a beautiful thing. For all of two seconds. Suddenly, it reminded

Carly that she didn't have a warm body to curl up with at night. No one to warm her cold feet on when she climbed into bed in the small hours of the night.

Carly stood and stooped to pick up her shoes and dress as she crossed the room.

"All by myself," she warbled before halting abruptly. "Talk about a pity party. Not an attractive trait, Carly."

Interplanetary love.

Would it be so bad taking one more chance? The email called to her like a tempting dessert or piece of chocolate. Not the artificial cocoa stuff, but the rich, full taste of the real product. Carly whirled and, against her better judgment, retrieved the email from her computer trash.

"Five hundred and fifty dollars," she muttered, reading the small print. Not bad considering she'd spent almost that much on a new dress and her share of dinner tonight. Carly sat in front of her computer, filled out the form and clicked send before she had time to second-guess. "Probably a scam," she said, watching the email leave her box. "Probably a rip-off."

* * * *

"I'm tired of grasping females. They're only interested in my reputation as a lover. They have no interest in me."

Rala Ramuk stared at her older brother in total disbelief. *Whining twit.* She tossed her gauzy, blue scarf over her left shoulder and straightened her gold embroidered tunic top with several sharp tugs. When anger continued to bubble, she leapt to her feet and paced the length of the receiving room, skirting a low wooden table with a wooden elephant perched on top.

Her parents were old-fashioned in that they adhered to the strict laws of the goddess of fertility and marriage. Rala glared at the likeness of Peti that smirked from a small alcove. Incense sticks burned, plumes of perfumed smoke rising to drift across the goddess' face and highlight the humor. The goddess-bitch thought her predicament amusing. Rala sucked in a huge breath. The incense smoke caught in the back of her throat and a huge sneeze erupted.

"You okay?" Ekim asked.

Rala gave a clipped nod, and he turned back to their father. No, she was not all right! The rules stated that children of a marriage must marry in birth order. Ekim showed no signs of giving up his single life while she had found her mate. And now she was stuck in limbo until Ekim found his mate.

"Rala, come and eat."

"Yes, Mama." Acting the dutiful daughter, she glided across the receiving room and into the formal dining room, trying to quell her irritation. She and Gregorius would never join if she didn't take action.

Interplanetary Love. She'd filled out the form in Ekim's name and chickened out at the last moment before sending it.

"Is there anyone special in your life, Ekim?" Mama asked, after the four of them were seated at the long table, all at the same end so they didn't have to shout.

"Leave the boy alone," Papa chided. "We will offer thanks for the good food and our health to the Goddess."

Topic closed, Rala thought. Beneath the table, her hands gripped her knees while she fought to stay silent. *Leave the boy alone.* Rala fumed. If she left the boy alone, she'd die an old maid. She'd never know what it felt like to hold her child in her arms or feel the slide of her body against Gregorius' in the joining bed. A leisurely loving. She'd remain confined to quickies whenever they could snatch them. She glanced at her brother and caught his arrogant smirk. In that moment, Rala decided to send the application form off to Interplanetary Love.

Chapter Two

"Ekim, would you chaperon me to a meeting with my friend from Earth?"

Why him? Ekim considered Rala's proposal and thought about the woman he'd seen skulking around his dressing room half an hour earlier. The blonde had winked suggestively when he'd seen her and mouthed, "Later."

Ekim shuddered inwardly. He was oral sexed out. His frustration levels were at an all time high. This morning's lover had left him weak and shuddering but not fulfilled. Rajah had certainly enjoyed being inside her mouth, but Ekim just felt empty. And she'd worn a perfume that made him have an allergic reaction. He'd coughed and spluttered until his eyes watered. The woman gave great head even though he hadn't come. She deserved a medal or an award. But then she'd started to work on Rajah again. She'd wanted more, dammit, when poor, limp Rajah had wanted a rest. Luckily, a stagehand had knocked on his door telling him he was needed on the set in half an hour. He'd left before the woman had demanded full vaginal penetration. Ekim fidgeted at the idea. He had no idea why he couldn't get Rajah erect enough to do a proper job. He'd consulted medicine man after medicine man. Mage after mage. They'd prescribed potions, delicacies to try, lotions to rub on Rajah, to soak him in, but nothing changed the facts. He couldn't have full sex with a woman. The joke was definitely on him. The planet Nidni's greatest lover couldn't get it up. The man with the honorary title of Nidni's greatest lover was a virgin. Technically.

Ekim ripped his thoughts off the worrying subject of sex and back to his sister. They'd argued so much lately, Ekim couldn't understand why Rala had sought him out now. "Where's your chaperon?"

Rala pointed at the elderly woman standing outside the doorway to the visitor's reception room. She watched each arrival with narrow-eyed scrutiny as if she expected them to spirit her charge away. Ekim wished! With her recent soaring moods, his sister was a pain in the backside, and Luci, the little katmer creature that she kept as a pet.... Ekim's thumb started to throb where Luci had bitten him two weeks ago during the family curry dinner.

Luci didn't seem to be with Rala today. Ekim directed his attention to his sister. "Why can't Aisha go with you?"

"I can't ask her to give up her afternoon off. She's visiting her daughter."

Good answer, Ekim thought with grudging approval, but something was wrong with this picture. Ever since Marisa had cancelled their betrothal, his sister had become increasingly sullen and resentful toward him. She blamed him for Marisa's departure. And after their last blowup, it was weird that she'd seek him out now.

"Please," Rala whispered, her brown eyes filling with tears. "I know this is short notice, but Carly is a cop. She works a lot of weird shifts." Her shoulder lifted in a delicate shrug. "You know what it's like. I don't know when we'll have another chance to meet."

Interest peaked in Ekim. A cop from Earth. She might give him some tips for his latest role. The alternative was a sweaty, embarrassing session with the woman in his dressing room. No contest really.

"All right," Ekim said. "I thought I'd drop in at home for dinner anyway. They don't need me on the set again until morning."

"Great." Rala tucked her hand on his forearm. "I think you'll like Carly. We've corresponded for ages."

"As long as she doesn't expect me to jump into bed with her," Ekim muttered.

A small brown hand flashed out to strike him over the head. "Ow!" Ekim turned to face Rala's irate chaperon. The woman had the hearing of a bat creature and moved like a shadow, sneaking up on a male at the most unfortunate times. "What did you do that for?"

"My baby is pure. You must not speak of sexual relations in her presence. Your reputation taints her."

"Sorry." Ekim glanced at Rala and saw her eyes were downcast. A becoming blush stained her cheeks. His sister had turned into an attractive woman and was probably resentful because she couldn't marry until he did. Family members on Nidni had to mate in strict birth order. To go against this law would bring down the wrath of the goddess. Ekim felt sympathy for Rala--he really did, but his life was no picnic. The constant parade of female sexual predators was wearing him out. And the paparazzi! Bah! Ekim forcibly shoved the evil creatures to the back of his mind.

"Give me five minutes to change." Ekim turned for the door, but Rala gripped his arm and tugged him to a stop.

"We don't have time. Carly's spaceship arrives at the main port in twenty minutes. Grab something to disguise yourself until we're clear of the reporters outside the studio. Oh, wait! I have a hat in my bag. You can use that." Rala opened a large black bag covered with yellow flowers, pulled out a floppy blue hat and zipped her bag back up.

Ekim glanced down at his tight black trousers and knee high leather boots. A black shirt hugged his chest. With his long dark hair slicked back he looked like a criminal or gang boss rather than the undercover law officer he was playing. The hat would clash terribly.

Sighing at the necessity of having a disguise, he accepted the hat. "All right, but I hope I don't scare your friend."

"I'm sure Carly will like you," Rala murmured. "My friends swoon over you. Can we go? I'm looking forward to meeting her in person." Rala tugged him in the direction of the door.

The thought of Rala's friends made him shudder. No wonder the females were so pushy if they started that young. His bottom had turned black and blue with bruises after a trip home coincided with a visit from Rala's friends.

"Ekim?"

Ekim shook away the remembered horror. "We'll leave via the rear exit to avoid the paparazzi."

"I'll leave by the front entrance," Aisha said, popping into the conversation with the stealth of a ghost cat. "Paparazzi will assume you stay here with brother."

Rala clapped her hands in delight. "Good plan. I like it."

"I'll need to grab my ID card and currency, but that won't take long." *As long as I don't have any unwelcome visitors in my dressing room.* They hurried down the stark corridors deep within the building, heading for Ekim's dressing room. When they approached, Ekim's gut started to churn. Hoping like hell that the loitering woman he'd seen earlier hadn't broken into his dressing room, he punched in the security number and cautiously opened the door. It was blessedly silent.

"Hurry up," Rala grumbled. "You know how long the rickshaw ride takes to the spaceport even with the new supercharged droids pulling them."

Ekim grabbed his ID and credit purse off a makeup-strewn counter. A small white envelope snagged his attention. That hadn't been there before. More fan mail left by his dresser. Or another nasty proposition. He stuffed it in his pocket to read later.

The back exit was paparazzi free. Ekim strode from the building and on to the street. A rickshaw driver leaned against a large oaka tree, his red and gold rickshaw parked and ready to hire. Ekim put two fingers to his lips and let out a piercing whistle. Acknowledging his signal with a casual wave, the rickshaw driver trotted over to them, his muscled body shiny with sweat from the seasonably warm day. Perfume from the large, white flowers that festooned the lill trees lining the street filled every breath Ekim took. He coughed, trying to forestall the building sneeze. It reminded him of the last woman who'd graced his bed. She'd made him sneeze too.

"Luckily I brought my parasol. Aisha will subject me to citrine and ass milk bathes for a week if I catch the sun. She treats freckles like a plague."

Ekim listened to his sister's mutterings with half an ear while he wondered about the contents of the envelope in his pocket.

The rickshaw driver started off at a trot, then turned on to the main thoroughfare. He spotted a gap and darted into it, smoothly switching to city speed.

The increased wind velocity tore Rala's parasol from her grasp. "Damn! Why couldn't you have summoned a covered rickshaw?"

An indignant shriek sounded, and Ekim glanced back to check the source. "Language," he scolded but without heat. Ekim grinned with unholy delight. Rala's parasol had hit Nisha Storrisome, one of the paparazzi, square in the kisser. The rail thin woman shook her fist, her gold bangles chattering like Rala's katmer in a bad temper. Ekim punched his fist in the air. "Good shot!" He forgot to hold his hat down and it sailed off his head, disappearing across the top of a juice stall.

Rala looked behind, her smooth brow creased in a frown. "Now they've recognized you. They're chasing us. Botheration. I wanted to talk to you."

"So talk."

"But they'll have listening devices trained on our rickshaw." She muttered a curse that raised Ekim's brows.

"I don't think that's anatomically possible," he retorted.

"You would know," Rala snapped back. "You being Nidni's greatest lover and pinup boy."

If only she knew. Ekim would give anything to have a normal relationship. Maybe the last medicine man he'd consulted on the neighboring planet of Indus had been correct, and Ekim's giant reputation was the cause of his disastrous symptoms. Rajah's failure to rise to the occasion was in his mind. Ekim scowled. He didn't like the theory any better this time.

Their rickshaw raced down the main highway, increasing in speed even further. They bypassed the main market area and sped through the upper class housing development with its large mansions and high fences. Once they left the confines of the city gates, the buildings gave way to trees and a lake. The hyper speed at which they traveled made communication difficult.

Since they couldn't talk Ekim gave into the impulse to read the contents of the envelope he'd found in his office. He pulled the envelope from his pocket, prepared to open it when a strident chatter drew his attention. "Did you bring that bloody katmer with you?"

"No!"

"I heard it. Where is it? In your bag?"

"Luci wasn't feeling well this morning," Rala said while she unzipped her bag.

A small pointy nose peeked out, then Ekim saw two black eyes. They narrowed to slits the second the creature noticed him.

"I didn't mean to sit on his favorite chair," Ekim muttered. "And I didn't stand on his tail on purpose."

An indignant chatter came from the katmer as if the wretched creature understood and strenuously denied Ekim's words.

Rala rubbed the katmer's glossy head. "Don't listen to my brother."

The katmer gave one last indignant squeak before starting a loud kitty purr.

Ekim grimaced and went back to his mail. He ripped the envelope and pulled out the plain white parchment inside.

I know your secret.

The words seared into Ekim's mind. He closed his eyes and opened them again. The words remained the same. Ekim stuffed the card back into the envelope and buried it deep inside his pocket.

Someone knew he couldn't get it up. Oh, man. He was burned chapattis. Ekim loved his job as an actor. It was the only thing that kept him sane. The sex and planet's greatest lover tag were a part of his career that had just happened. He hadn't planned it. The words danced through Ekim's mind.

I know your secret.

Blackmail? Horror chilled his body. The note hadn't said, but the threat was implicit. If someone knew his secret, they'd tell.

The rickshaw slowed to pass the exclusive houseboats moored at the far end of the lake before increasing speed again. Ten minutes later they halted at the spaceship security checkpoint. Ekim paid the toll entrance to the spaceport.

"Ekim, I have to tell you something." Rala grasped his arm. "It's important."

"Surely it can wait until later?"

"No." Her sharp tone drew his attention. Rala sounded worried. "Now." She hesitated before forging ahead. "Carly isn't really a friend."

"But you've corresponded with her." Ekim didn't have to pretend confusion. Rala refused to meet his gaze, and his bewilderment narrowed to suspicion. "What's going on?"

"I pretended I was you and signed you up for *Interplanetary Love*."

"The dating service?" Ekim's roar drew the attention of pedestrians entering the spaceport. "The dating service," he repeated in a terse whisper. Their rickshaw driver trotted toward the front doors of the spaceport.

Luci chattered in a warning fashion and that was the only thing that kept Ekim from throttling his sister--the thought of Luci's sharp teeth piercing his skin. "Explain. *Now*."

"I thought it would be nice for you to meet someone new. A woman who doesn't know about your reputation."

Better and better. Gut instinct told him Rala lied through her dainty white teeth. "Tell me exactly what you've done."

"I told her you were in law enforcement. But other than that I kept pretty much to the truth."

"How are we going to keep her from learning about my reputation?" Damn, he didn't need this.

"It will work," Rala insisted. "She's here for three nights. Don't take her into the city confines where you might run into the paparazzi."

* * * *

Carly noticed the man straight away. So did every other woman in the spaceport, but his attention remained on the petite woman at his side despite the heated whispering and come hither looks. A pang of envy pierced Carly. He was taller than Carly's six foot, and dressed completely in black. His black hair was slicked back to showcase the angles and shadows of his face. Carly stared at his mouth. The curves of his sensuous lips were made for kissing. Sighing, she turned her attention to the woman. Lucky lady, Carly thought as her gaze strayed to the man again to steal another hit of his hot sensuality. A shiver slid down her spine, delicious and naughty. Better than a morning shot of java. A woman just had to look at this man to know he'd be great in the sack. It was the way he held himself, the way he walked, all languid and lazy. It was in the charming smile and the dimples that winked suddenly at the corners of his mouth, wiping away the tough guy image. Carly resisted the need to fan herself. Oh, yeah. She wanted one of him in every flavor.

"Carly!" a voice shrieked. "You came!" Carly gaped as the petite woman who'd walked in with Mr. Hunk opened her arms and ran toward her. It was like a romantic scene from a corny movie--two lovers racing toward each other--and all Carly could think was she'd ticked the box specifying a heterosexual male.

She was sure of it.

"I'm so glad you came." The woman bounced up and down, looking like an exotic bird in her tight turquoise underblouse. Folds of material in contrasting blues and greens draped over her shoulder and fell to her feet, reminiscent of an Indian sari. A sheer scarf draped across her dark hair. She looked like an exotic bird, but not the bird for her. Carly steeled herself as the woman leapt at her, stealing a quick hug before pulling away.

"Please excuse my sister," the man escorting her said. "She's excited that you've managed to fit in a visit."

"Oh." That was all Carly could manage. The man was perfect. He looked good, he smelled great and his husky voice strummed right through her nerve endings. But after the greeting his sister had given, he probably thought she batted for the female side. Carly gave a feeble smile.

"I'm Ekim, and this is my sister, Rala."

This was Ekim? Carly's heart squeezed out an uneven pump. This was the man *Interplanetary Love* had hooked her up with? Every trace of spit dried from her mouth, and she could do nothing but gape. Luck had finally made an appearance in Carly Abercombie's life.

Chapter Three

Ekim tried hard not to stare at Carly. Rala was forgiven, not that he'd let her know too soon. His sister deserved to sweat. The transmitter in his pocket vibrated insistently.

"Excuse me, I need to take a call. Won't be long." Ekim turned away to take his call. "Ekim Ramuk."

"It's Yacel. How's the latest part going?"

"Fine," Ekim said to his agent. "It's a great part."

"Good. Good. The producers are thrilled with the publicity you're generating for this movie. They've decided to make it into a trilogy."

Ekim rolled his eyes. Nazrat, Cop had been shooting for two days, but with the paparazzi hanging around the set, publicity was through the roof. His bloody reputation.

"I've agreed in principle--all you need to do is sign on the dotted line. Whatcha say, big boy?"

Ekim cringed. "Sounds great," he said, forcing enthusiasm into his voice. He loved acting the part of a tough, no-holds-barred cop. But the bloody publicity, the constant pressure to perform with the women who threw themselves at him wore him down. He felt like a volcano ready to blow. They treated him like a toy.

Just for once, he'd like to be treated as a normal male. "I'll drop in at the offices tomorrow after shooting finishes for the day."

"Catch ya," his agent said, and after blowing a loud kiss, she disconnected.

"Sorry about that," Ekim said as he rejoined the two women. Interest spiked when he glanced at Carly. Tall for a female, she towered above his petite sister. Like him, she was dressed in black. Her trousers clung to her legs and hips while her tight black shirt revealed bountiful breasts. Brown hair with hints of red was pulled back from her face and tied with a piece of black cloth. Her mouth was wide, eminently kissable. Carly appealed to him on every level.

"Where are you taking Carly?" Rala asked, her expression bland.

A choking sound escaped Ekim before he regained control. The little minx. What would have happened if he'd refused to come with her this afternoon?

"I thought I'd take Carly for a drive before descending on the parents for a meal."

"Good idea. Can you drop me off at the vet? My katmer is feeling unwell."

Ekim hesitated, knowing he'd catch grief from Rala's chaperon if he left her alone, yet wanting to use the gift of time with this beautiful Earth woman.

"It's not far from the palace," Rala said in a wheedling tone. "The vet's sister will be present. She's one of my best friends."

"All right." Ekim offered his arm to Carly. "Right this way." She wavered for an instant before setting her hand in the crook of his elbow. Heat, sudden and unexpected, shot from her hand and seeped through the synsilk of his shirt. Rajah twitched insistently, and Ekim stilled, holding his breath. He glanced at Carly in astonishment. Was she the magical key to a normal sex life?

"Come on, Ekim. Stop day dreaming," Rala complained.

"Sorry. The rickshaw stand is this way."

They hired a closed rickshaw outside the main entrance to the spaceport. Ekim had no intention of allowing the paparazzi to glimpse Carly, not when their relationship was so new and full of possibilities. Ekim gave directions to the driver, helped Rala inside then Carly. He squeezed in beside Carly and tapped on the roof of the rickshaw to tell the driver they were ready to depart.

In the cramped confines of the rickshaw, Ekim smelled Carly's scent. It wasn't floral but more like something he would wear--

woodsy with a hint of cinnamon. Rajah stirred to life again, and for the first time in his life, Ekim worried about his erection showing. What would Carly think if she noticed?

"We can let the windows down once we leave the confines of the spaceport," Rala said. "The fumes from the spaceships cling to your clothes for ages."

Ekim arched a brow at Rala, and she winked in return. Good cover, he thought. He couldn't have done better himself. Three covered rickshaws had taken off at the same time, which would make the paparazzo's job difficult. They wouldn't know if their quarry had left or were still in the spaceport.

"I'm looking forward to seeing your planet. I hear it's very like the country India on my planet," Carly said.

Rala let the filmy scarf that covered her dark hair fall to her shoulders. "Nidni's founders are said to come from Earth."

Ekim watched Carly's expressive face, feeling excitement he hadn't felt for a long time. His woman, his mind shouted, and his heart echoed the sentiment.

"When is your flight back?" he asked.

Rala rushed into speech, a trace of alarm flitting across her face. "I'm sure you told me Carly was catching the night flight on Saint's day."

Ekim smothered a grin at Rala's attempt to cover. Her plan. Her problem. If Ekim hadn't liked the look of Carly, he would have found a way to extract himself. Work probably.

He turned to Carly, eager to learn more about her. "Do you enjoy your job?" Rala had said she was a cop, but what sort?

Carly smiled. "I told you in my letters. I love being a cop and making a difference even though the hours are long."

"You have a sexy voice. I wanted an excuse to hear it," Ekim murmured taking her hand in his. Her hand was warm and her fingernails clipped short and business like. They were large hands for a woman but they fitted with the rest of her frame.

Rala rolled her eyes at him from the far side of the rickshaw. If he blundered, it was her fault. Before he could stop, he imagined Carly plastered against him, their bodies moving together. A shudder swept the length of his body.

"Are you feeling the cold?" Rala asked, one delicate eyebrow rising in query.

Hell, no! Heat. Fiery heat spread to body parts and stirred them to life. Rajah danced a happy jig. While the phenomenon had occurred before, it had never happened with such vigor or rapidity.

Ekim shifted uncomfortably when he noticed the amusement on Rala's face.

"I think we could open the window now," he said. Scenery distraction. Good idea. He tugged on the window catch and let the window slide down. Fresh air swept into the interior of the rickshaw, but it did nothing to cool his ardor. This unfortunate rising of the Rajah pole had the potential for great embarrassment.

Carly glanced at his lap. She knew when a man wanted her, but the erection was a huge giveaway. She wanted to shout. She wanted to scream but resisted. Instead she sat calmly between brother and sister and tried not to squirm.

Finally the need to tease, to raise the stakes higher as it were, got the better of her. Carly leaned toward Ekim, pretending to look at the view. Not that it wasn't interesting because it was, but the idea of actually finding a male she liked right off had her in a lather. Literally. Her panties were damp and the V of bare skin at his neck teased and taunted. She wanted to lick. She wanted to bite. Oh, yeah. Carly wanted to use her mouth.

Instead, she leaned forward, pressing her breasts against his upper arm until her nipples brushed his biceps. The scenery flashed past her glazed eyes. Carly sucked air into her starved lungs but instead overloaded on his scent.

"That's the Blue Fort and the old part of the city. I can take you to the market later, if you'd like to do some shopping," Ekim said.

Shopping. Not if she had her way. What did she want with extra luggage on the way home? Oh, no. She had other things on her mind. If Ekim continued to impress her then no, there wouldn't be any shopping.

* * * *

Ekim's family lived in an honest to goodness palace that looked like the pictures she'd seen of the Taj Mahal apart from the color and the lush green plants and flowers in yellow and orange surrounding it. The palace was a beautiful honey color, and it gleamed in the afternoon light. Carly's breath eased out in wonderment as she stared. Then she laughed, glad none of her cop friends were present to witness her gaping mouth. How the hell had she lucked out with Ekim? She observed him from beneath lowered lashes. There had to be something wrong with him, but she had no idea what it was since there was no convenient sign on his forehead.

Carly sighed, trying to ignore the blast of cynicism that punched her in the chest. But it was true. Her track record was none too good with men. There had to be something wrong with this gorgeous man sitting at her side.

Ekim climbed out of the rickshaw before turning to assist Carly from the vehicle. Normally, Carly would have clambered down without aid. She was no pushover cupcake.

"I can do it," she murmured, good sense reasserting itself. But Carly miscalculated and tripped straight into Ekim's outstretched arms.

He gathered her against his muscled chest--close enough that she felt the uneven beat of his heart. She glanced up into his dark eyes. Carly pushed up on tiptoes to close the distance between them. His mouth was close, and she craved a taste.

A vibration against her hip made her eyes widen before realization set in. Ekim's phone. It wasn't a new sexual technique. Pity.

Grimacing at her pure neediness, Carly stepped away from Ekim to survey the palace again. She frowned, unhappy with her thoughts. Cripes, her emotions were closer to desperation than neediness.

"Can you pay the rickshaw driver for me?" Ekim handed her a handful of glittering coins. On seeing her helpless shrug, he smiled in understanding. "Give him all of the coins. It's the right amount plus a little extra for excellent service."

Ekim's smile made her insides tingle with awareness and anticipation. Warmth seeped into her cheeks bringing with it a sense of astonishment. Carly handed the coins to the driver and studied Ekim's face as he spoke into Nidni's version of a cell phone. She'd never felt this way before: the mixture of desire and the knowledge that this man could hurt her. She never fell hard and fast like this. Never.

Too full of a cop's cynicism and pragmatic with it.

Ekim finished his call, a broad smile on his kissable lips. "There's a problem with my case," he said in his husky voice. It made the hairs at the back of her neck stand to attention. "I don't need to go back into work. I'm all yours."

Carly heard sex loud and clear in his words, and her body rejoiced. Oh, yeah, baby.

"I promised my mama that I would take her on a pilgrimage to the Temple of Ynroh. It is a beautiful part of our country."

His mother! Disappointment soared through Carly, killing every bit of tingling anticipation in her nether regions. Talk about a

188

passion killer. His mother. "That sounds lovely." Carly knew her response was weak and attempted to raise it in the smile stakes.

Ekim lowered his head to whisper in her ear. "I know you're probably disappointed," he murmured. "I am attracted to you, but I'd like to get to know you before we advance any further. I hope you understand?"

Carly shivered at both his words and the moist air that skimmed the whorls of her ear. Oh, baby. Anticipation bloomed again along with a natural smile. This attraction wasn't one-sided. Suddenly getting to know Ekim sounded a whole lot better than jumping his bones straight off. Getting to know him indicated more than one date. It indicated a future.

Chapter Four

They caught a private shuttle ship to the village of Ytnelpxes where Ynroh Temple was situated. After disembarking, they walked through a short passage to an opulent room that looked like the frequent flier, first class lounges on Earth. Or at least they appeared similar to the rooms Carly had glimpsed while dashing through spaceports. Cops didn't travel in luxury.

"Ynroh is a special holy place for our people. Very sacred," Ekim murmured, taking her arm and ushering her up to a small counter to the right.

A young male in a pristine white turban and matching white tunic and trousers stood behind the counter. A selection of filmy squares of material, sorted according to color, sat in front of him.

"For the lady?" he asked. "What color would you desire?" His gaze drifted across her face and briefly across her shoulders. "Does memsab wish to match her scarf to her attire?"

Carly could have sworn distaste flickered across the man's face. She glanced down in case her buttons gaped or worse, her fly was broadcasting the type and color of knickers she was wearing. Nope. All intact.

"We'll take one to match her eyes," Ekim said, pointing to one in soft blues. Currency exchanged hands. "I'll help you put it on."

Ekim smoothed the loose tendrils of hair around her face and shook out the delicately embroidered scarf. He tucked one end under her hair, glanced over his shoulder at his mother and sister then pressed a quick kiss on her lips before he flicked the other corner of the scarf across her face. Carly would have argued about the scarf but noticed all the other women and men had their faces screened. It must be an etiquette thing.

"Couldn't resist a kiss," Ekim murmured near her ear. He pulled a black hat with silver stitching from his pocket and placed it on his head then turned to his mother. "Are you ready to go to the inn, Mama? Should I summon a rickshaw?"

"Not a rickshaw, Ekim. I wish to travel by bullock carriage."

Both Ekim and Rala groaned, and Carly caught Rala's chaperon grimace before her expression faded to neutral.

"As you wish, Mama." Ekim turned to her with a rueful grin. "You are in for an experience, Nidni style. Let's hope we can find an experienced driver. Would you like to come with me?"

Oh, yes please, Carly thought. Sudden heat in her cheeks let her know that the unfortunate trend in blushing was continuing unabated. Sex. She couldn't seem to stop thinking about the act. Carly glanced at Ekim. Specifically with him. The thought of running her hands across his bare chest made her hot, her nipples tight with need.

They made their way from the private room and stepped into the huge entrance hall where people waiting to depart hovered anxiously checking flights, mixing with hundred of excited arrivals. Ekim guided her through the crowds of excited pilgrims who had arrived to visit the temple of Ynroh. The scent of flowers filled Carly's every breath and the haze from burning incense made her eyes water. An elbow jabbed Carly in the ribs, knocking her off balance. Ekim drew her even closer, protecting her from the pushing and shoving of the animated crowd. Finally, they exited through huge glass doors. Outside, a stiff breeze blew, blowing and tugging at clothes, sending gauzy scarves fluttering madly.

"Hold tight," Ekim murmured in her ear. "It's the afternoon winds. They blow every afternoon for two hours."

Carly laughed. "Two hours? You're kidding."

"No, you can set your time piece by them. You'll see." He glanced past her and let out a piercing whistle that impressed the heck out of Carly. Whistling was one thing she'd never mastered. She blamed it on the tiny gap between her front teeth.

A whip cracked, audible over the sudden wail of the wind. A protesting groan followed then a loud squeak.

Carly's eyes widened in astonishment when the largest bovine looking beast she'd ever seen in her life pulled up in front of them drawing a beautiful glass coach that looked as though it belonged to Cinderella. Carly glanced down at her black combat boots. No Cinderella here, especially since her feet were a large, ugly sister size. A loud roar drew her attention back to the beast. Black. Huge. With its huge hump, it looked like a Brahman bull on steroids. The beast let out another roar and promptly lifted its tail. A steady stream of liquid waste dropped to the ground, splattering the coach. The stench was indescribable--something between a rubbish tip and a pigsty. Immediately, several small men appeared bearing shovels. The steaming pile was shoveled into a wooden cart and wheeled away. Another group of men arrived bearing buckets of water. Before Carly's startled eyes, they washed the glass coach until it sparkled again. Finally a group of women, the same height as the men, appeared with baskets of sweet scented flower petals. They tossed them over the beast and the coach driving away the horrid scent.

Carly shook her head as the tiny women vanished. Amazing. Nidni's version of a car wash.

Ekim ignored the whole process. He negotiated price with the wizened looking driver and after a long protracted discussion and much hand gesturing, gold coins exchanged hands.

"All set." He flashed her a grin that made her heart beat faster. "Wait here while I collect Mama and Rala."

Ekim strode back inside, and Carly seized the opportunity to check out his butt. Very grope-able. She sighed, the idea of waiting seeming like a bad idea when time was so short.

He returned almost straight away, pausing to hold the door open for several porters bearing luggage. Carly couldn't quite believe it was necessary for the few days they would spend here. A high-pitched whirring sound grabbed her attention.

"Load up as quickly as possible," Ekim called to the porters. They didn't seem to need the urging. Despite the bulk of the bags and packages they bore, the men scuttled about like busy ants.

"Mama, I don't know why we can't get a rickshaw instead of a bullock carriage," Rala grumbled.

"Stop complaining," Ekim said, his tone terse. He opened the door, extended the stairs and helped Rala and his mother inside, then Rala's chaperon.

"What's the problem?" Carly whispered.

His smile was grim. "Let's hope the driver is as experienced as he looks."

Carly climbed the stairs to enter the coach, feeling as though she was in the wrong story. She slid across the plush, fabric covered seat, smiling at Ekim when he entered the coach and sat at her side.

The luggage compartment groaned as it closed. A porter pushed the stairs back into place and slammed the door shut. Carly noticed everyone stood well back. She heard the sharp crack of a whip. Without warning, Carly found herself flying through the air. She hit her head on the wall of the coach nearest to her before Ekim grabbed her arm and hugged her tightly. The scent of exotic spices tinged with a hint of cinnamon surrounded Carly.

"You okay?" Ekim's warm breath tickled her ear.

"Took me by surprise, that's all." Carly struggled to move away and sit up.

Ekim's arms tightened around her. "Stay here."

"But what about--?"

"Don't worry. Mama, Rala and Aisha have all gone into a trance. They won't wake until we reach our destination in a half an hour."

Carly glanced over at the three women in surprise. She waved a hand in front of their faces and saw they didn't blink. They sat with a restraint belt around their laps, swaying gently with the movement of the carriage. "Why are they in a trance?"

"The ride might become rough. It depends on the skill of the driver and the mood of the beast."

"But if it's dangerous then why would your mother want to travel this way?"

"It's a status thing. She likes to go home and brag to her friends."

"Oh."

The bovine beast let out a cranky roar and swished its long tail. Without warning, it kicked up its heels, making the driver curse. The whip cracked and the beast roared again.

"How are you with heights?" Ekim asked.

"Okay." Carly peered in the direction he was staring and drew in a startled breath. "We're crossing that?"

If anything the winds were stronger, and the coach rocked in a dangerous manner.

"Yes."

Carly eyes the swinging bridge with doubt. Perhaps falling into a trance wasn't such a bad idea.

"Don't worry. Coaches have crossed this bridge safely for many years." Ekim ran his finger across her lips. "I've been wanting to kiss you all day."

"Okay." Carly's voice came out as an undignified squeak. Very uncool. Jeesh, her workmates would laugh themselves silly if they saw her acting like a girl. She attempted to pull up the cop look she wore when she interrogated a suspect. Her bad cop look.

A glint of humor flashed in Ekim's dark eyes, but before she had time to react his mouth covered hers. His lips tasted, coaxed, made her heart beat faster. Ekim cupped her face with one hand, stroking her cheek while his tongue slid between her parted lips.

Shimmers of sensation zapped through her bloodstream, converging and fuelling the flames that already burned and made her ache for him. She wondered briefly if her behavior made her a slut--kissing and throwing herself at him on their first date--then decided to worry about it later. Better to enjoy the magic while it sparkled through her body. Carly pressed even closer, elated to feel his erection prodding her upper thigh. They were in accord-- the attraction was mutual.

Ekim gently moved the gauzy scarf aside so he could run his fingers across her soft hair. If Rala had wanted to annoy him by arranging this blind date she'd miscalculated. Carly was beautiful. She was perfect. She tasted of tart lemons and sunshine and felt like heaven in his arms. Ekim explored her mouth, the softness inside her cheek and the contrasting hardness of her teeth. Her taste. Her scent. While they kissed, his hands wandered across her body, skimming her soft yet muscled arms. He thought about touching her breasts but decided he'd wait until they were alone, when he had a chance to unwrap Carly and savor her charms. He thrust his tongue a little deeper into her mouth before retreating. Goddess, the woman could kiss. But best of all, she had his full attention. Ekim wanted to howl his excitement out loud. Revved and ready to go, Rajah was very excited, and that was a rare occasion that demanded celebration. The latest potion he'd purchased from a mage in a small back street had done the trick, enticing Rajah into prominence.

"By the Goddess! Get a room! Eew, I'm not looking. My eyes are closed. Have you stopped exchanging spit yet?" His sister's voice intruded, forcing reality on Ekim. He was kissing Carly in a see through glass coach. The whole population of Nidni could see if they cared to look. Ekim pulled away from Carly and scanned the area for paparazzi. His sigh of relief eased out slowly. Luckily for them, not many paparazzi hung around the Bridge of the Single Strand.

Ekim glanced at Carly and wished his mother and sister and the chaperon were the other side of the planet. On second thought, perhaps it would be better if he and Carly were the other side of Nidni. He grinned. There was a couples only resort there that....

"Ekim!" Rala clouted him across the shoulder. "Get your mind out of the gutter."

"You'd better not let Mama hear you talk like that. You shouldn't have come out of your trance so early. We're midway across the bridge. Don't look down," he said innocently. Of course, all three of them looked down.

The bridge crossed a deep canyon. A swift flowing river forced its way through the rocks below, the white water surging and beating against huge boulders. The roar of the water was audible inside the coach. Huge crocobats made the canyon their home. Several hung from the rock walls while dozens swam in the water their jaws wide open to display sharp teeth.

Rala let out a feeble moan and promptly went back into a trance.

Ekim curled his arm around Carly. "You okay?"

"No problems for me. I'm a cop."

Ekim's gaze wandered from her eyes to her kiss swollen lips. "I'd like to kiss you again."

"Yes," she said, offering her lips. "I'd like that."

"I want to do more," he whispered, his gaze lowering to the curves of her breasts. He could see they were nicely shaped even though the black top she wore covered her from neck to waist.

"What?" Carly glanced at the other occupants of the coach before squirming closer to him.

Ekim smiled. "Let me tell you." He paused, pondering where he'd start his exploration, his gaze drifting to their surroundings outside the coach.

The wind howled. The coach rocked and the whip cracked constantly, forcing the beast to continue across the narrow bridge.

"Gedup!" the driver hollered.

Ekim turned back to Carly. "I think I'd start by loosening your hair and running my fingers through the strands. Maybe I'd take the time to massage your head in the Nidni manner. I'd press here." He tapped her finger at her temple. "And here, so the pleasure starts to swell and hum through your body until your sex weeps for my possession and aches for me to come inside you."

"What next?" Her blue eyes were wide, the pupils dark.

Ekim ran the pad of his forefinger across her mouth before tracing the curves of her lips. "I'd strip your clothes off very slowly and massage your skin with the finest Nidni oils while I discovered and explored your body."

"What scent?" The pulse beating in her neck quickened.

His finger popped into her mouth when she spoke and before he could remove it, she closed her lips, holding his finger in her warm heat. They stared at each other, scarcely breathing during the intense awareness. Rajah swelled, a taut and needy sensation springing to life in his balls. She ran her tongue across the tip of his finger and gently sucked.

Ekim gasped, the heat of arousal sweeping into his face. "I'd use a spicy oil mix," he whispered. "I'd get the perfumer to mix a special blend to suit your personality."

Carly sucked on his finger again before letting it pop from her mouth. "Where would you rub the oil first?"

"I'd want to do everything slowly. Allow the anticipation to build, but I know I'd feel impatience, so I'd dribble a little oil on your breasts. I'd massage your curves inch by inch until your skin absorbed every trace of oil. Then, I'd turn you over and massage your shoulders. I'd work my way down your body, rubbing the scented oil into your buttocks, your thighs and calves. Your feet."

"And then where?" Carly's voice was a needy whisper.

"I'd turn you over again and redo your breasts until your nipples were tight with need. I'd work my way down your body, maybe snatching a kiss or two."

"Then what?" Carly asked in a hoarse voice.

"I'd part your legs and give you an intimate kiss. But not straight away," Ekim said. "I'd want to touch and stroke on some scented oil the length of your cleft. I'd touch you everywhere except your bud."

"You'd tease me?"

Ekim pressed a kiss to her lips and followed the touch with a slow, lazy exploration. By the Goddess, he thought he might embarrass himself and explode if this went on much longer. And that would definitely be a first.

"I'd want us to both reach the ultimate pinnacle together. The little death. I'd stroke you and enter your channel with my fingers. First one finger and when you accepted me easily, I'd use two and then three fingers. By that time, I'd need to taste you so I'd lift you to my mouth and lick your juices. I'd kiss you, sucking your erect bud with my mouth. But I wouldn't let you come."

"Oh, man," Carly murmured, her voice not much more than a groan. "How long would this take?"

"How long do you think you will have here on Nidni?"

"Ekim." Carly buried her face against his shoulder, gripping his shoulders tightly as if she would never let go. "When can we do this?"

Ekim closed his eyes for an instant, savoring Rajah's insistent throbbing at his groin. Soon. Hell, he hoped it was soon.

Before he could answer, Carly said, "Maybe we can arrange for some time together this evening?"

"I'll see what I can arrange after we've visited the temple. I think you'll enjoy Ynroh. Most people do." Ekim scanned the road ahead. "Hold tight," he warned.

The coach hit a series of potholes in the road. The restraint holding the women opposite popped open. One after the other, Rala, his mama and Aisha bounced off the plush seat to land in a heap on the floor.

"We'll leave them there. They'll only fall off again. The road gets worse."

"But won't they be hurt?"

"The trance protects them. Don't worry."

A loud snort erupted from one of the women on the floor followed by a series of rhythmic snores.

"See what I mean?" Ekim muttered. "They're very comfortable down there. We're the ones that will suffer."

Chapter Five

Rala suppressed a groan and an unladylike curse. "I'm bruised all over," she snapped while she waited with Ekim for their room allocation. "Why didn't you strap us in again?"

"Because I couldn't keep Carly safe and grab the three of you at the same time. I'd quit complaining if I was you." Ekim cast a sly glance at his mother and Carly before turning his attention back to his sister. "Mama wouldn't be very pleased if she knew what you've been doing on your 'puter."

"But--" Rala grimaced and stared at Ekim through narrowed eyes. "Okay. You win this round."

"You make it sound as though we're in competition."

This wasn't a competition, Rala thought. It was a battle to win her love. Gregorius was too honorable to run off as she'd suggested, which is why she'd decided to take the situation into her own hands. Rala had no intention of turning into a dried up old appleberry, of no use to anyone except as a chaperon. Luckily, she'd been able to talk Gregorius into sex. A grin flirted with her lips at the thought. A memorable seduction indeed. Their weekly sessions were the only thing she had to look forward to these days. Rala felt the secret smile widen. She liked sex way too much to wait for her brother to decide to take a mate. And judging by the way her brother and Carly were sucking face already, her plan had worked. Gregorius, sex-god, here I come.

Pity that Ekim and Carly weren't forced into sharing a room. Unfortunately with Mama along plus Aisha intent on showing a good example, there would be no shenanigans between sexes.

But Ynroh Temple--now that was a different matter. Rala held back a smirk, knowing that Carly would get the shock of her life when she saw the temple. If the temple didn't give her some ideas of what she and Ekim could do together then the Earth woman wasn't the right one for her brother.

Rala couldn't wait to see the Earth woman's reaction. Could not wait.

* * * *

"This is Ynroh Temple?" Carly gazed at the erotic friezes on the temple walls, very aware of Ekim at her side. "Um ... it's ... um ... different." She had the absurd desire to fan the heat from her face.

Ekim's mother went on a pilgrimage to an erotic temple? Carly couldn't help a surreptitious glance at Ekim's mother. The woman looked like Carly expected a wife and mother to look--loving, ordinary--apart from the colorful dress she could pass for an Earth woman. She was like Carly's mother or one of her aunts. Carly took in the woman's beatific smile as she scanned the panels of the temple. The temple ... the erotic positions made her wonder about the woman's sex life. Did she? Carly's glance shot to the nearest temple wall again. The figures depicted were acrobats. They had to be with their limbs entwined and bent in that manner. Carly's legs and joints ached at the thought of emulating the figures. She was all for experimentation but this...

"Would you like me to show you around?" Ekim murmured next to her ear.

Carly nodded, wondering at the same time what one did on a pilgrimage. She gazed at the nearest frieze again and felt renewed heat crawl over her cheeks. They didn't have orgies, did they? While she wanted sex and would jump Ekim's bones in a heartbeat--if he gave the nod--she liked her sex on the private side. A kiss in public, like this afternoon, was about as adventurous as she liked. Give her cool sheets, one man and privacy and that was another story. Maybe, she'd stretch to two men if the circumstances were right. Carly glanced at the entwined couple carved in stone in quiet speculation. Maybe she was missing out by not having sex in public?

"What does one do on a pilgrimage to this temple?" Carly asked finally when curiosity became too much for her. She tugged at the scarf around her face, loosening it so she could feel the soft breeze on her cheeks.

Ekim's grin was wide and toothy, visible even though his hat screened most of his face and covered his dark hair. "What ever you like," he murmured, leaning close enough that his spicy scent surrounded her.

Carly suppressed a groan when his warm breath drifted across her ear. Who'd have guessed that an ear was an erogenous zone? She shuffled from foot to foot, the proximity of Ekim and the atmosphere of the temple making her all too aware of how much she craved the release of good, hot, sweaty sex.

Ekim grasped her arm and drew her gently away from Rala and his mother, deeper into the temple. Inside, it was much darker, more intimate. Torches tucked in wall sconces lit the way, but there were plenty of dark alcoves for amorous couples. Judging by the giggles and deep breathing when they walked inside, many of the private spots were in use.

"Some people come to learn while others come to socialize," Ekim said.

Carly digested his words and tried to apply them to his mother and sister. It was probably better to concentrate on this than the urgent need building inside her. She pictured mother and daughter.... Uh-huh. Imagining naked women wasn't her style at all! Ekim, now he was a different story. As she walked at his side, she was aware of his masculinity and the dampness between her legs.

"Does your father visit?" she asked, frowning at the breathy tone. She had to get a grip. Jeesh! Bad word choice. She did not need to get a grip no matter what her body craved. Her gaze darted to Ekim's groin and away again before he noticed. No gripping with body parts. Not here with his mother and sister behind them.

198

"Sometimes." Ekim chuckled. "He encourages my mother to visit. I think he enjoys the benefits on her return, but I try not to think of it, you understand. I'd rather think about you. And me."

That was it! Carly's control slipped. She grabbed Ekim and yanked him into the nearest alcove, uncaring of whether it was occupied or not. She slammed against his body, drew his head down and kissing him for all she was worth.

For an instant he did nothing, then his arms came around her and he held her tightly, kissing her back with gratifying urgency. Their lips slid against each other, nibbling. Tasting. Getting better acquainted.

Her hands slid under the hem of his shirt to explore his smooth chest. Muscles flexed under her exploring hands.

"By the Goddess. Carly," he murmured.

Her busy hands retreated to cup the impressive bulge at his groin. He groaned, thrusting lightly against her hand.

Hard rock dug into her back and cool air brushed the bare skin of her belly where Ekim had lifted her shirt. Carly didn't care. She wanted with an urgency she'd never experienced before.

"Ekim? Ekim!" Rala's voice intruded on their private moment. "Where are you? Ekim?"

Ekim pulled away from Carly but continued to hold her. Rajah was getting closer and closer to an explosion. Astonishment along with excitement made him desperate to continue, but he knew from Rala's tone this little episode was over.

"She's not going to go away," he murmured, pressing a lingering kiss to Carly's smooth forehead. "We'll continue this later." A success! The latest potion was doing the trick. He wanted to shout his exhilaration. Rajah was alive and kicking, ready to go out on the town.

The last time he and Carly had fooled around hadn't been a one off.

"Ekim?" Rala's panicked voice jerked him into action.

"We're here. What's the problem?" Ekim moved out of the dark alcove to join his sister near a wall sconce. When Carly joined them, he curled his arm around her waist despite Rala's presence.

Rala's glance contained uneasiness when she glanced at Carly. "There's a reporter and a cameraman filming a news segment for the news. I thought you and Carly might like to be filmed. It's going to be beamed all over the galaxy on the evening news." Although her delivery was full of excitement, Ekim caught the underlying subtext. He and Carly had to blow this joint or risk exposure. The hat and scarf probably wouldn't make it in the disguise stakes with keen-eyed reporters about.

"A cameraman?" Carly said in distaste. "I don't want to be filmed. I'd never live it down at work. Please, I'd rather not."

"You sure?" Ekim asked, trying to keep the satisfaction from his voice. A close call indeed. No wonder Rala sounded anxious.

"Very. I don't like crowds. Besides, it's a good idea for cops to keep out of the news if possible. I've helped put away enough crims that I have enemies. You must be the same."

Crap. He'd forgotten Rala's falsehoods for a moment. A subject change required. "We can go back to the hotel, or we can explore the far end of the temple. Not many people risk going there since some of the buildings are dilapidated."

"It seems a shame to return to the hotel so soon," Carly murmured.

"I agree," Rala stated. "Carly should see some of the planet while she's here, not just the inside of a hotel. Why don't you take her to the Widow's Whisper? With the vid-cam crew here at the main area, the Widow's Whisper should be quiet."

Ekim glanced at Carly. "What do you think?"

"I'm in your hands," she murmured.

Goddess, yes! He hoped so. Rajah jerked at the sound of her voice. He couldn't wait to see what her hands, along with his latest potion, would do when they stroked him.

"Wait here and I'll signal you when it's clear to leave. You won't want to get captured on film." Rala hurried from the temple leaving them alone.

Ekim leaned down to brush a kiss across Carly's tempting lips. He lingered and repeated the process, stroking his tongue across her lips and urging her to open to him.

"Cripes, are you two at it already?" Rala shouted from the doorway of the temple. "Everyone is at the main reception area. Hurry! You're going to miss all the fun."

His sister, the little conspirator. Ekim lifted a hand in Rala's direction signifying that he'd heard and understood. Taking Carly's hand in his, they exited the temple and headed away from the crowds, only easing up on the pace when Ekim saw the path leading to the Widow's Whisper was empty.

"What is the Widow's Whisper?"

Ekim grinned without warning, tightening his grip on Carly's hand. "It's a quiet place where I can kiss you."

Carly's glance was full of heat, and it felt as though she trailed her hand across his chest. His muscles tightened. Ekim eased out a breath. "Rumor says that a widow, deranged after her husband died, leapt off the cliff, falling to her death. It's said that she wanders the paths whispering to those who walk with their true love."

Carly's dark brows shot upward toward her hairline. "Are you a romantic? I haven't met a cop before who was."

Guilt wiped the humor from Ekim. By the Goddess, he hated lying to Carly. He opened his mouth to tell her the truth before changing his mind. If Carly knew he was a film star and famous on Nidni, she might behave differently toward him. Ekim liked her even though they hadn't known each other for long. Rajah liked her, dammit, and that was the important thing.

"If I'm with a woman I like to treat her well, give her my undivided attention so if that makes me romantic, then I guess I'm guilty. But I don't believe in the legend of the Widow's Whisper."

Carly chuckled. "Me neither, but it's a pretty tale. Cops are realists." She lifted one shoulder in a shrug. "Some people might call it cynicism."

A loud wail rent the air, making the hair at the back of Carly's neck prickle.

Ekim appeared startled too, glancing around the vicinity with a scowl on his face, his dark eyes narrowed in suspicion.

The wail repeated. A large gust of wind tugged at Carly's scarf. Ekim's hat blew off his head. He scrambled after it, grabbing the black hat an instant before it toppled into the ravine below.

"Carly and Ekim. Forever," a ghostly voice whispered.

Ekim stormed back to Carly and placed a protective arm around her shoulders. "Is that you, Rala?"

"Why would your sister pull a stunt like this?" Carly said, scanning every possible hiding place for signs of a prankster.

Carly caught the hint of red that appeared high on his cheekbones, and the way his scowl deepened. The man had a flaw. Carly wanted to smile despite the circumstances. Temper she could deal with since she had one of her own.

"My sister has a warped sense of humor," Ekim muttered. "You have no idea."

Another gust of wind tugged at their clothes and chilled their faces.

"Ekim. Carly. Forever."

Their names hovered in the air before fading. They echoed off the pale white cliff on the other side of the ravine, without warning startling Carly into a flinch.

Ekim's arm tightened around her shoulders, drawing her against his solid bulk. Carly cuddled close, her heart thumping against her ribs. That voice didn't sound like Ekim's sister to her, not with the way it was echoing around them coming from all directions.

"Rala wouldn't have had time to arrange such an elaborate trick," Carly murmured when the wailing ceased.

Ekim shrugged, but he appeared as uneasy as her. "Are you ready to go? There's a wonderful park on the other side of the village. We can get the hotel to pack us a picnic basket for dinner instead of having a meal at the hotel. I'll leave a message for Mama so she knows we are out for the evening."

"Just the two of us? Alone?" When Ekim nodded, a slow grin curled across her mouth, driving away the prickling skin caused by the whispers. "Sounds great."

Ekim kept her close, pressed against his side. Warmth from his body crept into her skin slowly--unfurling tendrils of heat. Promises of what was to come. Her nipples peaked against her plain cotton bra. The beat of her heart picked up in pace while Carly's skin became ultra sensitive wherever Ekim touched her. She hadn't felt such anticipation since ... since she couldn't remember when. And for a picnic of all things. She was a city girl. She generally started sneezing when she went anywhere near the countryside and green plants. But for Ekim, she'd risk it.

Chapter Six

The porter hailed a covered rickshaw and handed them the laden picnic basket once they'd climbed onboard. When Ekim tapped the roof of the rickshaw, signaling they were ready to leave, the driver trotted off down the street.

Inside the privacy of the rickshaw, the arousal from earlier intensified until she was a quivering mass of expectation. Carly was very conscious of Ekim sitting beside her--his scent and his masculinity. The urge to grab the front of his shirt and rip it off him thrummed through her with powerful intensity. The more time she spent with him, the more she wanted him in every way.

For a girl who was used to going all out for what she wanted, when she wanted, the waiting was torturous.

"Tell me about the park we're going to," Carly said. If she couldn't touch him in the way she wanted at least she could listen to his incredibly sexy voice and imagine he wanted to love her. Just listening to him made her hot.

"There's a walk along the edge of a stream, lots of beautiful flowers in all the colors you can imagine. A waterfall drops into a pool that's perfect for swimming. That part of the park might be busy but a little further along the stream, there's a smaller waterfall with a private clearing not far off the path. I thought we might dine there. If we're lucky we might see a tycat. They're tiny striped cats, not much bigger than my hand. It's said that luck will follow the person who sees a tycat."

"It sounds wonderful," Carly murmured. She'd popped a couple of pills when they'd stopped at the hotel. Everything would be fine as long as the anti-pollen pills kicked in. Nothing worse than a red, swollen nose when she was trying to look sexy and seduce a man. Tonight was the night she'd finally have Ekim's hands on her bare skin, touching her all over. Her shoulders. Her breasts. In the small, achy, very needy place that throbbed between her legs.

Twenty minutes later the rickshaw slowed before stopping. Ekim paid the driver, and they clambered down. In perfect harmony, they wandered hand in hand down one of the paths that meandered along the edge of the stream, before turning into a copse of trees. The tree trunks were brilliant red while the leaves on the trees were long green and red strands, almost like coarse hair.

"When does night fall?" Carly asked, dodging a branch that grew over the path. Although her watch showed the hour was late, a bright light shone high in the sky. Carly had no idea what they called their sun.

"We have hours before darkness falls," Ekim murmured. "During this time of the season cycle we only have two hours of darkness. Here we go. This is the smaller of the waterfalls. We came via the most direct route."

He placed the black bag containing their meal on the ground and squatted to open it. "I think we'll set up just over there."

Carly turned and saw he pointed to a small clearing that was perfect for a private picnic. If anyone chanced to walk along the path they wouldn't see them unless they stepped off the path. Carly followed Ekim into the clearing and stood back to watch him while he dealt with more practical matters. She didn't think she'd ever tire of studying his strong face, his tanned skin and his dazzling white smile. The man was centerfold material. The thought brought a frown and a reality check. From experience she knew good-looking men often played the field--her ex being one of her experiences. Perhaps she should put a brake on her runaway hormones.

"Sit." Ekim gestured at the blanket he'd spread on the soft, brown grass-like plant that grew along the edge of the paths. "I'll see what the hotel staff has packed for us."

"I'm not hungry," Carly said, leaning back on her elbows to study their surroundings. "Not yet, but you go ahead if you want."

Sudden panic assailed Ekim. Carly had a familiar glint in her blue eyes. Not that he minded the way her gaze lingered on his face, his body. The thing was ... what if Rajah failed him? Ekim reached for the leather straps of the black picnic bag and noticed his hand trembled. Shook, by the Goddess. His gaze drifted to trace the curve of Carly's cheek, the lush red lips and a sudden intense longing filled him. He'd never wanted a woman as much as he wanted Carly. Ekim attempted to unbuckle the straps holding the containers and bottles in place and frowned, trying to work out how she'd wormed her way into his affections so quickly. Part of the attraction was the fact that she didn't know of his film-star status. Although Ekim wasn't sure how long he'd be able to keep that from her. She was bound to see stories in the media at some stage or, even worse, they might run into the paparazzi. She'd appear in the media then, even if she didn't want to. The realization came that it would be better if he told her first. Now. He opened his mouth to spill the truth but shut it again before he uttered the words. His gaze hit her lips and lingered. She'd hardly want to kiss him if she found out he'd lied to her. Maybe he'd tell her later.

"I thought we might have a drink," he said, aware that Rajah had subsided and was fully at rest even though a beautiful woman lay at arm's length. Sighing inwardly, Ekim lifted a bottle out of the bag to check the label. "There's juice or eparg wine."

"I'll try the wine, thanks. I guess it's like Earth wine? Never mind. I'll try it." Carly lay back on the blanket and closed her eyes allowing Ekim to look his fill. The scarf had come adrift, leaving her hair to fall loose. With each breath she took, her breasts strained against the cloth of her shirt. Ekim swallowed, his mouth as dry as the deserts to the south of Nidni's main town. Jerking his attention away from the tempting sight, he reached for the bottle of wine. He screwed the metal cap to open the bottle. Ekim jammed the bottle between his legs to keep it upright and wiped his clammy hands. Nerves. Ekim gritted his teeth and tried to relax. The doctors and the mage he'd consulted had all told him he must remain calm. Easier said than done. He pulled two goblets from the bag and filled them both before replacing the lid on the bottle.

"Carly, you awake?"

"Just," she murmured, her voice thick with relaxation. As she spoke, her lids flickered and her eyes opened. She smiled lazily. "What?"

"You're very beautiful." And it was true, although not perhaps in the strictest sense, and not if he judged her by Nidni's standards of beauty. Her mouth was a little wide, her eyes not the pure blue that bespoke beauty and her nose was on the large side. But Ekim liked the way she looked, and he especially liked the way he didn't get a sore neck because of the difference in heights. Carly was self-sufficient. Confident. A cop.

She wrinkled her nose. "I don't think my ex-husband would agree."

Ekim shrugged, trying to push away the knowledge that Carly had prior experience of successful sex. He forced his hands not to squeeze the goblets so tightly. "His loss."

Carly sat up to accept the wine. Their hands touched during the transfer and to Ekim's surprise, Rajah stirred with enthusiasm once again. He couldn't help the cocky grin that sprang to life. Perhaps all was not lost.

"I try to keep telling myself that." Carly paused to take a sip of her wine. "Oh, nice. It has a hint of lemon. I like it."

"Your husband didn't deserve you." Curiosity prodded Ekim to ask more questions. "Is he a cop?"

"Not on your life. Cops have to start off honest. My ex doesn't have an honest bone in his body. That's part of the reason I left him. And he has a gambling problem and difficulty in confining his dick to one woman," she added in a tight voice. "The man doesn't tell the truth unless it suits him. Heck, he probably can't remember what the truth is because he lives so deep in his little fantasies."

Although her face remained expressionless, Ekim heard the underlying pain. He also realized that not telling Carly the truth about his occupation was going to lead to big trouble. Hell, not telling her about the deception that Rala had pulled would stir things up too. He sipped at his wine while he debated how to introduce both subjects. No matter how he shaped his thoughts he'd already passed the point of no return when it came to Carly. Ekim dragged the bag closer and examined the contents. Maybe he'd eat something. His hand came into contact with a piece of paper. He pulled it out and unfolded the single sheet.

I know your secret.

"What's that?" Carly asked.

"A list of the contents," Ekim said, folding the note up and sticking it inside his pocket. Another bloody note. He was being stalked by a phantom who left blackmailing notes. "Are you sure you wouldn't like a pakora or a samosa? Some cheese from the planet Franco?" Crap. Another lie to Carly. But even more worrying--how did the note get inside the bag? Who knew about Rajah and his virginity? "Or could I tempt you with some luscious berries?"

"Does anyone swim in the stream?"

Ekim stilled. "As far as I know there are no crocobats in residence this far up."

"I'm not sure what a crocobat is, but I'll take your word they're dangerous. It's much hotter here than on Earth. I thought I might go for a swim." As she spoke Carly unbuttoned her shirt and slid it off her shoulders.

Ekim gaped when she stood and unfastened her black trousers. They slid down her legs leaving her clothed in a pair of matching white garments. "You're going swimming?"

"Unless you have a better idea," she murmured.

Rajah stood to attention with such vigor that Ekim wanted to groan out loud. "Did ... did you have anything in mind?" he asked hoarsely.

"Wanna fool around?"

Ekim found himself nodding dumbly. Crap. When he messed up he did it big time. His big secret was going to come out whether he liked it or not if he didn't slow things down with Carly. Icy fingers of fear stroked his skin bringing a shiver despite the warmth of the evening.

Carly lay beside him on the blanket. "I'm all yours," she said with a wicked grin. "Do your worst."

Ekim's mouth watered as his gaze wandered her partially clothed curves. Desire battled with cowardice. What was the worst thing that could happen? She could laugh at him and do an interview with the paparazzi. His heart burst into a series of weird skips and jumps at the thought. No, he didn't think she'd do an interview. It didn't seem like the type of thing she'd do. Even though they hadn't known each other for long, her innate honesty and integrity were obvious.

Ekim couldn't remember ever being attracted to a woman so much. Her skin was a golden color as if she toasted in the sun. He wanted to touch so badly. Was it wrong to take advantage of her willingness and see where their relationship might lead? His thoughts drifted in turmoil. He dithered and wondered if she was that golden color beneath her remaining clothing. Then, he took a deep breath. Only one way to find out. He could do this. He could make love to her fully. And he would, by the Goddess! But first he'd explore with his fingers and hands, with his tongue. He'd enjoy himself and play a little while Rajah got in the mood.

Ekim tossed his hat aside, hesitated then removed his shirt. He dearly wanted to slide his chest across hers and feel naked skin against naked skin.

"I think you're the beautiful one," Carly murmured, her hands busy exploring his biceps. She grinned up at him, her blue eyes dark with devilment. "So, explore me. Do you need a map? Go on. You know you want to." Her gaze skimmed Rajah, and his cock reacted with unusual vigor.

See. The Goddess would take care of him. All he needed to do was believe. Ekim forestalled further discussion by kissing Carly. Immediately, Rajah pressed against the placket of his trousers, the pressure so great it was almost painful. His balls drew tight, and Rajah wept. He actually wept at the thought of becoming closer to Carly. Exhilaration poured through Ekim. He wanted to leap to his feet and dance a jig of celebration, but he didn't. Instead, he deepened his kiss, sliding his tongue between Carly's parted lips. She tasted of tart wine. Addictive. His hands cupped her face, fingers sliding through her soft tresses. His heart thudded while Rajah continued to plague him, urgently wanting to escape confinement. The unusual demand from his member was so unexpected and unusual, Ekim decided on a little torture. Payback! That would teach the critter to have a mind of his own....

Ekim pulled back so he could see Carly's face. Her lips were red and swollen from his kisses, and her nipples were puckered and easily visible through the cloth that covered her breasts.

"Let me take this off," Ekim said. It was going to be all right. It really was. Soon he wouldn't have a secret to worry about. His nimble fingers undid the back closure and freed her breasts. He drew the garment down her arms and tossed it aside.

"Kiss me again," Carly said.

Ekim kissed her eyelids and pressed his mouth to the tip of her nose. "That okay?"

Carly grasped his head between her hands and forcibly directed his mouth to one breast. "Kiss me here. My breast," she said, spelling it out.

Her nipple pouted, standing upright in a silent bid for his mouth. The dark pink tip trembled as he watched. "Are you nervous?"

"Yeah. I mean, I like sex, but I don't know you well. I don't usually jump into the sex straight away. What if I disappoint you?"

"You won't disappoint me," Ekim said with certainty. It was more likely he'd disappoint her, but he wasn't about to confess that little germ of information now things were getting interesting. "Let's take things slowly. There's no need to rush. Turn over and I'll help you relax."

"I don't want to relax. I need release," she muttered.

"Trust me. You'll like this."

Ekim pulled a small bottle of scented oil from the picnic bag. When he's seen it earlier he'd thought it was a strange addition, but then, maybe not. He'd noticed the hotel had included several aphrodisiacs and items for lovers within the basket. Being in the same town as Ynroh temple probably put most people in mind of sex.

He broke the stopper and tipped the bottle so the oil dripped the length of her spine.

Carly screeched, raising her upper body off the blanket. "That's cold!"

"You'll warm up soon," Ekim promised, smiling at the glimpse of plump breasts. Carly was beautifully formed, and he couldn't wait to get his hands on her. His mouth.

He set the bottle of oil aside and trailed his fingers across her shoulders. Silky soft skin greeted his touch. Ekim rose on his knees and moved to straddle Carly's hips. Rajah rejoiced in the position, pulling tighter than Ekim had imagined possible. He gritted his teeth against the surge of pleasure/pain. Goddess, he'd never felt the like. Breathing through the wave of sharp sensation, he placed his hands on Carly's back again and commenced light, feathering strokes. As the oil on Carly's skin heated, the scent of wild flowers rose up to Ekim. He smoothed his hands across her shoulder blades, and dipped to slide over the outer curves of her breasts, teasing them both.

"More," Carly murmured in a sleepy voice. She attempted to turn on her side so her breast filled his hand, but Ekim stayed her with a touch in the middle of her back.

"Soon," he promised. "Relax. Let the tension seep away." His hands kneaded the muscles in her lower back before hitting the barrier of her panties. "Let me take these off," he suggested. "Wouldn't you like me to massage all of your body?"

"Please." Carly's sigh made Rajah jerk insistently. Once. Twice. Three times.

Ekim's trousers were tented. Tight. He barred his teeth in a feral grin. It didn't sound as if he was the only one suffering. Ekim grasped her hips and lifted them high enough that he could slide the panties down her legs. He tossed them over his shoulder and settled her back on the blanket to look his fill. Her ass was a lighter gold than her arms and legs. A round, luscious handful. Ekim cupped both cheeks of her butt in his hands and squeezed lightly.

"Part your legs," he said.

She hesitated for long seconds before following his order.

In the instant it took her to part her legs, Ekim heard the shout of a child in the distance, his senses hyper aware. Overhead, a bird shrieked, the cry echoing through the clearing. The breeze rustled the leaves on the trees and the sun sank lower on the horizon. He backed up until he kneeled in the space between her legs.

"A little wider," he whispered. "Yes. Perfect. Just like that." When he looked down he could see her folds were damp with arousal juices. He leaned forward and trailed one finger down her backbone. She shuddered, and suddenly Ekim wanted to know what she was thinking. How she felt. "Tell me how you feel." The fact he'd voiced the words astonished him since sex was always done furtively and in a hurry--something sandwiched in between vid-cam takes. But he really wanted to know more about Carly.

"How I feel?" She sounded surprised.

"Please. What will make you feel good?"

"I'm so hot I want to touch myself," she confessed in a rush of words. "Yet you've hardly touched me. Embarrassed because I don't know you very well, but I'm desperate to have you thrust your cock deep inside my womb."

Her honesty made him squirm inside. Fear that he could lose any hope of forging a relationship with her, if he wasn't careful, froze him.

"Too honest for you?" She mistook his silence for something else.

"No," he said hoarsely. She wanted him to fill her with Rajah. Dammit, Rajah wanted in--the critter was demanding entrance to her love canal. Ekim squeezed his eyes closed. He prayed he didn't disappoint her. Nothing like a little pressure to make things interesting....

Chapter Seven

Carly wished she could see his face. His clever fingers sent a quiver the length of her body. Flames of heat licked her skin wherever he touched, stoking need higher and higher. She really did want to touch herself, to stroke her clit until she exploded. God, much more and she'd start begging.

"Where would you like me to touch you? Tell me exactly what you want." His thumbs dug into the muscles of her butt. Slight nips of pain that brought pleasure as well as a bite.

"I need to you touch my breasts. I want you to put your mouth on me, to take my nipples inside your mouth and suckle."

"Anything else?"

Carly caught the touch of humor in his voice and was relieved she hadn't shocked him. From the limited research she'd done on Nidni, she'd learned how reserved and old-fashioned the families were--no hubba-hubba out of wedlock. Or whatever the Earth equivalent was here. Of course, she supposed there were exceptions. And the guidebook she'd read had been old. Hopefully, they'd rewritten it since.

"I'm not touching your breasts yet," he said in a low voice. But he didn't sound as though he was laughing or making fun of her. In fact, his words hinted at other treats in store.

"I'm the kid that rattled all the presents under the Christmas tree before it was time to open them," she muttered. "I'm not patient."

"Ah, but patience will make your release better. Stronger. More explosive." His husky voice held promises and ... truth. "You'll enjoy it." His hands were stroking her butt like it was a pet cat.

The devil in her wanted to tell him her pussy was on the other side of her body, but she bit her tongue. The man spoke the truth. The longer she waited, the more he'd touch and stroke her hungry body, and the harder she'd climax. Her ex hadn't been big on foreplay nor had the couple of men she'd slept with since. Besides, everyone knew women were stronger than men. He'd crack first or her name wasn't Carly Abercombie.

His stroking fingers glided across her butt then dipped ever so slightly between her parted legs. A groan built deep inside her chest but it backed up behind the begging words she refused to utter. He could torture her as much as he liked. She was not going to beg for it. Suddenly, he stopped.

"What are you doing?"

"Patience, my sweet. Patience."

She heard him check through the contents of the black bag from the hotel.

"Ah," he said, a wealth of satisfaction in the sound.

Carly heard the crackle of paper along with the steady thud of her pulse rate. When he touched her again, she couldn't restrain the flinch.

"Steady," he said. "I promise I won't hurt you."

A steady trickle of oil landed on her butt. She knew it was oil because of the heady scent of flowers that filled the air. Ekim stroked her bottom until she wanted to purr with the pleasure of his touch. But man, she wished she could direct the traffic a little.

"Feel good?"

Oh, yeah. "Hmmm."

The strokes were going lower, progressively closer to her throbbing clitoris. Carly held her breath, the incessant weeping of her body telling her how close she was to orgasm.

She was easy. She must be if she could get off on having her butt fondled.

Ekim gripped her legs and pulled them even wider, exposing her feminine flesh to the great outdoors. Carly didn't care. All she wanted was to get off, and the begging words were getting closer and closer to the tip of her tongue.

"Let's see if you like this," Ekim murmured.

One of his hands left her bottom to touch her inner thigh. The other drew a line along the crevice between her butt cheeks, dancing over the puckered rosette of her anus and through her cleft to circle her swollen clit.

A groan escaped as tiny shards of tingling pleasure followed his touch. "Harder. More. Please." The words burst from her unchecked. Her eyes had closed, seducing her senses with a world of darkness. Anticipation hummed through her sensitized body.

"Impatient," he murmured, tapping her butt cheeks hard enough that it stung. He repeated the move again before she could protest, and damned if she didn't enjoy it.

Eew! She was a sad, sick woman, getting off on the thought of being spanked. A third slap on her bare ass intensified the pleasurable sensation dancing across her nerve endings. Okay. It was official. She was sick. Carly waited impatiently for the fourth blow but it didn't come. Instead he skimmed a finger around the swollen bundles of nerves that needed attention.

More, she thought, almost frantic. She moved her butt and pelvis upward, following the movement of his skillful finger, but he was too quick for her sly move. The subtle pressure of his finger disappeared leaving her unfulfilled.

What was he going to do now? Her breathing sounded harsh to her ears. Needy. Desperate.

The crackle of paper or plastic sounded. "I'm not sure if you have these on Earth. It will give you great pleasure. That, I promise you. You can turn over now, but you must close your eyes. Will you do that for me?"

"Yes," Carly whispered, curious and rebellious at the same time. She'd do almost anything ... anything to have him touch her right where she needed him right now. Anything.

Ekim helped her roll over onto her back. He parted her legs, then silence fell. The anticipation was exactly the same as when she waited for a takedown to unfold or when she apprehended a criminal. Adrenaline rush, big time.

"Bend your knees for me," he directed. His hands guided her moves until she was in the position he wanted.

The paper crackled again. Carly felt his hands on her backside, lifting. Oh, my. He was going to make her come with his mouth. She held her breath. Swallowed.

His finger ran the length of her cleft, gliding easily because she was so aroused and slick with her juices. His finger thrust inside her channel, and she arched upward to maximize the penetration. Damn that felt good. So good. Carly sensed that Ekim leaned closer and knew it for fact when a stream of warm air blew across her clitoris. She trembled, the urgency in her body quickening, intensifying until she thought she might scream.

His finger slid from her pussy.

"More," she whispered, her hips canting upward even further. "No more teasing. Please."

Ekim didn't reply, but the stream of air moved closer to her clit. She felt the delicate stroke of his tongue at the rim of her clitoris. A shimmer of sensation shot the length of her body, pulling her nipples tight.

"Carly," he whispered, his moist breath winding her even tighter.

Without warning, he popped something inside her channel. Cold. Intense cold made her still, then his mouth covered her swollen clit. Heat versus an icy chill. It was too much. Too much. One lazy sweep of his tongue and she shattered, exploding into an orgasm, the like of which she'd never felt before.

Carly came back to herself slowly, feeling as though something momentous had occurred. A masculine chuckle jerked her to full consciousness.

"Was that good?"

Carly smiled lazily. "You couldn't tell? Heck, I'm ready for round two."

Ekim's smugness faded. By the Goddess, she was no different from the other women. Give them one good orgasm, and they wanted a heap more.

"Come here," she whispered, crooking her finger at him.

Ekim held her gaze, part of him ready to run and part of him wanting to haul her into his arms and go from there. Even Rajah seemed enthusiastic about the idea.

He could do this. He wanted to love her. He wanted to thrust inside her body more than he wanted his next breath. Rajah wanted to taste full penetration.

Ekim rose from between her legs and tugged Carly into his arms. The sensation of her breasts brushing his chest felt wonderful. He cradled her in his arms, and Rajah cuddled close too.

A perfect moment.

"Papa, can we go for a swim here?" a high, childish voice demanded.

"As soon as Mama and I have set up the picnic site," a deeper, masculine voice replied.

"I don't believe it," Ekim muttered.

Carly clutched him more tightly then pulled away to stare into his face. Definite humor shone in her eyes. "Your ass isn't buck naked, so I don't know why you're worried."

"That's true, and I'm not likely to remove my trousers with that family setting up camp there," Ekim muttered.

Saved by a child.

* * * *

Two days later, Ekim helped Carly check her bag for her flight back to Earth. In silence, they walked over to study the departure board.

"I ... do you want to see me again?" Ekim asked in a low voice. He had to keep this discussion between the two of them. He'd found another of the, I know your secret notes in his 'puter inbox. After trying to trace the mail's origin, he'd finally given up. He wasn't worried enough to call in the cops. Not yet, but he suspected it was only a matter of time.

"Of course I do." Carly threw herself at him, giving Ekim no choice but to catch her and clutch her to his chest.

He wanted to get closer, but he couldn't kiss her here, not when any of the public could be a reporter in disguise.

It was obvious Carly noticed his reticence. "Have I misjudged the situation?" she asked in a low voice.

Ekim drew her over to a secluded corner and yanked her hard so she fell against his chest. His mouth was on hers before she could say a word.

When he finally pulled away they were both breathing hard. "Does that look like you've misjudged the situation?"

Carly's smile was a thing of beauty, lighting up her whole face. "That's great. I'll contact you via the 'puter web and let you know when I have my next long weekend."

This might work. As long as Carly didn't stumble across any stories about him. He was careful to wear a hat pulled low over his face these days or use a scarf to cover his features. It had been months since he'd seen a clear shot of his face in the media. On the screen was another matter, but Carly had mentioned she didn't watch much in the way of vid-coms. She didn't get time.

"I'll give you my communication number in case you get time to contact me in person," Ekim said.

"Carly! Ekim! I've been looking for you everywhere," Rala said, pushing her way between them. "Did you enjoy the visit to Ynroh Temple? It was so nice meeting you."

Ekim grasped his sister by the shoulders and attempted to shift her from between them. A loud squeak sounded. Ekim saw a flash of brown a second before sharp white teeth sank into his hand.

"Ow!" He jerked his hand away with Luci, the katmer still attached. "Get the devil creature off me. Dammit, Rala. We're attracting attention."

"Let me take, Luci," Carly said, and she gently removed the katmer from his hand. The creature glared at him, only subsiding with a purr when Carly stroked her head.

"I told you not to sit on her chair," Rala said, a trifle defensively.

"We'll discuss this later," Ekim snapped. "Now go away and let me say goodbye in private." Talk about frustration. He'd never spent a weekend with so many interruptions. Rajah hadn't had a chance to thrust anywhere near Carly's body--within or nearby-- and by the Goddess, he was feeling a mite testy because of the fact.

Rala took Luci from Carly, and stood on tiptoe to brush a kiss on Carly's cheek. "I hope you'll come to visit again." Her plan to mate with Gregorius depended upon it.

So far, the plan seemed successful. Carly and Ekim had spent most of the weekend together--the waking hours at least. The rest of the time they had spent in their separate beds with plenty of chaperons. And as for the little notes she was leaving for Ekim to find in his dressing rooms and 'puter.... The bribe to the hotel staff had been a masterstroke. Her brother was looking distinctly nervous. The plan had to work. It just had to. If her numbskull brother made of mess of this she was going to kill him herself.

Chapter Eight

Ekim hung up his communicator, a scowl on his face. Goddess, he missed Carly already. In the two months that had passed during her visit to Nidni, they had communicated via 'puter and hand-held that bounced messages from satellite to satellite. He preferred the hand-held because he liked to hear her voice. Low. Husky. It reminded him of synsilk sheets and the glide of skin against skin. It made him think of the unfinished business between them-- Rajah and Carly--full penetration. Making love. A familiar pang of anxiety speared his heart before fading. His head told him that this time things would work. Part A would slide into slot B without a hitch.

"Ekim, you're needed on the set."

"Coming." He checked his make-up. The fake blood had dried. They'd need to spritz it before he went on set to make the wound appear fresh. As he wandered down the corridor toward the section of the building they were filming in, his thoughts wandered to Carly. Something had to change in this long-distance relationship. He couldn't stand much more of being apart from Carly.

"You ready?" the director asked, peering up at Ekim.

"Yeah. I think my wound needs attention."

The director stood on his chair to check the make-up at closer quarters. "Make-up! Dammit, where's that boy when you need him?"

"He's coming," Ekim murmured, having glimpsed the boy from his greater height. A sharp tug on his sleeve made Ekim turn. "You've hit the scandal sheets again," his leading lady said.

"Oh, yeah?" He grinned at Tara with real affection. The lady had yet to throw herself at him in a sexual way. It made a refreshing change. "What are they saying this time?"

"They're saying that you're in love with a mystery woman."

Shock punched him square in the ribs. A hoarse gasp escaped before he resumed an enigmatic expression.

"Goddess," Tara whispered with a touch of awe. "They're right. Nidni's greatest lover has succumbed."

"No comment," Ekim snapped. "We have a scene to shoot. Let's put this scene to bed." Bed. An unfortunate word for him to use since Rajah reacted with enthusiasm. Thank the Goddess he didn't have to wear the tight black trousers for this take.

Ekim and Tara took their places in the middle of the room. Ekim sagged against a wooden desk while Tara hovered nearby. Furniture was strewn around the office set, a broken chair blocked the doorway, and files and papers littered the floor.

"And action," the director said.

"Nazrat!" Tara threw herself at him, sobbing loudly. "We have to get out of here in case they come back."

Ekim pressed his lips to her temple and held her for an instant before pushing her gently away. "Help me stand up." Ekim staggered to his feet, leaning heavily on Tara. When they were both standing, the music started up--the cue for them to launch into their musical number. Extras poured onto the set and flowed into dance. The music and dancing became loud. Frantic. A signal of the suspenseful scene coming up. Tara held the last note, strong and clear, then raised her arms high in the air in a flamboyant finale.

"And cut! Great! Well done, people," the director yelled. "We'll film the chase scene in fifteen minutes."

Tara strolled at Ekim's side as they headed back to their dressing rooms.

"Will you retire when you mate? Are you going to move to Earth?" Tara's eyes danced with lively curiosity while a smile that bordered on a smirk flitted across her lips.

Ekim frowned. "I don't know what you're talking about." But unfortunately, he did. He didn't know how the info had leaked out, but he hoped like hell that the story hadn't made Earth.

"I've heard rumbles of discontent from the female extras. You've been dodging them. No naughties. In fact, I heard a rumor that they're touting Kumar as Nidni's greatest lover. Better watch out if you want to keep the crown and fringe benefits." Tara waggled her eyebrows up and down.

Ekim managed a disapproving snort, glad they'd reached their dressing rooms. Sometimes silence was the better course of action.

"See you later when we shoot the night scenes."

Tara waggled a finger at him. "You can run, but you can't hide. I'll worm the story out of you. I'll wear you down."

"Promises. Promises," Ekim mocked. "And what would your mate have to say about that?"

"We have an understanding," Tara said with quiet dignity. "I'm allowed to look but no touching."

"But what about me? What does he think of you cuddling up to Nidni's greatest lover?"

"Second greatest lover, dahling." With a wave of fingers, she disappeared inside her dressing room.

A tabloid newssheet. Dammit, he needed one right now so he knew exactly how big the damage was. He wrenched his dressing room door open and found a copy of the newssheet along with another familiar white envelope.

"Damned sporting of them making sure I didn't miss out on the big news," Ekim muttered. He opened the sheet out. A huge face stared back. A photo of him taken during the South Universe Sector Entertainment Awards with his co-star at the time, Marlana Singh. Snooty little cow. Surely they didn't think he was involved with her? He scanned the story written by Nisha Storrisome and let out a sigh of relief when he came to the end. It was all speculation based on the fact that he hadn't appeared in public with a woman for over two months. His gaze strayed to the white envelope. The appearance the envelope at the same time as the newssheet made him wonder if his mystery note leaver had given the story to Nisha Storrisome.

"I don't understand why I haven't received a blackmail demand," Ekim muttered. He picked up the white envelope and ripped it open.

I know your secret.

Same message. Same paper. Same writing.

There were no distinguishing marks--nothing that gave a clue as to who had written the notes.

"Damn!" Ekim ripped the note into dozens of small pieces and discarded them. Only one clear course of action came to mind. He had to contact Carly and tell her the truth.

It was late when Ekim put the call through to Carly. He waited nervously while the telecommunication satellites connected. His palms were sweaty, and he wiped them down the legs of his trousers. During the delay he planned what he would say.

"Hello?"

"It's me. Did I wake you?" Of course he'd woken her.

"I'm awake now," Carly said, her voice still full of sleep. "What's up?"

"I wanted to talk to you."

"I can't wait to see you again, to kiss you. Touch you." Carly's tone softened to low and intimate.

They were both silent for a few seconds. Ekim swallowed. The lie. No matter how he dressed it up, Carly was gonna get pissed. She'd made it clear how she felt about the truth and men who were economical with it.

"Ekim, I miss you."

The confession froze on the tip of his tongue. "I miss you too," he managed.

"What are you wearing?"

Communicator sex? He smiled, a slow smile of appreciation. Rajah shot to full alert. Maybe communicator sex was the perfect way to see if Rajah had what it took to pleasure a woman.

Ekim propped up his pillows and settled back in comfort.

"I'm wearing a pair of synsilk trousers. Remember the trousers you purchased at the market?"

"I have them on," Carly whispered. "It makes me feel closer to you. Do you have a shirt on?"

"No, my chest is bare. It's hot here tonight." Goddess, what was he doing? He was meant to confess not think about sex.

"Slide your hand across your chest. Pretend it's me touching you."

Ekim inhaled sharply before slowly smoothing his palm across his breastbone. The tips of his fingers flicked across a flat masculine nipple. Rajah jerked as Ekim closed his eyes and slid deeper into the fantasy.

"Are you touching your chest?"

"Yeah."

"Imagine my lips following the same path as your hand. Imagine me kissing your lips. Slow. My tongue thrusting deep."

Ekim moaned. He had no difficulty imagining the picture she painted with her sultry words.

"Imagine my hand sliding lower, under the waistband of your synsilk trousers. My hand wraps around your cock. You're hot to the touch. Hard. When I touch you your cock grows even harder. I pass my thumb over the very tip. You're so eager to slide into my pussy that you're weeping for me. Can you feel all of that?"

"Yeah." Ekim breathed deeply and slid his hand down his belly, tugging the synsilk down to take Rajah in his hand. Rajah leapt at his touch, and Ekim's heart thundered in response.

"I strip off your trousers and unwrap you like a present. Now I'm sliding down your body and taking you in my mouth."

"Carly, that feels so good." Ekim swallowed. "I'm touching you too. My hands cup your beautiful breasts, holding them up so I can taste you. I pinch your nipples until they go hard and turn rosy red."

Carly's breathing sounded louder than normal. "Ekim, I love the way you touch me. And you taste so good. You fill my mouth. I'm licking you while my hands fondle your balls. They're hard and drawn up tight, close to your body. Can you feel how much I like having you in my mouth?"

"Yeah. It feels great. Hot. I feel like I'm going to explode."

"You do that, big boy," she murmured. "Come for me. Let me taste you properly."

Ekim pumped Rajah in his hand and imagined Carly with her mouth wrapped around his cock. The sensation built slowly but surely. His breathing became faster. Louder.

"I'm sucking on you, licking you like one of those Nidni icy treats we bought at the market. But you taste much better. Go on, Ekim. Thrust into my mouth."

Goddess, she didn't need to tell him! His hips jerked. His hand squeezed and pumped. Sensation increased. He could feel Carly's hair, soft like synsilk, sliding across his lap. Her hot mouth driving him higher. Further than he'd ever been before.

"Ekim, I can feel how close you are to coming. Come for me, Ekim. Please."

Carly's voice curled through his head. Seductive. Full of passion and desire. Ekim pumped Rajah again and exploded, his jet of semen shooting upward and hitting him in the chest.

He groaned, his heart thundering in his chest. "Carly. Can you feel me between your legs? You've made me so hot that I'm hard for you again. I'm drawing the tip of my cock through your juices and teasing your clit until it swells. How does it feel when I put the tip of my cock into your womb?"

"It ... it feels.... You're stretching me, making me feel full. I can feel your strength. Your heat."

"I'm pushing deep inside you now. Slow. Easy. You're wet for me. Tight, too. It excites me knowing you want me that much."

"I do," she whispered.

"Each time I thrust, I hit your clitoris. Does it feel good?"

"Yes. I'm so close to coming. Kiss me, Ekim."

"My lips cover yours and my tongue slips between your lips to taste you. I keep thrusting into you."

Carly gave a soft cry, her breaths coming in breathy pants.

"And I slip my finger between us so I can rub your button just enough to--"

"*Ekim.*" She was quiet, then sighed. "Thanks. That was amazing."

"Yes," he said simply.

Not the right moment to confess to a lie. A sliver of fear hit him without warning. The knowledge that he could lose Carly, if he wasn't careful, took all the pleasure out of talking to her and communicator sex.

"When is your next long weekend off?" he asked.

Carly sighed again. "Not until the end of next month. I have a week this time."

"Can you come to Nidni?" Ekim waited anxiously for her reply. Everything, his future--their future--depended on her answer.

"I wasn't sure if you wanted me to."

Ekim grinned at her uncertainty. Good to know there was confusion on her side too. "I was wondering if you'd be interesting in spending your time off at a resort on the other side of Nidni."

"With your mother?" A note of caution appeared. "And your sister?"

Ekim snorted. "I don't think so! I had something more romantic in mind. Just the two of us." *And Rajah.*

Chapter Nine

He'd thought the fuss in the media would die down. He'd been wrong. Ekim peered out the front window of his private dwelling. The paparazzi had erected a syn-vas shelter. His mouth dropped open. Goddess, they'd brought stones and set up a cooking ring with a fire inside. Ekim let out a disgusted snort and stomped over to attend to his pot of chai. He whipped the tin pot off the gas fire and poured the milky liquid into a mug. The tang of cinnamon and spices filled the air.

Ekim planted his butt on a high seat and contemplated his cup of chai with irritation. Not only were the paparazzi making his life hell by dogging his every move, his phantom note dropper had started contacting him on the communicator.

His announcement bell rang, making him scowl. Probably another impatient reporter demanding a story. The ringing stopped for an instant, then continued. They were leaning on the announcement bell. Ekim flicked the control switch.

"I'm not home," he growled.

"Ekim, it's me," his sister said in clear exasperation. "Let us in immediately."

Oh, great. That was all he needed. "All right," he muttered. "But secure the door after you. I don't want any of those villains inside." He pressed the button to open the door and sat back.

Rala marched indoors with Aisha following a full two minutes later.

The chaperon glared at her charge, her chest rising and falling rapidly while she fought to regain her breath. "It is not ladylike to run," she barked.

Rala ignored her reprimand, turning her attention on her brother instead. "Where have you been? Mama wants to know if you're coming home this weekend for the festival. She has tried to contact you all week."

Which was why the paparazzi were a mixed blessing. He'd guessed his mother would want him at home during the festival and had dodged calls so he didn't have to lie. "I have work commitments."

"Over the holidays?" Rala's dark brows rose to punctuate her disbelief.

"That's right," Ekim said, meeting her stare without a flinch. He intended to meet Carly, and nothing was going to get in the way of their romantic rendezvous.

"Oh. I was hoping you would invite Carly. I liked her."

Ekim's attitude softened for an instant. He liked Carly too. Very much. He thought of the approaching week that he and Carly would spend at the resort. *His hopes.* Rajah reacted with gratifying promptness at the thought of cozying up to Carly, and Ekim was glad he was seated.

"I talked to Carly yesterday. She has only one day off this week since she is working on a big case." Ekim matched her stare for stare, determined not to look away first. "We have to wait for another two months before she has a long weekend."

"So you are seeing each other?"

Ekim shrugged since he didn't like the gleeful expression on his sister's face. "We've talked a couple of times, but I think she's still in love with her ex-husband."

"Her ex-husband? Do you think so? She didn't mention him to me." A frown puckered Rala's brow.

Aisha scowled at her charge and tsk-tsked. "No catch male like that. Stay ugly if winds change."

Rala glared at Aisha before turning back to him. "I'll tell Mama you're working."

"Thank you." He could afford to act graciously now it appeared he'd escape the festivities. Goddess, he couldn't wait for the weekend.

* * * *

Bloody paparazzi. Ekim paced the length of his dressing room, trying to figure out how he would leave for the spaceport without gaining a posse. He'd never lose his virginity at this rate! A disguise was the obvious answer--that and a decoy to help him leave the studio with a minimum of fuss. But who the hell did he trust? No one yet, he decided. He'd try to leave the studio on his own first.

Ekim opened a drawer and pulled out a short black wig. He picked up a tub of concealer and applied it with a deft hand. Next came a bushy black mustache and sideburns, and finally, a bushy beard. He dressed in a plain blue pair of trousers and matching shirt. There, he thought, glancing in the mirror. He doubted his family would recognize him. Of course, he might have problems explaining his disguise to Carly but he'd face that problem later.

* * * *

Carly filed through the doors leading into the main meeting area of the spaceport, searching eagerly for Ekim. Her heart pounded and adrenaline pulsed, giving her a pleasant buzz of anticipation. She and Ekim had spoken to each other every few days via communicator, they'd had communicator sex several times, but it wasn't enough. Carly hungered for Ekim with an intensity she hadn't felt since meeting her ex. The thought sobered her for an instant. No comparison between the two men. Ekim looked tough and no doubt, he needed mental strength to do his job, but he contained an inner goodness. He was protective of his mother and sister, and he made her feel special. Ekim was a keeper. Carly experienced a sudden sliver of fear deep inside. Her heart was involved here. It had happened quickly and scared the hell out of her.

She couldn't see him anywhere. Carly switched her bag to the other hand, hesitating while she wondered what to do.

A man appeared, his face obscured with facial hair. He held up a sign with her name on it.

"You here to meet me? Where's Ekim?"

The man didn't answer but seized her bag and gestured for her to follow him.

"Wait! Where are we going?"

The infuriating man kept striding through the spaceport, detouring past a group of men holding up cameras, and Carly had to hurry to keep up. He stopped at a ticket counter and handed over tickets to the woman behind the desk.

"Now look here," Carly snapped. "I'm not going anywhere with you unless you tell me where Ekim is."

"Ekim? Do you know Ekim?" the woman behind the desk demanded. "Ekim Ramuk?"

"Yes," Carly said, before directing her attention to the bearded man at her side. His eyes widened with a trace of panic. Ekim's eyes. "We'll talk through the other side once we've boarded the spaceship."

The man relaxed noticeably, confirming Carly's suspicions. He'd had to bring work with him for some reason. Okay. She was fine with that. At least he hadn't cancelled. Explanations could wait.

"There's a reward out for anyone who knows where Ekim is." The woman licked her lips, her eyes glinting with greed and excitement.

"Really," Carly said. "He's a passing acquaintance. I don't know him well."

"He's so handsome," the woman gushed.

"Do you think so? Personally, I think his nose is too large and his ears stick out like an elebat's."

The man at her side snorted before taking her by the arm and dragging her away from the desk. They went through a door and boarded the waiting spaceship. A hostess showed them to their seats and brought them a glass of sparkling purple bubbles. Carly watched her walk off with a waggle of pert buttocks.

"My ears do not stick out like an elebat's," Ekim said with great indignation. "My nose is not big."

Carly saw he didn't sneak a peek at the beautiful woman, and this cemented him even more in her heart. They might have been apart for a large part of the time they'd known each other, but during their calls they'd talked about everything. Their hopes for the future. Their hobbies and interests. Their fears. Carly knew more about Ekim now than she'd learned about Matt during their three year marriage. She grinned and leaned over to plant a kiss on the tip of his nose. "It is on the large side, but I like it. What are you doing dressed like that?"

Ekim sighed, a scowl drawing his dark brows together. "It's a long story. Can we leave it for later?"

Carly shrugged. "We have all week, I guess."

"We certainly do." Ekim's voice lowered, the intimate edge sending a shiver of anticipation dancing the length of her body. "Do you know how badly I want to kiss you?"

"Yeah, I do," Carly said, eyeing his sinful mouth through all the extra hair on his face. "Because I want to kiss you just as bad."

Ekim took her hand in his and squeezed it tightly, his dark eyes lingering on her mouth. "Hold that thought," he said fervently.

* * * *

Rala paced along a market aisle with her silent shadow, Aisha following. She turned down another aisle full of stalls selling fresh flowers for the festival. Ekim had disappeared. Her brother was sending her spiraling down the path to madness. Where was he?

224

And why was he being so difficult about Carly? Couldn't he see that they were made for each other? She had to do something. But what?

After turning down a third aisle, she decided to go home via her brother's dwelling. She still had a spare key since she'd neglected to return it to her mother. Yes. There must be a clue as to his whereabouts in his dwelling place. Rala whirled about and stomped in the direction of Ekim's dwelling. Enough of the delicate manipulating. It was time to take a tough line--her future depended on getting her brother and Carly together. When she discovered where Ekim had disappeared, she'd set the paparazzi on him. That would teach him to mess with her.

* * * *

The resort was private and as beautiful as the advertising literature had promised. Ekim relaxed at the check-in desk and curled his left arm around Carly's waist. He signed the guest register.

"Thank you, Mr. Ramuk. I'm sure you'll enjoy your stay. If there is *any*thing I can help you with, please don't hesitate to come and see me."

Carly stiffened beside him. Ekim's eyes narrowed on the woman behind the check-in desk but she continued to meet his gaze with guileless blue eyes. "Do you have any suggestions of how to spend our afternoon?"

"Of course, Mr. Ramuk. I'd suggest a picnic lunch on the small island just off the beach." She flicked through a small black book. "None of the guests are using it at present."

Ekim glanced at Carly, and she nodded. "Sounds great. Who do we order the lunch from?"

"I will take care of that for you, Mr. Ramuk." She made a notation in the black book and reached for the phone. "What time should I tell the boatman?"

"In half an hour?" Ekim asked Carly. When she smiled and nodded, he said, "We'll be at the jetty in half an hour."

They followed a young boy who led them to a beachside suite with views of the cove. He showed them around the luxurious suite, then left them alone.

"I'm dying to kiss you," Carly said. "How about getting rid of the facial fungus so you look like the Ekim I know?"

Ekim's heart kick-started when he saw the promise on her face and the soft curve of her lips. He strode over to a mirror and grasped the edge of his mustache, ripping it off in one move. "Ow!"

"Don't be a baby. Let me help." Carly stepped close enough that he smelled the flowers in her hair. Her hand trailed across his cheek and an instant later, she held his beard in his hand.

"Ow!"

"Aw, want me to kiss it better?" She brushed soft lips over his stinging chin, and Rajah woke from his slumber. A second kiss from Carly on his lips turned Rajah hard as stone. He hardly felt the removal of the first sideburn. "One more to go."

"Ow!"

Carly chuckled. "I don't believe you're a big, bad cop when you're such a baby."

The guilt was instant. "I--"

"We'd better hurry. Our half an hour is almost up." Carly grabbed her bag and tossed it on the synsatin bedcover. Ekim admired her backside when she bent over to unzip the brown bag.

"Hurry up," Carly said, glancing over her shoulder and catching him ogling her butt. She shook her fist at him although Ekim thought his attention pleased her. "You can do that later."

Sounded promising. Ekim could hardly wait to get his hands on her beautiful curvy body. He turned to grab his bag and caught sight of the bed. One bed. Large. Made for two people--him and Carly. Rajah jumped with joy, and Ekim murmured a soft prayer. No chances this time. He rifled through the side pocket of his bag and pulled out a bottle of argaiv tabs. After unscrewing the top, he swallowed one tablet then another.

"What are those for? Are you sick?"

"Vitamin pills," Ekim said, uttering the lie without blinking an eye. Hopefully, the argaiv tabs would work. Goddess, he prayed he could get Rajah up and keep him up long enough to lose his virginity and satisfy Carly.

* * * *

The island was idyllic and private, although it wasn't far from the shore. They set up camp on the sandy beach on the far side of the island that faced out to sea. The waves ran into shore before receding with a gently whoosh. Over to their right, the putt-putt of motorboats sounded spasmodically, but the area around the island was off limits to the public.

"I'm not hungry," Carly said.

"Me neither." Ekim set the picnic basket down, his gaze following a lone llug bird diving for fish. He swallowed, feeling unaccountably nervous. Although he knew a lot about satisfying a woman with his hands and mouth, he worried about taking the next step. The argaiv tabs had kicked in, and Rajah appeared erect and eager to do the job. The widow's whisper came back to him. *Carly and Ekim forever.* Ekim was starting to believe the whispered affirmation. Ekim dithered, trying to decide how to proceed.

As if she could read his mind, Carly tugged her black shirt over her head and tossed it on the sand. Her breasts were unbound and swayed gently when she moved.

Ekim shook his head, pulling from his mesmerized state. "Let me undress you." His hands slid around her waist, pulling her flush with his body so her nipples brushed his chest. Under his fascinated gaze, they pulled to tight peaks, tempting him to take them into his mouth and suckle.

"You're a big boy," she whispered, her hand burrowing between them to grasp Rajah. "I'm so ready for you. It feels as though we've had months of foreplay."

Carly's hand tightened, and Ekim squeezed his eyes closed at the intense wave of pleasure.

"Take your clothes off. All of them. I never got to see you last time."

"Don't remind me," Ekim muttered, remembering being chaperoned by his mother and sister. "Talk about an aggravating weekend, but nothing compared to the frustration I'm feeling now." And it was true. Rajah throbbed, each squeeze and stroke from Carly stoking his need higher.

Carly fumbled with the buttons of his shirt, almost ripping the synsilk fabric in her haste to remove it. Ekim rolled his shoulders and allowed the shirt to drop to the ground. Her cool hands slid across his belly, slipping lower to tease Rajah. She unfastened his belt and tugged his trousers and underwear down his legs. He stepped out of them, self-conscious but proud of Rajah's performance.

"Nice." She smacked her lips, making Ekim imagine her mouth wrapped around his cock. Carly ran her hands down his chest before pausing to strip the last of her clothes off and toss them aside.

Ekim spread a blanket on the white sand, then lifted her in his arms and set her down. He leaned over. Their lips met and desire flared higher as they struggled to get closer to each other. Determined to savor his first time, he gently bit at her bottom lip, tormenting and tasting while her fingers entwined in his hair, tugging the strands from his queue.

"I've missed you," Ekim said. "The communicator calls weren't enough."

"I know." Her hands crept over his shoulders and down to cup his butt. For a moment Ekim worried about Rajah holding up but one glance at his groin told him he had no problems in that department. The argaiv tabs were working.

Carly's heartbeat lurched crazily while her hands took advantage of the prime male that hovered over her nude body. He nuzzled at the valley between her breasts before running his tongue in sweet, agonizing circles around one nipple. Each touch, each kiss became a primitive throb in her veins. She stirred restlessly, parting her legs in silent invitation.

"Do you know what I'd like?" he asked, the corners of his eyes crinkling in humor.

"What?"

"I'd like you to ride me. I want to see the sway of your breasts when we move together. I want to feast my eyes on your body."

"Yes." Her favorite position. She loved to take control, but most men liked to assume authority during the first time. "Yes," she repeated.

Ekim rolled, taking her with him so she ended up on top of him. She moved back a fraction so she had a better view of his cock. She closed her hand around his hard, hot arousal and shuddered. Soon, she'd impale herself on him. Carly sucked in a wildly excited breath. Not soon. *Now*. She'd anticipated this moment for months. They would take it slow next time. Carly grasped his cock, placing him at the mouth of her pussy. With one easy move, she pushed downward until he filled her.

Ekim groaned, his eyes screwed shut and a hint of red showing in his cheekbones. "Don't stop," he begged.

"I won't." *As if she could.* She lifted, then took his cock inside her again.

A motorboat sped by the island, but Carly didn't stop, her movements becoming increasingly frenzied. Ekim groaned, a dark sound that thrilled her. Carly set a steady rhythm, the frissons of excitement building so fast she knew it wouldn't take long to climax. Beneath her, Ekim shook.

"Look this way, Ekim," a feminine voice shouted.

Carly froze while Ekim cursed and almost threw her off his cock when he jerked upright.

"That's it, Ekim. Got the image. Who's the mystery lady, Ekim? Gonna give us a name?"

"Fuck," Ekim said, lifting her off him effortlessly. Both anger and worry flitted across his face. "Get dressed."

Carly grabbed her shirt and thrust her arms into it so she was partially covered. "Who the hell are they? I thought this was a private island."

"Paparazzi."

"Ekim! Yoo-hoo, Ekim!" a woman shouted from a second boat.

"Not her," Ekim gritted out. He, too, grabbed his clothes and rapidly dressed. "Let's go." He grabbed the gun the boatman had left with them and let it off, signaling the man to return to pick them up.

"What's going on?" Carly snapped, digging in her heels when he tugged on her arm.

"Happy to see Nidni's greatest lover still has the goods," the woman trilled. "The stories didn't have the same interest when our actor god wasn't providing us with gossip. Circulation has gone done, but these shots of your new lady will boast ratings. I can see the headlines now. *Nidni actor bares all in repeat role*. What do you think?"

Carly glared at Ekim. "What the hell is she talking about?" Nidni's greatest lover? Actor? She wanted answers, and she wanted them now.

Another boat appeared and pulled up on the beach beside them. Ekim tossed the picnic basket and the blanket onboard before turning to her. Carly ignored his outstretched hand and clambered onboard by herself. Ekim followed, and the boatman pushed the boat back out to sea.

"Can it wait until we get back to our room?" He glared past Carly, and when she turned, she saw the two boats were following.

"How about a clue?" Carly's hands clenched as she studied Ekim's grim face.

"Trust me. We'll talk as soon as we're in private. I don't want the risk of anyone overhearing."

Carly's mouth tightened. All sorts of scenarios chased through her head. None of them were good. *Trust me.* Yeah, right. Gut instinct warned her to run and not look back.

The silence stretched out between them broken only by the purr of the boat motor and the hollered questions from the boats that followed. Minutes later, they reached the shore. Carly jumped onto the sand and headed for their suite without looking back. Footsteps behind told her that Ekim followed.

Trust me.

Yeah, right.

"Wait up," Ekim called.

Carly didn't look back until she reached the door of their suite. The man was walking in a strange manner--hobbling really--and closer observation revealed he still had a hard-on of gigantic proportions. Typical man. Always thinking with his lower brain. If he thought they were going into the suite for a bout of sweaty sex he could think again.

Ekim opened the door and waited for her to enter before following.

Carly turned to see his trousers still tented. Perhaps she needed to throw cold water on him to put out the fire. She sniffed and gestured at his groin. "What is wrong with you?"

"I took two argaiv tablets before we went on our picnic." Ekim staggered to the bed and yanked down his trousers. His erect cock sprang free, and he groaned with pure relief. "I'm never going to do that again."

"We are not having sex," Carly snapped. "Who were those people? Reporters?"

"It wouldn't be sex. We'd make love."

"I want the truth," Carly said, ignoring the hurt expression in his brown eyes. "Tell me."

Ekim's chest rose and fell. "I'm not a cop."

"Not--" He'd lied. Carly's stomach roiled with apprehension and more than a hint of anger. This was it. He was a big, fat liar. Deep down she'd suspected Ekim was too good to be true. "Why did you tell me you were? For God's sake, you wrote it on your *Interplanetary Love* application form."

"I--I'm sorry. The truth is I'm an actor."

"And I suppose your latest role is a cop, right?" Carly's voice contained all the bitterness she felt. Hell, would she ever learn? She turned to her bag and threw in the few clothes and personal items she'd taken out earlier. An ache built inside her throat, and she bit down hard on her bottom lip. Dammit, she wasn't going to show a shred of emotion.

Ekim straightened, attempting to zip his trousers up. His cock got in the way, and he gave up. "What are you doing?"

Carly wrenched her gaze off him. "Packing. I know what I want, and it isn't a man who lies to me." She picked up her bag. "I'm going home." Carly walked to the door and opened it. Without looking at Ekim, she stepped through the doorway and kept walking, trying to subdue the acute sense of loss that weighted her every step.

Chapter Ten

"How did you meet Ekim Ramuk? Is he really as good in the sack as everyone says?"

Carly knocked the sleek blue microphones away from her face and kept walking, ignoring the members of the paparazzi and the flash of cameras as she made her way through the spaceport to await her departure to Earth. Talk about a nightmare. Another male dud. Did she have a tattoo on her forehead saying apply here--liars are welcome? Jeesh, if it weren't for the paparazzi, she would have found a quiet corner and sat down to howl. Huh! Perhaps she should have ticked the box listing preference for females. She sure couldn't do worse than her strike rate so far. The knowledge twisted inside her, icy pain reverberating until she wanted to scream. Carly sat in an empty seat in the waiting lounge and closed her eyes. It wasn't as if she pretended she was perfect. She wasn't. But she sure as heck didn't deserve this crappy bad luck.

"Memsab! Memsab! Please, won't you tell me your story?"

Carly opened her eyes to see a small, thin woman with bright red hair peering at her in concern. But the hard, avaricious eyes were a dead giveaway. This woman would screw her four ways to Sunday and probably laugh when she'd finished. If Carly let her.

"No comment. Go away." Carly closed her eyes and hoped they were allowed to board early.

"Nisha Storrisome of the Nidni Press. We'll pay well for an exclusive story. Ekim Ramuk doesn't do interviews with the press. He's so private, the only way we learn about him is through his lovers. We want to print your story." The woman's armful of thin gold bracelets rattled when she emphasized her point.

Carly shuddered inwardly, feeling sneaking sympathy for Ekim. It sounded as though they hunted and hounded him constantly trying to uncover facts about his private life. Then she hardened her heart. He'd lied to her. They'd known each other for three months and the whole time he'd kept up the pretence of being a cop. They'd talked about their hopes, Ekim's dreams for the future of writing a spy thriller, and covered every subject they could think of during their calls via communicator. So when had he intended to tell her the truth?

"Go on. Tell me how he rates in the lover stakes. The other women who've sold their stories tell us he's the best. He consistently tops the yearly poll for Nidni's greatest lover. You can't pretend you didn't know. His face sells magazines and papers. Go look in the spaceport gift shop if you don't believe me."

"I don't like gossip," Carly replied, not bothering to hide her distaste. "And I don't have time to read magazines."

The woman blew through pursed lips. "Well, lady. You're either dumb or stupid because I don't know how you missed the numbers of reporters after him all the time." She reached into her copious handbag and produced a business card. "Here. Take this. Ring me any time you change your mind."

"How much are you willing to pay?" Carly asked, curiosity finally getting the better of her.

"Twenty thousand gold coins." The smug look on the reporter's thin face pissed her off. Then the amount the woman mentioned registered, shocking Carly. Bloody hell. No wonder the other women had sold him out. But she wasn't like the other women.

Carly's flight was called and boarding commenced. She stood and attempted to walk around the reporter. The woman kept pace with her, trotting at Carly's side like an eager hunting beast.

"Remember if you change your mind, my name is Nisha Storrisome. Communicate with me at any time!"

Carly boarded the spaceship without looking back. Yeah, Ekim had hurt her, but she'd never sell him out to the press.

* * * *

Rajah took a whole night and a day to settle down. The next morning, Ekim glanced down at his groin with relief. Damn he was never going to pop *those* pills again. He'd rather die of embarrassment first rather than having a painful hard-on for that long. Self-pleasuring hadn't put a dent in Rajah's determination to get the job done, so in the end Ekim had tried to go to sleep. A groan escaped when he rolled over and climbed to his feet. His body ached as if he'd done stunts for one of his action vid-coms and had to do several retakes.

Ekim paced a circuit around the luxurious suite. Every step reminded him of Carly and the fact that she'd left him. No point staying here amongst humiliating and painful memories. Ekim started to pack.

Half a day later, he arrived at his parent's dwelling. The palace was decorated for the festival of the Goddess Peti with strands of colored lights, scented candles and burning incense pots. Family members had descended on the palace and they were everywhere, full of laughter and smiles. Ekim wanted to curse as he dodged out of sight. He didn't want family hanging off his every word and seeking him out just yet. It was difficult to pretend when he felt so bloody miserable. Perhaps he should have gone to his dwelling, but he hadn't wanted to be totally alone. Damn, why hadn't Carly listened to his explanations? She hadn't given him a chance.

He crept through the outer reception room and escaped his aunt and her five daughters by cutting through the formal gardens. Luck ran out when he came face to face with his sister.

"Ekim. What are you doing here?" Rala demanded. "I thought you were working."

"I lied," he snapped.

"Where were you then? Mama will be pleased you're here."

So she could parade him in front of the relatives and gloat about his reputation, Ekim thought with bitterness. "I was with Carly."

"Carly? That's wonderful." She clapped her hands together and bounced up and down with excitement. "I like Carly. How is she? Where is she? I want to say hello."

"She's not here." New anguish stabbed his heart. He'd known how she felt about the truth, and now it was too late.

Rala's mouth thinned. "What did you do?"

"I didn't do anything. The paparazzi turned up at the resort we were staying at. The pictures are probably out by now, and whatever rubbish they decided to print with them." He and Carly had been practically naked. "Mama's not going to like the pictures."

"Where's Carly?"

"Probably half way back to Earth by now."

"And you let her go? Imbecile!" Rala struck her brother on the arm, hard enough that he'd bruise. She rubbed her hand surreptitiously. "Why aren't you going after her?" Damn, did she have to draw the stupid man a picture? He loved Carly. Why couldn't he see it?

"She doesn't want to see me again. She told me."

And you're going to let her go without a fight. Rala's temper rose until it threatened to choke her. "Are you sure? Have you tried to talk to her?"

"She thinks I lied to her." Ekim glared at her. "This is your fault. If you hadn't meddled in my private life none of this would have happened."

Rala fought to contain her shrieks of anger as her brother stalked away. Her fault? He was the one who was dragging his feet. They were made for each other. Did she have to do everything? At this rate, she'd never officially mate with Gregorius.

Rala stomped after her brother, prepared to do battle. His shoulders were slumped as if he bore a heavy burden. Rala frowned and guilt surfaced. Perhaps she shouldn't have contacted the paparazzi and told them Ekim was at the resort. Of course she hadn't known he was with Carly. If he'd told her the truth when she'd asked, none of this would have happened.

Ekim stopped suddenly and whirled about to nail her with a glare. "Leave me alone. And don't ever try to fix me up with a woman again."

Rala stared after her brother. Of all the ungrateful louts. He hadn't minded when he'd seen Carly. Tears of helplessness formed and trickled down her cheeks. She wiped them away with an impatient hand.

Gregorius. He'd laid down an ultimatum. She refused to let their relationship end like this with no hope, before it had officially started. Her right hand screwed into a fist. Gregorius had told her he wouldn't see her again. He didn't agree with all the sneaking around.

And as for sex....

She'd dry up like an old berry from lack of use. Rala clenched her jaw, fighting a sob of despair. No! She was not going to give up without a fight like her stupid brother. There was a solution--all she needed to do was find it. Rala decided to go to her chamber and think until she found the answer to her dilemma.

* * * *

"Have you seen the latest issue of the Nidni Press?" Ekim hollered, shaking the broadsheet under Rala's nose. He quivered with fury, clenching his jaw so hard it was a wonder his teeth didn't break. "How could she do this to me? I trusted her, dammit."

"Do what?" Rala said, careful to keep her tone neutral and innocent. "Let me see."

Ekim slapped the broadsheet in her outstretched hand. "Carly speaks of truth and honor and integrity, then she talks to the paparazzi. Wonder how much they paid her?"

Rala knew to the last gold coin. Charity would benefit from the money the Nisha Storrisome had sent via special delivery to the address Rala had specified. The reporter had wanted photos, but Rala had refused and insisted on the interview taking place via communicator. A sense of guilt pierced her for an instant before she pushed it away. Her future depended on getting Carly and Ekim together.

"It can't be that bad. What does it say?" Rala skimmed the story, her eyes widening. "This is awful, and the pictures are so ... so...."

"Graphic," Ekim muttered. "Mama will have a fit when she sees this."

"She can't see it," Rala said in alarm. Her plan was going wrong. "Don't show the broadsheet to Mama."

"I don't intend to! But I think Carly should see the broadsheet."

"Carly?" Rala said with caution.

Ekim turned and strode to the door with real purpose.

"Wait! Where are you going?" Surely her stupid brother wasn't going to muck up this plan as well.

"I'm going to Earth to demand Carly gives me half of the money she received for selling our story to the paparazzi."

Chapter Eleven

Ekim waited for his cue to enter the scene. During the past two weeks while he wrapped up filming, Nazrat, the paparazzo had made his life a living hell. They followed him every time he left his dwelling. They peered through fences and bushes and lurked outside buildings. They accosted his friends and family. Nothing was sacred. Filming the closing scenes of the vid-cam had become a nightmare for everyone concerned. Although the director had closed the set, a determined reporter bribed a bit character to give a report. Ekim shuddered, recalling the resulting fallout. Another story. Highly exaggerated. A hysterical Mama. A furious Papa. An indignant sister.

"Ekim, you're on."

Ekim strode onto the set in cop mode to join his leading lady, Tara, who was playing Cami, Nazrat's love interest. *Cop mode.* Huh! Damned ironic that was, he thought as he slid smoothly into the role of Nazrat.

"Nazrat, you can't leave me like this." Cami wrung her hands in a dramatic manner.

"You lied." Yep, ironic.

"But Maddox threatened to kill me if I didn't follow his orders. He threatened to kill my family." Tara looked up at him with tears flooding her eyes. "Maddox threatened to kill our son."

"Our son?" Ekim blinked, wondering what their child would look like--his and Carly's. "We have a son?"

Cami's smile was hauntingly brief. "He's beautiful. He looks like you."

"Cami." Nazrat brushed aside a lock of her hair. "Why didn't you tell me?"

"The work you do is important. Putting Maddox and his gang away was more important than me."

"No, Cami. You're wrong. You and our son are what's important." Nazrat enfolded Cami in his arms and kissed her.

Music played and the bit players sang a serenade while the two lovers embraced.

"And that's a wrap. Great take everyone."

A smatter of applause filled the set before everyone dispersed.

"You could have warned me you'd eaten a plateful of garlic last night," Tara complained.

Ekim helped her stand. "I thought it might help keep the paparazzi away."

Tara flashed an impish grin. "Well, I have to tell you it's not working. The swarms are as big as ever."

The beginnings of a plan crystallized in Ekim's mind. It might work, but he'd need help from someone he trusted. Not his family since none of them for talking to him. But perhaps Tara? He cast a speculative glance at her.

"What? Am I drooling? If I am, it's your fault. Despite the garlic, I want to jump you."

Alarm sprang to life in Ekim. It spread rapidly, and he backed away from Tara. "Not you too."

Tara burst into laughter. "Joking! You're too easy, Ekim."

Which seemed like the whole problem all along, he thought. His plan, formed years ago, to build his fledgling career had spun out of control along with his reputation. He wasn't easy any more, and that was the problem. The paparazzi were making up stories. "Do you have a minute or do you need to go home straight away?"

Tara linked arms with him. "I'm all yours. Soj is working late."

"I've decided to go to Earth to visit Carly. I need the truth."

"Now wait a moment." Tara forced him to a stop by digging in her heels. "I'm not willing to help you if you're going to go to Earth and harangue the poor girl."

Ekim narrowed his eyes on Tara. "She sold the story to Nisha Storrisome."

"Yes, but why then? You'd known each other for months. What did you do to her?"

His lips parted, then closed. Goddess, she was right. He'd been that pissed with Carly, he hadn't thought everything through. Carly hated the press. That time at the temple she'd said as much. Now he thought about it, selling a story was out of character for the Carly he knew.

"Ah-ha! Made you think."

"I don't like smug women."

"Numbskull men aren't much better."

Ekim's lips curled upward in a grudging smile. "Touché."

"So how can I help you?"

"I need a disguise that will get me out of the studio without detection and on a spaceship heading for Earth."

"You've forgotten that the first Nazrat vid-cam is out on Earth. You've always been a pinup boy in this part of the galaxy but now you're famous on Earth too. Your disguise is going to need to fool Earthlings at the other end until you can get your lady on her own to speak to her."

"Any ideas?"

"As it happens, I have a wonderful idea." Tara led him into her dressing room and closed the door. "Take a seat while I get Magda to help."

"But--"

"I'd trust Magda with my life," Tara said, pushing him down into a seat. "Don't worry. This won't hurt a bit."

* * * *

All went well until Ekim found his seat on the plane. He'd booked top class, but he still had to share.

"Memsab! Allow me to take your bag."

Ekim smiled weakly, remembering Tara's stern instructions to play this like he'd play any part. Fine. Except he hadn't expected her to deck him out like a female. "Thanks," he murmured in the feminine voice he'd practiced with Tara.

Say little and flash those pearly whites, she'd instructed.

"Take the window seat, memsab," the hefty male said. Ekim noticed his cheeks were scarlet and the fumes of cati juice, Nidni's national alcoholic beverage, filled the air every time the man spoke.

"Thank you." Ekim inclined his head and smiled again. Probably not up to Tara's exacting standards, but damned if he was lowering himself to flirt. He slipped past the male intending to slide into the seat nearest the window. Without warning a masculine hand cupped his butt. Ekim let out a squeak that sounded feminine, and he wasn't even trying.

"I do like a female with a big ass. Yours is on the skinny side."

There was nothing wrong with his rear end. Ekim subsided into the seat before the male could pinch his bum again. The gleam in the male's eyes told Ekim he'd better stick up for himself before the man started groping him again. "Sir, enough!" If the male so much as breathed on him again, he'd slap him. Purely in a feminine way, of course.

"Sir, please take your seat," the seat hostess said.

The spaceship engines droned, and they took off. Ekim feigned sleep for most of the trip to Earth. Tired but determined to see Carly, he headed straight for the Central Station on Continent A where she was stationed. The transport he'd caught from the spaceport pulled up outside an ugly concrete building. Ekim paid the fare and climbed out. He strode up the rubbish-strewn steps in front of the building until a whistle from a group of men on the other side of the street reminded him he was a woman--or dressed like one at any rate. Slowing his steps, he reached for the door.

"Let me get that for you, miss." An arm reached past Ekim to yank open the door. A cop held it for Ekim.

"Thanks," Ekim said, mincing through in the slow, hip rolling steps that Tara had instructed him to use. The reception area inside was packed with people. An elderly woman sat on a battered wooden bench, her head bowed while she slept. A baby cried incessantly and a young man groaned, a scrap of blood splattered cloth wrapped around his head. Ekim joined a line waiting for the enquiries desk. Three-quarters of an hour later, Ekim reached the desk.

He smiled at the man handling the enquiries. "I'm looking for Carly Abercombie."

"Fifth floor. Report in at the desk up there. Next."

Ekim took the stairs. The closer he came to the fifth floor the more nerves jumped in his belly. What if she refused to talk to him? He'd never factored that into his plan. He hesitated, then strode through the doors and headed for the nearest desk. He'd make her listen to him--she owed him that much.

"Yes?" The man sitting behind the desk scowled.

"I'm here to see Detective Carly Abercombie," Ekim said. The man stared at him strangely, and Ekim realized he'd forgotten to stay in his feminine role. He flashed a bright smile and fluttered his lashes the way Tara had showed him.

The man's distaste never faltered. He nailed Ekim with a glare. "Wait there."

Carly walked in a door at the far end of the room. Today she wore a uniform. A slow, appreciative smile spread across Ekim's lips. Goddess, she looked hot. He loved women in uniform.

"Carly," he called, before freezing mid-step. Damn, he'd forgotten the female voice again. How the hell was he meant to remember when all he could think of was how hot Carly looked? Aw, shit. Even Rajah was getting into the act. Thank the Goddess, he was wearing a roomy skirt.

Carly's expression was blank as she stared at him.

Aware that every cop in the room had stopped to watch, Ekim swallowed. The biggest role of his life, and he was decked out as a female.

"Carly, is there somewhere private we can talk?" There he'd managed a better voice that time.

"Ekim?" Uncertainty shaded her voice along with a touch of vulnerability.

The knowledge that he'd hurt her had him striding the remaining distance between them. Damn, he wanted to erase the hurt and replace it with a broad smile. He wanted a kiss or two. For an instant he stared at her, reacquainting himself with her face. Huge purple shadows under her eyes told him she hadn't been sleeping well. Goddess, he hadn't either.

Ekim hauled her into his arms and slammed his lips down on hers in a kiss of possession, pouring everything he felt into that kiss. His frustration. His need. His desire. Goddess, she was kissing him back! His arms tightened, and he rejoiced in Rajah's awakening. Expensive drugs and potions weren't necessary. All he needed was Carly...

It was Ekim.

His arms wrapped around her waist, holding her in a firm grasp. Possessive. And his sinful mouth. That felt....

Suddenly Carly became aware of the catcalls. The whistles. The smart-ass remarks. She yanked away from Ekim with a loud gasp.

"Well, well," one of the sergeants said. "No wonder you refused me."

Carly glanced from face to face. She'd turned them down because she didn't want messy romantic complications in the workplace. And now they were circling like sharks, clear in their smug male minds as to why she'd refused them. They thought Carly Abercombie preferred women and *that* explained everything.

"Carly, it's okay," Ekim said, smoothing his hand over her cheek in a gesture of comfort.

"Is it?" She couldn't say much with the big audience of co-workers.

"Carly?" Samuel said, his tone incredulous. "Do you know this ... woman? She's a friend of the family, right?"

Good old Samuel, trying to find excuses for her lapse. The humor of the situation suddenly struck Carly. Her lips quivered as she realized how this must appear. Ekim's lipstick was smudged-- probably all over her face. Carly suppressed a giggle. "No. My parents haven't met ... her."

"Carly is a lesbian," a voice said from the back. "It's obvious."

Ekim tensed, but Carly stilled his objections by squeezing his shoulder. She straightened and turned to face her colleagues.

"There is nothing wrong with being a lesbian," she stated, "but as it happens, I'm not."

"Hard to dispute the evidence in front of us," the sergeant said. "You were kissing that ... woman."

"Pretty ugly woman," another said.

Carly chuckled. "Take off your blouse and let them see your chest."

The cops all stepped back as if they wanted to disassociate themselves from the situation.

"Are you sure?" Ekim whispered. "They'll recognize me. Besides, I'm wearing a bra."

"Take your wig off then," Carly said dryly.

Ekim's brows rose. "If you say so."

The circle of people around them moved back even further. Carly folded her arms and watched while Ekim undid his blouse and tugged off his brown wig to allow his black hair to fall loosely about his shoulders.

"Bloody hell! That's ... that's...."

"A friggin' film star," the sergeant said. "That explains everything. Why would she bother with the likes of us when she could have all his money?"

"You stay away from her," Samuel snapped. "You might be famous, but you have a lousy reputation. Carly have you lost your mind? The man has had more women than most men dream about. In his case he's bonked them. Nidni's greatest lover. Shit, Carly. Tell him to get lost. You don't need him. You're just another notch on his bedpost."

Carly cast an uncertain look at Ekim. It was true that he'd lied to her, but he'd come all this way to see her. He must feel something for her to leave Nidni.

"Looks to me like she's already succumbed," the sergeant said in a snide tone. "She's already a notch."

Ekim grabbed the sergeant at the same time Samuel did, their hands wrinkling the man's crisp shirt.

"Let me go," the sergeant squawked, his eyes bulging and face turning red.

Carly wanted to laugh but manfully held it back. "Let him go, boys. I'm capable of looking out for myself."

"Remember when she kicked her date in the balls?" someone whispered sotto voice.

The sergeant paled, and the whole room seemed to draw a collective breath.

"Are you guys gonna hold that against me forever?" Carly demanded. "Never mind." She took Ekim by the elbow and dragged him toward the door. "I'll order a cab for you. Here's the key for my apartment. Wait for me there. We'll talk."

Ekim nodded and put the wig back on his head. Carly called to arrange a cab and minutes later he was gone.

Carly returned to her desk. Samuel was waiting for her.

"He's going to hurt you all over again. You're going to be the same blubbering mess you were a month ago."

Carly glanced over her shoulder to see if anyone was listening. "We're going to talk. That's all." She tried to ignore the defensive note in her voice, but it was there and Samuel heard it too.

He cursed, long and loud. "Do what you want," he muttered. "You're going to anyway."

Samuel seemed so sure she was setting herself up for a fall. Doubt crept into her mind. Ekim was famous. And it was true he had a reputation with the ladies. He could have anyone. So why was he interested in a cop who lived for her job? A sharp pain made her realize she was torturing her bottom lip. And she had no idea what she was going to do.

* * * *

"Why did you give Nisha Storrisome an interview?" Ekim said, the minute she walked in the door.

Carly was pleased to see he'd changed into jeans and a shirt. The wig and makeup were gone, and he looked so damned sexy, she wanted to bite.

"Carly." His sharp tone dragged her from her lusty fantasizing. "Why did you sell me out to the press?"

"I didn't. *I wouldn't.*"

Ekim strode over to the table and picked up a newspaper. He thrust it at her. "Read that."

The photos of her and Ekim made Carly cringe. Thank goodness, her bare back was to the camera. But man, her bottom looked large from this angle. Shit, the story was infinitely worse. Carly glanced up to see Ekim watching her intently. "I had nothing to do with this story. Nothing. A reporter followed me to the airport and offered me a heap of money that I refused." He had to believe her. Carly reached the end. "There's one problem with this story." Proof of her innocence. There was a God. "I haven't seen your bare butt yet so I've no idea if you have a diamond-shaped birthmark, the color of it or anything else."

Ekim blinked. A slow smile, full of sexual intent and promises, crept across his face. "We'll have to remedy that." He prowled toward her as if he intended to do the job immediately, but Carly placed her hand in the middle of his chest to stop him coming any closer.

"Not so fast, buster. I want an explanation. Why didn't you tell me who you were? Talk about feeling a fool. I should have recognized you. I should have guessed something was going on since you avoided crowds." Carly caught the discomfort in him and wondered about it. Her eyes narrowed. "There's more, isn't there?"

"Yeah." His shoulders slumped before he straightened with resolve. "You'd better sit down."

Shit, it had to be bad. Her stomach jumped with apprehension, and she dropped onto a leather chair, her unease multiplying tenfold. Then, it hit her, and she drew in a sharp breath. He was married.

"I have this ... reputation."

"Yeah. Nidni's greatest lover. The guys filled me in before I left work."

Ekim laughed but the sound held little humor. "I'm a virgin," he stated baldly.

Carly's jaw dropped in shock. "A virgin?" Astonishment yielded swiftly to humor. A virgin. Nah, he was joking. He had to be. Carly searched his expression for signs he was teasing. There weren't any. Slowly, she leaned back in her chair, giving the appearance of relaxation. Inside, the apprehension returned along with an appalling eagerness to strip him of his virginity.

"My career took off suddenly. A small budget movie I starred in was picked up and distributed in the rest of the galaxy. I'd just broken up with my girlfriend at the time, and the paparazzo were dying to find dirt on me. They interviewed her, and she lied. She said I was the greatest lover she'd ever had. Suddenly, I had this reputation to live up to. I was a sex-god but hadn't actually done it."

"But we.... You gave me the best oral sex I've ever had in my life. How.... I mean...," Carly trailed off in confusion.

"I read a lot. But the minute it came to full sexual penetration, I couldn't.... Rajah went limp."

Carly chortled and slapped a hand over her mouth to halt the merriment. She swallowed to compose herself. "You named your penis?"

Ekim scowled, the picture of an affronted male. "So?"

"Um. Never mind." The paparazzi had caught them in the act. He hadn't had problems then. "But we--"

"I took some argaiv tablets." He gestured at his groin. "To keep it up."

"Oh." Carly's lips quivered.

"It's not funny." He wandered across to the window that overlooked the street and stared out. It took hours before the pills wore off."

"You could have just told me the truth."

"I tried, but it's not an easy thing for a male to talk about. Damn, someone's told the reporters I'm here."

"Well, it wasn't me!"

"I'm not saying that, but we are stuck here unless we want more publicity."

Carly laughed. He'd come all this way to see her, to make amends. Her ex wouldn't cross the road to apologize let alone fly across a galaxy. Damn, she liked this man. She could easily love him. "I have an idea for passing the time," she said, advancing on him and not stopping until they were chest to chest. She touched the bare skin in the V of his shirt and traced circles with her forefinger. "We could have our own private party here. Alone. Together." Desire stirred inside, then flared. Carly glanced up at his face to see how he felt about her idea. *A virgin.* Her eyes caressed his face: his dark eyes, his high cheekbones, and the sexy, very kissable lips. Not often a girl got to initiate a virgin. "What do you say?" She bent her head and licked the tanned flesh she'd been fingering. She heard the harsh intake of breath and his hands grasped her upper arms, drawing her fully into his arms. His cock pressed into her belly, thick and firm and full of promise. Carly shivered, excitement building enough to make her heart pound.

A virgin.

Carly undid the buttons of his shirt to expose his muscular chest. "Very nice," she whispered, peeking up at him through her eyelashes. "Cat got your tongue?"

"No! I mean, are you sure? What if Ra ... ah, *I* can't perform?"

"Come with me," Carly purred, taking him by the hand. *Rajah.* He'd named his penis Rajah. "All you and Rajah need to do is lie back and think of Nidni. I'll take it from there and make things happen."

She led him into her bedroom and toed off her shoes before sliding his shirt down his arms. It fluttered to the floor. Next, she unfastened his trousers and pushed them along with his underwear down his legs. "See." Carly grasped his shaft in her hand and stroked him. When she smoothed her finger across the very tip, a drop of seminal fluid formed. "Everything will be fine."

Ekim suppressed a shudder at the warmth of her hand and strength of her grip on Rajah. Desire unfurled in his belly while his heart thundered. She seemed so sure. Confident. And that in turn convinced him all would be well. "You're overdressed," he said, relaxing enough to enjoy the game.

"Easily remedied." Carly stepped away to whip off her clothes and then pushed him down on the bed. She grinned down at him, her gaze sweeping the length of his body. Rajah stirred. "I don't think we'll have any problems. I'm wet with arousal already. Just looking at your body does that to me. So long, thick and hard. Oh,

244

no." Carly licked her lips and slipped onto the bed beside him. "We're going to have lots of fun."

And Ekim believed Carly. He rolled so his chest brushed against her breasts and angled his mouth over hers. Their lips moved together. Clung. Mouths mated and tongues surged and retreated in parody of the act to come. For once Ekim forgot about performing and simply enjoyed the moment. His hand cupped her breast. Her soft flesh filled his palm. Ekim kissed his way down her neck toward her breasts, using his teeth and mouth.

"Mmmm. Kiss me here," she whispered, offering him her breast.

Ekim bit her nipple and drew hard. She sucked in a deep breath and released it on a moan.

"You do that so well," she whispered.

Her praise made him feel like a king. Following instinct, he petted her and teased her flesh. Kissing. Touching. Stroking until Rajah wept freely. Each accidental touch fuelled the driving need. His balls were tight and ached for release, but he waited. He parted her legs and delved in the sweet spot, probing her cleft and massaging the small bundle of nerves that would give her pleasure.

"No more," she said. "I want you inside me. I want to feel you fill me and stretch my womb.

"I want that too."

"Come inside me then. Love me, Ekim."

A moment's doubt made him hesitate.

Carly seemed to read him. "Do you want me on top?"

"Not this first time. Maybe later."

"That's a promise," she said in a throaty drawl that made him impossibly hot. "Please. Don't tease me any more." She parted her legs wider in a silent invitation, an invitation that he didn't want to refuse.

Ekim rose up, and Carly guided him to the mouth of her womb. He pushed inside a fraction, feeling the heat of her as she stretched to accommodate him. He bit back a groan, worried yet exhilarated. Her hands laced in his hair, urging him on. Ekim withdrew a fraction then thrust. "Goddess that feels good."

"For me too," she whispered, arching her body upward so on the next thrust he slid deeper.

A violent spasm of pleasure shook his body. She rocked against him, her tight, silken sheath massaging Rajah until he thought he might burst.

"Move again. Slow, even strokes. It will feel good," she promised.

Ekim followed her instructions, moving in and out, thrusting in a slow, even rhythm. The jolts of pleasurable excitement grew, coming together until he lived in a world of sensation.

"Ekim," Carly groaned. Her eyes were closed, her breathing rapid.

Ekim pushed inside her and felt the deep, rhythmic clench of her womb. Raw need and desire coalesced into an unrelenting ache that was both pleasure and pain. His hips jerked, and he managed one more thrust before Rajah exploded, spurting out semen in a powerful jet. A wave of love engulfed him as he clutched her tightly. Carly was his. He didn't intend to let her go. Feeling as weak as a newborn, Ekim rolled to his side, carrying Carly with him so she lay plastered across his chest.

"How do you feel?" she asked with a grin. "You're not a virgin anymore."

Ekim pressed a kiss to her bare shoulder. "Relaxed. You're very special, Carly. What if I said I didn't want to let you go? That I love you?"

A blaze of hope bloomed on her expressive face before dying. "We're too different. We live on different planets. You're famous."

"How do you feel about me?"

Carly sat up and stared at him. "I like you more than any man I've met. I ... hell, I love you, okay? And it scares the bejeepers out of me."

Ekim smiled. "We can work everything out as long as we love each other. Looks like *Interplanetary Love* has made a match."

Epilogue

Two days later.

"Yes! Yes! Right there, Ekim," Carly pleaded.

His nimble fingers slid across Carly's engorged clitoris while he pumped Rajah into her clinging, wet cleft. "Goddess, I'm never going to tire of making love to you."

"Oh, Ekim." Carly contracted around Rajah and swept Ekim into another explosive release. He relaxed for an instance before pulling out of Carly and tugging her into a tight hug. "Goddess, I love you, lady. I'm not looking forward to leaving and finishing my filming commitments."

"It won't be for long," Carly murmured. "Then we can get married."

Ekim's communicator interrupted the glow of the aftermath and the start of another kiss.

"I'd better get it. It might be my agent. Yeah?"

"Ekim, it's Rala. Where are you?" She sounded so grumpy he laughed.

"With Carly."

"With Carly?" she shrieked.

"Yeah. We're getting married."

"Married?" she shrieked even louder.

Ekim held the communicator away from his ear. "You'd better shout a bit louder. I don't think the paparazzo heard."

Rala's heart thundered so loudly she could barely think. Carly and Ekim were joining. At last, she was free to pursue Gregorius. Her nipples pulled tight at the thought of mating with him. "That's wonderful, Ekim. I'm so pleased for you and Carly. Mama and Papa like her very much. So do I. When will you join?"

"At the festival of Peti in three months," Ekim said.

"Can I tell Mama and Papa?"

"Sure, but don't tell anyone else. I don't want the paparazzo to start speculating. I arrive home in two days. Talk to you then."

Ekim disconnected, leaving Rala with a frown. Three months wasn't so long after waiting for years. A secret smile curved her lips, and she did a celebratory dance. Score one for Rala and *Interplanetary Love*. Yeah!

The End

Printed in the United States
44693LVS00001B/181-207

9 781586 087296